D0986713

GHOULJAW AND OTHER STORIES

HIPPOCAMPUS PRESS FICTION

W. H. Pugmire, *The Fungal Stain* (2006)
————, *Uncommon Places: A Collection of Exquisites* (2012)
Franklyn Searight, *Lair of the Dreamer: A Cthulhu Mythos Omnibus* (2007)
Edith Miniter, *Dead Houses and Other Works* (2008)
————, *The Village Green and Other Pieces* (2013)
Jonathan Thomas, *Midnight Call and Other Stories* (2008)
————, *Tempting Providence and Other Stories* (2010)
————, *Thirteen Conjurations* (2013)
Ramsey Campbell, *Inconsequential Tales* (2008)
Joseph Pulver, *Blood Will Have Its Season* (2009)
————, *Sin and Ashes* (2011)
————, *Portraits of Ruin* (2012)
Michael Aronovitz, *Seven Deadly Pleasures* (2009)
Donald R. Burleson, *Wait for the Thunder* (2010)
Peter Cannon, *Forever Azathoth: Parodies and Pastiches* (2012)
Alan Gullette, *Intimations of Unreality* (2012)
Richard A. Lupoff, *Dreams* (2012)
————, *Visions* (2012)
Richard Gavin, *At Fear's Altar* (2012)
Jason V Brock, *Simulacrum and Other Possible Realities* (2013)
S. T. Joshi, *The Assaults of Chaos* (2013)
Kenneth W. Faig, *Lovecraft's Pillow, and Other Strange Stories* (2013)
John Langan, *The Wide, Carnivorous Sky* (2013)
Simon Strantzas, *Burnt Black Suns: A Collection of Weird Tales* (2014)

Ghouljaw
And Other Stories

CLINT SMITH

Hippocampus Press

New York

Copyright © 2014 by Hippocampus Press
Works by Clint Smith © 2014 by Clint Smith
Introduction © 2014 by S. T. Joshi

These stories first appeared in the following publications:

"Ghouljaw," *genesis, the Art and Literary Magazine of IUPUI* (Fall 2009).
"Benthos," *Weird Fiction Review* No. 1 (Fall 2010).
"The Jellyfish," *Indiana Science Fiction* (2012).
"Double Back," *Something Wicked, Volume 2* (2013).
"Don't Let the Bedbugs Bite," *British Fantasy Society Journal* (Summer 2011).
"Like Father, Like . . ." *Denizens of Darkness* (2012).
"What Happens in Hell Stays in Hell," *Hell* (2013).
"The Tell-Tale Offal," *Weird Fiction Review* No. 4 (2013).
"Dirt on Vicky," "What About the Little One?", "The Day of the Earwig," "The Hatchet," "Retrograde," and "Corbin's Gore" are original to this collection.

Published by Hippocampus Press
P.O. Box 641, New York, NY 10156.
http://www.hippocampuspress.com
All rights reserved.
No part of this work may be reproduced in any form or by any means without the written permission of the publisher.

Cover art © 2014 by Jared Boggess.
Cover design by Jared Boggess.
Hippocampus Press logo designed by Anastasia Damianakos.

First Edition
1 3 5 7 9 8 6 4 2
ISBN13: 978-1-61498-065-0

For Jess. More than words.

"'There are stories,' he said, 'tales. There's all that nonsense.'"
—Susan Hill, *The Woman in Black*

"The presence before him was a presence, the horror within him a horror, but the waste of his nights had been only grotesque and the success of his adventure an irony. Such an identity fitted his at *no* point, made its alternative monstrous. A thousand times yes, as it came upon him nearer now—the face was the face of a stranger. It came upon him nearer now, quite as one of those expanding fantastic images projected by the magic lantern of childhood . . ."
—Henry James, "The Jolly Corner"

CONTENTS

INTRODUCTION

It was, I believe, in 2009 that Clint Smith sent me his story "Benthos." Finding it a remarkably powerful weird tale, I expressed approbation but at that time could not think of any publication in which it could appear. Soon thereafter, Jerad Walters of Centipede Press asked to edit an annual magazine, the *Weird Fiction Review,* devoted both to original fiction and to articles about weird fiction. I could not think of a better vehicle for the publication of "Benthos" than this, and it duly appeared in the first issue of 2010.

Then, curiously, I heard no more from Clint. Could he be, I thought occasionally, just a one-shot wonder? I will confess that my own canvassing of contemporary weird fiction—in magazines, websites, and other venues—is not exactly wide-ranging, so I was unaware that Clint was in fact placing his stories in any number of other journals, print and online. Then, about a year ago, Clint submitted to me this collection. I was thrilled. While in no sense do I credit myself with being Clint's "discoverer" (the title story of this collection had already appeared in 2009), I was delighted to be able to offer an entire volume of his work to the reading public.

Clint Smith's virtues as a writer are easy to detect: a fluid, mellifluous prose style that conceals its artistry by its seeming effortlessness; a power and originality in weird conceptions that grasp readers by the throat; a sensitivity to emotional pain, domestic trauma, and interpersonal conflict that mainstream writers would envy. Every story bears the mark of his distinctive literary style: you could not possibly mistake one of his stories for someone else's work.

I know little of Clint's literary influences: the pungent twist on Poe's "The Tell-Tale Heart" that he effects in "The Tell-Tale Offal" says no more than that he has taken to heart Poe's dictum on the "unity of effect" in the crafting of a short story. Clint's work is bracingly modern, but with a sense of the heavy hand of the past weighing upon the present (most evident, perhaps, in "Like Father, Like . . ."). Also like Poe (but like many others too, ranging from Ambrose Bierce to Laird Barron), Clint knows how to dance elegantly on the border-line of supernatural and psychological horror; indeed, his best stories fuse these ordinarily disparate veins of weird fiction. "Benthos" seems on the surface to be a cheerless story of drug taking, easy sex, and gang violence, but a supernatural undercurrent raises its head at the most unexpected moment. "What Happens in Hell Stays in Hell" uses the war in Afghanistan as a grim backdrop to unthinkable horrors unleashed in the parched sands of the Middle East.

I have no doubt that Clint Smith will be heard from in the future as a leading practitioner of the modern weird tale. The stories in this collection testify not only to his literary potential but to his already significant accomplishments. His subsequent tales (and, let us hope, novels) can only enhance his standing.

—S. T. JOSHI

Seattle, Washington
September 2013

BENTHOS

From the *Indianapolis Times,* September 15, 1997, Metro section, city edition:

> IMPD continues to search for twenty-two-year-old graduate student Amy M. Campbell (Indianapolis). Campbell was last seen Saturday evening, and was first reported missing Sunday morning. Campbell's landlord notified police after several neighbors complained about an odor coming from her apartment. Authorities searched Campbell's living quarters, and were later seen collecting evidence from the residence and nearby stairwell. Police have yet to comment on their findings. While not yet considered a suspect, investigators say they are now searching for Campbell's twenty-four-year-old boyfriend, Max W. Kidwell (Indianapolis), also missing since Sunday morning.

It's after midnight and the rain is steady as Max Kidwell stumbles off an empty downtown sidewalk and into an alley. It's late summer, but the brisk, night wind holds colder currents of autumn. Max has traced this course dozens of nights before, almost always after leaving a bar—too drunk to drive, too broke for a taxi. With octopodal panic—like a small, soft creature seeking safety in the shadowy corridors of coral— Max weaves through the darkness of the alley: a shortcut to his girlfriend's apartment, to Amy's apartment.

In Amy, where there was commitment and loyalty Max saw only suffocation. In Amy, where there was patience Max saw innocent gullibility. Over the past few years, Max has learned that if he sincerely reminds Amy that he *does* love her—and that he *will* finish school, that he *will* grow up, that they *will* get married someday—that there is nearly no limit to the things Amy would allow. And in her commitment and patience, Amy allows Max many things.

Tonight, Max's inebriation is unique.

Max—his flannel shirt soaked and his hair clinging to his forehead in dark tendrils—winces through nausea and blinks through the rain needling his face. Despite his attempts to focus, things have taken on an aquatic quality—he watches himself moving sluggishly, slowly, languidly. His head throbs. His eyes hurt, as if slowly and fluidly pulling away from each other.

Tonight, Max has subdued these symptoms with the sedatives of alcohol and smoke; but they're wearing off, and he's beginning to focus on the feverish realness of irrevocability.

With his shoulder against a brick wall, Max shuffles to the end of the alley, eventually catching sight of Amy's apartment building. *Almost there,* he assures himself, but the thought—the *voice*—gurgles up from the echoey depths of his mind. And while the internal territory is familiar, the voice is not.

Jerry McWilliams picked Max up around six o'clock, and when Max heard the phlegmy tick of Jerry's car outside in the driveway, he'd hustled out the door of his mom's house without saying goodbye. Max dropped into the passenger seat, the interior of the car smelling of stale cigarette smoke. Max, rolling up the sleeves of his flannel shirt, smiled and said, "Let's get this show on the road."

Jerry waited until they were safely out of Max's affluent neighborhood before producing and lighting a freshly rolled joint.

Jerry had made plans to attend a party in a neighborhood on the outskirts of downtown. And while Max was always glad to tag along, he suspected Jerry's motive was to go somewhere to sell the rest of his dope. Jerry McWilliams had recently come into a large supply of marijuana. Pounds of it, Max estimated, by the amount Jerry had been selling and by the amount the two young men had been smoking. They'd gotten high nearly every day since Jerry had luckily acquired the drugs several weeks before; and Max only asked once about where it had came from. "None of your goddamn business, man." Jerry had replied, squinting and grinning through a blue cloud of smoke. "Just enjoy it and be glad I'm not making you pay for it."

Although having gone to the same high school, Max and Jerry had never spoken to each other as classmates. And while both young men were essentially the products of comfortable, middle-class families,

Max privately viewed Jerry McWilliams as his suburban antithesis. What the two had in common, as far as Max could admit, was their status as college dropouts and their affinity for mild hell-raising. What Max could not admit (out loud, at least) was that they were both spoiled kids, unwilling to grow up and grow out. Max considered Jerry his drinking buddy, but was, by and large, ashamed to accept him as a friend. Max never dared ask about his hopes and dreams, and rarely posed such questions to himself. They simply occupied each other's mutually wasted time.

Max took a long drag from the joint before passing it back over to Jerry. "So where is this place, exactly?" Max asked.

Jerry cleared his throat and blinked rapidly, apparently stirred from his own thoughts. "It's in The Swamp, close to Creely Park on the southside, close to the city." Max nodded, vaguely picturing the run-down neighborhood.

Max was comfortable with the stoned silence that had settled into the car and turned his attention out the passenger window. As he savored the haze of losing lucidity, he watched the subdivisions and manicured lawns give way to warehouses and streetlights. He looked out west, where the salmon pastels of sunset were being overrun by a mass of storm clouds.

Max registered his inebriation by the slow-motion quality of what he was seeing. Only recently, when Max's mind began to drift, he saw the world as watery, peacefully listless; but the pleasant sensation would invariably be transformed into something uncomfortable, something foreign. His head would begin to throb and joints began to ache. In those moments, Max toyed with the impossibility of his skull—his bones—gelatinizing, turning into soft, malleable cartilage. In those moments, Max's anxiety translated directly into the image of an agitated black eel, straining against the flimsy walls of his midsection. The worst was when he thought about it too deeply or too solemnly. And if he did either, he could almost coax the creature into reality.

The dark gray rectangles of city skyline eventually appeared in the distance. His thoughts turned to Amy, and it suddenly occurred to Max that he should firm up plans for later.

"Do you mind dropping me off somewhere after the party?" he said.

Jerry was now smoking an ordinary cigarette. He frowned, exhaling a long stream of smoke. "Where the hell at?"

"Downtown, just off Broadway. It's only about ten minutes away."

Jerry frowned for a moment before his expression changed, as if suddenly understanding. "Oh," he said, "that *one* chick."

"Amy," said Max.

"Yeah—*Amy*," Jerry repeated the name delicately, as if the sylla-bles had a flavor. "Jesus, man, she's fine. Smart too. I thought you guys were history."

"Nah," Max said, smirking. "She's still in the picture."

Jerry was silent for a long time before asking, "Does she still let you crash at her place when you get fucked up?"

Max's grin faded slightly. He blinked a few times and looked out the window. "Yeah, she does."

Jerry snorted. "Well, when you're all done with her you can send her my way."

For the first time, Max seriously imagined Amy with someone else—someone like Jerry. And for an instant, Max felt the flutter of something like homesickness. But it was for Amy, a *her*sickness. He shoved the feeling aside. "Yeah," he said. "Sure thing."

The party-house was at the end of a dead-end street, choked with beat-to-hell, rust-scabbed vehicles, reflecting the shabby, counterpart quality of the houses which gave The Swamp its namesake. Because the narrow street was so crowded with cars, Jerry had to park around the corner.

When Jerry pulled the key from the ignition he said, "If anyone asks who we know here, tell them you know Winston, or that you're friends with Winston."

Max had his hand on the passenger-side door handle.

"Sure. Winston who?"

"Winston Kolb," Jerry said. The name sounded familiar to Max, and it took him a moment to register that this had been a guy from high school. "Winston's the guy who invited us—well, me; I didn't tell him you were coming with me, but it shouldn't be a big deal. He says he wants to *buy*—he said there's some people here who want a couple ounces." And as if that were that, Jerry pushed open the door.

The two walked down a cracked and weed-spiked sidewalk. Dogs intermittently barked from back yards and from inside the dilapidated houses. *Dogs are like the deranged crickets of the city,* Max mused humorlessly.

The houses here appeared to have been, at one time, noble looking. Now they merely maintained accents and elements of their original refinement—the exterior moldings, the severely pitched dormer windows, the intricate stone work. Now, all the dwellings could have easily passed for a child's idea of a haunted house.

The air was losing its humidity and the sky had darkened, both from encroaching nightfall and the approaching storm. The lavender tones of dusk were absent, having been replaced by thick, cobalt-gray clouds. Occasionally, they'd walk past a house with a large tree in the front yard—the leaves fluttering like shoals of fish, their pale palms twitching in pre-storm fits.

Max was beginning to hear the pulse of music now as they closed in on the cul-de-sac, and Jerry gestured toward a large two-story house.

A group of people were sitting on front porch, talking, their conversation falling silent as Max followed Jerry up the front steps. The darkness under the porch's roof was dotted with tiny orange embers.

"What's up?" Jerry said to the crowd. "Winston here?" Max thought Jerry sounded too smug for being an outsider.

Most of the heads turned toward a scruffy, hippyish guy sitting in a rocking chair—*the homeowner,* Max assumed—who was in the middle of passing a joint. "Who're you?" he said, sounding uninterested.

"Jerry. This is my friend Max." Max jutted his chin as a silent, collective greeting. The lethargic crowd appeared righteously fucked up.

The guy in the chair scratched his whisker-patchy cheek. "Jerry . . . Jerry," he said to no one, scowling—but then his face lit up. "Oh, yeah—*Jerry,*" he said, pushing a thin lock of oily hair behind his ear. "Sure, man, go on inside. Winston's in there somewhere."

Max glanced around the group, who remained silent as the two young men stepped inside.

A variety of different sorts of smoke and the steady thrum of music permeated the crowded house, which—despite abuse and neglect, and not unlike the other façades here in The Swamp—still had some hallmarks of its original nobility: hardwood floors, high ceilings, wood paneling, and lots of corridors and rooms.

Max and Jerry shuffled through the maze of partiers, Jerry occasionally stopping to catch up with an acquaintance. Max recognized no one and was comfortably cavalier about his anonymity. Most people were milling around, grouped in small clusters. Many looked to have been partying for hours. *A party in The Swamp,* Max thought—*like a frat party for Nascar fans.* Eventually, Max and Jerry wound up in the kitchen.

Winston Kolb was standing with his back against the refrigerator, in the middle of telling a joke or a story, gesticulating with a beer bottle. Several people smiled, stared, and laughed at Winston.

Now, upon actually laying eyes on Winston Kolb, Max remembered this guy more clearly. They'd gone to the same high school together, Winston being two grades ahead of Max and Jerry. His senior year, Winston had not only been kicked off the football team but had been kicked out of school. As far as Max knew, the guy had never graduated. Max only heard stories after that, and Winston had apparently maintained his reputation as a brawler, a drunk, and all-around small-town asshole.

Max and Jerry moved farther into the kitchen, and Winston became abruptly unconcerned with the group he'd been talking to when he spotted Jerry.

"Holy shit, man," said Winston, "you've got to be kidding me."

Winston gripped Jerry's extended hand and pulled the boy in for a half-hug, before hooking his arm around Jerry's neck in a good-natured half-nelson.

"I didn't think you were going to make it," Winston said, grinning. *Horse's teeth,* Max thought. *A bully's smile.*

After a moment, Winston, with Jerry still in a headlock, trained his attention on Max.

"I didn't know you were bringing somebody with you, Jerry." Winston squinted and lifted his bottle, taking a long swig of beer and sloppily wiping his lips before speaking. "Do I know you?" he asked Max.

Max started to speak but Jerry cut in. "This is my friend Max—he's cool, man."

Jerry was saying something about the two having gone to the same school together when Winston interrupted, tightening his headlock on Jerry. "This guy looks like a fucking narc, Jerry. You a fucking narc, prettyboy?"

Max's nervous smirk began to fade. He shot a quick, twitchy

glance at the other people in the now-silent kitchen. Music pounded the walls of the small space.

Max's stomach spasmed as he again paused on the notion of that tangled eel, struggling to squirm out of a ragged rent in his insides. *Fuck this,* Max thought—struck with the urge to turn and run. But Winston suddenly broke out in boot-stomping laughter. A few of Winston's kitchen disciples chuckled, nervously mimicking their alpha male.

"Aw, I'm just fucking with you, man," Winston said, letting go of Jerry's neck. "We all know Jerry's the *real* narc." More nervous laughter. "What did you say your name was?"

Max blinked and tried to regain some casual composure. "Max . . . Max Kidwell."

Winston nodded, turned and opened the refrigerator door, withdrawing a beer and extending it. "All right, Max, Max Kidwell. Want a beer?"

Max crossed the kitchen. "Yeah, I'd love one." He closed his hand on the bottle, but Winston held firm.

Winston's face had again gone wooden. "What's the magic word?"

Several ugly thoughts snaked into Max's mind. While he was several inches shorter and weighed comically less than the other guy, Max had the inebriated urge to attempt a joke himself—to say something about Winston's horsey mouth or about his caveman brow or about the old rumor that he was a closet queer. "Please."

After a moment of staring Max down, Winston switched gears again, smiling and letting go of the beer bottle. "Shit, I'm just breaking your balls, man. Help yourself, prettyboy."

I intend to, asshole. "Thanks, man."

Jerry and Winston then began to catch up, their voices drowned out by music. After the two young men appeared to agree on something, Jerry began to follow Winston out of the kitchen but split away momentarily, stopping to talk to Max once more.

"I've got to go chat with Winston and a few of his friends. Are you going to be okay by yourself for a while?" asked Jerry.

Max was a little surprised he wasn't invited to tag along. But aside from his recreational use, Max didn't know much about drugs or drug deals. He didn't know much about Jerry, for that matter. "Yeah, sure. I'll just hang out."

Jerry nodded, lightly bopped Max on the shoulder with his fist, and followed Winston out of the kitchen.

Max wandered around the party, moving from room to room and talking to strangers just long enough for them to offer him some of their dope. He'd take a few drags from their smoke, thank them and move to the next group. Max's headache—*a skullache,* he thought—ebbed and flowed as he drifted down hallways and in and out of rooms. There were moments where the headache was more pronounced— moments where the pain, if he dwelt on it too much, became a solidly tangible thing, extending from his skull and spreading down his spine, along his ribcage and leading out to his limbs. It was a blackly numb thought-sensation, and Max felt as if his bones were being compromised, being replaced by some more malleable substance. He saw himself floating fluidly through the party—his arms and legs slipping and sliding with tentacle-smooth agility.

In a flicker of semi-lucidity, it occurred to Max that he was overdoing it. Another fevery thought: *I should have told Mom I was going with Jerry. If Jerry ditches me, I'm fucked. It'd be a hell of a walk to Amy's apartment.*

He was on the way to the front porch to get some fresh air when he noticed the dark-haired girl over by the staircase.

She was standing with her back against the banister, smoking a cigarette and talking to another girl who was seated on the landing near the bottom of the stairs. As soon as Max noticed her, he deviated his course slightly to get a better look. As he passed, the girl took a long, squinty drag from her cigarette, her eyes lingering on Max. She smirked slightly, exhaling a stream of smoke. Max glanced at the other girl sitting on the landing, her head down, hair hanging over her face, and she was intently using a pair of scissors to cut out pictures from a stack of magazines. Slivers and chunks of discarded paper were scattered around her.

Max snaked through the crowd, aiming toward the kitchen; he crossed to the refrigerator and retrieved a beer. He considered the girl for a moment, the thought of her both sobering and intoxicating. But the sobriety was superficial, just a formal sort of clarity as his mind prepared his mouth to speak to her.

Max estimated that she was roughly his own age, maybe a little older. Her olive skin and dark features, to Max, suggested a Mediterranean or Italian lineage—*exotic* was the word that drifted into his mind. Her black hair hung down just below her ears in a 40s-style bob. The girl was tall and thin—long, slender legs and arms. A physique Max often associated with both ballerinas and artsy snobs. But more than anything, what exhilarated and distracted Max was her uniqueness—her *out-of-placeness*. And once again, the black eel in Max's stomach jerked, suddenly unknotting and twisting itself into a more comfortable position.

Max took a long swig of beer, reached into the fridge to grab another bottle for the girl, and started walking back to the corridor.

She was laughing at something when Max returned to the hallway.

Max slowed as he walked by the staircase, angling his attention down toward the girl on the landing—her face obscured by a brown, rat-tangle of hair—who was still cutting pictures from the magazines. He smiled as he came to a stop, feigning interest in her project. She was using a glue stick to paste the photos into different arrangements on a wide piece of posterboard. Max finally glanced up at the dark-haired girl, who regarded him with glittery, dark chocolate eyes.

She took her back off the staircase's railing and leaned in toward Max. "Do you like surrealism?" she asked.

Max frowned, edging in on her a little closer. He could smell patchouli and cloves. "What did you say?"

She spoke up over the music. "Do you like surrealist games?" she asked.

Max nodded. "Yeah—absolutely." He cleared his throat. "I knew lots of people who did collage projects in school." The girl's smile remained as it had, impassive and cruelly coquettish, and she nodded slowly, as if satisfied by the answer or by Max's obvious ignorance.

After a moment of silently scanning the hippie girl's collage, Max leaned in again. "I'm Max."

"Gina," the girl said, taking another methodic drag from her cigarette. The tips of her silky pinup-girl bangs teased her dark eyebrows.

Max twisted the cap from the extra bottle of beer and offered it to Gina, who gripped it with her slender fingers, glancing at the label briefly. She said *thanks* by cocking her chin down and blinking slowly. She kept her glazy eyes on Max for a few seconds before speaking. "I haven't seen you around before. How'd you hear about the party?"

"Me and this other guy were invited—Winston Kolb invited us. You know Winston?"

Glancing back and forth between the collage-girl and Max, she said, "Never heard of him."

Presently, the girl on the landing was carefully gluing a Humboldt squid over the face of a briefcase-toting businessman. Max paused on the animal's gray-and-red mottled flesh, on the orbs of its yellow-ringed black eyes. The tentacles.

Gina extinguished her cigarette on the banister. "That's Nancy," Gina said, gesturing toward the girl on the landing. "She's rolling."

Oh, Max bobbed his head, hoping to mask his obliviousness.

After a moment of scouring Max's face with silky precision, Gina said, "You don't know what that means, do you."

Max winced and shook his head. *You got me: guilty.*

Gina didn't seem surprised, but she didn't seem any less interested. "She's on Ecstasy."

Max lifted his chin in sudden understanding. "Oh. Cool." The surrounding pulse of music filled the space between them.

Gina leaned in again, slowly. "I've been watching you walk around by yourself."

Max made a *yeah-it's-tough-being-a-loner* face. "I don't mind. It's a decent party."

Again, Gina moved closer to the side of Max's face, her lips almost clipping his earlobe as she spoke. "Do you want to roll, Max?" He watched her pull away. Her eyes had gone to half-dreamy slits.

She's already on something. "Roll? With you?" he asked.

Gina's grin was mellow, content. She shrugged her shoulders, raising her eyebrows. "Maybe," she said, then bit her lower lip. The music continued to pulse wildly, and now Gina's shoulders were beginning to sway.

Max took a chance. "Can we go somewhere quiet?"

"Why," Gina said—it wasn't really a question.

Max cleared his throat. "I just want to go somewhere more private. We can come back to the party after we get . . . going. Okay?"

Gina's body continued to sway side-to-side, in sync with the thrum of music. She nibbled her lower lip again and nodded, *Okay,* and took Max by the hand, leading him up the staircase. They stepped around

Nancy and her scattered scraps of paper. Nancy—her face still hidden by her kelpy tangle of hair—began to giggle.

Max peeled off Gina's shirt as he edged her toward the bed. He was kissing her face, her ear lobe, her clavicle. Gina, breathing heavy and moaning in tiny bursts, shuffled backward, fumbling to unclasp her bra.

The room was dark, save for a phosphorescent glow streaming in through an uncurtained window; light from a mercury-vapor street-lamp outside washed the room—the water-stained ceiling, the bare white walls—in a weak, bluish-green tint.

After reaching the second floor, it had taken little time for them to find a vacant room. Gina had locked the door behind her and produced two round pills. She taunted Max for several minutes by holding out her hand, and as he reached out she pulled back. "Ah, ah," she teased him. "You don't think this ride's for free, do you?" Max smirked. *My move,* he thought. He inched closer to Gina, whose stony-black eyes glistened in the dim light. He leaned in, pressing her up against an oblong-mirrored vanity and kissed her. After a moment, Gina pulled back just long enough to feed the pills to Max, who washed them down by polishing off his beer and dropping it to the hardwood floor. Max moved in on Gina again—on her lips, on her nape, on her chest—and she acquiesced with seasoned fluency.

Now, as they neared the bed, Gina unclasped and slipped free from her bra—her breasts dropping and swaying loosely as she fingered the button and zipper on Max's jeans.

Gina suddenly pivoted, spinning Max around and shoving him back onto the bed. She crawled in on top of him, straddling him. At some point, Max produced a condom, allowing Gina to slip it on to him. For several sensual minutes, things proceeded the usual way.

Lying beneath her, he watched Gina's body arc and bounce over his—he cupped her breasts and in the anemic seafoam glow, watched her face contort with pleasure. The smell of her body was a mixture of smoke, peaches, and something acrid and mossy—like the mineral smell of cave water.

With flashbulb brevity, Max contemplated his luck this evening and, with equal brevity, thought of Amy. Compelled to keeping that mental door locked, Max gripped Gina's hips, savoring the sensation as they rotated with locomotive smoothness.

Max's world flickered. The room, for a moment, dimmed, and he was briefly pleased with the culmination of sensations. But this was different now—new. Max felt the dull twinge of his headache re-emerge and change into something insistent and serious. The long fissure of pain, which began as a distraction, quickly transformed into a blurring throb. Gina slipped Max out of her and dropped down to her side, rolling on her back and pulling him over on top of her. Gina moaned coarsely as she reinserted his sex, grasping his buttocks and roughly urging him to resume.

And now—through the fog of alcohol, smoke, and Ecstasy—he actually felt something, faintly tectonic, shift along his left temple. This time the pain was assertive and so significant that his thrusting ceased for a moment. Gina opened her eyes, scowling. "What?" she hissed, her chest rising and falling as she spoke. "Why'd you stop?—you didn't come, did you?"

Max shook his head, resuming his steady, but weak, plunges into the musky nexus between Gina's thighs. The room wobbled again, and Max blinked back the pulsing pain coursing across his skull. His stomach hurt, and he was again struck with the image of that livid inky eel, writhing as it squirmed in the black coral of his midsection—keen only on freeing itself from his insides.

Max looked down at Gina, who was suddenly no longer a beautiful girl but an emaciated hag, whose wiry frightwig hair fell over the pillow in a seaweedy mass. Her saggy breasts hung loose on her chest, under which the shadowy ridges of her ribcage her visible. Max flinched but the gaunt thing pulled him closer. He shuddered and closed his eyes; but when he looked again, she was an attractive, exotic girl again. "Don't stop," she breathed, "keep fucking."

Max fell forward, his spine was quaking, losing its shape—he convulsed, feeling muscles and bones begin to tremble, as if his entire body had suddenly become blackly obedient to the resonance of some unseen tuning fork.

The room was rippling, the gyrating shapes and shadows flickered and spun on all sides like an aquatic cyclorama. The electric ache was close to unbearable, and Max sank down on top of Gina, whose raspy moans turned into a boggy wheezing in his pain-lashed mind. Max made one last effort to right himself. Darkness closed in as something inside—something ink-smeared and slick—tore itself free.

Max woke to the sound of screaming and applauding. Lying on his stomach—cold, naked—he pried his eyes open and was met with a pervasive of numbness. The ache in his head had not subsided but had dulled a bit, as if it had spread itself evenly through his body. The room had, mercifully, ceased its watery wobble.

"I'd get the fuck out of here if I were you," Gina said from somewhere in the room.

Max jerked up toward the voice, instantly regretting the movement. It took a moment for his eyes to adjust. She had the sheet from the bed wrapped around her abdomen and was sitting cross-legged on the waist-high vanity, her back pressed directly against the oblong mirror, creating the illusion of two girls sitting back-to-back, like spinal Siamese twins. Her face briefly glowed orange as she took an agitated drag from a cigarette, her eyes glittering with nocturnal listlessness. The shouting and pounding music from downstairs continued to rattle the floor.

Max wanted to ask what had happened. Instead, Gina spoke through an exhalation of smoke. "The condom broke."

Max, momentarily paralyzed, hesitated before reaching down and searching his groin. His fingers stopped, sensing the damage. "Jesus . . . Christ," he mumbled, quickly shedding the torn piece of latex and flinging it, like a diseased piece of skin, to the floor.

Through the inexplicable numbness and restless soreness coursing through his body, Max, sickly galvanized, scrambled, as best he could from the bed, searching the floor for his clothes and shoes. He heard cheering. "What's happening down there?" he asked hoarsely, tugging on his jeans.

"Sounds like Winston's pissed off about something."

Max, struggling to pry on his sneaker, stopped suddenly. "You know Winston?"

Gina snorted—the ember of her cigarette glowed for a moment before she answered. "Yeah, I know Winston."

Max let that sink in. Everything in the room was at once crystallized and distorted. He found his flannel shirt and fumbled with the buttons. As he stood, he tripped and fell. Gina let loose a small chain of giggles. "Amateur," she said and clicked her tongue. "Winston was right about you, *prettyboy.*"

Wavering, Max got to his feet again, but now he was moving quick—panic propelling him forward. The light in the hallway stung his eyes with antiseptic starkness, and he teetered as he slid his hands along the wall, stumbling toward the stairs. The other girl, Nancy, who'd been at the bottom of the stairwell, was gone; but her collage still lay scattered on the landing.

People, standing shoulder-to-shoulder, were gathered down in the main hall. With his hand clutching the railing, Max craned his head above the top of the crowd, which seemed to be congregated in the living room near the front door. And now he could see what they were watching.

Winston Kolb had Jerry pinned-up against the wall near the front door. Jerry's face—having obviously suffered some trauma—was horribly florid; his lip was split and a rill of blood ran from his nose. He struggled against Winston, who threw a vicious, under-arcing punch into the smaller boy's stomach. Jerry slid down the wall, hitting the floor with both knees before doubling up in a fetal position. Max noticed the whisker-patchy hippie he'd seen when they'd arrived; he was drinking a beer and blocking the front door.

"You stupid, thieving motherfucker," Winston said, breathing in wheezy bursts. "You thought you could steal from *my* buddy and get away with it?" Winston gritted his teeth as he kicked Jerry in the lower back.

For the first time in hours—in weeks, in months—things appeared clear to Max. Jerry, of course, had stolen the drugs. Max shouldn't have been here tonight—tonight was a trap for Jerry. Winston was grinning, showing a bit of blood around his teeth. *Maybe Jerry tried to fight back.* The obstinate glee of the thought was remote and fleeting. As close as they were to the front door, it occurred to Max that maybe Jerry had tried to make a break for it.

"You poseur piece of shit," Winston said, readying himself to deliver another kick, when he glanced up toward the back of the crowd—Winston's face contorted, locking eyes with Max. *"That guy!"* he shouted, raising one of his meaty hands and pointing. "That guy came with McWilliams!"

Max's mind seemed to be catching up with his body, and it took him a moment to register that he'd wheeled past a few of the hallway gawkers and was now rushing toward the back door. Someone made a lazy attempt to stop him as he ran through the kitchen, but Max shoved the guy aside and burst through the back screen door.

The cold rain and night air steeled Max and steadied him as he darted across the unkempt back yard, ducking under a clothesline before slamming against a wooden fence. Max grabbed the top of the fence, his sneakers skidding against the damp planks as he hauled his body up and over, falling sideways into a row of trashcans.

There were people in the yard now. Frantically, Max pushed himself up and ran for cover in a small belt of trees that lined a junk-cluttered backstreet. Just as one of the pursuing partiers had edged over the top of the fence, Max clawed through a few branches and lost his footing, slipping and tumbling down a steep hill and landing in a soggy, leaf-choked creek. Covered in septic-smelling muck, Max stumbled forward, slinking up the other side of the ravine without looking back. Soon he reached a chest-high chain-link fence, lifting his leg up awkwardly and vaulting himself over, his body jarring as he landed on the puddle-pocketed gravel of a sidestreet. The shouting was still echoing out there in the woods behind him, but seemed disorganized and eventually began to fade. He waited, caught his breath and, again, struggled to his feet.

For over an hour Max stayed close to the back alleys, weaving through poorly lit sidestreets as he headed north toward the city—the twinkling skyline visible from time to time between rows of outdated houses in these outlying neighborhoods. Max guided himself toward the beacon of big buildings, knowing that if he could get close, he could make it to Amy's apartment. The rain was light and constant, helping to rinse some of the muck from his clothes. He only stopped once, overtaken by a savage wave of nausea. Max steered into an alley, vomiting intermittently for nearly a minute before absently wiping his mouth. His eyes—which had been blurred by retch-induced tears—quickly widened as he concentrated on the inky strands of bile on his hand and wrist. His eyes flicked to the ground, trying to comprehend what had spilled out of him—a great glistening pool of black, viscous liquid. Repelled, Max wiped his hand on his jeans, and through rain and pain and panic, he hurried on.

Max Kidwell stumbles off the dimly lit street and into an alley—a crooked, accustomed shortcut which leads to Amy's apartment. Max feels his skull softening, elongating. He looses his footing and falls, slamming down, palm-first, into gravel and broken glass. As he stands a large chunk of lacerated flesh tears away from his wrist and forearm. But there is no pain—Max is both detached and savoring the new sensation, prepared now to give himself over to it.

Reaching the apartment's lobby doors, Max searches his mind for the apartment number. He punches the call-button and, as he presses, the skin covering his finger splits open. After several seconds, he hears the voice of a girl. Amy says something, a gurgle sound. Then there's a buzz. Max is moving again—moving by some distant, rote memory— through the lobby, into the stairwell. Here he falls again, landing shin-first against the edge of a concrete step, causing a jagged, fleshy fissure to open up along his back. Most of the skin is violently sloughed off during the fall, but his clothes and ripped jeans hold most of him to-gether. Max reaches to touch his face, pressing his arms against the sides of his head, where he feels his large, bulbous eyes—his *new* eyes—are now. He has an ephemeral sting of regret about not hugging his mother goodbye earlier this evening. Even so, with cephalopedic ease he slinks up and out of the discarded tissue and sinew—out of his old body.

The second floor hallway appears concave through his new globu-lar eyes. The bronze number on Amy's apartment door is the one clear, remaining memory in Max's mind, like a nursery rhyme one learns as a child and can faithfully recite. He thumps the door. Amy answers immediately, and at once her sleepy face freezes, registers hor-ror, inevitability, resignation, and—*somehow*—recognition.

Amy begins to cry, silently, and takes several mincing steps back-ward, disappearing into the darkness of her apartment. The thing that was Max Kidwell edges into the room, raises several writhing, coiling appendages, and smears the threshold with gore as the ink-slick tenta-cles reach back and close the door.

GHOULJAW

There came a time, he realized, when the strangeness of everything made it increasingly difficult to realize the strangeness of
anything.

—James Hilton, *Lost Horizon* (1933)

1

I was drowning in the ocean under a bone-toned moon.

Those were the first words I had hastily scrawled on a legal pad,
sitting at my kitchen table in the middle of the night. It was my first
attempt to capture the details of my dream. Not just a recurring dream,
but the only dream that now exists.

I remember that first night, clinging to the dream, lingering in that
amniotic place between lucidity and oblivion. I remember being distantly aware of my fiancée's voice calling out for me to wake up, yet I
had endured the sensation of drowning, of sinking, because I wanted
to know where it took me. I wanted to see the bottom. On this night,
however, things were *too* dark. The black weight of water, the ice-cold
suffocation as the moon dimmed and I drifted down, was too much. I
began groping, desperate to find the lifeline of her voice.

"Paul," Gretchen said, as if calling after a wandering child. "Paul,
wake up." And with a sharp inhale, I did. Gretchen was propped up on
her elbow, caressing my chest. "Are you okay?"

"Yeah," I said, struggling to catch my breath. "Yeah, I think so."

"You had me worried," she said, sinking back onto her pillow.

My vision was beginning to adjust to the dim light in the bedroom.
Gretchen's dark eyes were intent. Her skin, the naked slope of her
shoulder, looked pale in the baby blue of the moonlight—the sort of
soft lambent light reflected off snow.

She yawned and tucked a few ribbons of dark hair behind her ear. "Do you want to talk about it?"

I blinked a few times and stared at the ceiling, listening to the low train-whistle wail of winter wind causing the windows to chatter in their frames. Even then, fresh from resurfacing from the velvet undertow of unconsciousness, the images began to fade—gauzy veils began overlapping, blurring the vividness of the dream. I told Gretchen everything I remembered.

When I finished I turned toward her. Gretchen was frowning; her mouth hung open. "Jesus," she said, "that's awful." She blinked and shivered.

After a while her eyelids softly bobbed shut and her breathing came in gentle exhalations. Carefully, I slipped out of the bed, pulled the blanket closer to Gretchen's neck, and crept out of the bedroom, easing the door closed behind me.

It was February—the icy marrow of Midwest winter. In the dark I found my robe draped over the recliner. The slick-chill hardwood floor creaked under my bare feet as I shuffled into the kitchen. It was three or four in the morning—the small hours, as my father used to call them. I had to get ready for work in a few hours. I had to get ready to be a teacher in a few hours.

I clicked a small lamp on near the counter, pulled a pencil from the drawer, and searched for something to write on. I spotted a yellow legal pad on top of Gretchen's briefcase.

I stared at its blue lines for a long time—struggling to retain some clarity before the dream's definition was choked out, struggling to sharpen the dimming images.

I see an umber-smudged moon in a starless sky, hanging over a tranquil body of water. The sand on the beach where I'm standing is black and glitters like powdered obsidian. I seem to float toward the water. Up ahead, rocking against the tide, is an old canoe. As I approach I see long, thick threads of seaweed hanging over the sides. There's something inside the boat. Lying along the bottom is a long burlap sack, stained with dark splotches and crudely stitched up along the seams.

The sack begins to move and shift as if something inside is squirming. Now and again, I hear a whimper, vaguely human, from within. I step into the canoe, balance, and push myself into the water, using a splintered oar to paddle into the soft chop of the ocean.

Some time passes. The shore disappears. Whatever is inside the burlap sack is writhing more violently now, and the muffled sounds almost form themselves into words. Noticing a skinny pickaxe lying along the floorboards, I discard the oar, grip the axe, steady myself, and stand. I lift the axe high and pause for a moment before bringing the beak-shaped spike down in vicious arcs—piercing the thing inside and puncturing the canoe's hull.

Then there is water. Night-frigid water. My body sinks, and with no thought of breathing, I give myself to the descent. Lambent shafts of moonlight stream through the black water but begin to fade as I float down. Despite the saltwater sting, my eyes somehow see clearly. As the slender, twitching fingertips of moonlight fade, they touch the surface of something down in the darkness—on algae-mottled limestone and buttresses, ornate spires and a steeple. It is, I see, a cathedral. Shadowy things move behind the shattered stained glass. The moonlight disappears completely and, as I sink toward the structure, there is the echo-gurgle eruption of a pipe organ. That's when I start drowning.

I scooted my chair closer to the kitchen table, pressed the pencil to the legal pad and wrote: *I was drowning in the ocean under a bone-toned moon.*

I only caught a glimpse of it, some gray shaky movement on the other side of the kitchen window. As I straightened in my chair the hazy thing slipped away like a piece of soot-stained fabric yanked from a clothesline. Still gripping the pencil, I stepped toward the frost-framed window and scanned the yard. Nothing. Nothing but swirling snow shaping itself into snake-shaped drifts. The neighbors' houses were dark. I glanced up at the moon, glowing crisp and bright behind black tendrils of winter-thin tree limbs, before pulling back from the glass to inspect my reflection. My eyes looked dark and puffy. My slim face looked drawn and pale. I was beginning to lose some intangible quality of youthfulness. I attempted to bring some dignity to my appearance by smoothing my disheveled brown hair.

I did not write much more that first night, but I did scribble down one thing. A name. I still have no intelligent explanation for its origin, only that it whisper-drifted into my mind that night, and now serves as a private, nonsensical moniker for the presence inside that sunken church: Ghouljaw.

2

What follows is something I recently remembered. For what it's worth, it has provided insight into what later happened to me. To Gretchen and me.

My father, after the separation and shortly before the divorce, moved out to the country. By that time, Mom (who'd given up trying to keep it a secret) had moved in with her boyfriend, who lived just a few counties over. I was young, ten or eleven at the time, so I split weekends between my parents.

In my innocence, and with my limited adolescent perceptions, I was only vaguely aware of how truly haunted my father was. And to what lengths he'd go to distract himself from his phantoms.

Dad's cottage-style house, a Brothers Grimm cobblestone affair, was pleasant at first, but it soon fell under disrepair, reflecting Dad's disorganization and disorderly tendencies. He filled the house with things he claimed he could fix: old radios, appliances, clocks. Every other weekend he had something new scattered out on the dining-room table, which had become more of an autopsy slab for debris than a communal eating space.

One weekend Dad had been working on the upstairs bathroom, and the shower was torn apart—one of his "projects." I had to use the utility shower in the basement.

Similar to the upstairs, the basement at Dad's house was a wreck—a dusty obstacle course of boxes and sheeted clusters of junk, meagerly lit by a few bare bulbs on pull chains. The shower stall was in the back of the basement.

Clutching my towel and clean clothes to my chest, I weaved through the cluttered maze, clicking on the hanging low-watts, which merely gave me enough light to get to the next bulb.

Once in the back room, where the shower was, I saw that the filmy shower curtain was shut, and I hesitated a second before gripping the mildew-stained curtain and yanking it aside. It was dark there. With the exception of a few cobwebs in the upper corner, the space was shad-owy but safe.

I twisted the knobs; water coughed and sputtered from the calci-fied shower head. I undressed and waited. The concrete slab was slick and frigid under my feet. Eventually, steam began rising from the stall. Pulling the curtain closed behind me, I wasted no time lathering up and washing my body, my hair, my face.

Over the hiss of the shower I heard a warbling, phlegmy giggle, like a pneumonia-stricken kid laughing softly on the other side of the curtain. I jerked my head toward the sound, squinting through soap suds; thin sheets of steam swirled around me.

"Dad?" I called out. Of course, no response. Just another con-gested chuckle.

I frantically rinsed the soap from my face and drew back the cur-tain. The lights blinked a few times and went out. My heart cranked up to a drumming throb. I remember not hesitating at all in my panic, but simply stepping out thoughtlessly—almost confidently—into the dark and reaching out for the pull chain in the middle of the room. My slick feet made it perhaps three steps before I slipped, pitching sideways and catching the back of my head on the corner of a shelf before my small body smacked down on the concrete. Wavering. That's all I recall: wa-vering in the darkness before going to sleep.

When I opened my eyes the lights were on. Pain, acute and in-tense, had sewn itself into a thousand fissures along my skull. I made the silly mistake of trying to raise myself onto one elbow before world-spinning nausea spilled into me. I twisted my body and vomited. Blood was on the floor. I was shivering wildly.

Just as I was about to cry out for my father, it came. It seemed to pour out from the darkest parts of the room—black things collecting into one single, corporeal shape that rose over me, blocking out the light and covering my body with its shadow.

It took me nearly two decades, but I remember it all now. It had been a black, undulating sheet before slowly gaining hideous definition. And from that diaphanous blackness emerged a pallid, gray face; its trans-lucent skin was marbled beneath by faint purple veins. A noble shock of white hair was swept back from a widow's peak. It—*he*—was smiling a greedy, goblin grin composed of thick crooked teeth. His large unblinking eyes were bloodshot and rheumy, set in bruise-shaded sockets.

Through the shock and shivering I discerned some sort of black cape or robe. Only now can I describe it as a two-tiered, pilgrim-style cloak.

Its dark lips twisted to an impossibly wide smile as it began to lower toward me; two corpse-pale hands slipped out from inside the cloak, and long fingers reached out as he glided down. I shut my eyes.

"Paul?" said a voice from far away. "Paul—you all right down there?"

I opened my eyes. As if viewing a video being rewound at high speed, I watched the black mass pull back, swirling apart in shadowy pieces and rejoining the dark corners of the basement.

Dad was with me seconds later, covering me with a towel and performing a trinity of cursing, crying, and apologizing.

At the hospital and after the stitches, the doctor explained that I had a substantial, but not critical, concussion.

I could not forget the slender scar on the back of my head, but I allowed the post-accident shower encounter to fade from my consciousness. *Repressed* is the more appropriate term—a term a therapist used in one of my sessions recently.

That day at the hospital was the last time I saw my parents speaking civilly to each other. Later, as a teenager, I told myself that if I ever got married that I'd never do what my parents did to each other. *Never.*

3

I met Gretchen a few years ago, shortly after moving to New Bethel to accept a teaching position at the elementary school. Back then, before being promoted to branch manager, she was an associate at the bank down on Main Street. I went in one afternoon to open a new account. Things happened fast after that.

(Despite her exotic beauty, unapologetic ambition, and attraction to ostentatious displays of success, she seemed satisfied with our placid town and with the meager income of a schoolteacher. She seemed satisfied with me.) I proposed three months after our first date.

We played house for less than a year before getting married. And we took our honeymoon in the Caribbean.

On our second night at the resort, Gretchen and I had wandered out onto our beachfront terrace. I held my new wife close as I surveyed the chalky shoreline and star-scattered sky. I peered out over the silver-rippled surface of the ocean. Far off were tiny green and red lights of some ship or barge moving slowly across the dark horizon. I inhaled the salty air and tightened my arms around Gretchen. I glanced down and saw her fondling her wedding ring.

"I wish I could afford more," I said, a confession I'd expressed before.

She tilted her face and smirked. "It's perfect, Paul." She inched up on her toes and kissed me. "Besides," she said, resting her head on my shoulder. "I can always upgrade for our anniversary."

We discussed Gretchen's recent promotion; whether or not my students missed me at school; and when we should think about starting a family. Eventually we grew silent. I was content listening to the gentle cadence of the tide. Rearranging my embrace, I pulled my wife closer and caressed her arms. We told each other, *I love you,* before making our way back to the bed.

I woke to the sound of Gretchen's peaceful breathing—a rise and fall that mingled with the soft sussurance of the surf outside. We'd left the French doors open after coming back inside, the long delicate drapes drifted languidly. The room was still and washed with pale blue moonlight. As I made a drowsy movement to get up and close the doors I registered the figure standing on Gretchen's side of the bed. In one jerky shift I rose up midway and went rigid.

Recognition of a thing I'd forgotten for twenty years spilled into me: the high-cheekboned, cadaver-gray face, the jagged rows of broken-porcelain teeth glittering between a rictus and lecherous grin. Its moist, unblinking eyes were fixed on me. The long, pilgrim-style cloak hung loose over its shoulders.

In a slick flash its gaze darted down to Gretchen. My stomach knotted and soured as it extended one of its purple-veined hands, fingering a few strands of hair from her forehead before making a single stroke across her clavicle.

I twisted and lurched up, leaping over Gretchen and grabbing the thing by its collar, yanking him away from the bed. His smile widened as he clasped his hands over my upper arms. We tangled up in the middle of the room. Gritting my teeth, I swung my body around and shoved him toward the terrace, knocking over lamps and furniture. We burst through the doors and pitched over the rail, landing on the beach and kicking up sand as I tried to gain some control.

And very quickly my bare feet sank into the soggy shoreline. With all the strength and leverage I could summon, I clawed into his cloak, shifted my weight, and tugged him down into the water, pressing a knee into his chest as a wave rushed over his face.

"Goddamn it," I grunted through my teeth. "My wife . . . fucking touched my wife." I saw a burst of bubbles stream from his beaky nose, as if he'd laughed. I tilted forward, pressing harder, driving him down. *Touched my wife.*

His arm, as if he'd not exerted an ounce of energy, shot up through the water, a slick hand latching over my throat; his slender, disproportionate fingers wriggled and worked and tightened. His arm began dragging me down.

Flailing, I drove my fists against his face. Then, holding what little breath I had left, my face was submerged. Everything went black and silent. I opened my eyes and stopped struggling.

In the underwater hum I heard, dimly at first, a distant echo. I heard the sonorous wail of a pipe organ, a single drawn-out note rising, sustaining, and fading. And as if that resonating note blended into a whisper, I heard, "Let go." That whisper poured through my mind with the ease of a serene tide washing away impressions in the sand. The twitching fingers loosened around my neck as, once more, I heard the words. *Let go.* And I did.

Hands grasped my shoulders and arms and my face broke the surface. There were frantic voices, a woman crying for help. I was being hauled onto the beach. I remember seeing wide-eyed people rushing from their beachfront rooms. Gretchen was there. Her face was tear-streaked and she held a hand over her mouth as someone settled me on my back. She knelt down next to me, pleading to know what had happened and why I had done this. Eventually her voice was drowned out as the sound of the ocean grew louder, and night rushed on, closing in around me.

4

Things got worse after the honeymoon. The dream got worse. Our marriage lasted about as long as our courtship, less than a year.

I'd always imagined myself being inconsolable—perhaps even physically violent—were I to be confronted with my wife's infidelity in my marriage. But in Gretchen's case, and considering the circumstances, I can't blame her. Lately, I've learned to let go.

I'd been sitting at the kitchen table one evening, staring at scratched-out words on a piece of paper, trying to scribble down an unsatisfying version of what you are now reading. I heard Gretchen's car pull into the driveway. It was late.

I can't remember what I tried arguing with her about when she walked into the kitchen, but I stopped when I saw her. Her eyes were puffy. She simply dropped her keys on the table and sank down in a chair across from me. She'd been seeing someone for months, some finance manager from another bank.

"Please, Paul," she said, sobbing, reaching out for my hand. "It's not your fault." I did not believe that then, nor do I believe it now. Several days later I moved out. In November, I received divorce papers.

Three weeks ago, the administration did my students, the school, and myself a favor when they fired me. My behavior had become too erratic and cruel to be considered acceptable conduct for an educator.

Two nights ago I was standing in the shower, leaning against the ceramic-tiled wall with my eyes closed, dozing. The door didn't open. It didn't have to. I knew what was waiting for me on the other side of the vinyl—what had been waiting all along. I opened my eyes and hesitated before drawing the curtain aside.

The black figure was slightly obscured by rolling clouds of steam. It was smiling, of course. Water streaming from the showerhead sputtered and changed color, turning black. Rivulets of inky liquid poured over me, branching down across my skin and collecting in a dark pool at my feet. The static hiss from the shower head grew louder. For the first time he spoke, and his voice was my voice: *I was drowning in the ocean under a bone-toned moon.*

DIRT ON VICKY

Everybody loved Chick Lorimer in our town.
Far off
Everybody loved her.

—Carl Sandburg, "Gone"

Bill Hughes watched the children fall under the storyteller's spell. The kids—Bill's eight-year-old son Casey among them—were sitting on an enormous rug, wreathed around the feet of the old woman weaving tales from a wooden rocking chair at the back of the library. With Halloween days away, tonight was the final installment of New Bethel's annual ghost story festival: *The Witching Hour.*

In an exaggerated wail, the woman said, *"Give me back my bones,"* extending her arthritic fingers toward her devoted audience. Casey twisted around to look at his dad. Bill supplied a brief, reassuring smile before his son hooked his own fingers into tiny claws and mouthed: *Give me back my bones.* Bill nodded, silently indicating that Casey should return his attention to the storyteller.

The combination of pausing at critical transitions, channeling eerie voices, and calling up the occasional witch's cackle brought an unsettling authenticity when paired with her austere features. To Bill, it was as if one of Macbeth's Weird Sisters had crawled off the page and slid into the creaking rocking chair. She was dressed in gray, a black shawl wrapped around her hunched back and knobby shoulders. Her wiry, iron-colored hair was spooled into an unraveling bun; the ghost of a smile played at the corners of her mouth as she peered at the rapt faces of her young listeners.

Nestled near the center of the town's prim bosom, the library had remained frighteningly unaltered since Bill Hughes had been a kid. Originally a courthouse, the building was a repository of custodial antiquity—marble floors reflecting the green gleam of reading lamps; massive, lacquered bookcases; the warm aroma of age-worn paper. Having lived here all his life, Bill was familiar with most of these stories. His own parents had brought him to these festivals when he was a kid, and he hoped Casey would find similar contentment with the provincial tales of ghost lights, phantom trains, banshee screams echoing under bridges.

He recognized a few folks here and there, deftly sidestepping the opportunity for anyone to strike up a conversation. Bill's threshold for tolerating these questions had grown narrow over the past three or four years. He didn't need to rehash his humiliation every time some busybody got nosy. Of course, none of them cared about him or Casey; they just wanted more gossip, more small town dirt on Vicky.

Bill's wife had been killed when Casey was three years old, and everyone in town, Bill was certain, had their own perverse account of what had happened—the maliciously myopic, grown-up counterpart of the children's story circle. While Casey wasn't the only youngster in town living in a single-parent home, he was the only kid whose father was a widower. Only in the past few years had Casey started articulating those painfully inevitable questions: "How come kids at school have a mommy *and* a daddy?" On these occasions, Bill sloppily cobbled something together to mollify the boy. But Casey was getting smarter, his innocent inquiries becoming more acute.

Throughout the evening, Bill abandoned being a member of the audience, opting to aimlessly pace the aisles in solitude. Lean and lanky, Bill had the aspect of a rangy farmhand. He'd played basketball seventeen years earlier in high school—the same school where he was now a science teacher—and had since strictly maintained the appearance (down to his high-and-tight haircut) of a soft-spoken ball player.

Bill checked his watch and then gave a glance through one of the skinny windows. The orange-to-mauve tint of October twilight had nearly faded completely. Night's lithe fingers had pulled darkness up to the town's chin. Despite this being a Friday (and despite neither father nor son having to cope with school tomorrow), Bill still had the uneasy urge to head home.

"All right, children," said the old spinster, steepling her crooked fingers, "are you ready for a final twilight tale?" The kids collectively acknowledged that they were. From a wicker basket near her feet, the woman produced a saddle-stitched chapbook. "Well then . . . our last story is a local legend . . . the legend of the Aikman Farm."

Bill's thin grin faded, his face slackened. *Good God,* he thought, *do people still talk about that place?* But why be surprised—the town had barely changed over the past three decades, why should its superstitions?

He half listened to the latest permutated tale of the Aikman place. Experimentally, he tried to imagine what Casey was envisioning—a gray, windowless farm house on a hill, under a sky the color of dirty wool. Drifting through knee-high witch grass, his mental eye floated across the yard, toward the house, through a black, coffin-shaped threshold beneath the shadow-draped porch. Bypassing a parlor covered with shattered plaster, dead leaves, and debris, his imagination is dragged up a crooked flight of stairs, slows on the second floor, and stops at a door with a gleaming brass knob. The door yawns open, revealing a narrow corridor of scuffed, severely angled stairs leading up to the attic, up to a figure standing at the top, up to Vicky. He twists his mind away before she can do something obscene.

The applause of children shook Bill from his self-induced trance.

Parents were converging. Casey rose to his tiptoes and caught sight of Bill. Grinning, Casey jogged forward, chattering in eager tones. Bill gestured for his son to slow down and lower his voice. Casey obeyed.

In a hush-rushed breath, Casey said, "Oh my gosh, Dad, it was so spooky."

"I'm happy to hear it. Did you thank the storyteller?"

Zipping his windbreaker, Casey turned toward the still-seated woman. "Thank you," he said, supplying a timid wave.

The old woman remained in character—part crone, part bucolic prophet—raising several feeble fingers. "You offered some very fine questions about the fables, my boy. Perhaps there's bit of a storyteller in you." Casey's face lit up. She flicked her rheumy gaze onto Bill. "You have a bright little light bulb on your hands, Mr. Hughes."

Bill was seized by a preposterous suspicion: that this was somehow *the same* woman who'd told stories at *The Witching Hour* when he was a kid. His left brain understood the impossibility of such a thing (that old fabler had been ancient thirty years ago). This idea was small, like a struck match momentarily flaring in a dark room, but it guttered with a dangerously playful possibility: that if Bill allowed his mind to get carried away, he could convince himself to believe it.

He patted Casey's shoulder. "Oh, yes. Too precocious for his own good." Bill cleared his throat, uncomfortable with how alive her eyes were. "Well, good night."

The frail woman remained rocking, staring, silent.

Casey was recapping the evening as they stepped out of the library. It was full night now. A breeze had picked up, anemically urging clusters of brittle leaves to chatter along the sidewalk.

"We better get home," Bill said, and shifted his voice to a light-heartedly sinister tone, *"before we drift into the witching hour."*

Appearing momentarily startled, Casey looked up at his father; but he obviously read playfulness in his dad's expression. "Yeah, right." As they passed under the amber halos of streetlamps lining the sidewalk, Casey drew his fingers into little claws and gave a mournful, imitative moan. Now it was Casey's turn: *"Give me back my bones!"*

They were nearly clear of Main Street when Casey said, "Do you believe in ghosts?"

"Well," Bill began, taking the same tone as when one of his students caught him off-guard. He glanced over at Casey, a sincere little frown between his large eyes. Sometimes he looked so much like Vicky. Panels of shadows passed over the boy's face as they moved through sparse light. "I suppose I don't." In his periphery he saw Casey's shoulders slump as he turned away. "But it's all supposed to be for fun, right?" Casey mumbled something. Bill scratched his cheek. "I mean, what would Halloween be without ghosts?" This time there was no reply.

Bill slowed at an intersection, idling under a red light for a few seconds before it clicked to green and he steered onto Northeastern Avenue. After several minutes without speaking, Bill said, "Do you believe in ghosts?"

Casey, hands folded neatly on his lap, peered out the passenger window. His small voice was resolute. "I think ghosts are real."

Bill gave an earnest nod. "And there's nothing wrong with that, son. *I* believed in ghosts at your age."

Casey shifted a bit, glancing askance at his dad. "Really?" His tone was more eager than incredulous.

"Sure," Bill said, steering onto the road which led directly home.

"You may not believe this, but when I was a kid—although quite a bit older than you—me and some of my friends used to ride our bikes out to the Aikman farm."

"Seriously?" Casey pressed forward against the taut seatbelt. "That lady wasn't making that up? The Aikman place is real?" He was beaming, the energy of their special evening returning.

"If I'm lying I'm dying," Bill said, trying to sound at ease.

"What was it like?"

"The Aikman place?"

"Uh-huh," said Casey.

"Well," Bill took a deep breath and squinted as if straining to see through fog. He was back in front of his classroom, back in control. "It was a deserted farmhouse out on Haymaker Lane, mostly a place kids dared each other to explore—coaxing one another to run up and knock on the front door on Halloween, that sort of thing. The house was"—he struggled for the right words—"exactly something you'd imagine a haunted house would look like: two stories with a few dormers around the top . . . a sagging porch around the bottom. I don't think anyone really knew why it'd been abandoned."

He trailed off. Bill didn't know if this was true or not. He'd always just accepted (and perpetuated) whatever legend or lie was circulating at the time: *The Aikman woman murdered her husband and kids and buried them in the root cellar before hanging herself from the rafters out in the barn. . . . The Aikman's eldest son came home from college during winter break and poisoned the entire family Christmas morning before dumping the bodies out in the limestone quarry out east. . . . The Aikman father smothered his wife and kids while they slept, placing their corpses in the cornfield shortly before tumbling them to pieces in the rusty pickers of his combine at harvest time.* Grim as it may have been, Bill had always relished the autumn elements of the last legend, but was reticent to share any of these particular tales with his impressionable son.

Yet beneath all this there was that persistent image—the impression he'd suppressed since long before the library—of Vicky at the top of the stairs, only now it had taken on the photographic effect of a negative—all the colors inverted . . . the whites to black and blacks to white: Vicky, her teeth now pearly black, her penetrating pupils had reversed to white marbles rimmed with black sclera, her once dark hair now shredded gray drapes. Bill stifled himself from murmuring, *Not real.*

"Dad?"

Bill shivered. "Hm?"

"Why do you keep saying *was?*"

Bill said, "How do you mean?"

"Like"—Casey licked his lips—"you keep saying *was* and *looked* and *used to be,* and I want to know why everything is in the past."

His son's question had momentarily rendered Bill without words; he haplessly stammered for a few seconds before saying, "Stories, tales, are written that way—with all those past-tense verbs—so that we can. . ."—he was desperate to conclude his impromptu lecture—". . . so that we can better understand the past, and help us know more about ourselves now in the present, and maybe far off in the future."

Casey's face was stern. "No, I mean, is the house still here in town? Is the farm somewhere out there?" He gestured vaguely at the screens of trees, at the passing fields of parchment-colored cornstalks.

Bill inadvertently twitched a frown, uncertain. "Yes." He supposed the sprawling property was still owned by the Aikman relatives. *But the house?* It was beyond condemned twenty years ago; it had surely collapsed by now. *Or it was burned down by hoods.* "I don't know why it wouldn't be out there."

Casey waited a while before speaking. "Can we go see it?" Bill was already shaking his head before verbally dismissing the suggestion, but Casey pounced on his father's hesitation. "Oh, please. We're already having such a good time . . . it would be like an adventure and it would be such a nice memory . . . please?"

Bill stopped shaking his head. *A nice memory.* Guilt now. Guilt again. An odious title wormed its way into his head: *widower's kid.* He sucked in a breath. "Casey"—his delivery was sober, determined—"if we drive out there, we're only going to look, okay? Nothing else—we stay in the car, got it?"

In the dim light cast from the dashboard, Casey's smile was radiant. "Oh, I promise, it'll only be for a minute."

Bill turned the car around in a gravel driveway.

A sepia-mottled moon was lying rather low on the horizon, giving the illusion of being trapped in the black lacework of tree limbs. They coursed along back roads, which grew narrower as they drew closer to the secluded Haymaker Lane; and each time that black-and-white image of Vicky reasserted itself, Bill distracted himself by entertaining Casey with another elaborately fabricated legend. All lies.

The house on the hill was worse than Bill could have imagined or described. Of all the things he'd told Casey, nothing could have prepared him for what the car's headlights fell on. A wood-decaying horror.

After finally arriving on the cattail-lined lane, Bill had pulled the car partway into an overgrown driveway. Casey complained that he couldn't see the house from the road. It was true—a jagged wreath of elms and pin oaks had created a barrier around the house, which was nothing more than a shapeless, night-shaded mass within the inky tangle of trees. Begrudgingly, Bill eased off the brake and the car crept forward. Making their way up the hill, he and Casey jostled and jounced over the rutted trail. Bill heard odds and ends rattling around in the glove compartment—matches, maps, junk.

Now, with the engine idling and the headlights creating a torn curtain of shadow against the house, Bill said, "Well, this is it," startled to find his voice so thin.

With the exception of the high attic dormers, the windows had been completely knocked out—by vandals, Bill assumed—leaving only shards of glass around the casings. With the mullions and sash bars having been broken away, the black rectangles gave the illusion of absorbing light; and even with that stark illumination falling over the house, it did little to bring any color to it. The paint had faded and flecked away, exposing rotting wood-plank siding, giving the exhausted structure a uniform slate appearance.

The whole place had been intimidating to Bill when he was fifteen, but now the dwelling had an almost cognizant quality to it. With the moon glowing on the other side of the house, the crooked columns supporting the sagging porch gave the illusion of crouching spider legs. And all at once, the circle of trees seemed like skeletal sentinels— vacantly faithful suitors holding a vigil at the skirt of this abused muse. It was remarkable but, in the silence of the car, Bill felt the image of the house transform into the medium of actual sound, a warbling whisper—the voice of the librarian. *Go away,* it repeated in a reedy cadence. *Leave this alone. Go away.*

A spell of silence had settled into the car. "Turn off the headlights," Casey whispered, his face fixed on the house, a smile playing at the edges of his mouth.

Bill surprised himself with the ease at which he complied. Yes: this had the potential of being an indelible father-and-son memory; but they were beginning to traipse too close to the sensible threshold of Bill's comfort zone. Under the moonlight, the wild lawn acted as a dark blanket spiked with slivers of chrome.

After a while, Bill said, "We'd better get going, it's—"

"I want to go up there."

This time there was absolutely no negotiation—with either himself or his son. He needed to regain some semblance of control. "No, Casey." He flicked on the headlights, re-illuminating the hideous face of the house, the open cavity that used to be the front door looked like a frozen howl. "I frankly feel a bit foolish for trespassing."

Bill was reaching for the gearshift when Casey said, "Dad?"

"Mmm?"

The boy's voice was soft, plaintive. "Will Mom ever come back as a ghost?"

After a second or two, Bill sank back in his seat. He'd rehearsed his answers for years, never properly polishing an adequate response. But each time, Bill had drifted back to the circumstances of Vicky's death, and his explanations had been distorted by embarrassment and perverted by resentment. What was he going to tell him?—*Your mother was sad sometimes, and it got worse after you were born. . . .* Never. *Your mother was killed in a car wreck . . . she'd gone out for cocktails after work with a man from her office, a man daddy didn't like. A clerk at a local hotel said they'd spent a few hours in a room that evening before abruptly checking out. The man was probably driving mom back to pick up her car when he clipped a guardrail, resulting in a really awful accident. The guy lived, your mother didn't. We went to the funeral . . . you were little, you didn't understand . . . we threw dirt on her coffin.* Christ—never.

As if a black straitjacket tightening around the fringes of his mind, the claustrophobic truth enclosed Bill's conscience.

"No," Bill said, "she won't come back." He glanced over at the pale shape of his son. Silence hung between them like a solid thing. Bill peered through the windshield, the moon's reflection making a silver Rorschach shape on the hood of the car. "But, son, you have to know that your mother—"

In a blur, Casey unfastened his seatbelt and shoved open the passenger door.

Bill stammered—"Casey!"—and fumbled for his own door handle, making a feeble attempt to give chase before getting yanked back down by his seatbelt. He had the brief glimpse of his son running through the untended grass before disappearing between in the columns of tree-trunk shadows.

Bill scrambled out of the car, sprinting up to the house. "Casey!" he called out, frantically scanning the front yard. Not knowing where to begin, Bill darted around the side of the house.

Casey was standing in the side yard, reverently facing a long row of broken windows. Bill's initial impulse was to forgo speaking to the boy, but rather clutching hold of his son and spanking him all the way back to the car. Instead, relief spilled in to Bill.

"Casey?"

His voice was hushed. "Yes, Dad?"

Bill was panting. "Damn it, don't ever do that again."

"Sorry, Daddy. But I wanted to see up close—I wanted to see all that." Casey gestured at something through the hollow socket that had once been a first-floor window. The tall grass made sibilant, hissing sounds as Bill sidled up next to his son, slipping his hand into Casey's. He was preparing to formulate some sort of scolding before glancing inside the house, into what used to be a parlor or living room. Bill was now as mesmerized as Casey. Helplessly, his mind was pushed backward, back down to his fifteen-year-old self; and while many of these memories had remained smudged and obscure, the sensation of physically confronting the Aikman place had the effect of adjusting focus, bringing definition through an internal lens.

A memory came. *The* memory came. A group of teenagers, Bill one of them, a gang of six or seven local kids who'd been running together that summer, a mix of guys and girls. Victoria Sanford was there. Since elementary school, Bill had had a crush on Vicky (most guys did), but she was "wild." *Wild*—that was the term Bill's mother often used. Bill's term would have been "out of my league." Although years later in college, he would learn a more accurate word: "indomitable."

Because of her exotic complexion, Vicky had always reminded Bill of a firmly built Indian girl: nutmeg skin, long, coffee-colored hair, and eyes so deeply chestnut that they verged on black. Throughout their elementary and middle school years, he liked most everything about her. Except, sometimes, her laugh. It took on a coarse quality as they entered their teens. It was as if there was something bitter inside her laugh now, like specks of glass in an otherwise welcomed breeze.

And there had been gossip—by adults, mostly—that Vicky's "wild" behavior was a result of her parents' separation and eventual divorce, something about her father—something he did; there were even hushed discussions about "it" being something he'd done to Vicky.

It had been overcast that afternoon in July, the sky an endless tumble of soot-dusted cotton. The group leaned their bikes against trees in the front yard of the abandoned farmhouse. Inside the former dwelling they found only a few interesting items—a rust-rimmed sink with some shattered plates, a fireplace in which someone had tried to burn a shoebox full of Polaroids. The floorboards had creaky-weak spring to them, as if a section might collapse and send someone plummeting into the root cellar.

It had been Vicky's suggestion to explore the second floor.

Once upstairs they split up, giddily searching rooms. Bill was leaving an empty bedroom when he heard Vicky hiss. "Hey, Bill." He spun around. She was down the corridor a bit, peeking around a corner; she jerked her head. "Check it out." Bill pursued, rounding the elbow of wall. Vicky was now at the far end of the hall, standing in front of a door, palming its brass knob. Her face held the expression of a magician's assistant preparing to reveal some sort of wicked trick. Vicky was wearing cut-off jeans, clipped so high that her pockets showed from under the frayed lips of her shorts, and a black Def Leppard T-shirt, the logo from the *Hysteria* album. Bill approached but said nothing. She turned the knob and the door yawned open. A staircase. The attic. "Come on," she purred. "You've got the guts to go up with me, don't you?" Bill fidgeted, suddenly aware of the possibilities. It was humid up there, her cinnamon-tinted skin looked sweat-filmed. For only a moment, Bill was crippled by hesitation. But a moment was all it took.

The other kids were curiously converging now. The attic windows let in some meager light up there, a dust-and-shadow diffuseness. Silence wore on for stretch as Vicky scanned the group, her unnerving gaze settling on Bill for a second or two before rolling her eyes. "Jesus, you guys. Who's coming with me?" The teenage gang murmured non-committally. "Fine," she said with no hint of disappointment. She dashed through the threshold, bounding up those scuffed and creaking stairs as the group watched her ascension until she was at the head of the narrow passage, supplying an impromptu victory dance. "Come on, guys, take a look," she said. "It's spooky as hell up here."

And then Vicky Sanford tugged up her T-shirt and peeled down her bra, providing the group with an improvised peepshow. With something very much like awe or admiration, one of the girls, Darlene Zukowski, said, "What a crazy bitch." Vicky laughed, an abrasive, teasing noise that Bill would become acquainted with in the years ahead. "Hey, fellas—I'll give you another peek if you come up and join me." Blood rushed into Bill's face, his pulse already hammering in his throat as Vicky—this time swiveling her hips with slow, sensual finesse—lifted her T-shirt again, this time cupping her heavy breasts. Bill's mouth went dry at the sight of her chest, the inverted-heart-shaped curve lining her cleavage and tracing the lower crescent of each breast, the firm indention between her sternum and belly button.

The small crowd of teenagers chortled, and Bill remembered one of the guys—Luke or Davey—whistling, egging her on, making a joke—"Better get it while the getting's good"—before stepping into the corridor. Most of the others followed, including a couple of girls. Only a few kids remained on the second floor, Bill being one of them, milling around while footfalls, muffled laughter, and other noises issued from the attic.

Bill never heard the story of what actually happened up there. He never asked.

Even though Vicky was in most of his classes that autumn semester, he never asked. In the years ahead he reluctantly listened to rumors—the pregnancy rumors that, as far as Bill knew, never turned out to be true; while other stories, the parties where Vicky got drunk, got out of control, were unshakably accurate. During those four years of high school, Bill watched Vicky pass herself around their small group of friends, and still Bill didn't ask. And despite their chance meeting at the nearby college—"*So, Bill . . . when are you going to get sick of acting shy and ask me out for a drink?*"—and the dates that followed, the quiet out-of-wedlock miscarriage, the hasty and tumultuous marriage,

Bill never worked up the courage to ask.

Bill only had the courage to *tell*—he told Vicky what her problems were. After completing a few college courses, he started using words like histrionic, latent, borderline, disorder, and promiscuous. For Bill, her agreeing to marry him became an opportunity to fix—to teach—that wild girl exposing herself at the top of the stairs.

Now, standing next to his son in the untamed yard in front of this decaying house, Bill shuddered and clenched his teeth, forcibly pulling his gaze away from the high attic dormers.

It was little more than a whisper, but Bill nearly screamed at the abrupt emergence of Casey's voice. "Dad—Dad, do you see it?"

Bill bristled. "See what?"

Casey lifted a finger, "It's right there," indicating a spot within the house. "See it? See it? It's moving."

Bill winced, growing impatient, not understanding. "Son, I—"

And then Casey squeezed his father's hand. "Dad, look—it's right *there.*"

Squinting, Bill scoured the fractured ribcage-interior of the house. A breath carrying a question was strangled in his throat, his mouth hung open. Something was . . . *there.*

The harder Bill gazed the more vivid the thing became. Vaporous at first, it gathered itself up from the overlapping gloom, squirming shapes contracting into a gauzy figure. It was drifting across the parlor now, a slender shrouded thing.

Bill's breath caught as a face swam out of that ragged blackness— an angular, expressionless face, like a dirt-smudged cameo carved from bone. A gray hand slid from within the undulating cloak, its fingers hooked and reaching up, revealing a cadaver-pale throat, sliding further down now, exposing a gray slash of collarbone. Bill clasped his free hand to his mouth, his other hand still gripped with Casey's.

"Do you see it?" Casey said.

Bill spoke, but it was little more than a whimper. "Yes."

Casey tore his hand away and raced forward, running up to the open cavity where a window had once been and, as if to hoist himself inside, clutched hold of the lower lip of the sill. Casey cried out, spinning around and thrusting his hand at Bill.

"Daddy—I'm sorry, Daddy, I'm sorry."

In the moonlight Bill saw blood glistening in Casey's palm. Bill remembered the shards of glass in the casings of the empty window frames. He cradled Casey, calming him, guiding him back to the car, doing his best to disregard the rag-and-shadow figure hovering in the parlor.

Bill settled Casey into the passenger seat and rummaged through the glove compartment, locating a stack of napkins to stanch the bleeding.

Casey was sniffling, still apologizing. "I just wanted to get a closer look."

Bill was nodding. "I know it, I know it. It's my own fault for coming out here." He dabbed the napkins against the small laceration, seeing now that stitches would be unnecessary. "You're a curious kid . . . it happens. Keep pressure on it . . . like this." Casey winced and nodded.

Bill used his knuckles to gently swipe at the channels of tears on his son's cheeks. He was moving to close the glove compartment when his hand froze, his fingers a few inches away from a tiny box of Ohio Blue Tip Matches. He picked it up. Bill inadvertently flicked his eyes at the house and heard a witch's whisper. *Burned down by hoods.* The matches gave a bone-dry rattle as he gave the box an experimental shake.

"Dad."

Bill trembled, shifting his gaze to Casey's tear-swollen face. He dropped the matches back in the glove compartment and slapped it shut.

The headlights quaked as the car shook over ruts on the overgrown driveway. Bill checked the clock on the dash before giving a glance in the rearview mirror. He stared at the vibrating, rearview reflection of the house on the hill. With moonlight glowing from behind, the house's silhouette appeared sharp-edged, as if crookedly cut from black paper. Something separated itself from the dwelling, a shroud shape floating into the yard, lingering in the knee-high grass. "Casey?"

His son had been facing the passenger window; now he turned, his expression and the set of his small body at ease. "Yes?"

"Will you tell me what you saw back there?"

Hitching in a breath, Casey told his story, and Bill listened. But with each bump along the narrow country road, Bill heard the box of matches shuffling around in the glove compartment, the brittle rattle of bones.

Don't Let the Bedbugs Bite

Sundays have become unbearable. But before this Sunday—that is to say before *this morning*—the only thing I seriously needed to worry about was nursing a hangover. Now things have become . . . complicated. Now what I need to focus on is neglect, and maybe consequence. Either way, this Sunday was different. Worse.

I should probably explain what you're about to read—not a confession, I have no doubt what happened will affect others. But this is also a custodial exercise—an attempt to keep things as clean as possible, as sane as possible.

I'll start here: this morning. I live in the country, in an old house. Not quite a farmhouse, although I am surrounded by fields and farmland. I woke early, feeling achy and lousy, my mouth still soured from last night's beer. The light seeping in from the windows was dim and blue. I lay there for a while, drifting in and out of sleep, listening to the wind make the windows chatter as it rushed up along the eaves. The wind—making a low-moan sound, like blowing over the lip of a beer bottle—had picked up overnight, and I didn't have to look outside to know it brought more snow with it. I listened to other noises too, old house sounds—the pinging and popping of joists up in the attic. From time to time, I could hear scuttling up there. Coveys of field mice, no doubt, taking refuge for the winter. I imagined other things up there in the attic, in the walls. Web-nests of spiders; wing-wrapped bats nestled in clusters. Twitching termites munching on wood.

I tried not thinking about the cemetery. About Julie.

So I continued distracting myself with the winter-sounds I was hearing all over the house. Okay, right: the bugs. That got me thinking about that urban legend (although I guess out here it'd be consider a "rural" legend), the claim that dozens of bugs and spiders crawl in your mouth at night while you sleep.

I asked Uncle Jasper about this the first time I'd heard it. I was probably in middle school. (I always asked Uncle Jasper about that sort of stuff. My dad was pretty useless for advice, especially back then. Now he's just useless. Uncle Jasper sort of adopted me by default. I never had a problem with that.) Uncle Jasper, sitting at the table in front of his typewriter, crinkled his already wrinkled forehead (because of his prematurely gray hair, most kids thought he was my grandpa) and said it was nonsense. "Besides," he'd said, waving off the story, "somebody would have to do a DNA test on a person's stomach to find out if there really was an abundance of bugs that had been digested. And that can't be cheap, Dennis." Uncle Jasper always did have a reliable built-in bullshit detector.

Anyway—like I was saying: It was the noises in the attic that got me thinking about the bugs in the first place, and it's the bugs that got me writing this now.

Trust me: I'm not a writer. Sure, what you're reading here might be serviceable, maybe even competent, but it's nothing more than the result of private practice. (For the last few years I've been maintaining a journal, which I keep fiercely private.) Now Uncle Jasper on the other hand—he's a writer. I've read the stuff he's written (poems, essays), and he's good, smart. He says he started writing after Aunt Susan died (cancer). I always admired that: Uncle Jasper's resolve after Aunt Susan passed. He was . . . honorable. And even though I'm not as good a writer as Uncle Jasper—or as good a widower, for that matter—I like to think I'm like him in other ways.

We were both born and raised here—here being Deacon's Creek, what I used to think of as a blue-collar-nowhere place when I was younger. But I've grown to appreciate it, or at least what it used to be. So Uncle Jasper's been here sixty-seven years; me: thirty-six.

And just as Sundays weren't always this way, Deacon's Creek wasn't always a town on the verge of financial and social emaciation. Now Main Street's just a slow-beating heart with withering arteries stretching out to other more bucolic towns. Oh sure, a few years ago some civic groups got the bright idea to transform Main Street into something more contemporary—something to draw in tourists on their shopping trips between Chicago, St. Louis, and Cincinnati. A popular fast-food chain replaced the flower shop; Harlan's barber shop was taken over by a commercial shoe company; and the grocery store (where I was hired for my first job) was converted into a high-end antique boutique. But none of them succeeded, and the outsiders just left. Now we're stuck with empty stores, empty houses.

Even the farmers are having trouble maintaining their small-town roots. A lot of the small-scale growers have had to sell their farms, or at least their fields. After some of the big-time companies came in, the families' business models collapsed and they had to sell out. For the last few seasons, outside parties have been using that land. Uncle Jasper says these commercial guys have been using weird chemicals on those fields—DDT, anhydrous ammonia, stuff like that. He said the seeds they've using have been genetically altered, and that the corn can survive massive amounts of herbicides. Here, in my clumsy explanation to you, I wish I'd have listened better to Uncle Jasper. About a lot of things.

One of those cornfields skirts the edge of my backyard. They've been using those chemicals for several seasons. It gets me wondering about what the chemicals have done to the insects around here. Honestly, in the past few years, I've seen what I thought were rabbits and other animals skittering about within those stalks of corn. Now I wonder if they were rabbits at all.

But I was talking about Sunday mornings, and about Julie.

I met Julie in college, and that was the only time I lived outside of Deacon's Creek. I dropped out after a year, came back here, and got hired with the landscaping company (where I still work); but Julie and I kept in touch. Eventually, I talked her into letting me take her to dinner; we dated for about six months before I proposed and convinced her to move to Deacon's Creek. She found a teaching job at an elementary school.

We loved Sundays. We were married for a little over five years, so that gave us about twenty seasons together as husband and wife. We really had some wonderful mornings with each other.

One of Julie's favorite things to do was clean house on Sunday mornings. We'd wake up, maybe make love, then drive into town, eat breakfast at a café, and return home. Julie would turn on the radio (a college station was her favorite, one that played two hours of Beatles music: "Beatles Brunch," they called it) and open the blinds, letting the light stream into the living room, what we would have eventually called the "family" room—I know she wanted that: a family. I know she wanted to turn this dilapidated place into a good home to raise kids.

Anyway. Julie would make her rounds—dusting, laundry, vacuuming. I'd lend a hand where I could, but really, Julie did most of the work. She just seemed . . . content. I should have (and could have) been a better helper.

Julie died in a car accident. Maybe reading that and telling you that seems abrupt, but so was the accident. She'd been coming home from work. It happened out on County Road 700—a car full of teenagers, speeding, lost control of their car; it was a head-on crash. The three kids were hospitalized and lived. The doctors said Julie probably died instantly. Of all the things I avoid recounting, that's the worst—whether or not Julie suffered.

That was six years ago, seven years this coming spring.

Uncle Jasper, having already gone through the process of coping with Aunt Susan's death, tried to help me through Julie's death—the funeral arrangements, the money, those sorts of things.

In those first few months after the accident, I'd go out to the cemetery every Sunday and take flowers to Julie. I'd sit, I'd cry, I'd talk to her. And at first, I was eager to go out there. At first, it felt as if I was actually talking to Julie, and she was listening; but then it started feeling lonely, as if I were just talking to a cold rectangle of marble; then it just felt like I was talking to myself. And that was like talking to no one at all. So—even though Uncle Jasper said it was good for me, and good for the memories I had of Julie—I quit going out there.

Memories are funny like that. Why do you think people hang up pictures in their house?—they need physical proof to validate memories. We all do. That's another reason I'm writing this now, to sort of keep what happened this morning glued together. I'm writing this now not only as an exercise to maintain sanity, but to bring keener clarity to what I saw this morning. Because if I lose my mind, then I can kiss my memories of Julie goodbye.

I'm downstairs in the den right now; but I can still hear them—upstairs, in the walls. You might say a smart person would have called an exterminator. Maybe so. But knowing what I know now, a smart person would have never had time to call, because a smart person would have run.

Here's a silly thing I used to do from time to time: Back before Julie, back in high school—and during my first and only year of college—I'd make a chronological list of all the girls I'd ever kissed or had sex with. (Admittedly, in high school it was a pretty slim list.) It was a physical list of physically intimate conquests—a list running from my first kiss (Kelly Baker, first grade) up through Nikki (which I'll discuss in a minute).

I'm not proud to admit it, but in the years since Julie's been gone, and in my widower's loneliness, I've shared my bed with several women.

Let me say that none of these women were the kind that leave sweet notes in the morning. Not like Julie. These women never said sweet things before falling asleep. I have fond memories of Julie leaning over and whispering, "'Night, 'night, Dennis."

"Sleep tight," I'd say.

Then she'd reply softly, "Don't let the bedbugs bite." I've missed that little routine more than I can express here to you.

That being said, this morning, lying in bed—and further distracting myself from confronting the issue of going out to the cemetery—I began making another, more recent list.

There was Abby, who I met at the library in town. She was shelving books, and we somehow struck up a conversation. Abby had the blackest, straightest, silkiest hair I've ever seen or touched. We saw each other for about a month or so, but things didn't work out. She was intelligent. I don't think my being a college drop-out was a turn-on for her.

After Abby was Vanessa. I was at a tavern down on Main Street one night with a few guys from the landscaping company. Vanessa was sitting at the bar by herself. I bought her a drink. And even in the neon-dim light of the bar, her eyes twinkled green, almost emerald—so green they affected sobriety, albeit briefly. Things were short-lived with Vanessa too. She didn't ask a lot of questions and didn't expect a lot of answers. She liked meeting at hotels a lot. I think she might have been married.

Then there was Nikki, a waitress at a chain restaurant a few counties over. Nikki was the youngest and the kinkiest—the worst and the
last. Nikki and I lasted for almost six months; but if things would have
continued, Nikki would have been trouble for me. While she had a
sort of fleeting, injured tenderness about her, she was, more than anything else, a casually cruel girl. Besides her frequently changing hair
color, the most memorable characteristic about Nikki was her tattoo—
a large, elaborate praying mantis that ran from the outside of her thigh
and wrapped up around her back, its long spiny legs extending up over
her lower back.

Only once did I inquire about the tattoo's significance. I was driving her home one morning when I asked. She was in the middle of
lighting a cigarette when she looked over at me, froze for a few seconds before laughing—laughing as if she were watching a child doing
something adorable and totally foolish. It was a laugh I'd grown tired
of. I kept driving. Eventually Nikki quit giggling, sighed, and lit her
cigarette. I saw Nikki at a bar not too long ago; she'd been playing
pool with a couple guys, or rather *acting* like she didn't know how to
play pool—letting one of them repeatedly reach around her from behind to show her the proper way to use a cue.

It's occurred to me before, although I haven't had the language to
explain it until now, that there seemed to be some form of emotional
parasitism with these last three women—some sort of lonesome anesthetization.

Sometimes, particularly when I avoid dwelling on Julie for days on
end, I have dreams that she's returned to our bed (the bed I've disre-
spected), slowly materializing in the depression where she used to
sleep, like fog drifting into a gully at dusk. Sometimes, in my dream-
eager need to communicate, I speak; and as I do, my breath curls the
delicate features of the phantom and the fog dissipates. As little use as
I have for religion and superstition, I often find myself praying for that
phantom to stay.

The goddamned thing is this: once you give license to old wives'
tales and the supernatural—once you sincerely marry mental energy
and commitment—there's no telling what will break through.

Most of these Julie-dreams have been pleasant—some of them
even felt therapeutic. But sometimes they're bad; or rather, their es-

sence is bad. The tone is all wrong, and that *feeling* invariably carries over into the next morning, setting the miserable tone for a miserable day. It was almost as if, through the dreams, Julie had been dictating what kind of day I'd have when I woke up the next morning. Last night I had a bad dream.

So let me finally get out of bed, or at least tell you about when I finally got out of bed this morning. Let me get back to what this is really about: neglect.

Rousing myself from those cold sheets, I yanked up the blinds at the window and stood there, looking out over the countryside. Sure enough, it had snowed overnight, and the wind was rustling some of the broken stalks spiking out of the cold, white blanket covering the empty field (again, I think about the chemicals—the bugs). The belt of trees out west was all blacks and browns and grays under the pigeon-colored sky, which hinted at more snow to come. I closed my eyes and gently pressed my forehead against the frigid glass—the icy contact having a pleasantly sobering sensation.

I started in with my usual litany of resolutions: no more casual sex . . . no more barroom arguing . . . no more blackout drinking. But then I stopped. I realized I was just making another list. Resolutions?—I needed to start making *promises*. Promises I could keep, especially if they were for Julie.

I pulled my forehead away from the window and opened my eyes. I'm going out to the cemetery today, I promised. And I'm going to clean the house. So I decided to start here, with the house.

After showering, I pulled on an old pair of jeans and a worn-out flannel and walked downstairs. When it comes to accomplishing dull tasks, I've become a creative practitioner of delayed momentum. And at first, I found a few things to distract myself from the *real* job of housecleaning. I started a pot of coffee, laced up my boots, and stalked through the snow and out to the mailbox to get the Sunday newspaper, and came back inside and started a fire in the cobblestone fireplace. Soon, the house was filled with good smells—the acrid percolation of chicory and smoky-warm fire scents. I turned on the radio to some static-lashed jazz station. At this point I could have easily given in to old habits—I could have dropped down in the recliner, started reading the paper, maybe turned on the TV. But this morning—more so than usual—I had self-disgust on my side. I stoked the crackling logs in the fireplace a few more times before setting the tongs down on the hearth.

I parted the drapes hanging over every window on the first floor, noticing that a few gold spokes of sunlight were now piercing through the gray-wool clouds. Dim light streamed into the house. I began spraying and wiping down the windows, the panes regaining their clarity. I went into the bedroom, tore the sheets from the mattress, and tossed the bedding into the laundry machine. Now with washer going and the antiseptic light revealing dust and spider webs, I set out to re-arranging the living room and picking up clutter. After that came the next chore—dusting. I went from room to room, removing items from shelves, pulling novels from the bookcases and wiping down all exposed surfaces. Copious amounts of disturbed dust filled the house—glittering motes swirling in the gray shafts of sunlight streaming in through the windows.

Now that I recognized some semblance of Julie's tidy and cozy Sunday-morning home, the work came easier. I whistled along with the staticky jazz station playing in the kitchen.

After dusting everything, I prepared to start vacuuming.

I couldn't remember the last time I'd vacuumed the house. (Months? Last summer? I still can't recall.) Suffice it to say, the vac-uuming—like the whole issue of cleaning—was something I'd ignored for far too long. The old vacuum (a long disused domestic totem, which Julie and I had received as a housewarming gift) was in the back of the hall closet, standing behind a curtain of coats.

I pulled the dust-caked device from the closet—the outdated thing protesting with a few plastic creaks—and unwound the cord. I waved away some floating particles that the flimsy dustbag had shaken off, trying to avoid breathing in too much of it, before flipping a switch. The vacuum, with a sustained wheezing, rattled to life. I began work-ing over the carpet with smooth lunges, making my rounds from the den to the bedroom to the living room. At one point I realized I was smiling at the thought that Julie might be proud of my progress.

This would be an appropriate moment to tell you something else. It was the dust that got me thinking about it then, and it's the dust that gets me thinking about it now.

I've had all day to turn this over in my mind, and had it not been for what happened, I might have completely neglected a conversation I had had with Uncle Jasper a couple months ago. It had been a Saturday night. I was at Uncle Jasper's house for our monthly chess match, which, as usual, essentially amounted to me getting my ass kicked. It was my night to buy the beer. He was craning over the chessboard, his heavily lined forehead summoning more wrinkles as he studied the pieces. At some point I glanced over at the coffee table, at a stack of magazines. The one on top was an issue of *Scientific Frontiers;* I slipped it off the table and flipped through the pages. An article caught my eye: "Dust In the Wind, Scientists Wonder What Will Happen."

I scanned the article, absent-mindedly mumbling one of the enlarged excerpts. "Common dust travels thousands of miles, over continents and oceans." Silently, I continued reading about new research into how dust was altering the environment. Tons of the stuff—from smoke, soot, and soil—make "transport events" through the atmosphere which can even be seen from space. Pollutants like dust and smoke are evidently responsible for thousands of deaths in some countries.

"Skin," Uncle Jasper said abruptly, startling me, "is the body's largest organ."

Wondering where he was going with this, I looked at him from over the top of the magazine. He was still scrutinizing the chessboard but was no longer scowling. "A while back I read something very interesting, Dennis." Of course he had. Uncle Jasper—the consummate reader, the blue-collar scholar. He continued speaking without peering up at me. "The reason dust starts off light in color before turning darker, eventually turning black, is because so much of it is made up of *cells.* That is to say, decomposing skin cells." I watched him watching the chessboard, wondering if he was trying to distract me or if he'd had too much to drink. "The cell that makes up skin—keratinocyte, I believe—is the same cell responsible for keratin, which forms nails and hair."

Now I knew this was some sort of distractive tactic. Nevertheless, I set down the magazine, picked up my beer, and let him continue. "We lose about one hundred hairs a day, Dennis." He ran his arthritic fingers through his wiry tangle of gray hair. "Each week we lose about, oh, a gram of dead skin cells, and we lose tens of thousands of skin cells each passing minute."

Drunk or not, I smirked at him. "Why are you telling me this?"

"Because skin, my dear nephew," Uncle Jasper reached out and grasped his black bishop, "isn't the only thing you're losing at this moment. Check—and if I'm not mistaken—mate."

As I said, that conversation with Uncle Jasper took place months ago. I wish I'd remembered it sooner. But I'm not sure it would have done any good anyway.

I was thinking about that dust-discussion when the vacuum began making an awful noise: a low, weepy moan. It occurred to me—too late, of course—that I had neglected to replace the dustbag. The whimpering din continued as I clicked the power button, which was stuck. So I grabbed the cord and yanked the plug. Now the mechanical noise from the machine died away, but was replaced by something else. Something worse. At first it sounded as if a cat or some other animal had been stitched up inside. The mewling grew louder. I pried off the plastic cover and stopped short of detaching the bag. Something was shifting and squirming inside—as if filled with writhing knots of irate snakes. I'm sure anyone witnessing my reaction would have described it as something preposterous—something from a movie: me, wide-eyed, slowly lifting my hand to cover my mouth and inching away.

As the mewling grew louder and the squirming became more frantic, another sound emerged. And although I write this to maintain some sharpness in my sanity and to bring keener clarity to the thing I saw—the thing *I know* I experienced—there's one thing of which I'm incontrovertibly certain: the voice. The voice that suddenly shaped itself from a ragged, nonsensical whisper. And that whisper-hiss said my name. *"Den—niiiissss . . ."*

A thin laceration appeared on the dustbag. From the slit emerged the tip of what looked like an ink-dipped porcupine's quill. But now I have a more accurate description: a black widow's leg, slender, segmented, shiny. Seven more slits appeared and seven more legs poked out of the bag, which was rattling to pieces like a dried-out beehive. I could see an oblong smoothness inside, and think now of the bloated tissue of a satiated tick, the grayish flesh covered with dark, hairy bristles. There were other things imbedded in its skin—calcium-colored pieces of teeth and bone, like half-formed elements growing within the soft, timorous tissue. Then I saw an eye—a black, glistening eye, as large and a smooth as an obsidian billiard ball.

I was unable to move. What I was seeing was impossible. But it was *real.* And in that awful dissonance between the impossibility and reality, a single sustained howl broke free in my mind—a sound that made me feel both alive and nauseous. Maybe you'll see and feel something like that someday.

I summoned enough of my threadbare faculties to shake out of my paralysis, making a staggering twist toward the fireplace, reaching out and grabbing the bronze tongs on the hearth and spinning back around. Despite myself, I made a few confident strides toward the kitchen. The bag was completely detached from the vacuum now, and the spider-tick thing was on its back, its legs making desperate, wriggling swirls in the air. In what may have been panic, the thing started excreting a viscous web on the floor, made of thick strands of dark silk.

Just as I opened the tongs, the thing righted itself, flopped over, and grappled the floor. In a foul-smelling burst of dust, the tick-thing vomited a pool of spiders and beetles. Small black scuttling things spilled over the floor, darting in different directions. I felt the first sick tickle of something crawling up my shin, and by the time I swatted at it, I felt something working its way up my stomach, my chest, my collarbone. I slapped at something on my chin, feeling a wetness smear greasily near my lower lip.

Holding my breath, I stepped forward, my boots crunching the black carpet of bugs on the hardwood floor, and made a wincing grab for the spider-tick with the tongs, pinching it around the bloated abdomen and shuffling toward the back door, holding the bag with the tongs and reaching for the doorknob with my free hand. The black-widow quills were wriggling, gyrating in eight directions, slashing at the air. I twisted the knob, took one step onto the porch, and pitched the thing out into the snow. It rolled and tumbled for a moment before balancing, those black legs quickly making a mincing retreat toward the barren field, trailing a cloud of dust behind it.

I shuffled off the porch and took a few steps into the snowdrift-thick yard.

Through the visible puffs of my rapid breathing, and through the low-lying cloud of vacuum dust, I caught a glimpse of black bristles on the thing's back, and of dozens of multi-colored, arachnid-dotted eyes glittering in the weak gray light as those ink-dipped legs carried the thing across the snow.

I stood there for a moment, trying to catch my breath, watching the knee-high weeds part as the thing scurried into the forest that fringes my property. I heard—as if coming from numerous mocking mouths or mandibles—the distant echo of tinny giggles. *"Night, 'night,"* it said, *"night, 'night—'night, 'night . . ."*

Suddenly imagining the sensation of dozens of delicate legs crawling inside my clothes, I began swatting at my body, panic-slapping the back of my neck, my arms, shaking my hair and scratching my scalp.

Eventually, stillness returned. I was still. Dust from the shredded vacuum bag dissipated in thin wisps toward the sky, mingling with the pencil-scratch trail of smoke and ash drifting from my cobblestone chimney. Somewhere over in the woods, a bird gave up a jerky sounding squawk.

That was this morning. It's evening now. When I came back inside I didn't see any of the bugs on the floor. But I could hear them. In the cabinets, in the walls. Rustling under the carpet.

I thought about calling Uncle Jasper. He might know what to do. I still might call him, but right now I need to clean up the mess around here. I thought about leaving this document for him. Maybe if he finds it (and can't find me) he could clean it up a little bit, turn it into something that makes more sense to someone who reads it.

I've locked the door to the bedroom upstairs. The sounds are the worst in there. I have no doubt they're in the mattress. But before I do anything else, there's one more chore I have to accomplish. One more promise to keep. After I write this I'm going out to the cemetery. Do me a favor. If you happen to drive by the cemetery, check in on Julie's grave. If there's a cluster of fresh flowers in front of her tombstone, then everything's okay. If not, and you're reading this, then something's happened here. And I probably deserve it.

RETROGRADE

As the weatherman on the eleven o'clock news begins delivering his forecast, Wayne Webber, stretched out on his side in bed, stares at the television and contemplates two things—one: how magnificent and unpredictable sex with Bridgette used to be; and two: how fortunate and grateful he is that his wife, Nancy, never discovered his indiscretion. *Indiscretions*—the plural, he corrects himself, opting to inculpate himself for each illicit instance rather than the affair in its brief entirety.

Wayne vacantly listens to her now, Nancy, in the bathroom getting ready for bed—the steady hiss of running water hypnotically braiding itself with noise from the television. According to the cheery meteorologist, a low-pressure system has stalled out and is circulating over the region, the cold front's retrogressive condition will apparently trigger a week-long stretch of rain. Thinking his wife might like to know, Wayne says, "It doesn't sound like you'll—"

"It doesn't sound like I'll have to water the plants for the next few days," says Nancy, her toneless, almost vacant voice reverberating inside the white-tiled walls of the bathroom. Wayne shuts his mouth, the side of his face remains nestled the pillow's cushy indentation. She'd been doing that a lot lately—cutting him off, interrupting him mid-thought to unapologetically complete his sentences. Synchronistic things like that, Wayne reminds himself, should be a noble inevitability after over twenty years together. *Which one was it?—familiarity or proximity that bred contempt?* Wayne couldn't recall, but acknowledged the bygone sentiment.

Wayne hears Nancy turn off the running water and waits for the predictable pill-rattle of her medication as she shakes it from the bottle. Then comes the brief, closing squeak of the mirrored medicine cabinet.

There's a lengthy, perhaps thoughtful, stretch of silence before the rectangle of light from the bathroom door is extinguished with a snap, and save for the mercury coruscation from the television, the room is dark now.

The bed frame creaks as Nancy crawls in next to Wayne, mattress springs yawning as the slim figure slides in toward her husband. Wayne doesn't budge and continues facing the TV as Nancy slips her fingers into his gray-threaded hair, her slender fingers massaging his scalp. He feels her breath on the nape of his neck, the gentle pressure of her breasts against his upper back. Nancy places her lips next to his whisker-stubbled cheek and whispers, "I love you, sweetheart." Wayne closes his eyes, ignoring the forecast, wondering if they might try tonight—wondering if she might summon the inspiration to instigate physical affection toward him—wondering if she might reach over his shoulder, her hand moving across his chest, down his sternum, her lithe fingers finding him, slowly stroking him.

On nights like this Wayne sometimes wonders how different things might have been—how different their marriage might have been—if Nancy had just maintained this sort of sensuality. And though part of him acknowledges the success and emotional equalization elicited by the medication, Wayne wants to believe her tenderness is genuine, natural, spontaneous, not some synthetic affection thanks to an amber tube of bi-colored pills in the medicine cabinet. Their therapist had explained that Nancy's new medication would likely change her perception—not only about herself but about he dualistic dynamic of their marriage.

How much of Nancy's depression is biology? How much of it is me? Wayne had posed this Janus-mask pair of questions to himself well before betraying Nancy, and had maintained the detrimental nature-nurture riddle—sometimes insouciantly, often times sincerely—throughout his illicit liaisons with Bridgette.

He fears tonight will be no different from those in recent months, where he finds himself waking sometime in the dead hours, only to stare at the frail, emotionally emaciated shape of his sleeping wife: the soft, cyclic breathing acting as a reminder of Bridgette.

On one of those torment-troubled nights, Wayne had slipped from the bed and wandered the dark house—their home echoing with metronomic ticking of the grandfather clock—for a period before surreptitiously removing his wife's Ouija board (a ridiculous gift from her ridiculously credulous sister) from the hall closet and padding away to his den. Under the small green dome light on his desk, Wayne, feeling foolish and admonishing himself for yielding to this desperate impulse in his self-conscious quest for answers, asked this preposterous device several questions—*Will we ever see each other again? Did she truly care for me?*—and watched or willed the ivory planchette to reveal its nonsensical responses. In the end, the embarrassment was too much, and he solemnly returned the preposterous toy to its place on the top shelf of the closet before taking to the couch in the study, covering himself with a quilt, and ceding to warm waves of sleep, surrounding himself with vivid images of a young woman sitting in the back of the lecture hall.

On nights like this Wayne Webber's mind compels itself to return, again and again, to Bridgette.

He'd initially noticed Bridgette Harless (difficult not to notice)—a grad student in one of his evening lecture sessions at the university—last August. It was at the conclusion of a class in October, as Wayne was gathering his notes and a few reference paperbacks, when the attentive, ballerina-bodied girl from the back row cautiously approached the podium. As her peers shuffled from the lecture hall, she—the *she* was in her mid-twenties, Wayne guessed—cleared her throat and spoke. "Excuse me, Professor Webber?"

Despite having had similar interactions with attractive, ostensibly innocent students, Wayne—in tone, expression, and overall academic affectation—had made his lack of interest in succumbing to cheap charms very clear. Even so, Wayne found that he could not muster the humility to correct the young lady's presumptive distinction between professor (which he was not) and painfully average lecturer.

But of course he had noticed her these past few weeks, hadn't he? This young woman—*What was her name . . . Miss Harless?*—bore a startling resemblance to his wife as she, Nancy—the poised posture, the delicate fluidity of her gesticulations—had appeared when they had first met two decades earlier. But there was something about the girl that was different, the way she smirked, the almost deceptive gliding gait. Something compelling impish and fundamentally naughty, perhaps.

Wayne felt an errant, adolescent flutter in his midsection, and had done his very best to honor a level of professional indifference. Their conversation had been awkward. This young lady had submitted two papers thus far—both sincere but pathetically executed—but now Bridgette's small-town banter moved from class, to art, to her interest in Native American history, due in great part to her grandmother's heritage. Wayne stopped short of mentioning his wife's own Cherokee lineage. Wayne stopped short of mentioning his wife at all.

And these after-class chats continued: Bridgette waiting as Wayne patiently entertained lingering, marble-mouthed questions from a slew of slouching students. Back then—before Wayne had agreed to meet her for coffee, and before those meetings progressed to glasses of wine, eventually ending at her apartment—Bridgette had been re-served, almost woefully shy, self-consciously stroking long ribbons of raven-pitched hair as she addressed her instructor. Later, Bridgette would simply stride past or through her dawdling classmates gathered near the podium, meeting up at a discreet location for a drink before taking him to her apartment.

Discretion, or rather devoted attempts at discretion, had been part of their pact. It was implicit that no one suspect anything untoward. Once, immediately following the conclusion of class, Wayne, wanting to know a little more about this mysterious little creature who had casually imposed herself as his concubine, followed her to her car. There was no car. Rather, he watched Bridgette slide into the passenger seat of a waiting vehicle. The figure of a young man was positioned behind the wheel. And at that moment Wayne had intentionally made himself visible, confidently ambling across the parking in such a way that he would have to come within pointed proximity of the car on his way to his own.

The car slowed, allowing for Wayne to cut through its headlights. He gave a hearty smile and a wave and a split-instant glance at the black silhouette in the passenger. Of course, the next time they were alone together Bridgette provided an explanation. "I bet you're curious about who I got in the car with the other night, huh?"

After a moment of feigning recollection, Wayne shrugged. *The curiosity, my dear, has driven me to the point of distraction.* "No, not really."

"That was Doug. A friend of mine. My car's at the mechanic's and he gave me a ride." Wayne opened his mouth as he prepared to say that it was none of his business when Bridgette, perhaps sensing one last, lingering question, cut Wayne off. "He's gay, Wayne"—the trace of a comely smile appeared at the corners of her lips—"you have nothing to worry about."

Bridgette was gleefully indecent, and sex with her, Wayne had convinced himself, was like therapy. (He had difficulty, though, committing himself to whether it was sex with her body or sex with her spirit that provided the anesthetic effects.) Nancy had her methods of coping with their unhappiness—her therapist . . . her cache of meds . . . her close companionship with her bohemian, Ouija-board wielding sister, who had convinced Nancy to begin reading spiritualist books about her "inner path," stuff (Wayne had gathered) pertaining to meditation, the power of positive thinking, astral projection, and other witch-doctor nonsense. Wayne had no healthy outlet, no companionable release valve, until compromising his steadfast fidelity and acquiescing to Bridgette's coquettishly aggressive advances.

On some of those nights in Bridgette's bed, just before climax, Wayne, his face slacked with ecstasy, would savor Bridgette's body: her slender torso and creamy skin grafted with the razor-slashes of shadow and orange, sodium-vapor light seeping in from the courtyard through the mini-blinds. When she was on top, the black strands of her hair, like rivulets of spilled ink, covered her shoulders and hung between and around her breasts, which rose and fell in an eager-anxious cadence with the rhythm they created.

On one strange occasion, Wayne had drifted into a post-coital drowse and had become overwhelmed with the sensation that his body was levitating, slowly floating up toward the ceiling, away from Bridgette's bed. Wayne was aware of this unfolding as a sort of semi-lucid prelude to sincere sleep; but he was also paralyzed, unable to move his arms or open his eyes. After a time, Wayne—feeling as though he were trapped in the chapter of one of his sister-in-law's meditative self-help books—focused on the synaptic command to simply peel open his eyelids and *look*. And so Wayne opened his eyes.

He was still floating, but his back was against the ceiling now, and he was hovering face down above Bridgette's bed. Two female figures lay on top of the tangled sheets—each with their backs to each other, facing away from one another, each loosely curled on their sides in fetal positions. It was as if a mirror had been placed in the center of the bed, reflecting one of the frail, dark-haired women lying there. *A Rorschach test,* Wayne thought distantly. *Or the top-view of the brain's corpus callosum.* Yet as identical as the figures appeared, he began to discern that one was older, the splayed hair wired with streaks of gray. Everything in this scene, this half-dream aberration, had been absolutely still, but now, with arresting slowness, one of the figures began to twist her head, rotating her face away from the pillow to stare at Wayne's form floating above the bed. Of course it was the familiar visage of Nancy; but as Wayne recognized this, his body began descending, Nancy's portentous expression contained something like devastation mingled with expectation. Her face was painted not by shadow but smudged and smeared with what looked like jaggedly applied war paint. Wayne had seen this sort of mask on the faces of Cherokee shamans. A thin layer of smoke, or perhaps tendrils of incense, appeared, creating a phantom cloud to permeate this slow-motion spectacle. And now Nancy's body was no longer wrapped in crumpled cotton sheets, but was enveloped in a black bear pelt, the animal's palate and upper skull capped over Nancy's head; and as Wayne fell toward her, it was no longer his wife, her face streaked by mystic designs, but simply the open maw of a black bear. The curve-clawed arms sprang toward Wayne as he fell inexorably toward the black cavern of sharp, gleaming teeth.

Dreams, he had told his students each semester. *Never dramatize dreams.* But this really hadn't been a dream, had it? *Come now. No.* Some type of hybrid between hallucination and image-muddled musing.

The affair continued into the first few weeks of December, and Wayne had achieved a confident disposition in concealing his liaisons—always meeting Bridgette somewhere far from the familiar thoroughfare of faces, and only on nights after class. Nancy, typically, would already be in bed when Wayne got home, not budging as Wayne slipped into the bedroom, and appearing not to have stirred even after Wayne had showered, washing away the scents of sex.

On the night of his last lecture with Bridgette's class Wayne, having deemed this a providential coincidence, seized the opportunity of Nancy being out of town—visiting that reclusive, incense-burning sister who lived out by that backward town Colfax—and decided he'd spend the entire night with his kinkily agreeable young lover.

So: the morning after that last class, Wayne woke in Bridgette's bed, his head throbbing and his tongue residue-soured from some questionable brand of Bordeaux. The phone was ringing. Bridgette twitched awake and clambered for her cell phone. She picked up and made a few monosyllabic responses before clasping the mouthpiece with her hand and saying one last thing and hanging up. "Listen," she hissed, "you have to get out of here. My friend Doug's out front." Wayne hadn't risked asking too many questions when it came to the possibility of her sleeping with someone else—someone her own age. Even this Doug character. Bridgette's expression was soberingly unapologetic. "I forgot I told him I'd go to the opening of the Pawnee exhibit up at the museum," she said. "He's waiting outside for me to buzz him in."

Translation: *You are* not *to be seen;* but still he asked, "What do you want me to do?"

Bridgette slid from the bed, partially wrapping herself with the sheet in which she'd been twisted moments before. She crouched and clutched the bundle of Wayne's clothes. "Just go through the courtyard." Bridgette flitted her fingers toward the window. "It'll be easier that way," she said and flung Wayne's slacks to him. Still distantly assuming this might be some sort of joke—*escaping through a first-floor window . . . this has to be a*—Wayne had time to slip into his pants and fasten his belt as Bridgette ushered him over to the window.

It had snowed lightly overnight, leaving a feeble layer of dusty accumulation on the trees and sidewalk in the courtyard. Clouds of various gray smudges stretched out above the apartments like a smoke-tattered shroud.

Bridgette yanked up the window and appraised "professor" Webber. Wayne was tempted to lean in for a kiss, but thought better of it; he swung a leg over the sill. He was gathering his faculties to make a joke about how ridiculous he must look, but he lost his balance and tumbled into the shrubs below the window, the wiry cluster of branches raking his bare shoulders and face. As he rolled into the snow-peppered grass Wayne thought he heard Bridgette stifle a giggle. Or maybe it was just a gasp. He got to his feet, cradling his remaining clothes to his chest. He quickly brushed snow and dead leaves from his slacks. Wayne looked up to say goodbye, maybe even taking the risk of investing the sentiment, *I love you.*

Bridgette had already shut the window and dropped the blinds behind it.

In the following days Wayne continued his business at the university—conducting end-of-the-semester meetings, arranging appointments, generally preparing for break. Initially, Wayne dismissed the less flattering aspects of his first-floor retreat and instead envisioned the scene at Bridgette's apartment with a fair amount of levity—fleeing, he mused, from the ravaged bed of some clandestine lover like a modern-day Casanova.

Wayne spoke with Bridgette on the phone, briefly, after turning in his final grades. She had apologized for the awkward scene at her apartment. Wayne—succumbing to some pathetic possibility that she might instigate another chapter in their relationship—had all but guaranteed a perfect grade for the class.

That had been four months ago.

Bridgette never called again.

Nancy is still massaging Wayne's head, her slender fingers gently coiling and loosening, flexing sensually. With his eyes still shut and the mercury hue of the TV playing on his face, Wayne allows himself a faint smile. He hopes the tepid spell between him and Nancy is over, and that he can share and return his wife's attempts at affection (catalyzed by medication or otherwise) as he had so many years ago. He begins to rotate his upper body toward her. Wayne opens his mouth to verbally reciprocate—*I love you too*—but again, Nancy cuts him off and whispers, "I know, darling. You don't have to say anything—I know." Wayne's smile widens. He thinks about new things, about an uncertain but ultimately companionable path together. *This could be our second act.*

Nancy's fingers, still threaded through Wayne's hair, suddenly contract and coil—her grip tightening on the crown of his skull. In the periphery of his now bulging, searching eyes, Wayne sees a silver flash as Nancy's free hand moves over his shoulder, under his jaw, between his ear and the pillow. And gracefully handling the pearl-handled straight razor that Wayne instantly recognizes from its place on the narrow shelf of their mirrored medicine cabinet, Nancy places the chilled, obscenely sharp steel against the strained cords of his throat, and with a single, elegant stroke, slowly slides the blade to the other side.

WHAT ABOUT THE LITTLE ONE?

The nimbostratus moth wings out west
has become the undulating Rorschach test
I've expected for months. It's hard to tell where it all
begins—where that exam ends. I know Fall

like dreamers know the ocean floor
peace and the aquamarine torpor
of the Kraken's embrace—like the stray dog
seeks the burlap solace in a hollow log

after a morning of fruitless looting. The hound knows:
ear cocked with the hope of a far our howl; nose
to the ground as he crosses the dead-bladed plain
of this frost-peppered property. He returns to the remains

of his hermetic campsite hidden in a wooded nook,
and to the comfort of that aforementioned oak.
Our pup props his jaw upon his paws and joins the dreamers
—drifting off against the green-glow fire made of femurs.

Things began deteriorating after the dog got knocked up. Of course, Lewis only made this association after it was too late. Doing the gestational math—one of the only reliably rational methods that proved useful to Lewis in this particular predicament—the dog had certainly been impregnated on the night he and Maggie had gone sledding on Hatcher Hill.

That had been a Friday night, and on Fridays Lewis Brewster had a routine: finish recording his students' grades for the week, hustle out of the high school as early as his contract stipulated, take a well-worn shortcut to a nondescript liquor store, and drink a generous portion of the purchase along the narrow backroads on his way home. It was a routine he'd established shortly before his separation from his ex-wife and which was later ratified in the midst of a tidy divorce. But then Maggie came along, and Maggie presented an entirely different sort of routine.

On this frigid Friday in February, Lewis had made it home and was sitting in his recliner, easing into inebriation, reading a book about the Johnstown flood, waiting for Maggie to call.

His cell phone rang just as the sun was declining behind the leafless tangle of tree limbs and the steep-pitched roofs of the nearby houses.

"Put on some warm clothes," Maggie said. "I've got a surprise for you."

Maggie. Full of surprises. It had been about six months earlier that they'd initiated their difficult-to-define relationship. Following the divorce, Lewis—having gained the judgment that spending too much time alone would only exacerbate his growing talent for slow-paced psychological self-destruction—had acquired the compulsion of remaining in public places, surrounded by the white noise of the vox populi. He had even taken to writing poetry at a coffee shop on the other side of town, solemnly scribbling bitter, disjointed material, the caliber of which he would have frankly criticized had it been composed by one of his own high school students.

He was a stranger in this part of town, though, and found solace in assuming the role of mysterious poet, a sort of poseur Byron—mad, bad, and dangerous to know. Yes, Lewis was mad, but he wasn't bad, and the only person he was a danger to was himself.

It had been a genuine surprise during one of these self-obsessed writing sessions when someone had casually bopped a fist against his shoulder. Lewis turned to discover one of his former students.

"Well, well, Mr. Brewster," Maggie Boyd had said (it would only be a few more days before Lewis insisted she begin addressing him by his first name). Her voice was distinctively hoarse and seductively husky. "Hell of a surprise to see you here."

Two years earlier as a senior, Maggie Boyd had been precocious and, more often than not, difficult to discipline and unceasingly argumentative, but had a trenchant independence that Lewis found compelling. He'd vaguely suspected that there existed some difficulty in her home life outside of school that fostered her peculiar maturity. In that unexpected moment in the coffee shop, as Lewis extended his hand to shake hers, the thirty-year-old divorcée found himself quickly calculating their age difference—ten years, give or take—and registered a sense of unease about being seen in public with a former student. His unease wouldn't last long.

She hadn't changed much. The tongue ring was new. Her eyeliner and makeup were what Lewis would have described as "Goth lite." She had darkened her hair and fashioned it into a punky, pixy thing. Maggie was wearing a Siouxsie and the Banshees T-shirt and her Bettie-Page bangs tickled the top of her eyebrows as she spoke and gesticulated. Maggie Boyd had a stout body and chest—a mix between farmer's daughter and roller-derby chick.

It was a surprise—during the second week of these coordinated encounters, which increased with frequency, eventually culminating at Lewis's house—to discover Maggie's nipple rings and a slender tattoo of intricate script on her pale stretch of torso. The single line of song lyrics was apparently from a band called Dashboard Confessional. (As with most of Maggie's day-to-day playlists, Lewis was unfamiliar with this particular band.) A few nights after glimpsing the tattoo, Maggie had used her new tongue ring on him with a fascinating, dark-gaze proficiency. They quickly achieved a sophisticatedly tacit variety of sexual stasis (Lewis's students would have slangily classified the arrangement as "friends with benefits").

"A surprise, huh?" Lewis leaned back in the recliner and fingered the slats of the blinds. Though the ember-orange sunset was visually comforting, a swollen expanse of pigeon-colored clouds were gathering in the southwest. "Can you give me a hint?"

"I just did," she said. "God, don't be dull as dishwater. Put on some warm clothes and I'll pick you up."

Lewis thought about it for a second. "I'm wiped out, kiddo." Then he thought about her pale torso in contrast with his dark bed sheets. "But you could stop by in a little while if you want."

Maggie made a dismissive noise. "Have you been drinking?" Though she rarely discussed it at length, Lewis had gathered—among other anecdotes about her immediate family—that Maggie's father was not only bound to a wheelchair but was also a ferocious alcoholic.

"Not really."

"Whatever. Come on, be spontaneous." Notwithstanding her lusty and limber contortions in the bedroom, Lewis had grown weary of Maggie's spontaneity. "Put on a sweater and some boots."

Lewis slowly stretched his neck. "Are you bringing Zooey?"

"Yep."

Of course. Maggie brought her dog, a hyperactive black lab, everywhere it was allowed on a leash. She even began leaving one of the worn, leather leashes at Lewis's house. "What time are you picking me up?"

"Like an hour or something. Just be ready." Maggie claimed to be an only child. Her old man had clearly spoiled her.

That was a Friday night. And how had Nabokov put it?—that Friday everything went wrong.

Maggie drove a 1987 Jeep Wagoneer with faux wood-grain paneling. It had been passed down by her father and she'd freely received the vehicle four years earlier when she turned sixteen. Maggie had no job but was a full-time student at a neighboring university. The only thing he could figure was that Maggie's "daddy" (never *dad* on the rare occasions when she mentioned him) paid for everything.

Night now. Maggie was behind the wheel and they were slowly coursing along snow-coated country roads. Delicate flakes of snow had just started drifting through the yellow shafts of the old Jeep's headlights. Sitting in the passenger seat, Lewis twisted around to glance past the panting, tail-wagging dog to study the two snow sleds stacked in the back—antique-looking, wooden slats with red, metal runners. Lewis cocked his head toward Maggie and in low whisper rasped, *"Rosebud."*

Maggie's face screwed up with smile. "Huh?"

Lewis shook his head. *"Citizen Kane,"* he said at last. Maggie merely raised her eyebrows, clearly anticipating an explanation. Lewis waved a hand. "Never mind."

Despite the frequent disparity in pop-culture references, Maggie was sharp; she'd even caught Lewis off-guard once or twice. For instance: her dog's name, Zooey. Shortly after purchasing the animal last autumn from a classified ad (which we'll come back to shortly), Maggie explained the name choice—a Salinger novella. The title had been lost on Lewis, but he feigned recollection, nodding his head as if retrieving the tale from some great distance.

Lewis found the dog to be mind-numbingly irritating: hyper, obnoxiously eager to please, and desperate for attention. Once, when Lewis and Maggie had been preoccupied in the shower, Zooey discovered Lewis's watch on the dresser and used the leather strap as a gnawing novelty. But Lewis tolerated the animal, certain that as long as he did so, his bucolic concubine would remain as biddable to him as servant to master.

Maggie had chosen a leisurely route through the back roads, and Lewis surmised that she was taking him to Southeastway Park. *Of course—Hatcher Hill*, thought Lewis. "Where'd you get the sleds?"

Maggie was quiet for a several seconds. "They were my parents'." So like the Jeep, the sleds were a hand-me-down from her father.

Maggie rarely talked about her father and divulged even less information about her mother. Drugs, other sorts of substance abuse had been vaguely hinted at.

One Sunday evening months before, Lewis and Maggie had just finished and were lying naked on the living room floor. "I don't even like thinking about that fucking bitch," said Maggie, her cheek resting on Lewis's chest.

Lewis—relaxed, eyes narrowed to slits—shrugged. "You're not on trial here, kiddo." But he was curious now. "What about the rest of your family?"

When it came to discussing her family Maggie's responses unpredictably pendulumed anywhere between the cryptically Delphic to the downright defensive. Maggie had lain quietly, breathing softly. Finally she propped her chin on Lewis's chest and waited for him to look at her. "Let's put it this way," she murmured. "My cousins are sort of like my half-siblings, okay?"

Lewis twitched a frown. "You mean like—" He made a quick calculation—*So your mom has kids from your dad and his brother?*—"Okay." He tried to conceal his dismay and failed. Maggie stared at Lewis for a stretch, her expression registering shame, disappointment, and something else—confirmation perhaps—before nimbly sliding away and slipping back into her jeans.

Now, with the question of the sleds, Lewis was aware that he should give the subject of her parents a wide berth. "So," Lewis placed his hand on Maggie's leg, clawing at it playfully. "Southeastway Park, huh?"

Maggie smiled but kept her eyes on the road. "It was probably never a shocker, was it?"

Southeastway was a two-hundred-acre park managed under the state of Indiana, and as such was closed after dusk. Lewis could not suppress his didacticism, nor could he avoid sounding like an overcautious candyass. "You know we'll be trespassing after dark, right?"

Maggie's face, softly lit by the diffuse candlelight from the dashboard, wrinkled with mischief. "I know."

Maggie knew about a horse trail on the cornfield fringes of the park's property. She slowed the Jeep and steered sharply onto a rutted, tree-lined lane that Lewis had never noticed in his decades of living in New Bethel. Maggie cut the headlights and, after several minutes of jouncing over frozen, snow-filled ruts, the vehicle emerged from under the low ceiling of tree limbs just outside an open, snow-cushioned meadow. From time to time, a ragged break in the clouds allowed enough moonlight to cause the wide expanse of snow to glow. Maggie twisted the key from the ignition. "Okay, handsome." The interior light popped on as she shoved open the driver's side door. "You grab the sleds, I'll grab the dog."

Hatcher Hill was insipidly called "Sledding Hill" by park officials and unimaginative locals who had either outgrown the folk story or were too young to comprehend the original legend. But for those like Lewis who had grown up with the story—and for those who had helped perpetuate and alter the details of the tale—this steep, tree-topped slope would always be Hatcher Hill.

Lewis hadn't been here for ages, probably since high school, and knew that the truth behind the nickname had been sadly simple: one afternoon back in the early '80s, a high-school kid named Toby Hatcher had been sledding with some friends and somehow managed to veer off course and into the wooded shoulder at the bottom of the hill. Hatcher sped headlong into a tree trunk, fracturing his skull. His friends rushed to the guard station, an ambulance arrived from nearby New Bethel.

Following the funeral, kids around town (Lewis included) began reproducing the story, embellishing it with macabre adornments. One of Lewis's favorites permutations was this: Hatcher had overturned and been decapitated by one of metal runners on his sled (not true; it was a flat, cheap, plastic thing) and that sometimes—*on a frigid winter night . . . just like tonight*—Hatcher's headless body could be seen sledding down the hill, the torso leaving a dark streak in its wake as the pale, floating orb of his disembodied head unblinkingly watched from the nearby woods.

Lewis did not believe in hauntings any more than he believed in luck or love or prayer or the vows he exchanged in front of that ghastly pastor eighteen months earlier. People haunted their own houses, bewitched their own woods. People, if they were careless, were apt to make the real unreal (or vice versa).

Nevertheless, for an indulgent moment as he and Maggie postholed their way through the snow, and with Zooey eagerly loping and tugging at her leash, Lewis briefly entertained himself by surveying the woods and conjuring the unlikely image of Toby Hatcher's blue, blood-drained head gliding within the stilted screen of trees.

Maggie had tied Zooey's leash to a tree at the top of the hill. Down below, Lewis and Maggie, peppered with flecks of white, caught their breath following an impromptu snowball fight. "Hey," said Maggie as she wiped snow away from her pink nose and cheeks, her breath visible in short-lived bursts. "I want to show you something."

Lewis sniffed. "More surprises, huh?"

From her puffy coat Maggie produced a small flashlight, which she clicked on. "Come on," she said and started walking toward the tree line.

Lewis took a few steps but looked over his shoulder, up toward the hill. Zooey was still visible, her skinny body bouncing and tugging at the generous length of her leash. "What about the dog?"

Maggie didn't slow. "Zooey will be okay. Besides," she said, jiggling the flashlight's beam at Lewis, "this is something special. Just for you and me." Lewis followed Maggie into the shadow-latticed mouth of the woods.

Twigs snapped and snow crunched under their boots. They hiked for twenty minutes through an overgrown warren that could hardly be considered an honest trail. Yet Maggie clearly knew where she was going. But just when Lewis was about to ask how much farther they had to go, Maggie clicked off the flashlight and stopped. "We're here," she said.

Lewis frowned, but his eyes acclimated quickly. Up ahead through the trees was a small stone footbridge. Lewis, wide-eyed, adjusted his knit cap and shuffled forward. "How'd you find this?"

Maggie shrugged. "I think it's been here forever." She giggled at that. "Kidding. I think it's like a relic or something from the old Pentecostal campground."

Up close Lewis saw that the bridge and its waist-high railing had been constructed with large cobblestones with a crooked maze of mortar holding them together; several boulder-size rocks served as walkway markers at either end. Beneath the bridge ran a skinny creek, frozen over and sheeted with snow, and the distance between the banks allowed a narrow gap between the overarching tree branches. Now and again a breach in the clouds allowed for ragged shafts of moonlight to fall over the bridge.

Almost reverently, Lewis and Maggie stepped onto the footbridge, both leaning over the railing. Maggie gave Lewis a searching look. "What do you think?"

Lewis smiled, sincere when he said, "Amazing."

Then Maggie looked down, scanning the walkway. She crouched and picked up an errant stone, which she clutched to her chest. Lewis watched as Maggie shut her eyes for several long seconds before opening them and lobbing the rock out onto the frozen creek. The stone clinked off the frozen surface, creating an uncanny echo that reverberated into the woods, giving Lewis an unexpected chill and eliciting a shudder.

"Okay," said Maggie. "Your turn."

Lewis hesitated before acquiescing, searching the snow-dusted bridge and eventually finding a baseball-sized stone. He briefly imitated Maggie's silent mantra before rearing back to throw, but paused when Maggie said, "Don't forget to make a wish." Lewis pitched the rock out across the creek. There came a glassy shattering and splash as the stone broke through the surface of the ice.

The two looked at each other and began laughing. Lewis finally said, "So what's that mean?"

"It means you still get your wish." Maggie slowly inched in on Lewis. "You know, you can be a lame old man sometimes, but you've got potential." Then Maggie slid her arms around Lewis and pressed her chest against his midsection. Lewis leaned down and kissed her. Maggie's upper lip was moist with perspiration from the hike. Once the moment had concluded, Lewis began to pull away, but Maggie tightened her grip.

She was staring at him, her inky eyes luminous in the moonlight, and something about the solemnity of her expression startled Lewis. He blurted a nervous laugh and smirked. "What?"

She tilted her chin. "You know, we've been friends—*real* friends— for a while now." *Holy shit,* thought Lewis, *here it comes.* He nodded, exhaled. "And we've been doing *this*"—Maggie cocked her head to the side as if the curt gesture were casting its meaning back across the fields, the winding backroads, neighborhoods, all the way back to Lewis's house, all the back to his bedroom—"since the end of summer."

Lewis said, "And it's been a lot of fun."

Maggie smiled. "Yeah. It has been. But"—she bit her lower lip— "like, if you started seeing someone else, or if you *are* seeing someone else, I think that would make me uncomfortable. You know?" Lewis nodded. Again her expression grew almost severe. "Do you think it will stay this way forever?"

Sometimes you can be so innocent. "I think as long as we keep making our own rules, then yes, we can keep being friends and keep having fun." Aside from slightly loosening her grip, Maggie was intolerably unresponsive. "You know"—*Let's try another route*—"at this time last year, if someone would have told me that my marriage was on the verge of falling apart and I'd be divorced before the end of summer, I would have leaned into their face and laughed." He felt her posture shift but she continued staring at him. "But the good thing about uncertainty is that we have the flexibility to change at any time."

Maggie's delicately furrowed brow suggested she was trying to decipher the context of his bullshit response. She said, "So the future is just supposed to be a surprise?"

Lewis contemplated that. "Yes. A surprise."

He thought this might serve as a nice conclusion, but Maggie renewed her embrace. And now, training her dark, solicitous gaze on him, she said, "I love you, Lewis."

This was something he'd deftly avoided for months, but he'd been so immersed in the unconditional dating and carefree sex that he'd never devised a way to deal with the subject of love when it inevitably emerged. So. Here we are.

Lewis's exhalation escaped as a thick phantom of fog as he gently clasped Maggie's upper arms. He frantically tried to assemble some sort of concessional manifesto that might prohibit any further articulation of commitment while simultaneously sustaining the equilibrium in their tacit pact of guilt-free sex.

Here, standing at the apex of the footbridge and enveloped in an almost unnatural silence, it was as though he'd returned to that scene on his wedding day with Beth, to that odious ritual at the front of the church. Lewis was not religious at all, but he'd done as he'd been asked. *Please, Lewis . . . it's just a formality . . . my family insists . . . do it for me.* He wanted to make Beth happy. *He* wanted to be happy. The least he could do was be a cooperative collaborator. But as his brief tenure as a husband came to a close, Lewis vowed he'd never deliberately return to being a victim—promised he'd never invest in that sort of precarious, self-shaming suffocation—swore he'd never have to risk enduring the sneering taunting confession of infidelity from someone he truly loved. He was sick of playing the role of noble, domestic soldier. For once, he wanted to be the Big Bad Wolf. *Mad, bad, dangerous to know.*

But she's not asking you to marry her, a voice prompted. *Christ, man, she just wants to hear* the words. But what if he did tell her what she wanted to hear? The answer was quite simple: verbally reciprocating this memorialization would only lead to more promises, more pacts, all resulting in an exponentially diminishing leash around his throat.

With a feeble streamer of silver-and-blue breath, Lewis uttered this bloodlessly insufficient response to Maggie's confession of *I love you:* "I know."

The dog was gone.

On their way back from the bridge, Lewis had made meager attempts to talk to Maggie, who remained in front of Lewis, rigidly marching forward. Several times Lewis had nearly coaxed himself to grab Maggie and profess that he was a coward and an asshole and that he loved her too. They were about halfway up Hatcher Hill when Maggie stopped and gasped.

Part of the leash, appearing to have been chewed through, was still attached to the tree; on the ground was a radius of trampled dirt and snow where the dog had struggled to free herself. Then Lewis noticed something. "Maggie, look," he said, pointing to a single set of tracks leading downhill, the sleek, distantly spaced indentions suggested the dog had taken off in a straight-line sprint.

"Zooey!" Maggie cried, aiming her flashlight at the tracks and running in the same direction.

Lewis was running behind Maggie along the bottom-hill boundary of trees, but as she ran ahead Lewis slowed, certain he'd heard something in the woods. He stopped and narrowed his eyes, concentrating on the noises—crunching underbrush, twigs splintering softly, and then a low-level clacking. The sound elicited the involuntary image of rattling porcelain, which ceded to the aspect of teeth—black teeth—chatter-clacking in the cold. Unmistakably a tall figure, moving with a jerky, deformed ambulation, eagerly lurched forward just a few yards within the scrim of trees. Lewis staggered backward. "Maggie." His intended shout came out as a whisper. He cleared his throat. "Maggie . . . I think I hear something."

Maggie jogged up, the beam of her flashlight quaking on the spot Lewis had indicated. "What?" she said, her face screwed up in impatience. "I don't hear anything." Now neither did Lewis.

Just then in the distance, over on the far side of Hatcher Hill, a slow-moving black shape crept out of the woods.

Lewis pointed. "There she is." Lewis began to follow Maggie but faltered, warily assessing the overlapping stilts of gray tree trunks that faded into the black folds of woods. And this is what did it: the sound was barely audible at first, not unlike the hush in a seashell, but then came the slow, seething swell of a whistle—an echoey, discordant keening that caused Lewis to clap his hands over his ears before twisting at the waist and running away.

The dog was limping but picked up speed as her owner closed in. Maggie tossed the flashlight into the snow and dropped to her knees, wrapping her arms around the dog's neck and caressing her face, kissing her snout and rubbing her ears. Zooey whimpered softly. Lewis was breathing heavily as he jogged up, but his relief at finding the animal was short-lived as he noticed the dark, speckled trail that the dog had made in the snow. He picked up Maggie's flashlight and aimed it toward the dog's backside. Lewis could only utter, "Maggie," as the beam shakily played over the red specks freckling the snow and the bloody substance streaking the animal's hindquarters.

Back at the Jeep, Lewis tried to be useful by spreading out a blanket to create a makeshift bed. He attempted to help Maggie lift the dog, but she recoiled, fixing Lewis with a alarming expression—a warning not to touch her. "She's my dog," Maggie hissed through clenched teeth. "I can take care of her myself."

While Lewis was certainly concerned for the dog, he was wary about touching the viscous blood congealing on the animal's backside. And though he could not detect an actual wound, Lewis guessed she'd injured herself in a thick tangle of thorns or possibly on some rusty barbed wire along one of the old fencelines. But then he thought about the distorted figure creeping through the woods. Suddenly he wasn't so certain exactly how the dog received the injury. He had tried to get Maggie to examine this disturbing discovery more closely, but she'd ignored him, opting simply to cradle the whimpering dog and carry her back to the Jeep.

They were quiet on the drive back to the suburbs. Lewis's attention alternated between the hypnotic swirl of falling snow slashing through the Jeep's headlights and snatching glimpses of Maggie's impassive face. He tried to conjure the thoughts that accompanied her expression—*What a fucking fool I am . . . first I humiliate myself by spilling my guts to this creep and then Zooey gets hurt.*

Lewis settled his gaze on Maggie's face and licked his lips. "I'm sorry."

Maggie didn't bother glancing over and simply kept her eyes on the snow-blown country road. After a while she sighed. "I know."

It was a Thursday morning the following week when Lewis received a text message from Maggie. His students were occupied with an assignment while he—*Mr. Brewster*—tried and failed to use his cell phone inconspicuously.

From: Mag
Received: Thursday Feb 21, 8:55 a.m.
Priority: Normal
Zooeys sick – skipping class to take care of her

To: Mag
Sent: Thursday Feb 21, 9:07 a.m.
What's wrong?

From: Mag
Received: Thursday Feb 21, 9:10 a.m.
Puking

To: Mag
Sent: Thursday Feb 21, 9:13 a.m.
Anything I can do to help?

From: Mag
Received: Thursday Feb 21, 9:20 a.m.
No. Will call U l8r

Maggie's spring break as a university student came two weeks before Lewis's spring break as a high school teacher. He'd known for months that Maggie and a few friends had been planning a trip to some debauched locale in Florida, and he had reluctantly harbored an increasing anxiety about the impending week-long vacation. Although she was no longer in high school, Maggie, he was certain, would succumb to the Girls-Gone-Wild climate of that requisitely hedonistic nightlife. *When in Rome.*

At one point, Maggie had suggested that he take a few days off from teaching and fly down to meet her. "It would be like something from the movies," she'd said, curled up on the couch next to him as they watched an old black-and-white called *Dracula's Daughter.* "Just imagine, a handsome older man stepping off a plane, buying me a martini in the airport lounge before whisking me away to his hotel room."

Lewis chuckled. "My boss would dock me on an evaluation for taking off that kind of time two weeks before a contracted break."

Maggie nudged him. "Oh, come on. Live dangerously. It'd only be for a couple days. What's the worst that could happen?"

Lewis made a face. "Well, if I get too many piss-poor evaluations I get fired."

"So?"

"So I'd get fired, couldn't afford the house, and I'd be forced to find a job as a short-order cook or something and go live in a shitty apartment."

"Good," said Maggie, grazing her nose over his collar bone. "I know someone who'd love to be your roommate."

"Oh yeah," Lewis said, playing along. "Who?"

Maggie stretched up and kissed him.

Lewis was a mess the entire week Maggie was in Florida. And for the first time in his life, his low-key brand of concern had morphed into outright anxiety, and that anxiety had eroded into a foreign sort of obsession.

During that long week Lewis maintained contact with Maggie through occasional text messages and several profile postings on Facebook, but for the most part their routine—well, Lewis's routine of sex and distractive companionability—had been crippled. The house was painfully quiet, and Lewis had even grown to miss Zooey's overzealous and mercurial behavior. He idly wondered who was taking care of the dog while Maggie was away.

As the voyeuristic accessibility of the Internet was wont to stoke everyone's inner stalker, Lewis stayed up late, sitting in front of the computer, repeatedly refreshing the browser to keep tabs on Maggie. And it was with an aggressive effort that Lewis, through the spiderweb haze of inebriation, restrained his drunken impulses to contact Maggie and tell her he was thinking about her.

She was clearly having fun, posting pictures of her and her friends (and her *new* friends) on the beach, late-night parties. Lots of guys. It occurred to him that Maggie might be attempting to exact some sort of sophomoric revenge for what transpired that night on the footbridge. He hated pretending that her behavior had no bearing, but he maintained this indifferent vigil as a trial, a sort of commitment litmus test to explore the boundaries of possible monogamy with her. One afternoon toward the end of the week, she finally called: "Hey, stranger. What's new?"

"Not much." *Be cool—be neutral—keep your distance.* "Looks like you're having fun."

"Well, well, Mr. Brewster. I'm doing just fine, thanks for asking. Do I detect a rumor of jealously in your voice?"

"Far from it."

"Liar."

"I've outgrown jealousy."

Maggie sighed. "It's actually been pretty dull—I've just been reading my anatomy book and collecting seashells for you on the beach."

Now Lewis sighed. "Right, anatomy."

"Have you missed me?"

"Of course."

"Well, just so you know, I haven't slept with anyone."

"Yeah, sure."

"I promise."

Seriously? "Seriously?"

"Cross my heart and hope to die."

With an uncontained pulse of relief Lewis said, "We'll have to do something about that when you get back home."

"Back home, huh?" A long pause. "Why wait?"

"What do you mean?"

"Oh, come on, don't tell me you've never had phone sex." Lewis, in fact, had not. "Lindsey and Brittany went to meet some people." Maggie's vampy voice turned pouty. "I'm all alone in this big hotel room." Through the connection came a soft, shifting sound. Lewis vividly envisioned Maggie, cradling the phone between her neck and ear, wriggling out of a pair of cut-off denim shorts and thumb-tugging down her panties. "Come on, Mr. Brewster . . . let go . . . it's easy."

Lewis laughed, but despite himself his hand had absently moved to the zipper of his jeans. Maggie's voice grew husky, bewitching. She told Lewis what to think about. He closed his eyes under the impromptu spell of this erotic enchantment. After a few minutes Maggie murmured, "Now."

Nothing was the same after Maggie returned home. She seemed to have been fortified by her stint of independent travel, and that air of autonomy only exacerbated Lewis's stubborn unease. There had been, as he feared, an irrevocable shift in the dynamic of dominance. Over the course of several weeks, phone calls between them went missed or ignored, and soon things settled into a dichotomous obstinacy. And despite their exploratory attempts to get back to where they'd been in the nascent days of their relationship, nothing was the same. Nothing had been the same since that night on the bridge. One of them had to capitulate. One of them had to submit.

Lewis was driving home from work when Maggie called.

"I think I need your help," Maggie said, sounding as though she'd been crying.

Lewis said, "Sure. What's the problem?" And the next words he expected to hear: *I'm pregnant.*

Maggie said, "I haven't been honest with you." Lewis waited. His mouth was dry and he alternated the phone from one to the other. He suddenly wondered how many other guys she had and how many he'd never known about. "Zooey got pregnant."

Son of a bitch, he thought with a lurch of relief, *is that all?* For the moment he ignored the stalemate state of their relationship. "Well," he said, affecting a teacherly tone, "it really could be a lot worse than a knocked-up dog."

Maggie's exhale hissed over the connection. "You don't understand, Lewis. She got pregnant a while ago." Silence. "It's bad."

And then Lewis recalled the period last fall when she'd bought the dog after having seen a photo in a classified ad or something. Internally, Lewis permitted himself a cursory comment about buying animals from disreputable, puppy-mill hillbillies selling dogs in classified ads. "I thought you said she was spayed."

"She was," said Maggie with a bit of nastiness, clearly not allowing Lewis to use any of his didactic tactics. "It doesn't matter because this is something different."

On the few occasions that Maggie had visited Lewis since she'd returned from spring break, she hadn't brought the dog around at all. *Wouldn't your dad notice?* From how Maggie had described her perpetually intoxicated father, maybe not. "Okay, so what—do you think your dad's going to be pissed or something?"

Maggie snorted a you-just-don't-get-it laugh. "He doesn't know about this."

Though Maggie was obviously distressed, Lewis was at ease, even eager in the certainty that his behavior in the next few hours would determine the reestablishment of their relationship.

Lewis slung his wrist over the steering wheel and with a smirk said, "What do you need me to do?"

Forty-five minutes later, Lewis met Maggie at Hatcher Hill.

It was late afternoon, inching toward evening. At the park a temperate, late-April breeze threaded its way through the profusion of trees.

Maggie had parked her Wagoneer on a curve near the giant hill and was standing with one hand in the pouch pocket of her hooded sweatshirt, the fingers of her free hand pinching a cigarette that dangled at her hip.

Lewis locked his car and slowly crossed the grassy plain at the foot of the hill. As he neared he produced a nervous smirk. "I hope you're not planning on going sledding again."

Maggie sniffed and shook her head. She wasn't wearing makeup, and the absence of it made her look more childlike than usual. She took a deep drag from the cigarette and smashed it into the grass with her sneaker.

On impulse Lewis stepped forward and hugged her. For a moment, Maggie did not move, but something, an unkindled energy, suddenly bloomed between them; she lifted her arms and wrapped them around Lewis's torso.

"Let's talk, kiddo," said Lewis. "What's the big deal about the dog being pregnant?"

Maggie exhaled, her fingers taking a stiff swipe at one eye. "Because she'd already had the baby."

Lewis's smile faded at the strange use of "baby" as a substitute for "puppy." "What do you mean *baby*?"

She gave a dismissive gesture. "Damn it, Lewis, that's why I wanted to see you." Maggie's chest rose and fell. "I don't have anyone else."

* * *

As he'd done roughly two months earlier in the frozen marrow of February, Lewis followed Maggie along the secluded path in the woods. The cobblestone footbridge eventually emerged through the huddled trunks. Dangling vines and ropy things hung here and there in this overgrown portion of the property, and the canopy of tangled limbs were pricked with slender green buds.

At the sight of the bridge Lewis replayed what had transpired that winter night in rapid succession. His midsection was pierced with a sudden flush of feverish guilt. Maggie beckoned Lewis over the bridge; he gave a cursory glance at the clear, languidly flowing water beneath.

Maggie crossed the bridge and advanced a few yards into the forest on the other side of the bridge; Lewis followed but slowed to a cautious stroll when he heard a noise. A thick, navy blue blanket was draped over a large, rectangular object positioned against the bole of a tree. Maggie began making hushing, soothing sounds—*"It's okay . . . everything's okay"*—and gently peeled back a portion of the blanket. It was Zooey's travel crate.

"Lewis," said Maggie, turning and appraising him. "I don't know what to do."

She explained that Maggie had gotten pregnant sometime last winter. "It takes about two months for a dog to give birth after conception." The way Maggie recited all this made it sound as if she were reading gestational information from a pamphlet in the waiting room at a vet clinic. Part of Lewis still assumed that Zooey was here somewhere, surely in the crate; but then again, the way Maggie was staring at him . . .

"Where's Zooey?" he said.

"She's at a friend's house," Maggie said, cocking her head, her expression and body language mingled in a patient plea. "Zooey gave birth a few days ago. And if you count back about sixty days . . ."

Lewis's mind was already tumbling back to the night they'd gone sledding, to the mysterious injury the dog had received on her hindquarters, and Lewis had to move his lips to dispel the numbness that had settle on his jawline. *The dark, deformed figure . . . the high-pitched whistling.* He didn't have to ask what was in the crate.

"Zooey was sick. I guess I thought she might be pregnant, but she didn't have most of the symptoms I'd read about. Even her belly didn't look ... big"—Maggie made a frustrated gesture toward her own abdomen—"or bloated ... until last week. I didn't want to bring her around your house and bother you about it." She gave a curt exhale through her nose and paired it with a hopeless smile. "I didn't even know what *we* were. And I didn't want to scare you away." Lewis opened his mouth to respond, but Maggie seized the moment. "And I didn't want to expose her to my dad because then he'd know I fucked up about getting the dog from some goddamn ad in the paper." Maggie locked eyes with Lewis to fortify her statement: "I didn't make a mistake about her being spayed, Lewis—I saw the scar." A single tear coursed down Maggie's cheek. She explained that she'd brought Zooey to the park for a walk but the dog had gone into labor. "It was ... awful. She started crying and twitching and collapsed." The few seconds of speechlessness were filled with the sound of birds, branches rustling together, and the eager panting of the thing in the crate. Maggie looked over her shoulder. "It came out quick. Zooey only yelped once when it"—she swallowed hard, clearly having difficulty recalling the details—"*crawled* out of her."

With great effort Lewis reversed his impulse to back away. Instead he took his fisted hands out of his jacket pockets and shuffled forward.

"He's peaceful when he's in the dark," she said evenly, "but he just howls if he's in the sun too long." Gently, Maggie peeled the heavy blanket away from the front of the crate, agitating a small cloud of bluebottle flies.

Lewis cautiously closed in, and just as he hunched down to peer inside, the animal, with a scrabbling of nails, lurched forward.

The smell alone—a damp, peaty reek—would have been enough to make Lewis recoil, but the unsettling aroma paired with the revelation of the small creature in the cage arrested his attention and stifled an otherwise impulsive retreat.

If it had been a split-instant glimpse Lewis would have described it as a starved, black mutt. Instead Lewis squinted, scrutinized. It was standing on four, doglike limbs that seemed to be too thinly out-of-proportion for the rest of its frame. Its black fur was matted and in several places exposed patches of gray, almost translucent flesh. The corrugated ribcage of its carriage was startlingly pronounced, but the creature did not appear to be uncomfortable, and despite its disturbing state Lewis could see a tail—or some sort of thin, swishing append-age—wagging happily within the cage.

But it was the face that Lewis had the most difficulty contending with. The dog-thing's long snout and angular head were lowered slightly as it peered up through the bars of the cage; and though its skull was clearly accented in the vein of some coyote or other vulpine variety, its pointed ears looked leathery, like splayed batwings, ragged on the fringes. Its prominent eyes were unnaturally blue, offensively expressive and unblinkingly fixed on Lewis.

Lewis was preparing to turn away when the creature's upper lip wrinkled and curled back, its jaws yawned open, exposing not sharp, fang-shaped canines but glistening squared-off incisors. Human teeth.

"Wha—" Lewis began.

There came another scraping sound as the animal lifted and gently stretched out one of its thickly tendoned forelimbs. Lewis's eyes wid-ened when he saw that each digit on the padded paw contained a long, glossy, talon-curved claw, which slowly contracted around the wire bars of the crate.

Lewis's voice was a croaky whisper. "What happened?"

Maggie's response was muffled behind a wadded tissue. "I don't know." Another sniff and swipe at her eyes. "He just came out of Zooey that way."

Though dizzy, Lewis was careful about appearing sturdy by staying on his feet; he kept his hands on his knees as he continued examining the animal.

"How long has it been out here?"

Maggie moved toward the cage, her voice calm. "Like I said, since Zooey gave birth to him. About a week."

Lewis shuffled backward, looking over at Maggie for a reaction. She'd obviously spent some quality time with this creature. *She called it* him. "What are you going to do?"

In mid-movement Maggie cast a stricken glance at Lewis. "What am *I* going to do?"

"I mean—"

Maggie lowered her head and turned away. Silence descended in their isolated space. "I'm going to take care of him."

Before he could stop himself Lewis said, "What have you been feeding"—he licked his lips—"what have you been feeding *him?*"

Maggie didn't answer as she rearranged the blanket over the crate. The animal's eyes remained trained on Lewis as shadows refilled the cage and the dark fabric fell over the front.

"I know this can't be real," said Maggie, crossing her arms and remaining with her back to Lewis. "I know that you and I don't make sense, and it would take a lot of work to keep us together. You've been a decent friend and a pathetic boyfriend. But I'm just asking for you to stand with me to help sort this out." Lewis opened his mouth to say something but stopped. "I'm a big girl, Lewis. I'm not your pupil anymore and I'm not going to follow you around anymore. If you want to leave, now's your chance."

Lewis didn't budge, feeling his heart pulsing as he considered his options. And as if from high above, up within the trees, he saw himself step forward and embrace Maggie, saying nothing, making a selfless pact through nothing more than selfless action. He knew the creature in the crate was an incomprehensible impossibility. But Maggie was real. The enduring, ember energy between them was real.

Instead, twigs and underbrush began cracking and snapping as Lewis turned on his heel and walked away.

That had been spring. Now it was summer.

Lewis was on his summer break, but it was intended to be a permanent break from teaching high school. He never planned on returning. Lewis had the prescience to understand that, among other things, he wasn't cut out to be a teacher of any sort.

During the day Lewis spent most of his time in the yard, mowing the lawn and mauling the landscaping with nonsensical projects. Yet at night he inexorably gravitated to the computer, aimlessly searching for information on Maggie. They were no longer connected by any sort of social media, so Lewis had to settle for scraps of script in search engines. Lewis spent the remaining sad chapters of his evenings sipping whatever booze was hiding in the cabinets and attempting to refine his writing—a drunken mix of prose and pitifully amateurish free-verse poems. Lewis was invariably ashamed of what was on paper when he groggily reread it the next morning.

He slept fitfully, shudder-jerking awake at the sound of a barking dog in the neighborhood—tree limbs scratching the siding became the clawing of paws, wind rattling the windows and transformed into panting. On several occasions during those panicky moments in the dead hours, Lewis had restlessly thrown his legs over the edge of the bed and the dust ruffle skirting the mattress had caught his bare ankle, causing Lewis to scream at the sensation of a wagging tail swishing against his lower leg.

The feverish existence that had commenced with her absence had reached its deteriorative peak.

He'd discovered that Maggie was working part-time at a video store. It had taken him weeks to devise a way to approach her, a few more weeks to write something for her, and several nights of crouching low behind the steering wheel as he staked out the video store to estimate the rhythm of her schedule.

On a stagnantly humid evening in August, Lewis parked outside the store. Maggie, wearing a dark blue polo shirt tucked into a pair of khakis, was stationed in front of the cash register when he finally summoned the wherewithal to confront her. In one hand Lewis shakily clutched a homemade gift for Maggie.

She was preoccupied and didn't look up when he walked in; nevertheless, she offered a compulsory corporate greeting. A young guy about Maggie's age repeated the greeting and grinned at Lewis before returning to his task of stocking shelves.

Lewis's midsection roiled with a sickening, electric acidity as he absently paced the aisles; he slowed when he spotted a copy of *Dracula's Daughter*. After a few seconds he warily lifted the film from the shelf and rounded the corner on his way to the register.

Maggie's hair was longer now and held no signs of dye or neon highlights; absent too were the facial piercings and heavy eyeliner. Her self-possessed appearance nearly made Lewis steer directly for the exit.

Maggie was still engrossed in whatever she was doing as Lewis placed the movie on the counter. "Did you find what you were looking for?" she said and looked up then, her smile disappearing and her upper body sagging. "Hey," she said, her voice and expression were flat, containing no emotion except for perhaps a civil sort of tolerance.

Lewis had practiced everything—his facial features, his modulation, his overall body language. Things fell apart. "Do you have a minute?"

"We can talk while I check you out." She slid the movie across the counter and scanned it.

Lewis glanced at the frattish guy stocking the shelves before lifting the gift for Maggie—an antique picture frame. Under the glass was a handwritten poem on vintage paper.

Maggie looked at the frame as if it might be capable of infection. "What's that?"

"I made it—I wrote it—for you," he said, trying to quell his vocal quiver. "I didn't know how else to say"—he swallowed, self-consciously glancing over at the guy stocking the shelves—"I'm sorry."

Maggie exhaled and snatched the frame. "Thanks," she said and resumed the checkout. Handing over the video she said, "This is due back in three days."

Lewis feebly gestured at the video. "Do you remember the night we watched that together?"

Maggie drew in a patient breath and looked at the title. "No." She shifted her position in preparation to show Lewis to the door but went rigid when Lewis said, "How's Zooey?"

Maggie's eyes grew dark, but something indefinable had softened in her aspect. "She's fine."

Lewis leaned against the counter and lowered his voice. "How's . . . the *little* one?"

Maggie lifted her chin and glowered at Lewis. She gave a glance at her coworker before soberly regarding Lewis. "I don't know what you're talking about."

And for a swooning, vertiginous instant Lewis wasn't certain what he was talking about either. He passed a hand over his face. "I'm talking about Zooey, about her—"

From behind came a braying voice. "Zooey's a hyperactive psycho."

Lewis flinched and pivoted. The other polo-shirted employee, the good-looking young guy. He was grinning at Maggie with his horsey teeth.

"Shut up, Craig," said Maggie, a soft pink flush appearing on her cheeks and throat.

Craig snorted, shook his head and went cheerily back to stocking the shelves, never quite acknowledging Lewis.

Lewis's lips and forehead tingled and his mouth was dry. As he walked past Maggie he gathered enough of his faculties to ask once more, "What about the baby?"

Almost imperceptibly, Maggie's lower lip trembled and she cocked her head as if hearing some distant whisper. Eventually she simply offered Lewis the movie and said, "I'm sorry. I don't know what you're talking about."

Lewis teetered away from the counter, remotely aware that his legs were carrying him to the door, to the dark parking lot, to the car. He left the video and the antique frame behind.

Several weeks later, when the wretched, dream-wracked nights have reached their most perverse peak, Lewis wakes early and drives out to Southeastway Park. One of Zooey's old leather leashes is limply coiled on the passenger seat. The August theater of verdant, silk-leaved cornfields is already humid and filled with the aroma of wet grass as dawn stretches out in a peach-and-baby-blue yawn. At the park he crosses the flat, dew-damp tract at the foot of Hatcher Hill as he retraces the path on which he'd twice followed Maggie, each irrevocable encounter culminating in irretrievable regret.

Lewis eventually reaches the cobblestone footbridge. Crossing it, he pauses at the apex and considers the crystal-clear creek smoothly sluicing over stones. After a time, he directs his attention toward the opposite side of the bank, at the boxy object cloaked by a weather-beaten blanket. He is enveloped by a haunting silence as he approaches the crate and, inhaling deeply, peels back the stiff, moss-caked cloth.

It's empty. No. That's not quite right. Something's inside. He unlatches the wire door and reaches through the shadowed opening, carefully withdrawing the object, appraising it in the morning light.

An antique frame. A poem under glass. Lewis stares at the words here, *his* words—*He returns to the remains*—rereading them for an uncountable time; but the letters shiver and disassemble, scattering and rearranging themselves into the words he should have spoken on that snowy night in February.

With a tormented howl Lewis flings the frame into the creek and raises his tear-streaked face toward the canopy of crisscrossing tree limbs, examining those crooked branches as he tightens his grip the long, leather leash looped around his clenched fist.

After a time he wipes his face with the back of one hand and levels his gaze straight ahead, appraising the dense maze of tree trunks. Movement in the distance—a crouching figure soundlessly creeping between the trees—seizes his attention. Lewis is suddenly aware that the dimensions and proportions of the figure bear an alarming resemblance to his own.

Lewis casually unravels the leash from his knuckles and ambles forward. And as he ventures further into the shadowy belly of the woods he senses the trunks growing more huddled, occluding more light, tightening like the rough-hewn bars of some crude cage. Lewis licks his lips and places a palm next to his jaw, and the unnatural silence is shattered as he calls out in a steadily serene voice, *"Here, boy . . ."* He repeats the summons, his voice reverberating through the forest. *"Here, boy . . ."* Then comes the echo of a whistle.

DOUBLE BACK

1

Deacon Stilwell stood inside his dark apartment, staring out the window, trying to ignore the figure standing in the shadows behind him. Deacon was clutching a glass of whiskey but hadn't taken a drink for several minutes, hadn't moved for several minutes. He was waiting for the thing behind him to speak. For a short time he attempted to calm the rapid rhythm of his heart, which drummed uncomfortably in his ears and throat, by focusing on what he saw outside: the unique, cobalt-gray hue of Chicago light pollution; slanting sheets of snow dusting the sidewalk and street below; in the windows of several apartments, nearby and in the distance, he noted twinkling Christmas trees. The exercise was futile and didn't last long.

"Hello, Deacon," it said. It was a monotone sound, issuing from a congested-wheezy windpipe. "Merry Christmas."

Earlier that evening, on his way home from the university, Deacon had taken a three-block detour to a familiar, nondescript liquor store—a darkly Pavlovian digression that had, in recent months, increased in frequency. But as habitually consistent as this had become, what grew ever more erratic were Deacon's reasons for these cyclic trips. Deacon Stilwell would stitch together a list of conditions that necessitated his desire to drink. And lately it had started this way:

He'd be on a bus downtown, sitting on a sticky seat with his face tilted over a book, trying to dismiss inane, one-sided cell phone conversations; or standing in a crowded el-train car, jostling shoulder-to-shoulder with clusters of commuters, listening to vulgar-speaking people and watching vicious arguments unfold before him. And when these mental vignettes were inadequate Deacon turned on himself, ruminating over his own personal misfortunes. He found solace in calculating his existential injuries—in sliding the black beads of self-pity along his internal abacus. *How can a man of consciousness have respect for himself?* He enjoyed repeating that phrase while inwardly sneering at people. He'd read it once, somewhere. It was from a Russian writer—Tolstoy or Dostoevsky or Turgenev. He'd always gotten them mixed up.

Deacon, particularly after living on his own for a year or so in the city, considered himself both: a man, and a man of consciousness. In truth he was a young man, whose intense eyes and coarse disposition contradicted his boyish, delicately vulpine features. He attempted to carry himself with the indifferent swiftness of a metropolitan, but succeeded in merely looking the part. Inside, since becoming ostensibly urbane, he'd developed nasty suspicions about the commonplace: every sidelong glance on the subway became accusatorial, each crosswalk collision became intentional.

As for consciousness, Deacon was pitifully unaware of this revelation: that he was a mediocre poet and a myopic artist, merely proficient at sketching self-serving metaphors—at observing relationships—which fostered disdain and kept the black dog of culpability at bay.

That's how things always started. That's how things started earlier this evening.

He'd entered his apartment, stomping off snow and yanking off his knit cap, uncovering disheveled, unevenly cropped hair; he'd slipped out of his coat, dropped it on the floor, and—cradling a wrinkled brown bag—walked into the kitchen, turning on the small light above the stove and retrieving a tumbler from the cabinet. He'd proceeded into the living room, not bothering to turn on any lamps or lights, and pulled up the blinds, the darkness softened by weak light—a pale orange phosphorescence cast up by sodium-vapor streetlights lining the sidewalk below.

Deacon had pulled the bottle from its paper husk and filled his glass with amber liquid. He'd drunk slowly, steadily, for several minutes before his nerves began to untangle. The phone had begun ringing, and Deacon answered to the voice of his younger brother, Paul. Of course, he thought, it was Paul. It was always Paul.

As with most of their conversations, it had started with Deacon asking his brother the same rote set of questions: about the weather, about Paul's surgical residency with the hospital, and so on. And as with most of their conversations, it had started to unravel when Deacon began reciting a litany of excuses about why he couldn't come home, why he couldn't come to see their mother. At one point Paul had asked Deacon about his health, his mind.

"Have you been drinking again?" Paul had asked.

"No," Deacon lied.

Deacon had briefly wondered if Paul asked those kinds of questions because he was training to be a doctor, or if it was the other way around.

The dialogue had nearly deteriorated when Deacon, stopping mid-sentence, noticed something in the reflection of the window, something standing behind him—the silhouette of a figure backlit by meager light from the kitchen. Paul, likely taking Deacon's lengthy silence as indignance, had hung up.

Deacon's lips had grown numb. His heart pulsed erratically, and it had taken him several seconds to lower the dead receiver from his ear and place it back onto its cradle.

He had listened to the figure's breathing—a lacerated, slashed-cord rattle. But for the savage quality of the sounds, the figure remained unnaturally still. It had simply stood there—a mannequin propped up in a poorly lit living room. After a while, it spoke. "Hello, Deacon. Merry Christmas."

Deacon heard it make another noise, a cough or a laugh or something, before continuing: "I would ask what's new but it appears the answer is very little," it said. "You know, our previous encounter ended so unfortunately. I wanted it to be our last, didn't you?"

Deacon remained silent.

"Are you still smoking cigarettes?" the thing asked.

"No," Deacon cleared his throat, trying to sound more formidable. "I quit a long time ago, years ago."

"Well," it croaked, "that speaks volumes about your self-control. How are your studies at the university?"

Deacon remained silent.

"Come now," it proceeded, "the two of us should talk. I'd like to see your face." The thing lunged forward with jerky, stilted baby steps, as if its limbs were being clumsily tugged by unseen wires. It made damp sounds as it moved across the darkened living room toward Deacon.

"Stop," Deacon said. "Please, stop."

It did. A few seconds passed before it spoke again. "What has been tormenting you?"

Deacon said nothing.

"Would it help if I turned on the light, Deacon?"

"No," he hissed, pivoting slightly, nearly turning around. In the stagnant orange light he caught a glimpse of it, of pale skin—of a baby-blue flannel mottled with dark stains. He swiveled back toward the window.

"Fair enough," the thing said. "So tell me, Deacon—do you know why your brother Paul called tonight?"

"No," he said, before correcting himself. "Yes, I do: to taunt me, to make me feel ashamed. To talk to me like a dog, or like one of his patients."

"I'm afraid your perception is addled, boy. But this is a symptom of your condition, is it not? You know, of all the things for which you occlude yourself, I'd submit that you *do* understand why Paul called. And I'm certain you understand why I'm here."

Deacon swallowed and moved his lips, trying to summon some moisture in his mouth. "Sure."

"We both know that articulation was never your strong suit. Do you need some help, son?"

Deacon snorted at that, lifted the glass of whiskey and swallowed what remained in the glass. He winced against the pungent sting; when he opened his eyes he was unsurprised to see that the thing's reflection had moved closer—that *it* had moved closer. In the window's reflection, in the pale orange light, Deacon could discern black strands of hair hanging out of a narrow, elongated head—a *dolichocephalic* skull, Paul might say, having examined it. It had milky-moist eyes, as if cataract-covered, set in bruised sockets. The thing's skin was pale, fish-belly white, and stood out in stark contrast against the shadows and darkness behind it. The flannel shirt was covered with black streaks and splotches.

"Why did Paul call tonight?"

Deacon answered after uncleaving his tongue from the roof of his mouth. "He asked when I was coming home."

"Yes, he did," the thing croaked. "But there is more." Somewhere down on the street, a car alarm began wailing. "What did he say about your mother?"

Deacon lifted the bottle from the sill and poured another drink. "He said she wasn't doing well—that he was having a hard time taking care of her. He said nobody blamed me, but he always says that."

"Do you believe him, your little brother?"

Deacon took a deep breath. His head swirled from the whiskey. "No."

"You lied to him tonight."

Deacon said nothing. He pressed his index finger against the cold window, and watched a foggy corona slowly blossom around his fingertip.

"You lied to yourself tonight," the thing began again. "And you are lying now."

Deacon raised his chin, dropping his finger from the window. The hazy halo faded. "You don't understand the things I see." He paused, his words echoing uncomfortably. "The things I see about people." He gestured toward the window, out at the city. "These goddamn people treat each other like animals."

"The best definition of man," the thing said, "is a being that goes on two legs and is ungrateful. Would you agree with that?"

Deacon hesitated, frowning slightly. "Yes."

"Does it sound familiar?"

"No."

"Those are the words of one of your beloved writers—from Dostoevsky: one of the many authors you often quote but to whom you rarely devote study. You murmur their phrases, from time to time, when they suit your mood. But do you know exactly the context with which you're employing these convenient little epigrams?" Silence hung for several seconds. "Deacon: you have been misusing your mother's money and you were wrong convincing her to allow you to come here. Your brother is correct: you have no business at the university. You have no business here in this city."

To hell with this fucking thing. Deacon bit his lip, began to turn and froze.

The thing calmly rested its hand on Deacon's shoulder. "You still answer questions like a child." Deacon angled his gaze to the pale hand, which was covered with some sort of black streaks. The fingers were out of proportion, several inches too long. Its nails were filthy and appeared to have been crudely chewed. "Let's put on some Christmas music."

"No," Deacon whispered.

"We're almost there, Deacon. But you need to gather your faculty. Let's think about the day we first made each other's acquaintance, yes?"

Deacon said nothing, closed his eyes and shivered.

2

Deacon Stilwell raised his fingers, bending down the brittle mini-blinds, and stared out a window overlooking a pothole-eaten parking lot. It was an early Saturday morning in late August. It would be humid and overcast; but the sun, still hunched along the horizon, sent pastel scarves—peach and mauvy—against gray, low-lying clouds. He panned down to the dusty window sill, where bluebottle flies lay dried-up and dead, their eyelash-thin legs turned upward, as if appealing something in the throes of their tiny death.

Withdrawing his fingers from between the blinds, Deacon dug into his pocket, retrieved a pack of cigarettes and his lighter. And just as he inserted a cigarette between his lips, he was startled by a voice.

"We only allow smoking outside on the veranda," a woman said, not unpleasantly. She was carrying a Styrofoam cup in one hand, a clipboard and a thick stack of almond-colored file folders in the other. "Besides we're going to get started here in a few minutes." She wore brilliantly white tennis shoes, which exaggerated each dutiful step as she buzzed around the small meeting room.

Deacon immediately poked the cigarette back into the pack, and the pack back into his pocket.

The white-sneaker woman—who Deacon recognized from his previous visits as the program coordinator—was now arranging folding chairs into a large circle. He thought the fluorescently-ill light and muted colors made the room feel more institutional, more nauseating.

People get sicker here, it occurred to him suddenly. The haphazard botanical pattern on the carpet looked like a garden designed by a disturbed person.

Feeling useless, Deacon asked, "Do you need some help?"

"Yes," the woman smiled but continued unhindered, "that'd be nice."

Deacon pulled a couple of beige chairs from the wall. The two worked quietly. When the circle was complete the woman exhaled and glanced around, as if in approval.

"Okay," she said, retrieving her Styrofoam cup. "There's coffee and refreshments across the hall. Help yourself before the meeting." She didn't wait for Deacon to respond as she walked out of the room. He sat down in a folding chair and fiddled with his lighter.

Nearly every chair in the circle was occupied.

Nearly every rehab program, at one point or another, utilizes a similar therapy exercise where group members in outpatient therapy— whether drug addicts, alcoholics, or both; whether here voluntarily or by court sentence—spend hours dwelling on and describing the circumstances for bringing them here. Very little time is devoted to exploring what will happen next.

The stories were, of course, varied—*diverse,* one counselor said brightly—but each tale was similar in that they contained pain, usually at the expense of others, and were narrated by unreliable speakers. Deacon recognized some of the members from previous sessions, but most were new. He sat upright, arms folded, and listened to the stories of the people forming this sad wreath. He was easily the youngest person here.

He listened to Tom, a high school swimming coach. "My son," the big gray man said, "told me if I didn't quit drinking that he'd move in with his mother." Tom's wife, apparently, had left him several months before. She now lived in a different state with a different man.

He listened to Kenny, whose nickname was *Fancy,* discuss crack. Kenny was HIV-positive and at the clinic because a judge said so. He spoke frankly and eloquently about his affection for the drug, and delineated ratios and reactions between cocaine and baking soda with the precision of a chemist.

He listened to a booze-weepy widow named Gloria, who dabbed incessantly at her heavily mascara-lined eyes. She cried about everyone else's story as much as she did her own.

These stories—these people, Deacon thought, couldn't be more different from me. The rotation eventually made its way around to the young man.

"Please," the program coordinator said. "It's your turn to share."

Deacon told his story—a vague patchwork of half-truths intended to evoke sympathy. He talked a little about his parents' divorce, about his younger brother Paul moving away to pursue medical school. "I got into trouble a while ago," he said when he sensed the people around him were growing uninterested in his bullshit. "There was an accident. My family suggested I come here, that I complete this program."

"Do you think you need to be here, Deacon?" asked the woman with the white sneakers.

Deacon frowned, refolded his arms and scanned the room. "Drinking, for me, is . . . recreational. I admit, it's bad to medicate yourself; but I think if I had my own place—"

Why don't you talk about your mother?

Deacon's eyes widened and his upper body stiffened. "What?" He began to scowl after no one responded. "Who said that?"

I did. Deacon saw, sitting directly opposite him, an ill-looking young man who presented a small mocking smile when Deacon leveled his gaze at him. *Your mother is nearly a cripple, now. Why is she that way?*

Deacon blinked a few times and leaned forward, trying to rein in focus, preparing to mentally square-off with this asshole.

After the sickly ashen young man lowered his hand he sat perfectly still. He had slick black hair, parted on one side. Bangs clung together in clumpy strands and hung over his brow. His skull was shaped funny. His skin was pale—white like a cadaver, Deacon thought, readying himself for some sort of hateful exchange. The guy was wearing a baby-blue flannel, an ink pen stuck out of the breast pocket of his shirt; his long thin fingers clutched his knobby kneecaps. Deacon inhaled, as if to say something, but was cut off.

Why does your mother spend most of her time in a wheel chair, Deacon?

Deacon's heart wound up, but his anger was slowly replaced with fear. He realized that the person speaking to him was growing perceptibly paler, second by second. And that he was not a young man at all, nor a teenager; and he was not older. He was, somehow, no age.

Tell us a story, Deacon. Be honest with us.

Deacon's chest rose and fell rapidly with his breathing. "This . . ." he managed, "is a fucking waste of time."

Some people in the circle glared or frowned. A few slid forward in their chairs.

The pale person, the sick thing, across from Deacon gave up a chuckle that quickly turned into a harsh, muddy sounding cough. Deacon watched him, it, regain some composure before smiling again—a botched incision framing two rows of uneven teeth, which, to Deacon, resembled jagged shards of tea-stained porcelain.

I assumed you'd do this. So allow me to tell a little story, yes?

Shifting in his chair, Deacon remained silent.

This is the story of Boy X. Boy X grew up in a small town not far from here. He grew up with his mother and father and little brother. Family X was happy for many years—there were vacations, snow days with snowmen, birthday parties, and Santa arrived each Christmas—but something happened when Boy X was a teenager. The father wanted to live with a stranger, another woman. Does any of this sound familiar? The mother and father, after months of Pyrrhic fighting, separated. On the day their father was packing suitcases, Boy X watched his little brother, crying, rush down the hall and grab hold of his father. 'Why do you have to leave us?' the little boy asked, again, and again. The father had said that he loved his sons, that he would always love his boys, but he had to make a hard decision that was impossible to explain.

A divorce followed shortly after. Boy X, unable to cope with the deterioration of his family, of what he'd come to know as normality, began drinking as anesthetization. Should I stop there?

Deacon wanted to say something ugly. But just then he caught sight of the pen sticking out of the thing's breast pocket. The pen started bleeding, pooling along the pockets stitching. Black ink bloomed and spread down his shirt like tendrils of black ivy.

Boy X's alcohol consumption grew increasingly excessive. Boy X's little brother tried to warn him—tried to, as much as one can as a little boy, help his big brother.

But here's what everyone really needs to know: One Saturday night in June— shortly after his high school graduation—Boy X acquired a bottle of whiskey, got into his car, and tore off into the country. Boy X lost control, ripping through a fence and slamming sideways into a tree. When police and paramedics arrived they found a barely lucid teenager behind the wheel, covered in broken glass, and an empty bottle on the floorboard.

Because Boy X was so young—and because he'd spent the entire weekend in the county jail—the judge ruled that the young man receive five years probation, a suspended license, and that he stay on, as he said it, the straight and narrow. Vowing to keep Boy X on that straight and narrow path, his mother, whom he still lived with, was resolute in keeping her son in school; she enrolled him in a local college, but because his license was suspended, she'd personally see to it that he go to class.

The ink was still spreading. Deacon was no longer listening, just watching the black liquid spill across the flannel material. Its skin continued to grow paler and was now nearly translucent—dark purple veins were visible under its diaphanous flesh. Deacon's gaze panned up, to the thing's livid face. Its nose began to bleed.

Boy X continued to drink, discovering that it wasn't difficult to conceal from his mother. She was, in her way, doing the best she could. She made a sincere effort in making sure that Boy X successfully complete a semester of school. One morning in early December, Boy X's mother came into his bedroom to wake him for class. He'd been out drinking the night before; he smelled of smoke and the acrid odor of alcohol. His mother, clearly hurt by her son's irresponsibility, dragged him out of bed, began tossing clothes at him and demanded he gather his books and get into the car. Boy X stumbled into the driveway, into his mother's automobile. She drove toward the city. Boy X, still vaguely intoxicated, said outrageously malicious things to her. She wept, begging to know where she'd gone so wrong. Christmas music was playing faintly on the radio as Boy X continued to raise his voice, excoriating his mother, blaming her.

It was the dump truck's fault, of course; and his mother hadn't even seen it coming. The truck slammed into the car, on the driver's side. Both Boy X and his mother were taken to the hospital. And while Boy X would be treated for a concussion and superficial wounds, his mother would never be quite the same. The nerve roots of her spine had been severely damaged—she would suffer, indefinitely, from Cauda Equina syndrome, the doctors said; and if she weren't completely crippled she would regain limited use of her legs slowly, painfully. She'd need assistance and therapy for the rest of her life. And the only thing she'd asked for after leaving the hospital—after the surgeries, after the beginnings of her comfortless recovery—was that Boy X get some help. But let's not forget what's important: that Boy X got his point across on that bleak December morning on the way to school. Do you like my tidy little story? Am I forgetting anything?

Frozen, choking back tears, Deacon stared at the thing—its upper lip was covered with blood, which continued to trickle from its nose, drip down its chin, and soak into the front of its shirt—and took a deep breath. Deacon watched its smile contort into an insane rictus grin.

"It wasn't like that," Deacon whispered through clenched teeth. His eyes looked watery, feverish. "You tell lies."

"Deacon," the program coordinator finally said, lifting the clipboard, recrossing her legs and affecting an expression of deep thought. "It takes a lot of courage, and a lot of trust, for people to share their thoughts and feelings inside the circle . . ."

Oh, what is she jabbering on about? She should have her mouth sewn up . . . just as the doctors sewed up your mother.

Deacon sprang from his chair and lunged across the circle. Tom, the swim coach, was the first to grab him, followed by several others who pulled him to the floor. Deacon, his vision tear-blurred, strained to catch sight of the thing across the circle. The chair was, of course, empty. Deacon started cursing, screaming for everyone to leave him alone.

3

The thing still had its hand on Deacon's shoulder when he opened his eyes. The snow was still falling. The car alarm had stopped. He looked down at his glass, the amber whiskey, and the half-drunk bottle sitting on the sill.

"Why did Paul call tonight?" the thing asked.

Deacon thought about taking a drink and paused. His throat constricted slowly. He winced, choking back a surge that threatened to rack his body with waves of tears. Leaning forward, Deacon pressed his forehead against the frosted window. The cold calmed him, sobered his senses a little. The thing, whose grip had before been almost tender, now tightened on Deacon's shoulder. "Speak, Deacon."

He stared at the snow—at the random descent of white flecks sailing across streetlights and tree limbs and layering the ground. Like leaves, he thought, like autumn. Deacon thought about the sound of leaves chattering across the pavement at twilight. He remembered one Halloween, when he was eight years old, he'd convinced his father to

take him to a haunted house—a cheap, small-town thing. Paul, mimicking his older brother's excitement, wanted to be included too. Citing
the boys' age and delicate impressionability, Deacon's mother had
been reluctant. It'll be harmless, his father said, wrapping an arm
around his wife and kissing her on the cheek. It'll be a guy thing.

The Stilwell family arrived at sunset. Deacon's mother, still object-
ing, said she'd wait outside. As the line wound toward the entrance,
Deacon listened to the screaming, the torture chamber noises, and
concocted all sorts of horrors that might be in store. From time to
time he'd glanced down behind him, at Paul—his small solemn face
obscured by tall shadows.

They were several yards from the entrance when Deacon's father
laid a large hand on his shoulder and leaned over. "Don't be afraid,"
he'd whispered, "they can't hurt you. No one's allowed to touch you in
there. It's all just make-believe—just for fun, okay?" Deacon nodded.
A few seconds before they stepped through the entrance, his dad said,
"Watch after your brother." Deacon peered down, held out his hand,
and Paul took hold.

The cloying atmosphere inside—the lurching strobe lights; the
sour smell of sweat and latex; disguised people looming over him,
breathing heavily under their masks—had been too much, and Deacon
kept his head down until it was all over. Eventually they exited through
a thick black curtain, stepping into cool evening air. Deacon quickly
spotted his mother, who'd been waiting on the leaf-littered sidewalk
next to the parking lot. Her expression, as she approached, became
pained, sympathetic. He followed his mother's gaze down to Paul, who
continued to grip Deacon's hand while wiping away tears from his
small, swollen face. Deacon had been too disoriented to notice. Shaking his head, Deacon's father had immediately, and repeatedly, apologized to his sons and to their mother. I didn't know it'd be that bad,
he'd said. *I'm sorry, boys.* Deacon wanted to put some distance between
himself and the awful noise that continued to spill from the building—
noise that had seemed to grow louder, more discordant. He'd turned
and started toward the parking lot, trying to yank free from his little
brother, whose tiny hand clasped tighter.

The thing loosened its grip on Deacon's shoulder.

Deacon, head pressed against the window, nodded.

"Speak, Deacon."

"I'm sorry," he said.

The thing, again, coughed or laughed, making a phlegm-ragged sound. "Do you know what to do?"

"Yes," he said.

"Besides," the thing said, its hand slipping off Deacon's shoulder, "you would have been a piss-poor poet anyway."

Deacon straightened up, grabbed the half-empty bottle, and whirled around. He caught an inky glimpse of something writhing, blending with the shadows, as he heaved the bottle across the darkened room. Glass shattered against the living room wall. Deacon reeled forward and fell, smashing through the coffee table. The orange-tinted ceiling swirled above him, and the smell of whiskey—which was trickling down the wall, bleeding into the carpet—permeated the tiny room. He got to his feet and scrambled for the hallway. His coat, still damp, was crumpled on the floor near the door. Tugging on his cap and yanking up his collar, Deacon half fell, half staggered down the stairwell. Soon he was outside, his frantic breathing visible in foggy bursts that trailed behind him as he weaved along the sidewalk—doubling back over a path he'd trampled only hours earlier. His footprints long erased by a sylphic blanket of unceasing snow.

Deacon walked for blocks, to the L station. He walked unevenly, pushing through the turnstiles, stomping up the fenced-in stairs. He made his way to the wood-planked platform, to the edge overlooking the black railway tracks. A silver train, its headlights twinkling through slanting snow, came to a stop in front of Deacon. The doors slid open and he stepped in. Deacon dozed as the train swayed, traveling south, toward downtown.

Deacon exited the train at a subway station, emerging on a street just west of the city. Walking a little steadier, he squinted against the snow and leaned into the wind, intent on the small hazy canopy of light a few hundred yards away.

Deacon, shaking snow from his coat, stepped into a run-down bus station. Long fluorescent lights buzzed overhead as he approached the ticket counter.

Behind the smoke-smeared sheet of Plexiglas, a black-haired attendant, dressed in a blue shirt and red necktie, swiveled away from his computer and smiled. "Can I help you, sir?"

"Yes, please," Deacon said between sniffles. His cheeks were pink. "I want to go home."

The attendant furrowed his brow and smirked, not unkindly. "Sure. Where's home?"

Deacon swallowed. It was warm inside the bus station. "New Bethel."

The attendant nodded once and typed something into the computer. "Closest I can get you is Indianapolis tomorrow morning."

Deacon tugged off his knit hat. "Yes, thank you. I'll wait." He shuffled toward a bench and sank onto the seat. A short time later he was lying on his side, sleeping—knees tucked up, hands folded under his head. Christmas music droned through static-lashed speakers.

THE TELL-TALE OFFAL

If you're reading this then I'll consider you a friend. My name is Wallace Crenshaw, and since you're a friend, you can call me Wally. So, friend, my first confession: Owing to my craft, I have butchered and dismembered more animals than I can (or care to) count. Yet, with the exception of dropping a languidly struggling lobster into a stockpot of boiling water, and aside from the cookery and consumption, I've never taken honest responsibility for the food I'm utilizing. I've never undertaken accountability for killing. At best, I've been a middleman; at worst, an accomplice.

I could say this all started with fungicides, with cattle infected with some sort of unclassified virus or bacteria. (Lately I've been reading about contaminated cattle feed, virulent strains of E. coli outbreaks making people sick, killing them.) I could say this started with Lacey Raymond (who I'll get to in a minute). But in truth, this all started with Joe Moss.

I met Joe Moss about eight years ago when I was a line cook at Cobblestone Creek Country Club. I was twenty-six years old, just a bit older than Moss (because of the boot-camp parlance in the kitchen, most of us simply refer to grunts by their last names).

Unlike me, Moss was a product of formal education, part of a new breed of culinary youngbloods who'd grown up watching "celebrity chefs" on TV.

Moss looked as if he were destined for celebritydom. He was a good-looking kid: tall, dark red hair, and a scattering of sandy freckles across his nose; a quick, cocksure smile. His sinewy, well-muscled forearms and rangy physique suggested some sort of athleticism, as if he'd run track a few years before in high school. You've heard the phrase *never trust a skinny cook*. It's apt here, but not for the reason you might think.

And while Moss began his informal apprenticeship with predict-able youthful ambition and delusions of grandeur (I'd been there my-self at his age), he also, I'm reticent to admit, swiftly began making his bones and earning our respect.

But even college boys make mistakes.

One day while we were prepping between lunch and dinner shifts, Moss casually said, "So, Wally, how long've you been working here?"

I'd been hesitant about disclosing too much about my personal life to a rookie, but the kid was disarming. "About six years." Moss raised his eyebrows and bobbed his head, not glancing up from his cutting board. We had a scratched-to-hell Anthrax CD playing on the beaten-to-hell stereo. "Why?"

Moss shrugged. "I don't know. You've been here a while, you ob-viously know your stuff. I'm only curious why you're still here on the line."

Translation: "I'm only curious why you're still *just* a cook." Let's get one thing straight: I liked being *just* a cook okay, friend? Cooks have always been a marginalized, blue-collar class. It wasn't until televi-sion started "gourmeting" our culture that pop-poseurs like Bobby Flay and Rachel Ray began elevating cooking from a proletarian utility to a bourgeois novelty. By and large cooks never make it out of the trenches. I wanted to tell him that I liked it in the trenches. It kept me close to the heart of my craft.

I'd been chopping mirepoix for a batch of chicken stock. "Are you asking me why I haven't been promoted?" I said, trying to sound unin-terested.

"Yeah, I guess so."

At the time, we had an executive chef who was in charge of every-thing. Below him was the sous chef, Drew, what you might call the "under chef." "I like where I am," I said. "Besides, I don't want to have to worry about all that responsibility."

Moss didn't answer immediately, as if crafting some response. "Yeah, but, there'd be more money in it for sure. Plus you'd have a title."

A title. Something to scribble on a résumé. In my heart, I was already a world-class chef.

I smirked. "But if I was the sous chef, then I'd be your boss."

Moss reacted immediately by giving a hearty laugh. "Sure you would. But what if I got the job before you?" His smile was a convolution of misguided confidence and countryish innocence.

Now I laughed a bit uneasy. "Kid, I've got seniority." In the kitchen meritocracy, it was true; but it was also tacit and tentative.

Wiping down his cutting board, Moss snorted, "Seniority." We were quiet for a little while before he said, "All I'm saying is that if the opportunity presented itself, I'd pounce on a promotion to sous chef."

"Maybe I will," I said, lugging a hotel pan brimming with chicken carcasses to my work station. "Maybe I'll be your boss someday." And then, humorlessly, I said, "Here's a sneak peak," and flung the hotel pan of raw chickens onto his work station. "Get your ass to work breaking down these chickens."

While I'm on a roll with admissions, I'll tell you something else: All cooks are petty thieves. The fancy word for it is pilferage, and it's pervasive.

But aside from thievery and alcohol and drug abuse, another thing our industry has a reputation for is widespread promiscuity.

Maybe it's just that cooks are more sensual people.

You've heard the adage *you eat with your eyes,* right? Owing to the importance of aesthetics in the food service industry (fine dining in particular), Cobblestone Creek hired young, painfully attractive front-of-the-house staff. Diners like eye-candy (especially wealthy, bourbon-buzzed middle-aged white guys, which comprised roughly 98% of our members). Depending on the rhythm and chemistry at a particular interval, there is usually some sort of illicit, intra-restaurant sex occurring.

It'd been about six years before. Back then I was the star of the club—young, energetic, idealistic.

In her early twenties then, Lacey Raymond was a cosmetology school dropout: *"I'm only taking a year or two off, save some money, go to business school."* The only sort of business she discovered was the restaurant business, and her ambitionless sabbatical found her in an industry with the rest of us dropouts and misfits.

Lacey had set her sights on me early on. Flirting led to drinks at a local tavern, drinks led to the occasional hook-up at my apartment.

As a receptionist, Lacey's job was routine: jot down reservations, schedule walk-throughs for potential wedding receptions, wear a satiny blouse and black slacks, laugh at the members' bawdy jokes, look pretty.

This industry has a tendency to chew people up and spit them out. If it weren't for her moxie, she would have survived a shorter time than she did.

It was a Saturday night, just before the restaurant closed. On this particular night we'd run a dinner special: Steak Diane—pan-seared filet mignon—shallots, morel mushrooms, brandy sauce. A classic. Moss had been off the night before, but he'd called in sick for his Saturday shift; his absence filled me with a lukewarm sort of glee—the opportunity to give him shit about flaking out.

After I finished scrubbing down the gas range, I checked over the requisition order for the following Monday, knotted up a couple garbage-pregnant trash bags and headed for the back dock. This was late spring, the night-cool air felt like a reward after a long day in front of the stove. Off toward the golf course came the raspy chatter of cicadas. Next to the dumpsters, grassy scents of late spring mingled with the fruity-putrid aroma of garbage.

I was about to hoist one of the trash bags up into the dumpster when I heard someone whisper, "Hey, Wally."

Startled, I dropped the bag in mid-lift. Moss's pale face was visible in the shadows between the wooden fence and a stand of shrubs. "Jesus, Moss," I squinted at him. "That's a good way to get your ass kicked."

"Sorry," he said, his voice uncharacteristically meek. There was a buzzing mercury vapor light above us, bugs orbiting around it. Moss shuffled closer and I got a better look at him.

He resembled a handsome corpse. His face was gaunt, which made the scattering of freckles on his nose stand out, the dark scallops under his eyes made his sockets appear bruised. Moss wore dark clothes—a pair of jeans, a dark blue T-shirt—and they looked wrinkled, damp.

Inadvertently, I stepped back and said, "What the hell, Moss? You okay?"

Moss took a deep breath as he dug a crinkled pack of Marlboros out of his pocket. "I don't know, man," he said, lit a cigarette, and exhaled a short-lived streamer of smoke. "I came to talk to you, Wally."

"Oh, yeah," I said, relaxing a bit, wondering if he was just coming down from some shoddy dope, or riding out some hideous acid trip. Combined with his calling in sick, this was just more ammunition to break his balls. "You look like you've got the flu or something."

A smile cracked across his waxy face, a curt laugh tore out of him. "I wish." The cherry of his cigarette glowed. "I felt bad about calling in tonight, but . . ." he trailed off.

"No sweat, man," I said, "we didn't have that many reservations on the books." I smiled, my tone lighthearted. "Besides, slow as you are, you'd have been dead weight anyway."

Moss fixed his eyes on me. My own smile sagged. "Listen, Wally," he said. "I need your help."

For the seven or eight months that I'd known Joe Moss, he'd been completely capable and confident, never asking me for help with anything. "What are you talking about?"

He took another drag from his cigarette and started to pace along the side of the dumpster. I crossed my arms and gave him some space, moving as he moved, keeping my eyes on him. Our distorted shadows took turns stretching and dancing under the light. "I think I'm in trouble."

I suddenly had the feeling that Moss was baiting me for some sort of practical joke. I glanced around to see if anyone else was around. "So this is where I say 'what sort of trouble?' and act like I'm interested. Moss I—"

"I stole some food from the walk-in fridge after my shift Thursday night."

I held my gaze on him for a second before laughing. "Food? That's what you're worried about? Moss, man, I know you're sort of a pansy, but this is too much." I didn't care that he wasn't laughing along with me. Honestly, at that moment I wanted him to relax. "Listen, nobody's noticed anything missing. What'd you steal, a couple potatoes?"

"Meat," he mumbled. "A plastic bag of steaks."

I'd stopped chuckling and was only grinning. "The filets?" Moss nodded, he was talking about the filet mignons for the Steak Diane weekend dinner special. "We didn't sell hardly any tonight." I explained that Drew was unlikely to notice a couple of missing pieces of meat.

"No," he said and briefly pinched the cigarette between his lips. "That's not it . . . exactly."

"What then? Spit it out."

Moss's chest rose and fell. "Thursday night, I swiped this plastic bag from the walk-in. Glancing at it—by the shape of it—I thought it was a few filets. The plastic was sort of murky." He paused, his gaze grew distant, and he cocked his head slightly, as if hearing a dog whistle. "Anyway, I wasn't on the schedule Friday night, and I had plans. You know that girl, Lacey? The receptionist?"

Lacey. My heart sank, quickly understanding his motivation for stealing the steaks. "Yeah," I mumbled.

"Yeah, well, we've been hooking up lately. She sort of suggested that I cook dinner for her, a real fancy meal. I said she should come over Friday night . . ."

The code of conduct is rather flimsy among cooks, sort of a *what's-mine-is-mine-and-what's-yours-is-mine* mentality. I suppose in our little country club coterie, it was only a matter of time before Lacey moved on to the next young stud. He was supplying some anecdote about Lacey's body. *Been there, done that, pal.*

"Get to the point, dude."

"Right. When I got back to my apartment, I went to the kitchen and unwrapped the bundle and it . . . it wasn't what I expected." I stared at him, hoping my unamused expression would urge him along. "There was a tiny steak in there but most of it was . . . offal."

A brief digression for the uninitiated: *offal,* noun, pronounced the same way as "awful"—internal organs or trimmings removed from the skeletal meat after butchery. In other words, brains, liver, kidneys, thymus glands, spleens, tongues, feet, intestines . . .

Moss blurted out, "There was a heart in there."

I was suddenly hesitant to ask why he'd called in sick to work that night. "So what?"

"So . . ." he scanned the back dock. "I want you to come to my apartment so I can show you."

"Just tell me what—"

"You have to see it. You have to . . . help me, Wally."

Moss insisted I ride with him. After some profanity-peppered deliberation, I agreed.

Joe Moss lived in an apartment complex called The Beaumont, which at one time may have evoked a sense of regality—with its exposed timber exteriors and ornate, Tudor-style touches—but now looked jilted, like a woman who'd preposterously decorated herself for a suitor who never arrived.

Without a word Moss pulled into a parking space, killed the engine, and got out of car. I'd discarded my sauce-spattered chef coat back at the club, but still reeked of food. I followed Moss along the sidewalk, over to a narrow corridor within an open-air breezeway.

As Moss mounted a paint-flecked staircase, he gave a furtive glance. I suddenly had the absurd notion that he was leading me into some sort of impromptu *ménage à trois*. The thought made me vaguely nauseous—not just him and Lacey together, but me as some sort of sexual second-fiddle. As some sort of accessory.

My heart began to beat in sync with my footfalls as I recounted the story Moss had supplied on the drive out to his apartment.

Moss, shifting in the driver's seat, had glanced over at me and said, "Have you ever had food poisoning?"

If this truly was a practical joke, I'd play along until the last minute. "Not that I know of."

"Did you eat any of the meat this weekend?"

Of course—it's a cook's responsibility to control the quality of what was leaving the kitchen. "Nope."

Moss sighed, and then laid it out.

After discovering that the plastic-wrapped bundle was a meager piece of meat along with a heart, Moss had thought about throwing the whole thing away. Instead Moss had sautéed the filet, eating it while he watched a late-night cooking show. When he was done, he returned to the kitchen.

"There was blood all over the counter."

"The heart."

Moss nodded. "I'd left it on the cutting board, just sort of forgot about it. I should have pitched it then, but . . ." He smirked. "I had this urge to keep it. I thought if Lacey was going to come over, I'd gross her out or something." Moss brought up a jittery hand, his fingers curled into an open-palmed claw, as if invisibly clutching the mass of muscle. "It was gray," he said, his tone decreasing as if talking to himself. "Blue and purple veins crawling all over it. Stubby valves . . . black chambers." He dropped his hand suddenly. "It was kind of cool. So I kept it. I slipped it in a big freezer bag and put it in the fridge." Moss said he drank a beer before heading to bed.

"I woke up the next morning, went out to the kitchen, and it . . ." Moss swallowed hard. "It was everywhere."

I had a guess, but still I asked. "What?"

"Blood," said Moss. The pale green glow cast from the console made his face look ghastly. "It was like the fridge had hemorrhaged."

"Did you look inside?"

"Sure. The heart was there, in the plastic bag where I'd left it. But the bag had split open, or burst." He looked at me for second. "It wouldn't stop bleeding."

I said, "Please tell me you threw the damn thing away."

"Hell yes," he said, as if I had just asked a preposterous question. "I tossed it in the garbage and got some towels to clean the floor. But"—Moss winced—"when I checked on it the garbage bag was already filled with six inches of blood."

"So then what?"

"The only thing I could think to do was drop it in the sink."

In the sink. "And?"

"*And?*" he said, his tone suggested I should fill in the blanks intuitively. "It won't stop bleeding. It's just been . . . draining into the garbage disposal."

We were quiet for a while as Moss weaved along nightroads. Finally—in my best don't-fuck-with-me voice—I said, "Moss—if this is some sort of joke—"

"It's no joke, man."

I didn't want to sound too insecure or desperate, but I eventually said, "What happened last night . . . with Lacey?"

"Canceled. Told her she'd have to take a rain check on her classy dinner." He snorted a laugh. "I couldn't have her in the apartment with that thing."

Silence settled into car. Moss's admission echoed in my mind: *It wouldn't stop bleeding.*

Now, on the second floor corridor if his apartment building, Moss fished a key from his pocket as we approached his door. The long walkway was intermittently lit with faux gas lamps; set in vintage sconces, they had the guttering effect of turning the hallway into a shadowy, turn-of-the-century alleyway.

The teeth of the key scraped into the deadbolt. Moss hesitated, still facing away from me. He canted his head as if listening intently. I could only hear the overlapping baritone of bullfrogs off toward a ravine. TV voices reverberated down the hall. I'd had my hands dangling uselessly at my sides, but now I clenched them into fists.

Moss cleared his throat and twisted the lock.

I waited at the threshold for Moss to flip on a light before I entered, lingering in the narrow foyer. Moss was just about to round the elbow of wall when he said, "Close that"—meaning the door—"I don't want any bugs in here."

Moss had disappeared around the corner, and I eased down the hallway. Now I could smell it. I thought of a poorly maintained, poorly ventilated butcher shop. I thought about the dumpster back at the country club.

A light came on up ahead. "In here," Moss said tonelessly.

The kitchen was lit by a couple overhead banks of fluorescent tube-lights, the anemic glow reminded me of the anonymous sterility of an autopsy room. The floor was far from sterile.

Moss was standing just outside a kiddie pool–sized puddle of blood. He'd tried to use some towels and T-shirts to sop up the liquid. Now they were saturated and clumped around the outer edge of the gruesome little lagoon.

The linoleum was smeared and streaked with varying shades of crimson, some dark and dry, some vibrantly red, slick and glossy.

Without looking at me, Moss said, "I told you."

I exhaled slowly, shifting my attention from the floor to appraise the kitchen—the tell-tale signs of a cook: a cluster wine bottles, oils, a faced row of seasonings. I noticed the silver handle of a pan sticking out of the sink. Mounted on the wall under the cabinets was a magnetized strip: a knife rack that held a collection of cutlery—a meager assortment for a professional, but passable nonetheless.

I looked at Moss. "Where is it?"

He jerked his face in my direction, as if I'd only now arrived, his eyes feverish. "Where's what?"

I clenched my teeth for a moment and then said, "The heart."

"Oh," he said, and tilted his head toward the sink. "Where I left it." He began walking toward me, skirting the outer edge of blood. "Go ahead, see for yourself."

I kept my eyes on Moss as we traded positions in the kitchen, waiting for him circle the puddle before approaching the sink, giving the blood a wide, wary berth.

I edged up on the sink. On the right hand side was a dirty sauté pan, a couple of utensils. The left side of the sink was empty.

I spun around, no longer able to tolerate this. "Moss, where is it?"

"Wally . . . it wouldn't stop—"

I cut in, raising my voice, "I know, I know—you've said it a dozen times—'it won't stop bleeding'—"

"*NO,*" Moss shouted, his face suddenly fixed and ferocious, "it won't stop *beating.*"

We stared at each other for a long time.

I said, "Moss, listen, man—"

"I have been listening!" He winced and clasped both hands to the sides of his head, his fingers clawed over his temples. "It just keeps . . . pounding . . ." he closed his eyes, breathing raggedly through his nose.

I tried to inch away from the sink, but my shoe squeaked on the linoleum and Moss's eyes snapped open. Absently, his hand drifted up and he slipped a large knife from the top of the refrigerator. He stood between me and the corridor leading to the front door.

Moss waved the knife. "The meat, Wally, did you eat the meat?"

Yes. Only a bite. "No."

For a split instant, his expression was stricken with disappointment. "I should have thrown it away."

"Where is it now?"

"In the tub," he said, and then his pasty lips yanked up into a leering rictus. "They're both in the bathtub." *Both?* His grin melted away, his tone became scholarly. "Well . . . part of it, at least."

"Part of what?"

"The heart," and then he added in a rush. "I ate some of it."

I had a hard time getting my mouth moving. "When?"

"In the middle of the night on Thursday." Moss looped the knife as if writing cursive in midair. "Sorry . . . forgot to tell you that." He took a step toward me. "It was like the heartbeats became . . . whispers. So I went out to the fridge, sliced off a piece and . . ."

"What happened to Lacey?"

Moss stopped moving. With mock astonishment he said, "Seriously? I already told you." He grinned. "She's in the tub."

He was shuffling toward me again.

"Moss—maybe you're hallucinating . . . or sick."

"Oh . . . I'm sick, man. Feels like worms are squirming in my goddamn skull."

"Let me help . . ."

"You're going to help me, Wally. Just like Lacey helped me last night. But I'm going to need you to hold still—" He lunged, darting across the pool of blood.

I twisted away, looking over in time to watch the knife come down on the lip of the sink. Moss grunted and took a back-handed swipe at me, which I somehow ducked before shoving into his midsection, sending him back far enough for me to stretch out and grab a sauté pan from the sink, which I had time to bring up like a shield when the blade came down again. The knife hummed like a tuning fork and fell from Moss's hand. I wrenched the pan over my shoulder and struck Moss alongside his head. He went limp, collapsing into the pool of blood.

Verbal altercations aside, I'd never been in a physical fight, let alone one where my life was at stake. I was trying to breathe, trying to think.

I stepped over Moss, already clawing for my cell phone. I was in the entryway when I slowed and stopped, my thumb on the keypad of my phone. *She's in the tub.* And by merely recalling Moss's words I felt as if I'd invoked something. I imagined I heard a low, steady beating. Moss had planted an awful question in my head: *Did you eat the meat?*

I clicked the phone shut.

I gathered myself, looked at Moss (not budging), and took a few steps toward the inner chamber of the apartment.

From the weak kitchen light issuing from behind me, I could discern on the left a slatted set of bifold doors (the kind used to conceal water heaters), and two doors on the right, the first of which was open, a bedroom. I peered in, waiting for anything, movement, a sound; but the only sound I heard was that hypnotic pulsation. The door at the end of the corridor was closed.

I inched down the hall, the beating growing louder now. I should have run. Instead I clasped the doorknob, twisted, and let the door yawn open.

A roadkill aroma spilled out of the black space. I winced, swatting at the inner wall for a light switch, which my fingers found. Lights—the same morgue-florescence from the kitchen—buzzed and stuttered to life.

A murky shower curtain was drawn shut; it was filmy with residue, but clear enough to see that the tub was filled with dark liquid.

And then came sloshing, the surface jostled. The beating persisted, the thrumming muffled, as if hearing my own heartbeat while holding my breath under water. Something began emerging from the dark liquid. I backed into the doorframe, lamely bringing my hand to my mouth.

Through the opaque plastic drape I watched a slender figure rising slowly, almost sensually, to stand fully erect, shin-deep in what I knew was blood. There was a viscous dripping as liquid ran off her body in thick rills, exposing patches of grub-white flesh.

I could distinguish the clumpy, once-blonde hair hanging over her shoulders, barely covering the crescent mounds of her breasts.

Her arm began rising, and I saw that her thin fingers clasped an object—smooth, glistening, pulsing. The heartbeat mingled with a small giggle, and I saw the ivory flash of teeth on the angular face behind the curtain. Her other hand clutched hold of the curtain, smearing it with streaks of red.

I shoved away from the door and scrambled down the hallway.

As I sprinted through the kitchen I gave a brief glance at Moss. He was still sprawled on his side, crumpled in the pool of blood. His eyes were open—fixed on me, unblinking. Moss was smiling. Without budging, his gaze followed me as I fled. And then I was in the hallway, in the entryway, in the second-floor corridor. I ran down the stairs and raced out the breezeway, the night sounds of insects along with my frantic footfalls eventually drowning out the laughter that had followed me out of the apartment.

I didn't have the heart to call the police.

In fact, the only phone call I dealt with that night (aside from phoning my brother to pick me up, his only comment: "You look sick, man") was from Moss, who left a voicemail:

"Your fingerprints are on the sauté pan you clocked me with if you're thinking about calling the cops." His voice was reedy but composed. *"I know you can use this message as some sort of evidence, but I could say the same thing about your footprints."* He sounded as if he were about to hang up when he hastily added, *"Bon appetit, pal."*

Again I thought about eating from the same batch of steaks as Moss. I disconnected the phone and steered into my bathroom where I was tidily sick.

No one ever heard from Lacey Raymond again. Moss simply stopped showing up for work.

The closest I ever came to doing the right thing was actually visiting The Beaumont, dropping by the front office under the guise of inquiring about apartment availability.

There were vacancies, according to a chit-chatty manager wearing a pink polo shirt. As ignorantly as possible, I asked about a particular apartment on the second floor.

"Afraid not," he said, dismissing it with a lisp. "That space is occupied at the moment." The manager leaned toward me conspiratorially. "Had a resident about six months ago who wrecked the place."

My breath caught. "Oh, yeah?"

Pink polo shirt was smirking. "When his lease was up, the facilities crew said he'd vandalized the place; they ended up calling the cops." He raised an eyebrow. "They did some sort of analysis on residue found in the bathroom."

I swallowed. "What was it?"

In a husky whisper he said, "You'll never guess."

"Try me," I said a bit too eagerly.

He shared this last secret by lifting a stack of envelopes to the side of his mouth. "Blood," he paused dramatically, "from a bovine." It was unnecessary, but he added: "Cow's blood."

Here's something that recently occurred to me: Because of the meticulous nature of those famed eviscerations, there's a theory that Jack the Ripper was some sort of physician; but I wonder why no one has ever suggested that Jack the Ripper was a world-renowned chef.

About four years ago, after the sous chef, Drew, resigned from the country club for some ritzy job in the city, I was promoted to sous chef. If I have anything to thank Moss for it might be for the lingering residue of his culinary guts and ambition.

Before I finish, there's one more component to disclose: This is the only story I've ever written. I'm not illiterate, but I'm ill-suited to be a writer. I am a chef. Although I've agonized over these contents with bloodless scrutiny, the essence of my confession—the "meat" of my story—remains intact.

By now, friend, your suspicion has transformed into certainty that my name is not Wallace, and that my former comrade's name is not Joe Moss. I see him from time to time in a food magazine or on a cooking show. He's a celebrity now (the diseased heart had apparently sharpened his senses—not destroyed—not dulled them). But I won't confess his real name. I couldn't cope with promoting his career.

LIKE FATHER, LIKE . . .

The central artery of Deacon's Creek, which is Exchange Street, runs north and south between a vast patchwork of fields. Most of these tracts are empty, dormant bodies waiting to be renewed by this season's rotation of soybeans or corn. Sooner or later, the narrow networks of country roads widen and branch off, running their crooked courses to steadily streaming motorways, pulsing back to life as they channel into flourishing communities that flaunt their vicarious promises of hope and rejuvenation—promises this infertile town can no longer fulfill.

Walking down the sidewalk, Ray Swanson slows his stride, squinting against the late-morning sun as he half-heartedly surveys the tightly huddled buildings along Exchange Street. Not for the first time since his recent return, it occurs to Ray that nothing has changed here, and not just the buildings—the market, the post office, the taverns, the newspaper suite—but the people themselves. Being Sunday, nearly all the businesses are either closed or closing early. Being Sunday, most folks are at church.

He glances up the street, at the Tudor-style façade of the restaurant where he and Heather had their first date. In fact, the more he considers it, just about everything along Exchange holds a bittersweet memory of Heather.

Ray fishes his car keys out of his pocket, opens the driver's door, and places the brown grocery bag on the bench seat. He's about to slide in when he catches sight of the barber shop.

A gentle breeze disturbs the striped awning hanging over the face of the shop.

Three weeks ago, the day before his father's funeral, Ray had slipped away from his parents' house—crammed, by that point, with casserole-toting townsfolk and estranged family members offering low-toned condolences—and made a break for the outskirts of town. If he was going to be a pallbearer, he'd need a presentable haircut. And a few drinks. He'd driven nearly twenty miles before reaching a familiar little community in the neighboring county. Finding the least obnoxious barber shop, Ray asked for a simple haircut, something as anonymous as he. The day after, Ray helped slip his dad's casket snugly into the ground out at Evensong Cemetery.

Now, Ray stares at the ancient barber shop on Exchange Street, the wind ruffling a few unruly bangs hanging across his forehead. Curious, Ray jogs across the street.

The barber pole attached to the brick exterior of the building is spinning slowly, listlessly. The sign painted directly over the glass reads, *Vaught's Barber Shop, Est. 1928,* and a smaller sign hanging over the door: *Sorry . . . We're Closed.* Ray mumbles, "Of course you are," making a note of the shop's weekly business hours. There is some sort of cheery Bible verse along the lower sill of the window. Ray ignores it, but catches sight of his reflection in the storefront. He doesn't want to admit it but he looks . . . old—his boyish features have somehow faded without consent. A black thought scurries through his mind: *I hope I don't look like Dad when I get old.*

He shifts focus to peer at the interior of the barber shop. There's too much glare, so Ray steps forward, pressing his forehead against the window and cupping a palm to his temple. Despite the warped glass, Ray can distinguish the layout: the wall-to-wall mirror running the length of the shop, eliciting the illusion of a wider room. Beneath the mirror is a long shelf covered with bottles, tonics, elixirs; low-lying coffee tables with a scattering of magazines; the vague rectangle shape of a painted-over door. He begins to pull away but pauses, squinting harder. There's a figure sitting in one of the barber's chair, a featureless silhouette, indistinct in the shadow-cauled gloom.

Ray pulls his face away from the window and reappraises the exterior of the shop. Rechecking the hours posted on the door, Ray's gaze drifts down and settles on something he's never noticed before. Painted on the glass on the bottom corner of the door is what looks like a number seven, with a curly tail and a small band over the middle section. He frowns, cocks his head—it was nearly unnoticeable, but now that he's caught sight of it, Ray can't help but wonder what the hell it is and begins to stoop and inspect the little symbol.

Shuffling footfalls sound on the sidewalk, but Ray doesn't turn from the window until a man's voice says, "This certainly is a pleasant surprise, Ray." He turns, instantly recognizing the couple standing here. The man extends his pale blade of a hand. "So nice to see you enjoying this glorious day."

Herbert and Hazel Steinhauer. Ray had gone to school with their son, Travis. But like most post-graduation relationships, they'd drifted apart once the flimsy structure of high-school customs disappeared. He'd lost touch with Travis but really hadn't given it a second thought. This isn't the first time he's run into the Steinhauers. Like many in town, they'd attended his father's funeral weeks earlier. Ray produces a polite smile and shakes the man's hand.

"Good to see you again, Mr. Steinhauer," Rays says.

"Now, now. Please, call me Herb. Hazel and I were just leaving church, out for a walk."

Ray would have been satisfied to keep looking at Herb, but feels obligated to offer a well-mannered nod toward Mrs. Steinhauer.

The woman's overwrought features had shocked Ray at the funeral, but now she looks worse, genuinely ill. She's pallid, and her faded blonde hair is threaded with gray and looks poorly washed. Dark purple crescents underrim her eyes. Her neck appears strained, the cords standing out, as if she is tentatively biting her tongue. The woman's eyelids have retracted from the eyeballs, giving the illusion that she has no eyelids at all. But the worst part is the makeup, which appears garish and gaudily vaudevillian—her gray skin looks as if it's brushed with baby powder, prominent cheekbones smudged with rouge.

Ray's breathless hesitation is brief, but before he can strike up a friendly response, Herbert clears his throat, his eyes ticking from Ray to Hazel, from Hazel to Ray. "Hazel has been . . . unwell, lately."

No shit. "Oh," Ray whispers. *If she's so sick, why are you dragging her all over town?* "What's wrong?"

"Thyroid," Herbert says, caressing his wife's back. The thin fabric of her dress flutters in the breeze, clinging to her willowy frame. "Graves obitopathy. It's affected her voice and her eyes . . . the doctor calls it *proptosis.*" The man sounds weary, as if this explanation is something he's recited for a long time. "It has been a struggle." Herbert looks at Ray. "Of course, nothing like your family has experienced during the last few weeks."

"Yes," Ray says. "Mom still has her moments, but I think she enjoys having me around the house."

"Of course," Herbert answers. "One must attend to the living."

Silence is suspended between them. Ray finally clears his throat. It occurs to him to ask about their son. "How is Travis?"

"Well," Steinhauer exhales, "Travis decided to follow your lead, as it were, and light out on his own." He smiles. "Who knows? Perhaps our son will make a prodigal return one day." His smile fades as he appraises Ray.

Silence. The red-and-white barber pole twirls slowly.

"Well, I'm afraid we must be going," says Herbert. "Please give our regards to your mother."

Ray and Herb exchange a parting handshake. He assumes the couple will resume their Sunday morning stroll, but neither budge from under the shadow of the barber shop's awning.

Ray crosses the street and gets into the car. Before taking the corner and steering away from Exchange Street, he glances in the rearview mirror. The sidewalk in front of the barber shop is empty, the red and white pole is twirling slowly.

Ray stands over the sink, scrubbing dishes after dinner. His mother is still at the dining room table, solemnly leafing through a stack of old documents and bills that have accumulated in the last few weeks. His mom seemed relieved when Ray had agreed to stay in town until things got back to normal, or at least as normal as possible without his dad around.

Through the window above the kitchen sink, daylight is dimming into the dreamy tints of dusk, the meticulously manicured lawn looks lush and lurid, the sharply defined shadows along the hedge inching toward the house.

In the six years since his initial departure from Deacon's Creek, Ray would occasionally return, stay for a couple of days, and leave, each departure being a substantially less dramatic reenactment of his original adolescent exodus. Those visits were always more miserable when they coincided with an appearance by his older brother, David.

Of course, Dr. David Swanson had flown in from Florida for their father's funeral.

At the wake, Ray watched his brother engage in long bouts of seemingly sincere discussion with family members before shuffling a few paces, only to be seized by another cluster of mourners. In the moments when David broke away, he'd tried making conversation with Ray. But there was nothing Ray could say. In his heart, the only things they had in common were the blood-ties of siblinghood and parentage. In Ray's heart, his only accomplishment in twenty-four years was forking over fifty bucks at the bus station and escaping Deacon's Creek.

"Ray?"

He's clutching a food-smeared plate, the faucet hissing as water gurgles into the drain. "Huh?" He sets the dish down and twists off the knobs. "What? Sorry about that. I was . . . daydreaming."

His mother offers a tired smile. "It's too late to be daydreaming."

Ray smirks, "Sorry," patting his hands dry on a tea towel and walking into the dining room. "Something wrong?"

"Well," his mother lifts a pair of reading glasses, "I found this check in some of your father's things—it's made out to Wendell Harper."

Ray remembered Wendell, the old butcher at Crenshaw's Market, where he'd spent his younger years as a stock boy. "Does Wendell still work there?"

"Heavens yes," his mother says. "They'll have to drag him out of there someday." She hands the check to Ray. It looks old, ink-faded. There's no date, only Wendell's name, his father's signature, and a dollar amount.

"Do you think Dad forgot to pay for something?" Ray shifts his eyes from his father's signature on the check and over to his mom.

"As busy as your father was, it wouldn't surprise me if he'd overlooked something." She gestures vaguely at the haphazard scatter of papers. "And it wouldn't surprise me if Wendell was too polite to ask."

Ray chuckles. "Wendell?"—shakes his head—"polite?" He's quiet for a few moments. "Do you want me to run into the market and find out what it was all about?"

His mother sighs. "Oh, that would be such a help, Ray. Maybe some time this week? Whenever you're free."

Aside from playing handyman around the house, Ray has nothing but free time. "Sure thing. Tomorrow or the next day, maybe."

Ray appraises the cluttered table, noticing a shoebox full of photographs. He lifts a small stack of pictures, flipping through them casually. They're mostly of him and David as kids. Ray pauses, staring at one particular photo. It's of him as a toddler—his first trip to Vaught's Barber Shop. His small, tear-streaked face is frozen in mid-cry, cheeks flushed, a little spittle on his lower lip. There's a white barber's cape fixed around his neck, and the cushioned chair looks enormous in contrast with his tiny body. Ray's mom had always thought this photo was adorable. Ray's attention flicks to the margin of the picture. His dad's there, just out of frame—his arms and big hands reaching for Ray, presumably to keep him from struggling out of the chair—a harsh, domineering gesture. Ray drops the stack of photos back into the box and sets the check on the bookcase before returning to the kitchen and finishing his chores at the sink.

Later this evening, Ray is sitting in his father's recliner. The TV drones with a primetime game show. His mom is sitting across the room, on the couch, contentedly reading her Bible. People around here turned to scripture—to God, Ray supposed—in search of answers when self-reliance failed. Part of him wants to let her be, to allow her to sustain her healing as long as she needs it. Another part of him wants to stroll over there and remove that book from her lap—and save her from dwelling on empty promises.

It's not lost on him that he is quietly, and if only proximally, filling in for his dad. This is a ritual, Ray realizes. *This is mom's grieving.*

Deacon's Creek did not cope well with grief, let alone surprises. Ray's faithless exodus six years earlier had been no surprise, but Roger Swanson's fatal heart attack had been a small-town shocker. It had been predictable arithmetic that the all-American Roger Swanson would end up courting, and later marrying, the equally virtuous Alice Burkhart. Roger and Alice were married, and with almost divine swiftness they discovered she was pregnant. David arrived—healthy, perfect. Roger and Alice had originally agreed to have two children, but after the first, they'd decided that one son would suffice.

Abortions were unheard of in Deacon's Creek—unheard of not because they never occurred, but because they went unspoken. After David, Alice's subsequent pregnancy had been a "surprise." But when Ray was old enough to decode the discontent in his parents' little euphemism, he automatically translated "surprise" to "mistake." Later, Ray figured he wasn't so much a disappointment as something they hadn't prayed for. After all, praying only got you so far.

Over on the couch, Ray's mother occasionally makes a soft *hm* sound, as if discovering some passage or platitude that pleased her. Now she gently closes the book and looks up at Ray. "Thank you for staying, Ray."

He doesn't know if she means staying in the living room to keep her company or remaining in town. He twitches a smile. "Sure, Mom."

"You may doubt it, but your father was so . . . *proud* of you."

His smile fades a bit, not out of anger. Maybe she'd intended that comment to be a heart-wrenching sentiment, but it was a bit far-fetched to be true. "That's very kind to say, Mom."

"He loved you and David so much. But your brother was always so distracted"—she makes a dismissive gesture—"with his career, all that." From the TV comes the ding-ding applause of the game show. "He loved you both the same, but that love was different. Does that make sense?"

No. "Of course, Mom."

After a while, Alice says she's going to bed, and Ray hugs her goodnight.

Later, with night fully pressed in against the windows, Ray creeps down to the basement to fetch a bottle of wine from his father's stash. He selects a dusty one from the cobwebby rack, one with a hard-to-read label, and returns to the chair in the living room to watch some TV.

As opposed to David's old room, Ray's boyhood bedroom has gone virtually unchanged since he left roughly six years before. Some of his old clothes are even hanging in the closet. Clumsy from the wine, Ray turns down his bed and surveys the claustrophobic space. Posters from his teenage years have remained hanging here and there—White Zombie, Motörhead, Rage Against the Machine.

Ray glances over at the bookshelf lined with some old paperbacks, a few yearbooks. He pulls one of the yearbooks from the shelf, the one from his junior year—that would have been a year before the accident. It's not the first time in recent weeks that he's indulged in this sort of sentimental time-travel, which fills him with a giddy trepidation, as if he might stumble onto something that will make sense, that might be a sign, that might fix things.

But Ray—thanks to some snooping on the computer—had kept track of the present. He knew that Heather lived two counties over, close to Indianapolis, and he'd done his best to keep tabs on the cyclic nature of her love life—the boyfriend/boredom/breakup rebound rhythm of her relationships.

He flips open the yearbook. Because both their last names began with S, he gives a cursory glance at Travis Steinhauer. But no matter how much Ray distracts himself with these antiquated memories— these people trapped between these faded pages—he finishes each pointless return by staring at the black-and-white photo of Heather.

In his dream, Ray is driving. Not his car, but his father's black '69 Chevelle convertible, a yellow racing stripe painted down the middle. The angle of the sun and the mildness of the air suggest it's morning. He's coursing along a lineless road, curving smoothly through hilly woods. Overhead, spokes of sunlight flash in and out between a low-lying canopy of tree limbs; but in a visual trick, the color of the leaves steadily alternates between the chlorophyllous greens of spring and the autumnal tints of orange, gold, and burgundy, creating a kaleidoscopic effect that mesmerizes Ray, making it difficult for him to keep his eyes on the road. He hears the radio—Springsteen, he's sure of it. The second track from *Nebraska*. The combination of aural and ocular sensations makes him grin. Just as he extends his hand to turn up the volume he notices his passenger. Heather smiles.

Ray's heart begins to drum and his dream-respiration becomes feathery. Random mosaics of shadow and morphing shards of sunlight pass over her face; her brown hair lifts in the gently rushing breeze. She's poised daintily, with her legs tucked up under her. Her skin tone is something between peach and nutmeg, as if she's been lying out by the pool all morning. Heather's heavy-lidded gaze grows seductively severe as she murmurs, "Better keep your eyes on the road, Ray."

The lineless road snakes on, an endless artery of S-curves. But it's no longer black, and now looks to be covered with a slick layer of crimson.

Ray fumbles for the right thing to say. On the radio, Springsteen's still singing, a mellow tune, one of Ray's favorites—the one about everything dying, everything coming back, the one about Atlantic City.

Again he goes for the volume knob, but this time a pale hand clasps his wrist. Ray fixes his eyes on the hand and follows it up to Heather's face, which is no longer tanned and healthy, but waxy, wasted, as if she were in the throes of some fever.

"Ray," she says, "you have to pay attention. You have to leave me alone."

"Why are you sick?" To his ears, his voice sounds as if he's talking under water.

She shakes her head impatiently. "I'm not sick." She frowns. "I'm not sick because I didn't stay." Heather lets go of his wrist. The dream-sun sinks with alarming swiftness, as if light were being extinguished with one simple exhalation. Under the Chevelle's headlights, Ray can see the crimson-coated road as he continues coursing through the tunnel of trees. He steals a glance at his passenger.

Heather's complexion suggests she's been dead for weeks. Her gray, vein-riddled flesh looks bruised in spots, putridly supple in others. There's a glossy spot just under her scalp where he thinks the skin has sloughed away, exposing portions of her skull. Her sunken, unblinking eyes are filmed with baby-blue cataracts, and her features are made more livid by the weak glow from the radio.

Ray tightens his grip on the wheel. Heather opens her corpse-purple lips to speak. "Ray—" she starts, but stops when a thick line of moss-colored drool dribbles out of her mouth. Heather quickly cups a hand to her chin. She wipes her mouth primly, as if embarrassed, and offers a demure smile. "Oops."

Despite her deteriorated exterior, and dream or not, Ray thinks she's lovely.

When she speaks again, her voice is mud-curdled. "You know Daddy will never let you see me again." Leaves begin falling from the ceiling of tree limbs. "Ray?" says the boggy voice next to him, but he does not look over. He tries to think of what to say, because he has the suspicion that with the right words—with healing words—he can fix things. He can bring her back. *I've changed, I've grown up. It's not too late.* The radio grows static-lashed, and there is someone speaking just under the hissing white noise.

Again the voice comes, "Ray," but it is no longer Heather's.

Roger Swanson, wearing the suit he was buried in, is casually angled in the passenger seat, unchanged since the funeral: dark hair slicked back, a mortician's veneer of powdery makeup, a salesman's grin showcasing rows of shark-glossy teeth. "Son," he says, his tone casual, conversational. "You certainly are a fuck-up."

Ray swallows and looks away. Just under the radio's static, he can make out the sermonic cadence of a shouting preacher: *"By faith Abraham, when he was tried, offered up Isaac . . . and he that had received the promises offered up his only-begotten son . . ."* Ray imagines a jowly face beaded with sweat.

"Your mother and I were always so disappointed in you."

Ray exhales thinly. "I know." His voice is lost under the droning pulpit-pounding preacher. *"And Abraham took the wood of the burnt offering and laid it upon Isaac his son . . ."*

Even in his awareness of the dream, Ray still has to summon the courage to say, "You had a very small heart when you were alive."

As if he hadn't heard, Roger says, "You could have killed that girl, you know that? And who in the hell gave you permission to drive my car?"

". . . So Aaron came to the altar and slaughtered the calf as a sin offering for himself . . . his sons brought the blood to him and dipped his finger into the blood and put it on the horns of the altar . . ."

It only now occurs to Ray that he might be able to stop the car. He stomps down to where the brake pedal should be, but his foot pushes into something moist, like water-saturated peat. He presses frantically, uselessly. The headlights and dashboard gauges flicker and fade. Cold, meaty fingers close around Ray's throat, fetid breath inches in on his cheek. But when the voice comes it's not Roger Swanson, but Heather. "You know Daddy will never let you see me again."

Ray shudders awake, the soft hue of dawn powdering his bedroom with gray light. Ray drops his legs over the side of the bed and runs fingers through his long, sleep-matted hair.

Ray and Heather's car wreck had been a serious accident. But in the sequence of things, the car wreck was really the second accident—going to the hospital exposed the first.

They'd been dating for over a year when they found out she was pregnant. Unplanned, of course. For a couple of seniors in high school, they had kept it a secret in order to formulate a solution of how to tell their parents. Neither believed it would be well received.

They went for a drive. It had been a Friday, late in the night by that point. What was supposed to be a date had turned into a debate about how to break the news to their mothers and fathers. They were cruising country roads when Ray brought up the possibility of adoption or abortion. Heather dismissed this immediately, appalled that Ray would even contemplate such things.

He was trying to explain that he wasn't suggesting they do either, but they should at least discuss it. Voices were raised, ultimatums were issued. Ray was looking over at Heather when her eyes went wide. Ray ploughed into a deer, the car spinning into a tree before flipping sideways into a ditch.

Sometime the next morning, Ray woke in the hospital. His mother was in a chair next to the bed. He could hear his father's strident voice down the hall. Hours earlier in the ER, after blood work was pulled, it was determined that neither had been drinking. However, it had been discovered that the seventeen-year-old passenger was several months pregnant, and that the fetus had been lost.

Ray sat up in the hospital bed and winced, drawing his hand up to his head, feeling some sort of gauzy wrapping there. He demanded to see Heather. With his mother trying to stop him, Ray staggered out of the room and into the first triage stall he could find, throwing back the curtain to discover a haggard man reclining in the bed, his rheumy eyes appearing amused by Ray's uncoordinated entrance. A tangle of liquid-filled tubes hung from machines and IVs, all leading down to his frail, liver-spotted forearms. Ray fell against the side of the wall, staring at the old man as if for some sort of answer. The frail man lifted one of his tube-needled arms, extending a crooked finger directly at Ray. A smile appeared, exposing long nicotine-tinted teeth. Heather was gone.

An hour after shaking away the residue of his dream, Ray is sitting at his parents' kitchen table, leafing through a stack of newspapers. One is the local paper, the others were from closer to Indianapolis. Closer to Heather. Most of the jobs are in the city publications.

Ray returns to the local paper, a headline catching his eye: EVEN-SONG CEMETERY VANDALIZED.

He is almost finished reading the thin column when he hears his mom's bedroom door open. A few seconds later she shuffles into the kitchen, and they mumble good-morning greetings to each other.

His mother pours a cup of coffee. "Anything interesting?"

Frowning at the newspaper, Ray says, "Not really. Someone vandalized the cemetery, knocked over some headstones and stuff."

His mom had just taken a sip from her mug. "Really?" Her tone suggests revulsion. "Some people just have no . . . conscience." Silence. "And, you know, that's not the first time that's happened." She moves around toward Ray's side of the table and peers out the window at the crisp, blue-orange morning. "I hope they left your father's spot alone."

Ray says nothing; but, out of simple decency, has a flicker of agreement. His mom clears her throat and seems to shake the news away. "So, any *good* news in the paper?"

Without glancing up Ray says, "A job. Maybe. I need some cash." He gives a sheepish grin. "Help with rent money and groceries."

His mom sighs a laugh. "Oh, Ray. You can stay for as long as you like—you know that."

"Tell you what," Ray says. "I'll stop by Crenshaw's, deliver that check to Wendell, and then go fishing for a job."

Steam curls from Alice's coffee mug. "You know," she says, tousling Ray's unkempt hair, "you could use a haircut before you go out and conquer a new career."

Ray smirks, conceding his rough-around-the-edges appearance. "I know, I know."

After taking a sip, his mother lowers the mug. "Harlan Vaught certainly could use your business," she says, and adds, "Best haircut in town."

Ray returns to the classifieds. After a second or two he says, "Sure, more like the *only* haircut in town."

On his way to Crenshaw's Market, Ray decides to run by the cemetery, curious about the condition of his father's plot.

As opposed to the dozen or so toppled headstones in the cemetery, Roger Swanson's marble maker remains undisturbed. The ground covering his grave, on the other hand, is a mess.

Crossing a grassy area just off a gravel path, Ray spots a groundskeeper. Ray approaches, offhandedly noting that they're roughly the same age. The groundskeeper says, "Good mornin'," a grin cracking under the bill of his ball cap.

Ray gives a curt nod. "Morning."

"Come out to check on somebody?"

Ray hesitates. "Sort of."

The guy's sunglasses reflect the sun as he bobs his head. "Yeah. Already had some people drop by this morning. Who you looking for?"

"My da—" Ray licks his lips. "Swanson. Roger Swanson."

The groundskeeper jabs a thumb over his shoulder. "Just got done with that one. Vandals didn't mess with the headstone, but they sure did trample the hell out of the dirt."

Ray paces a few yards to get a closer look. Sure enough, the mound of dirt had been gouged and scattered, but the polished marker remains untouched. Ray's eyes move to the dates of his father's lifespan. The groundskeeper sidles up next to Ray. "You his son?" Ray squints, and after a moment nods. "Don't worry, man. I set down some more seed on his spot." Ray had already noticed the fresh, wheat-colored specks of grass seed.

"Thanks for that."

"No problem. Hell, your dad was an easy fix. He's one of the lucky ones." He gestures toward the haphazard destruction. He spits to his side and wipes at a small trail of saliva hanging from his lower lip. "Some assholes have no respect for the dead."

The pickled pigs' feet are kept in brine. But Ray knows, from his formative years working at Crenshaw's Market, that the proper terms for these butcher-friendly solutions are sodium nitrites, nitrates, and sulfur dioxides. Preservatives, in other words—the formaldehydes of the food industry.

The pigs' feet are displayed on top of the curved glass above the rows of steaks and other cuts of meat. Nothing's changed. It's always been this way.

Ray waits at the meat counter for a few seconds before a stout old man with youthful eyes emerges, parting a hanging curtain of clear plastic strips.

"Can I help you?" the old man says. He's wearing a paper butcher's hat and a red, chest-to-knee apron. Ray smiles, and recognition spreads on the man's face. "Well, I'll be damned! Raymond, how the hell are you?"

"Not bad." Ray extends his arm over the glass counter and Wendell Harper applies a hearty handshake. "I was hoping I'd catch you here."

"You kidding me?" Wendell says, feigning indignation. "They never let me out of this place." His wrinkled features twist with a mischievous grin. "You look good, Ray. What can I do for you?"

"Well"—from his pocket Ray produces the personal check from his father—"my mom found this in my dad's things . . ."

Wendell adjusts his paper cap as he interrupts. "Listen, Ray, it was an awful thing that happened to your dad . . ."

Ray cuts in, shaking his head: "No need, Wendell. Me and mom are doing fine. In fact, it looks like my dad had some unfinished business with you." He hands over the check.

Glasses attached to a chain are hanging around Wendell's neck; he lifts the spectacles, resting them on his nose. He scrutinizes the check. "Where'd you say you found this?"

"Mom found it in a pile of paperwork."

Wendell's gaze lingers on Ray for several long seconds before he flicks his eyes back to the check. "And your mom sent you here?"

Ray shrugs. "I just told her I'd take care of it. Check in on my old pal."

It takes a moment, but Wendell finally responds with a weak grin. "Tell you what, Ray. Give me a minute. I'll take a peek in dry storage, see what we have in safekeeping. Stick around for a few minutes, okay?"

"No problem."

Wendell blinks, opens his mouth as if to say something else, but instead turns and disappears through the strips of plastic that serve as a curtained threshold.

Ray slips his hands in his pockets and paces along the front of the glass counter, idly appraising the selection of meat, casually scanning the aisle of the old-fashioned market, where cashiers still manually ring up purchases and bagboys walk people to their cars.

Ray bristles. At the far end of the aisle he sees Herbert and Hazel Steinhauer.

Herbert is crouched down, inspecting something on a shelf. The man's mouth is moving, but whether he's talking to his wife or himself, Ray can't discern. Hazel, her garish makeup still appearing hastily applied, is standing next to her husband, her willowy frame rigid, one hand clutching her purse, the other arm hanging at her side. Her bulging, unblinking eyes are trained directly on Ray.

Even from this distance the sick woman's condition appears to have deteriorated since he saw her at the barber shop a few days earlier. A dingy, short-sleeved dress hangs loose over her bony body. And now Ray notices something else: the inner portions of her forearms are noticeably jaundiced now, as if she's been smeared with—*What the hell is that stuff they smear on you before surgery?* Clinically distant as it is, the word crawls into Ray's mind: *Betadine*. Ray spots a cluster of livid bruises, the sort of marks people receive from intravenous injections. Perhaps the result of some recent hospital visit.

Ray swallows and lifts his hand to wave. The corners of Hazel's lipstick-smudged mouth tug up in the pantomime of a smile. Her eyes are avid, unnerving, the effect bringing artificial life to her gaunt face.

A voice from behind Ray—"Daydreaming?"

Ray flinches and turns around. Wendell. He smiles at the butcher. "Yeah. Just sort of spacing out I guess."

The old man hefts a brown bag, slender-shaped, tied with a piece of twine. "I think I found what you were looking for."

"What is it?"

"Wine," Wendell says, peering over the top of his bifocals. "And nothing cheap either. This stuff's imported." With a thick finger, the butcher points at a note on the bag. "Looks like your dad was sending it as a gift—says it's supposed to go to old Vaught down the street."

Vaught. The barber. "Really?"

Wendell nods.

"I'm going there anyway." Ray smiles and gestures at his hair. "Why don't you let me deliver it?"

Wendell eyes Ray for just a moment and then shrugs. "Suit yourself." The butcher hands the brown bag over the counter.

Ray is about to say goodbye but stops short. "Do you need any help around here?"

Wendell adjusts his paper cap and scratches an eyebrow with his knuckle. "You mean like a job?"

"Yeah," Ray says, "maybe for just a little while. Something to help me get out of the house, maybe get my own place."

Wendell passes a hand over his face and crosses his arms. He's quiet as he seems to consider this. "I can't pay you much."

Ray grins, "Anything's better than nothing. Besides," he says, thinking of his bygone days here in the market, "I could do most of this stuff walking in my sleep."

Wendell smirks. The two share one last laugh. "Why don't you stop by later this week and we'll talk." They exchange handshakes.

As he's leaving, Ray sees Herbert and Hazel in a checkout line. Herbert is chatting with the cashier, but Hazel is still watching Ray, her bulging eyes following him. Slowly, drowsily, she lifts an arm, her slender fingers gently scraping at the air. Her oddly stilted mechanics make Ray think of strings on a marionette. Ray returns the wave.

Hazel Steinhauer smiles.

The barber pole is spinning slowly, hypnotically, in front of the barber shop.

On the sidewalk beneath the shadowed underbelly of the awning, Ray hesitates before clasping the door handle and entering Vaught's Barber Shop. A tiny bell rings overhead. No customers.

Ray glances around. Nothing's changed. The long mirror making the place look twice its size, walls still covered with antique memorabilia: wooden signs—*Colonel Ichabod's Conk Tonsorial Artistry for Fashionable Gentlemen*—a vintage metal placard advertising "Cupping and Leeching"—*Hot Bath 5¢*. There's an old chalkboard listing an array of services: *Haircuts, Flat Tops, Wet Cuts, Shampoo, Beard Trim, Tonic, Razor Shaves*. Ray is conflicted between a comforting sense of nostalgia, and a creeping unease with the shop's stagnation. A radio is playing softly in the rear, some staticky big band tune. There's a hallway back there and a door that's been painted over, presumably leading to a basement or storage closet.

"Hello?" Ray calls out, his voice reverberating in the narrow space.

Someone clears their throat. A tall, thin man emerges from the corridor on the other side of the shop. "Pardon me," he says, his raspy voice and wild gray hair suggesting he's been drowsing. He takes his horn-rimmed glasses from his face and begins wiping the lenses on his white smock. "May I help you?"

"Yes, sir. I don't know if you remember me or not, Mr. Vaught, but my name is Ray Swanson."

"Ah yes . . . Roger's youngest boy," he says, his tone grave. "I didn't have the opportunity to impart my condolences at the funeral, son. But you have them now. Your father was a good man."

Ray nods, not knowing what to say. He lifts the brown bag. "I think this belongs to you." Ray offers the bottle. "I think it's a gift."

Vaught's eyebrows twitch as he looks back and forth from Ray to the paper-wrapped bottle. Almost warily, the old man takes hold of the package, unties the twine, and gently slips the bottle from the bag. "Oh . . . *my*," he says. For the first time Ray sees that the dark bottle has no label, but instead displays what looks like an embossed number seven. The top of the bottle has been sealed with burgundy wax. Up close, Ray gets a better look at the barber's austere appearance—a mortician in Buddy Holly glasses, Ray thinks. "Do you mind telling me"—Vaught licks his lips—"how you came across this *gift?*"

"My mom found a check addressed to Crenshaw's Market. Wendell Harper told me my dad had reserved this bottle for you, that it was some sort of present."

Smiling, Vaught shakes his head in what might be disbelief. Silence for several long seconds. "And what a generous gift it is, my boy. And since you are the one delivering it, I will thank you as my benefactor.

Now," he says abruptly, placing the wine bottle on his narrow work shelf in front of the mirror, "it would be impolite if I did not offer my services to you." Vaught slowly spins the barber's chair, his long hand inviting the young man to sit. Ray doesn't mention that he'd planned on getting his haircut anyway, but instead smiles and sinks into the bulky barber's chair, all chrome and cracked-vinyl cushion. In the mirror, Ray watches Vaught swipe a black cape from a hook on the wall and, with an old-fashioned flourish, snaps the cloth in midair and drapes it over Ray, fastening it around his neck.

The old man moves to his work shelf, lined with colored bottles and jars containing creams and tonics. In addition to several neatly arranged instruments, there's also the tall, ever-present glass jar of Barbicide filled with the requisite blue disinfectant.

Vaught lifts a pair of electric clippers and begins whistling along with the low-playing radio.

Ray shifts in his seat, getting comfortable. "I was afraid you wouldn't remember me."

"Nonsense," Vaught says with a dismissive gesture. "In fact, I remember your first visit to this very chair." He clicks on the clippers and moves behind Ray.

"Really?" he says, sounding a little more incredulous than he'd intended.

Vaught addresses Ray's reflection in the mirror. "Why certainly. My goodness, you threw a fit."

Ray huffs a laugh. "Oh."

Shaking his head Vaught says, "Lord, you just bawled." And Ray recalls it clearly, that old photo—the picture commemorating his first haircut at Vaught's barber shop: his round, tear-smeared face pinched in mid-cry, freshly trimmed bangs hanging across his forehead. And again his mind's eye moves to the margin of the snapshot—once more he sees his father's big arms reaching in. But now, Ray thinks, there's nothing harsh or severe in that frozen motion—those arms are not restraining him—those hands are cradling him, trying to soothe him. Ray is clutched by a cold contemplation: If he'd always been wrong about the interpretation of that photo, what else had he been wrong about?

Ray is shaken from this vivid image when Vaught whistles through his teeth. "Yep, your daddy took good care of you that day, and every other time he brought you. I tell you that man sure loved his boys, you in particular. Always said you were his special boy." Vaught thumbs off the clippers and returns to his cluttered work shelf.

While the man has his back turned, Ray winces, his chin sinking to his chest.

Vaught must have glanced in the mirror because the old man has been silent, peering at Ray's reflection. "You all right, son?"

He looks in the mirror at Vaught, who turns slowly. Ray swallows hard, knowing that his expression, his eyes, betray his true feelings. After a long pause, Vaught simply nods solemnly. "We all go through that, son." With his long fingers laced through the eyelets of his scissors, Vaught walks back behind the chair, speaking to Ray's reflection. "Sometimes we don't realize how much we love someone until it's too late." Silence. "All that matters is that your love is sincere in your heart."

Ray takes a rough swipe at his eyes and sets his forearms on the armrest. "It is."

Vaught is reverently silent for several seconds, and then slams his foot down on something.

All this happens very fast.

There's a metallic *clack,* and Ray's forearms are restrained from the sides of the armrest. The same thing happens to his shins. Ray's heart lurches and he begins to thrash.

Vaught pulls off the black barber's cape; now Ray can see his wrists clamped with stainless steel cuffs. The armrests have opened to reveal slender troughs, each containing a shallow drain positioned under his forearms.

Ray's eyes dart to the mirror to see Vaught standing behind the chair, smiling. *"HELLLLPP!"* Vaught reaches down, reemerging just as Ray sucks in another breath. *"HEL—"*

Vaught slaps a piece of duct tape over Ray's mouth. "You might as well knock off that racket, son." He strolls over to his work shelf. From a drawer he removes a worn leather strop. "I'd appreciate a little cooperation, and I know your daddy would too." He places the strop over Ray's forehead, latching the ends to the neckrest.

The big band music fills the barber shop.

On the shelf, Vaught opens a wooden box and removes a silver straight razor with an ornate ivory handle. Ray flexes and bucks against his restraints. "I assure you it's no use," the barber says.

Vaught retrieves the wine bottle and uses the razor to peel back the wax. With another instrument he removes the cork. The man sniffs at the lip of the bottle and smiles. "In vino veritas," he says. Ray watches Vaught remove the blue Barbicide jar from the shelf, revealing a small, funnel-shaped receptacle. The barber upends the bottle, inserting it into the small drain. Ray hears liquid flowing, gurgling as it travels through what sounds like tubes or pipes, just like a sink draining.

"A long time ago," Vaught says, scrutinizing the bottle as it depletes itself, "members of my guild were called barber-surgeons. And we performed more than just haircuts, we were more like novice physicians—we had our hands in pulling teeth, bloodletting, tonsillectomies, Caesarian sections, amputations. Did you know that?" Ray's chest rises and falls rapidly. "No. I didn't think so." Apparently pleased with the progress of the draining wine, Vaught lifts his razor and approaches Ray. "Back then, the key was to convince people of the doctrine of the four humors: black bile, yellow bile, phlegm, and of course blood. It was necessary that these four elements remain balanced in order for a person to be healthy. Or at least *think* they were healthy." The old man adjusts his glasses. "The number four carries great symbolic significance, son—the four stages of life, the four seasons." He chuckles softly. "I could go on and on."

Ray screams under the duct tape as Vaught lowers the straight razor. With a practiced movement, the barber carves a design—what looks like a curled number seven—across the inner portions Ray's forearms. Blood courses down and into the armrest-troughs. "These symbols," Vaught says, using the razor to gesture at the intricate lacerations, "are fleams—my guild's cherished instruments for bloodletting."

Ray thrashes and shakes his head, blinking back petals of darkness blossoming on the fringes of his vision. "And now"—Vaught sweeps his hands wide like a conductor—"to complement one pagan consecration with another: *By faith Abel offered to God a more excellent sacrifice than Cain . . . and through it he being dead still speaks. By faith Abraham, when he was tested, offered up Isaac, and he who had received the promises offered up his only begotten son . . .*"

The sound of Vaught's recitation grows distant, and Ray's head begins lolling. The last thing he hears is the tiny bell above the door as someone enters the barber shop.

". . . For the life of the creature is in the blood . . ."

Monosyllabic chants. Whispered scripture.

Ray urges his eyes open. The duct tape has been removed and he can breathe through his mouth. He's cold. It's dark here—scents of soil, rust, and rot. Lying on his side, Ray squirms, feeling dirt on his cheek and under his fingers. Through his slitted eyelids he sees guttering lights, flickering thinly as if from lanterns. The walls are thickly mortared stone, slick with moisture. This is a cellar, he thinks. Or a dungeon. Ray tries to move and winces against pain pulsing through his forearms. They feel bound or bandaged now.

". . . and I have given it to you to make atonement for yourselves on the altar . . ."

Amber light pulses at the far end of the room. Ray tries to focus on the reverent whispers. He squints across the cellar, seeing them now, their figures defined by the weak light from bull's-eye lanterns.

Ray hears his mother, the sound of her voice blending with the words of Harlan Vaught. Ray realizes that he's in the basement below the barber shop.

With the last of his strength, Ray struggles up on his elbow. Now he notices the tangle of thin, liquid-filled tubes hanging from the ceiling, dangling like IVs. Wine. Blood. Something else. He follows them down to a long wooden bench, to the crumpled row of corpses— huddled shapes in varying degrees of decay.

His mother and Vaught are standing at the far end of the bench, leaning over the body of Roger Swanson, the corpse still dressed in its funeral suit, its sleeves rolled up to expose forearms riddled with plastic tubes.

". . . it is the blood that makes atonement for one's life . . . because the life of every creature is its blood."

And with that incantation, Roger Swanson twitches and slowly raises his head, viscous fluids seeping from his nostrils and mouth. Alice Swanson gasps. "Amen," she says, reaching out to her husband. "Amen." Vaught delicately disconnects the needled tubes hooked into the cadaver's arms, and dark liquids weep from track-marks along its forearms.

With vertiginous understanding, Ray summons an image of Hazel Steinhauer. Intuitively, he knows that Travis Steinhauer is one of those hunkered shapes slumped along the wall.

Tenderly, Vaught helps the thing that was Roger Swanson to its unsteady feet. After a moment, Alice steps in and the two begin shuffling toward the basement stairs. Vaught strides forward, and Ray is hoisted up and dragged across the dirt floor. And there, between two mold-mottled corpses, Ray replaces his father as he is settled into his special spot on the bench.

CORBIN'S GORE

Where to begin? Where to begin . . . ?

Well, we could start with Cassidy, she was wealthy—that is to say her family, the Davenports, were wealthy—and that has some bearing on all this, because Corbin would have been rich too, by way of nothing else but relational proximity, if he would have just been a little more ambitious, if he would have just cooperated, if he would have just capitulated. *If only you could see the big picture . . .*

On second thought, maybe we should begin with the Gore, or at least the old gypsy-witch woman at the end of his fifth-floor apartment hallway. Corbin Hollis had noticed her on the first day after moving into that dreary, uptown dwelling. Of course she was no gypsy or witch at all, but as she resembled somebody's mummified but animated hippie grandma, sometimes staring vacantly down the fifth-floor passage, it was difficult for Corbin not to conjure a few entertaining associations.

Northern sections of the city were funny like that: there was always some weird block or two where the eccentricity of elderly affluence commingled with the voguishly antisocial segment of artsy punks.

Corbin was neither elderly nor artsy nor affluent. Corbin couldn't tell you what he was, and frankly didn't give a fuck about it—about anything, really.

His hometown of Colfax, Indiana, was a dismal, social-noose of a community that hung around residents' necks just waiting for the trap-door of independent thought or—God save us—self-reliant deviation to open up beneath their feet. Corbin hadn't waited for that to happen as it did to his mom and dad, and he'd departed on an existential exodus as soon as he could. That had been about three years ago.

But he had only lived in this uptown apartment for the last nine months or so. Last fall, during that first week here—the first week following his clumsy retreat from Cassidy's impeccably decorated apartment—Corbin had been walking home from an underwhelming day with the moving company—packing, stacking, lifting, and wheeling (repeating this routine several times a day)—when, from the sidewalk, he happened to glance up to the fifth-floor corner window of the weathered brick façade of his building, up to his apartment window. Corbin stopped walking and narrowed his eyes. An old, ill-pallid woman was standing there, looking out the window. Because of the overcast sky reflected in the already hazy-wavy glass, she seemed immaterial at first, as if floating in a frame of smoke-swirled murk. The curtains were parted on either side of her. *A ghost can't move curtains, can it?* But there was no mistaking it—fifth floor: northwest corner— Corbin's apartment. Even from the sidewalk Corbin was startled by how ghastly-gray the woman was—a scrambled bulb of white hair haloing her gaunt face—standing with her arms dangling at her sides staring down at the street below.

Sprinting through the lobby, Corbin took the steps two at a time as he ran up the stairwell, jogging along the jaundice-tinted hallway and fumbling for the right key on his key ring. Corbin carried a backpack with him to work, which contained a few handy pieces of equipment for his gig as a mover: pair of gloves, lifting belt, couple sets of ratchet tie-downs, a few other things. He already had the heavy-duty box cutter out and had thumbed open the razor blade as he burst into apartment 505.

Somehow (maybe it was all the brainless horror films he'd watched alone late at night) he knew that no one—a ghoulish, fanged hag . . . a psychopath cross-dresser in a gown wearing garish makeup to resemble a frail old female—would be in the apartment when he ambled in, breathing heavy, box cutter raised and ready at shoulder level. And of course no one was. No *thing* was. The drapes in his bedroom were pulled to either side, but Corbin was unsure whether or not he'd done that before he'd left that morning.

And as sure as Corbin was that there would be no living soul when he bounded into the apartment, he was just as certain that it had not been a ghost or a phantom or some other ridiculous, insidiously spiritual entity. Catching his breath, Corbin walked over to the window and looked down toward the street. He felt no disturbing sensation here—

no phantom pocket of apparition-iced air, no half-flashes of grim visions. His breath was beginning to fog the glass now, and he took a few steps back and watched the cloudy patch draw in on itself and fade away.

He'd made a mistake, that was all. He'd made a mistake.

Corbin walks into Cassidy's immaculate apartment—what he has slowly gained the confidence to call their apartment. He hears Cassidy's voice somewhere in here, in the kitchen. He finds her talking on her cell phone, her tear-streaked face rosy and puffy. "I got to go," she says to whoever she's been talking to and disconnects. Corbin blurts out, "What's wrong?" Cassidy sniffles, takes a wadded tissue, and runs it under her nose. She makes an attempt to smile, but it just makes her face more pained. When she speaks, her voice is composed and seductively saccharine. "Sit down, Corbin, please." At first, he assumes it's one of her grandparents— sick, taken from the nursing home, and sent to the hospital or something. But as he slides into the chair at the table he notices the pamphlet. He hears Cassidy speaking. Hears the words pregnancy test. *After an excessive explanation, Cassidy breaks out into a fresh series of sobs. Numb but alert, Corbin stands and rounds the side of the table, sinking down to one knee and pulling Cassidy toward him. He wants to tell her it's going to be okay, that they have nothing to worry about. Most of his mind believes that, but it sounds flimsy even as he silently recites it to himself. It's going to be okay.*

Corbin twitched awake to the sound of a crying baby.

Irritated, he squinted at the clock—three in the morning. Corbin rubbed his eyes fitfully and twisted in his sheets, taking a deep breath and staring at the ceiling. The arc lights lining the street below filled the room with a feeble-diffuse furnace-orange glow. First it was the bawling baby but now, adding to his agitation, his ear picked up on a blaring car alarm echoing somewhere in the neighborhood. Then came the domino effect of contemplation—his mind moving from the whimpering infant to the car alarm to this shitty apartment complex with its attendant shitty residents, which made him think of Cassidy's place. Then his dwelling inexorably tumbled toward the tragedy of him and Cassidy in general.

But it had been his choice, right? *I mean, it's not like she kicked me out and told me never to come back.* No. Most of Corbin's undoing was Corbin's doing. It had been a choice to walk out, rejecting the possibility of returning to that plush apartment and reconciling with Cassidy. It had been his choice to fork over most of his savings as a down payment to live alone in this decaying box in this ancient building and living down the hall from a demented version of an elderly Joni Mitchell. Throughout all that upheaval, Corbin had somehow maintained his job at the moving company. It was predictable, rewarding work—it was how he'd met Cassidy.

Just by glancing at the stuff he'd been toting he knew they were doing a job for some moneyed maiden. Sure enough, as he and a few of the guys had wheeled in those belongings into the impressive Evanston apartment, the girl hung around, supervising every movement and maneuver, frequently correcting the movers, unable to make up her mind as to where to place furniture. When he was in high school, he had despised this sort of spoiled, upper-class piece of ass. But something had occurred in the intervening years—a degradation in self-value, perhaps—that gave Corbin pause when considering girls like this, as if they might possess the potential to make him better. Corbin had had sense enough to understand that there was one variety of life waiting for him down in Colfax, and possibly another life somewhere else. But his lack of commitment resulted in his current state of stagnant, in-between existence. Besides, who the hell was he to judge this girl?

She had kept her eye on Corbin. And it was she who had ambitiously instigated a hasty conversation at the end of the day, following Corbin into the stairwell and, after some antagonizing small talk, offering him her phone number.

It took some time, but Corbin eventually figured out that Cassidy Davenport's attraction to him was twofold: 1) Corbin was compellingly deviant—not quite dangerous, but just roguish enough so that by partnering with a guy like him worked as a sophisticated mechanism of revenge toward her strict and overbearing parents; and 2) Corbin Hollis, in her mind, was a worthwhile project—rough around the edges but potentially malleable enough to mold into an in-law minion for her parents and to groom into an upper-class lapdog for herself.

Taking another deep breath, Corbin shoved the covers aside and slipped from bed, shuffling into the darkness of the hallway. He walked by the sliding door of the hall closet, absently noting some of the things stored in there from Cassidy's apartment—a few unpacked boxes, an old vacuum. Cassidy had been really good at that—buying *stuff.* After reaching the kitchen, Corbin poured himself a glass of water. The water smelled strong and strange in this apartment—a mineral mix of age and earth, infused with a whiff of ozone. The sound of the baby was beginning to fade. He drank deeply, placed the glass on the counter.

He was in the corridor next to the hall closet when the crying baby suddenly let loose a wild wail that caused Corbin to stop and go rigid just outside his bedroom. The crying was so intense—a series of *wah-wah* gulping sobs—and so desperate that Corbin imagined its pinched face, its extended arms, and tiny fingers helplessly flexing at the air, desperate to clutch something secure. He couldn't detect whether or not the crying was coming from above or below, next door or down the hall by the stairwell. It sounded as if it was coming from everywhere.

Corbin had to go to work in a few hours and hoped the kid's parents would just rock the damn thing to sleep already. He slipped back into bed and began to doze. And as he drifted away he tried and failed to recall which of his neighbors actually had a baby.

It's spring. Corbin and Cassidy are at a restaurant—a humble, unassuming taqueria near the red line L station. They sit across from each other, the small formica table in front of them cluttered with chips, salsa, sodas. Cassidy has made it clear that she's not in the mood for food. Nevertheless, they need to talk.

"My parents will lose their minds," says Cassidy. "My mother is going to be so disappointed. And my father—" She lets out a prissy-callous laugh. "My father will be fucking devastated." Cassidy shakes her head and crosses her arms. "My parents are just going to die, Corbin."

Corbin thinks, but doesn't ask, Will your parents die because a) their precious, promiscuous princess got herself pregnant, or b) their daughter's deadbeat boyfriend is the father? *He wants to convince himself that it might be more likely that it's a timing issue, that their well-to-do daughter is midway through grad school and unengaged to a guy they'd never met. But Corbin, in that deadbeat heart of his, knows better.*

"But that's not why we should make this decision," he says. Somehow he finds himself saying, "Your parents are important. But they shouldn't"—he makes a face, struggling for the words—"shape the life we make."

Cassidy's posture is pert and alert. She has the business-set composure of a woman in a critical business deal—a hostile takeover, maybe. Just like her old man. *"And what are we going to do, Corbin?"* *The sophisticated subtext of her tone serves to criticize Corbin's intelligence—or lack of intelligence as the case may be:* This is partly your fault. So what's your brilliant plan, genius?

Corbin thinks he can see through her precocious posturing and knows he loves the girl underneath. He's no angel either. This was the first relationship he's ever been in where he has so much to lose, and lately he lets Cassidy do all the fit-throwing. She's the one with the business degree, *he frequently reminds himself*—she's the one paying for the apartment. She's the one paying for everything. *To illustrate this he unconsciously adjusts the hood on the Chicago Bears sweatshirt she'd bought for him recently.*

Her question—what are we going to do?*—flutters through his mind, darting, swooping in and out of shadows like a trapped bat.*

Later, when he thinks back, Corbin will understand that his response had helped decide Cassidy. Corbin says, "I think we should get engaged."

She looks at Corbin—looks through *Corbin—as if catching a glimpse at some celestial event blossoming in the sky over the city. A demure smile appears, making the bloodless implications of her statement all the more unsettling. "You work for a* moving *company, Corbin."*

He allows the soundtrack of bustling conversations and ranchera music to play while he clenches his teeth for three or four seconds and levels his gaze with Cassidy. "I make decent money."

Another nasty little snort. "Your brand of decent doesn't mean dick-all when you're going to be a dad."

Plates clatter in the kitchen. One of the sauce-spattered line cooks slides a plate onto the pass and rings a bell. "I'll get a second job. I can find my own money." Cautious to retain some pride. *"We can make it work."*

Cassidy begins blinking rapidly, her shoulders sag slightly, as if slowly exhaling a pent-up breath. She tilts her head forward to look at Corbin from under the eaves of her brow. A thin, nearly imperceptible smile plays at the corners of her mouth. Again, when Corbin recalls all this he will still wonder if her threadbare smile is sutured to her face by reluctant relief or simple pity.

The name of the old gypsy-witch at the end of the hall was Barb.

Corbin stepped off the elevator and turned left toward his apartment; but as he walked along the narrow, shadow-paneled corridor, he was seized by the sensation of being watched. He twisted and looked over his shoulder.

Down at the other end of the hall, standing in the open-door threshold of her apartment as she sometimes did, was the odd-looking old woman. Though momentarily caught off-guard, he had become used to her presence by now. She was not a tiny creature but rather tall, just about eye-level with the twenty-four-year-old who'd now slowed to a stop to reciprocate her stare. Her long hair was silver-white, parted in the middle, and sheaved over her shoulders in wiry cables of cronish neglect. She stood with her hands resting in the pockets of a maroon, lint-pebbled cardigan that was too large for her. And even from this distance Corbin spotted several pieces of ostentatious jewelry—the dangling earrings, a few beads braided into her scraggly hair, a couple of necklaces looped around her loose-fleshed neck—that held all the hallmarks of a time-displaced bohemian.

Corbin found that he could not pry his attention away from her. Feeling as though he'd lost this installment of the staring contest, he said, "Do you need something?" It came out a little harsher than he'd intended.

The unusual smile on the woman's weathered face became more pronounced. "I saw you walking on the sidewalk," she said. "About thirty minutes ago or so."

Corbin bowed his lower lip and shook his head. "Not me." He'd just come from the first-floor lobby not three minutes before. "I just got home."

He was preparing to turn and leave when the old woman's expression changed. She smiled casually, and to Corbin it was something unusually warm and inviting. "Oh well, it doesn't matter. As long as you're here now." Corbin waited. "This building is full of old people and crawling with selfish young shits with wires stuffed in their ears who aren't aware of anything larger than the damn screens on those damn phones." Corbin instantly thought the comment funny but revealed nothing. The witch said, "Are you one of them?"

Corbin shrugged. "Am I an old person?"

Her smile turned into a wry smirk. "An old soul, perhaps. But no—are you too preoccupied with your gadgets to assist your strange neighbor?"

With his fisted hands shoved into the pockets of his hooded sweatshirt Corbin quickly pondered the long-range implications of rejecting the request. "What sort of assistance do you need?"

"Lifting sort of assistance. I thought living down the hall from a competent mover might have its benefits."

Corbin frowned. "How'd you know I was a mover?"

The hippie-witch slipped a hand from the pocket of her cardigan and used a knuckle-knobbed finger to gesture at Corbin's head. "That cap of yours. You do work for that company, don't you?"

Corbin's hand involuntarily came up and pinched the brim of the dark green ball cap, which was embroidered with the logo of two back-to-back dollies, forming a pair of mirror-imaged Ls. "Oh. Yeah." He adjusted his cap, already approaching the open door.

The interior of the old woman's apartment was unshockingly similar to her externally folksy appearance—unkempt, outdated, and adorned with antiquish trinkets. As Corbin cautiously followed the old woman into the belly of her dwelling, he noted the writing on the cardboard boxes stacked all over the place, label-scrawled in shaky black ink: one marked DEEP PURPLE, one marked LEADBELLY, ENCHANTED COTTAGE, STEREOSCOPES, CUBS GAMES, POSTCARDS, J. M. WHISTLER, stuff like that.

The drapes were parted, tingeing the clutter-filled room with the amber light of late afternoon. The old woman spun on Corbin and extended her long-fingered hand. "I'm Barb. Whitaker. Barb Whitaker."

Corbin, still inwardly wary but outwardly aloof, casually gripped the wrinkled, vein-and-bone hand. He simply supplied, "Corbin."

The gullied map of wrinkles covering Barb's face shifted as a grin drew up on her cheeks, and belying the manifest signatures of advanced age were her eyes, which glittered with mischief and dormant youth. "Well, Mr. Corbin. As you can see, I have a bit of hauling I need help with. An acquaintance has arranged for someone to pick up these items on the condition that I deliver them to the lobby." Corbin wondered briefly if the translation here was that she was being chaperoned to a nursing home somewhere. "I've been known to be quite the bruiser, but it would be a time-absorptive task to drag these things down five flights of stairs." Corbin crossed his arms, took a deep breath, and appraised the maze of boxed-up junk and bric-à-brac-lined bookcases. He opened his mouth to speak but Barb cut in. "I may appear like a peasant but I assure you I can compensate you handsomely."

Corbin smirked, blurted a tight laugh. "You don't look like a peasant."

"Ah." Now Barb was the one appraising Corbin. "Just a wee bit crazy, then."

The smirk Corbin was sporting spread into an awkward smile. "I don't think you look crazy."

"Demential, perhaps."

Corbin uncrossed his arms and returned his hands to his pockets. His smile slackened a degree or two. "Never crossed my mind."

Barb gave several slow nods. Her sincere smile didn't waiver. "Well, nevertheless, it's nice to make your acquaintance."

Watch her closely, pal. "You too."

"So"—she laced together those long, mood-ring studded fingers— "do we have a deal?"

Corbin considered the extra cash. Yes, they had a deal.

Ninety minutes later—ninety minutes of elevator-and-stairwell circuits broken by bouts of small-talk banter with Barb—Corbin was nearing the box-toting finish line. On one of his final trips, Corbin found the old woman in her now nearly clutter-free living room, the coffee table containing two highball glasses, both filled with punch-tinted liquid and garnished with a couple of maraschino cherries. Barb waved at the remaining boxes. "Take a break for a few minutes." She offered Corbin a drink. "I may not be much in the way of physical labor these days, but I can still lift a drink or two." Barb made a mock-astonished face. "Please tell me you're old enough to drink."

Corbin licked his lips, not immediately accepting the beverage. "Yeah. Beyond it." But after a few seconds he gently clutched the glass. "Thanks. What is it?"

"An old-fashioned. Some bourbon, few dashes of bitters, some club soda, couple of other things—nothing complicated. Cheers." Barb extended her glass.

The impulse to incredulously sniff the drink crossed Corbin's mind, but he simply eyed it for a moment before clinking glasses with his strange new friend and taking a sip. After a few seconds of savoring the pleasantly potent concoction, Corbin said, "Thank you."

"I'm glad you like it." She took another sip, passed a hooked finger across her lower lip, and swirled the ice, making a sharp, glassy sound. "This drink brings back good memories." Barb gave a distracted glance over Corbin's shoulder, over toward one of the bookcases, before batting her eyes and producing a thin smile. "It was Emily's favorite."

Corbin nodded once and turned a bit in an attempt to casually follow the distracted direction of Barb's eyeline. It took Corbin just a few seconds of scouring the room until he spotted it. He froze and narrowed his eyes, absently cocking his head as he scrutinized the framed photo on the shelf.

The large black-and-white picture contained two smiling women, one of them a younger version of Barb Whitaker dressed in a similar— *maybe the same*—bohemian ensemble. But that's not what made Corbin inadvertently hold his breath. It was the other woman: smaller than Barb, smiling and postured in a way that seemed reluctant to pose for the picture but still contained genuine affection. Her bulb of curly hair was partially suppressed by a folded paisley bandana. The women were shoulder to shoulder, leaning against each other, and their hands were clasped together, their fingers intertwined in what was an unmistakable gesture of intimacy. But beyond this was the recognition—recognition of this other woman in the photo. He'd seen a slightly older version of this woman before, last fall, when she was standing in the window of his apartment.

Suddenly aware of his paralytic pause and the silence that had drifted into the room, Corbin cleared his throat, took another pull from his drink, and turned to face Barb.

She was staring at him, not unkindly examining him. Corbin felt compelled to say something. "Is that who *that* is?"—he angled his head to gesture toward the framed photo—"Emily?"

Barb still seemed to be gauging her guest. "Yes." She straightened up a bit, as if to give a declaration. "Emily and I were devoted partners for over thirty years." A spell of silence returned. "I'm sorry," Barb finally said, "have I made you uncomfortable?"

Corbin had no problem contemplating the relationship of the pair of aging lesbian lovers in a photo. No, that's not what unsettled Corbin at the moment. "No, that's not it at all. I just . . ." He tried arranging his words in the least insane sequence possible. All that came out was, "I thought . . . I thought I recognized her from somewhere."

Barb nodded tersely, her smile dispirited.

Corbin scrambled for a sophisticated way to ask, *Is she dead?* But before he could say anything, Barb said, "She passed away some years ago." But Corbin knew this already, didn't he? "Cancer, of course. She had been—*we* had been—coping with it for years." After about thirty seconds of pondering something she added, "Best friend I ever had."

Corbin was preparing to wrap things up here by downing his drink and hinting at compensation. Barb said, "Why did you think you recognized her?"

A bit of the cocktail dribbled onto his lower lip, and he used the back of his hand to wipe it away. "I don't know. I think she might just have a familiar face."

Without hesitation Barb said, "I've seen her down the hall, wandering around by your apartment."

Branches of ice broke out under Corbin's skin. His lips and the back of his neck began to tingle. He stammered, "Excuse me?"

"Oh, come now." Barb made a dismissive noise and gently touched Corbin's forearm. "You can cut the shit. Don't tell me you haven't seen her." Corbin's face was impassive as he thought about the frail gray figure in the window. Barb said, "I've seen her down there, lingering around by your door, but she doesn't pay me any attention." Corbin said nothing. "Or perhaps you've heard things—strange noises?"

Before he could catch himself, Corbin mumbled, "Crying, sometimes." Having inadvertently consigned himself to this dialogic insanity, Corbin cleared his throat and refined his statement. "Sometimes I hear a baby crying at night."

Barb nodded slowly, sympathetically. "Do you have the wherewithal to talk about it?" she said.

Corbin acknowledged that he did by shakily lowering himself to the patched and faded sofa.

"They're not ghosts," Barb said. "Or least I don't think they're ghosts. It's something else. I've often thought it was more like a Gore."

Corbin listened—*had* been listening for twenty minutes—to Barb Whitaker's fluent monologue. "I grew up out east, out near New England, but I moved out here decades ago to be with Emily." She peered out the window, but shook her head as if to get back on track. "Anyway, back home, back out east, there are these places—or really these *non*-places—called Gores, little pockets of land that don't belong to anybody." Corbin made a face he hoped elicited further explanation. "Decades and decades ago, when the land was being portioned and divided, the surveyors made miscalculations, mistakes in mapping when they were charting townships and villages and so forth.

"Most times these sorts of no-man's lands ended up being a neglected field or something or other. But sometimes the Gores were dense channels of forest where acreage went disputed, claimed by some but technically belonging to no one." Barb shifted on the patched couch. "When we were children we cobbled together legends of these Gores that we'd heard from our parents and grandparents. One of the big things to do was to dare each other to run through a segment of woods, the idea was that if you ran though the wrong pocket you'd disappear into, well, nowhere or somewhere—some place not *here*."

With a weary thread in his voice, Corbin said, "So this all has to do with maps?"

Barb sighed. "Yes and no. Some maps, some boundaries, are just arbitrary anyway. Sometimes it's just perception. Sometimes it's just ink." She chuckled. "Did you ever wonder where the magic came from in magic markers?" Corbin blinked a few times. Barb cleared her throat and scanned the room. "It's a bit like that box over there," she pointed, "the one marked MATRYOSHKA. I would probably have to tell you that it's full of these Russian toys called nesting dolls, all shaped the same but all different sizes, tall to tiny, tiny to tall. Are you familiar with them?"

After a few seconds Corbin said, "You mean those little souvenirs you stack inside each other?"

Barb smiled. "Precisely. Well, you may be imagining that the box is full of these cute little pear-shaped dolls just because of what's written on the outside. You're certainly picturing them right now." Corbin blinked a few times, only nodding his head as a courtesy. "But what if that's not what was inside at all? What if it contained, oh, I don't know . . . just a bunch of mason jars filled shrunken, trepanned heads floating in formaldehyde." Corbin had no idea where she was going with this, and his expression seemed to signal as much to Barb. "I suppose what I mean is that after a while most folks begin to believe in boundaries just because of ink."

Things were quiet for a while. The muffled sound of a television pulsed from the apartment on the floor above them. A door slammed down the hall. The old woman took an ice-clinking sip of her drink before carefully placing the glass on the coffee table and resting her hands on her lap. "There is something down that in your corner of the building, something parallactically skewed. There's something like"— she winced—"an asymmetrical screen."

Corbin shrugged. "So what's it have to do with me?"

"Nothing maybe. I don't think you're special and I don't think you're the only one who's experienced something. I've seen things. I've seen Emily. I've watched people come and go quite quickly from leasing that apartment down the hall. But I also believe it's a matter of seeing the right—or seeing *wrong*—geometry."

Corbin caught himself off-guard as a series of thoughts rushed into his head: *Maybe it's something in the angles of the building itself. Maybe it's something connected to the actual body of the building—the mortar, the clay of the bricks, the pipes and plumbing—some sort of radiation.* But as quick as the unbidden thoughts came Corbin shoved them away, as if the mere assembly of these notions carried a deranged complicity with what this old woman was suggesting.

Wrinkles near Barb's eyes crinkled as she made an almost pained face, appearing to struggle with a way to convey a final thought. "You seem to be a reasonably bright boy, but I don't expect you to be acquainted with some of the thinkers of my day." Corbin didn't really know how to react to that. "But after the first time seeing Emily loitering down there by your apartment I've reflected on the connection between dwelling and building—dwelling as a place to *live* and dwelling as a place to *be,* as an act of always staying anchored to things. But dwelling, I think, eventually gives itself to constructing things, to growing things." Barb suddenly barked a laugh. "You must really think I'm swimming in senility now."

You have no idea. "Not at all," he said, his voice unexpectedly shaky. He finished his drink in a single swallow. "But whether you're nuts or not, I still have to get going."

Barb smiled. "Fair enough."

She followed Corbin to the door and handed him a folded bundle of money. Corbin glanced at it, peeled through it, and almost protested. For the small amount of moving he'd done, it was too much. After a second of inspecting the cash he said, "Thanks. This is really too generous."

"Ah. Well, you've been very generous and very patient to have listened to the rambles of a loony old lady."

Corbin gave a curt nod and a tight smile. "Okay, good night."

He was halfway down the hall when Barb called out: "Would you mind if I came and visited some time?"

Corbin could feel the old woman's young eyes on his back. He turned, contemplating the large sum of money in his pocket. "Sure. Stop by any time." The stiff drink had tilted his thinking.

The old woman waved, shuffled out of the threshold, and closed her door.

Back inside his apartment, Corbin tried to confront the interior of his living quarters with sober objectivity. He wanted to shake her words out of his head. *Gore. Dwelling. Emily.* Corbin dropped his backpack on the floor and flipped on a few lights. He flung his green ball cap on the couch and crossed the living room, turning on a lamp near the window. He lingered there, near the window, peering through the blinds. Evening was in its last gasp of purple-orange light. Corbin scanned the urban horizon before angling his attention to the sidewalk below. A few people down there, walking dogs. A couple holding hands on their way somewhere. And then came a solitary figure that broke away from the other pedestrians. The figure—a male as far as Corbin could tell—was wearing a dark hooded sweatshirt and jeans, and was toting a backpack. Corbin's eyes widened and his mouth inched open. The figure was wearing a green ball cap, the white moving-company emblem only discernible at this distance because of Corbin's daily familiarity with it. He recalled Barb's outrageous assertion that she had seen him on the street below, long before he actually arrived in the building.

With a vertiginous sense of horror and acceptance, the fifth-floor Corbin watched his sidewalk-self steer toward the building as it had hours earlier—striding toward the lobby of the apartment complex and disappearing below his field of vision.

In the weeks following their initial discussion about keeping the baby, Corbin has tried to acquaint himself with the idea of becoming—and actually being—a father. He's aware that he must prove his sincerity to Cassidy, and so he picks up more hours at the moving company and has been looking for a second job. He's even made an appointment with an advisor at one of the community colleges out near the suburbs. He's preoccupied with work but assures her it's for a good reason. Corbin has a plan to propose to Cassidy—an engagement: this is the one thing he thinks he can't screw up. Commitment. Initiative. Vision. Resolve. The hallmarks of the businessman, the jargon of the businessman.

Corbin arrives home to Cassidy's apartment one evening. He has no ring, but he has a small amount of money and a plan. On his lunch break earlier that afternoon, Corbin had scrawled down a few ideas on an index card—ideas about how they could make things work with the baby, with school, with Corbin's menial jobs and Cassidy's unfinished degree. This reality has a lean grimness to it. But, at the very least, the inked-up index card will show Cassidy that he's serious about the two of them—the three of them, he thinks—and their life together.

Walking in the door, he calls out for Cassidy. No answer. Again—clutching his coffee-smudged index card—he calls out, happily trying on the honey-I'm-home guise of a family man arriving at suppertime.

He finds Cassidy on the couch, sitting upright, leaning forward with her elbows on her knees. Cassidy's plum-brown hair is pulled back in a ponytail, her eyes scrubbed clean of mascara and eye shadow—all this, along with the sweatpants and T-shirt she's wearing, carries the effect of a girl in the first few stages of getting over a fevered illness, the fresh, after-shower sterility of a little girl who's had a tummy-ache. Cassidy is positioned in front of the coffee table, her slender fingers laced together as though she's preparing to flip a non-existent tarot card or shift an invisible chess piece. Check. Mate.

Corbin opens his mouth, but Cassidy goes first. "I went to the doctor, Corbin." About a hundred heart beats fill the silent space between them. "I did it," says Cassidy. Another hundred heartbeats. "It's gone."

Her eyes—that blackly impassive, impenitent expression—tells him that there is no misunderstanding. She's serious. Corbin's chest begins hitching up as if a dense balloon is expanding beneath his ribcage, every pulsing hitch making it more difficult to breath. For a moment, Corbin is overcome with the nauseating wobble of falling out of a tree, the impact jarring his spine and the back of his skull in a single wind-blown thud. The index card slips from his fingers.

Cassidy is talking, furnishing her explanation with business-proposal gesticulations. "If you could only see the big picture." The swirling hiss of numb noise reaches a crescendo and ceases. Corbin steadies himself; he ignores Cassidy; he scours the room with evacuative urgency. Corbin doesn't need a lecture. He knows why. He is childish and possibly mentally defective to believe an index card could have stopped any of this. For Cassidy, living with Corbin and a baby would be like raising two children at the same time. This whole thing is an inexorable, unrepealable intervention.

He owns nothing here. A book or two. Some clothes. Essentially nothing. Cassidy has purchased nearly everything, even the hooded sweatshirt he's ashamed to be wearing this instant.

Cassidy's still talking. And in his despondency, Corbin notices his pathetic reflection in the window across the room—a motionless boy listening to a lesson. His attention darts over to the bookshelf, to a marble bookend. There is a synaptic flash in his conscience, and in that flash Corbin—with objective lens clarity—sees an alternate self lifting the bookend and cudgeling Cassidy's shampoo-scrubbed scalp—hammering down with smooth, repeated arcs until the mineral-swirl of that marbled embellishment is coated with streaks of viscous crimson.

"It would never have worked," says Cassidy. "Neither of us—" She swallows, licks her lips. She takes a hostile tissue-swipe at her nose and fingers a cable of hair from her eyes. Now she just simply repeats the words. "It would have never worked."

*It isn't just the baby, Corbin muses meagerly. It's everything. Through all this, Corbin understands he has one last decision before she can decide for him. Corbin strides across the living room and faces the bookcase, grabbing the ornate bookend and hefting it—*I'll start my own goddamn library somewhere—*and then moving on to the next room. Cassidy is protesting but remains seated on the couch. He awkwardly fills a trash bag with what few clothes he has, some of his toiletries from the bathroom.*

As Corbin begins his final march to the front door, Cassidy, standing now, reprises her business declamation—things about keys, bills, cell phone accounts. Corbin stops as he nears the door and spins on Cassidy, now silent in this abrupt change in momentum. With his hands full, Corbin tries to slam the door as best he can.

Night. A vacuum of blackness. And from that all-encompassing noth-
ingness came the suppressed sound of a crying baby. Though this distant distress call has become familiar, almost expected, the stygian
weight of sleep deteriorates as Corbin flinches awake with alert lucidity.

Tonight the baby's cries were clearer, crystalline, and contained a
more starkly defined sense of urgency.

Corbin threw back the sheet and threw his legs over the edge of
the bed. The baby's cries grew louder. Corbin was in the hallway by the
time he fully surfaced from sleep, and that's where his momentum
hitched to a stop. Tonight, there was no doubt—the cries were coming
from inside his apartment. Near. He suddenly understood with a flinch
that the sobs were close—close as in several yards away. Corbin angled
his gaze toward the sliding doors of the hall closet, just a feet from his
face. The narrow passage was now filled with the panicked weeping.
Corbin slowly drew up to the closet door. The distressed mewling was
coming from inside. Inches, it seemed, separated Corbin from the
source of the cries.

Corbin held his breath and took a tug at the door. It didn't budge.
Scowling, planting his feet apart, Corbin began prying at the door, trying to slide it open. This variety of panic coursing through him was a
new thing, and part of him wanted to admonish this insanity, this un-
sound hallucination—*What the hell are you doing?*

Corbin tried again and merely felt a strange, caulish yawn, as
though the door were covered with some kind of unseen membrane.
The baby's cries had turned into a rapid-fire series of yelps, as if it were
running out of air and could only submit sharply pitched pleas.

Corbin heaved against the door and examined it with a furious assessment. The cries continued. He clenched his teeth, recoiled a fist,
and delivered a vicious, knuckle-studded punch into the door. Nothing. As he wheeled back and twisted away from the sliding door, his
eyes searched the shadowed hallway. Desperate, Corbin scrambled
from the corridor and staggered into the living room, dimly lit by diffuse orange light from the high-arc sodium vapor streetlamps, his
chest rising and falling, his gaze tracing the furniture and objects in the
room. He froze, his attention settling on something smooth-curved
and glinting on the bookcase on the far wall. Corbin rushed across the
room and snatched the heavy marble bookend from the shelf.

The scale of the cries were diminishing when Corbin returned to the corridor, as though the baby itself were fading away; but the unmistakable register of urgency—of fright in the face of finality—remained. Corbin took a deep, teeth-bared breath, drew the marble bookend over his shoulder, and drove it into the door. The plywood crunched with a slim, dark scar. Corbin growled and hammered down again, throwing his upper body into the movement and following through—this time the crescent trajectory of the swing resulted in a ragged, splinter-rimmed hole in the wood. The baby's cries pealed out of that access and echoed into the hallway. Corbin dropped the bookend and began tearing the hole, ripping away jagged chunks of plywood with an intensity that mirror-matched the urgency of the child's cries.

As he continued tearing, Corbin could now see that there was absolute blackness inside the closet—pure blackness, unpolluted by illumination. The depth of that darkness startled him. He curled all his fingers around the splinter-fringed frame and began to pull, his face straining as a large panel creaked, splintered, and finally broke free in a wide plank. Corbin tossed the wood aside and lunged toward the door, gripping the outer edge of the hole and peering inside. No longer astonished by what he might find, he drew his face closer—distant, twinkling, mercury-flicker light; he could feel cold whirl somewhere deeper within; but his attention was still on the baby. The hole was large enough for both his shoulders to fit through, so Corbin plunged his head and upper body in, his face and forearms bitten by frigid air and his movements inhibited as if underwater. It occurred to him that the proximity of the—he thought of Barb: *region . . . boundary*—was eclipsing proximity and he began to search frantically, his arms swirling against the black, fluid resistance within.

His fingers brushed against flesh. With a desperate lurch, Corbin wrapped his hands around the limb of a chilled-skin thing and began extracting his upper body from the hole. He placed his bare foot on the door and kicked, recoiling from the almost elastic connection, falling back and sinking to the floor. And in his hands Corbin cradled a pale form. The crying had ceased. From his modest bank of knowledge Corbin recognized, judging by its weight and proportions, that it was maybe nine months old. A baby girl. She had a dark-swirled pad of hair on her small head, and her prominent, inky eyes were fixed on

Corbin, gazing at him, blinking from time to time, breathing soft and steady now.

Corbin's heart was ticking with adrenaline quickness, and his first reaction was to exhale a sound that was part awe and part disbelieving laugh. There was the brief howl of cold air paired with the fleeting whiff of ozone, and then the narrow corridor was quiet. Corbin glanced over at the hall closet; within the hole he could barely make out the limp columns of hanging sleeves, and a beat-up, dust-covered vacuum was propped in the corner.

Though still cold, the baby was making contented, whimpering noises; its eyes—alert and as dark as the space from which it had emerged—searched Corbin's face and seemed to return the reverence in his own expression. Corbin rose slowly, carefully, supporting the baby's head with impulsive instinct.

In the faint light of his bedroom, Corbin searched for something to wrap around the baby. He spotted the hooded Chicago Bears sweatshirt hanging over the back of a chair. He tossed the garment on the bed and gently settled the infant onto the cotton material, tucking the heavy fabric securely around her.

The baby continued fidgeting contentedly at the air, its dark eyes searching the ceiling as though visually absorbing this strange place. Eventually, Corbin lay out across the bed alongside the infant, never taking his eyes off her. He listened to the sound of its breathing and lightly placed his hand over the infant's chest, savoring the delicate yet enduring cadence of its tiny lungs. Soon, Corbin began blinking slowly, watching the baby before giving himself to the dark susurration of unconsciousness.

Corbin shuddered awake. It was early morning—the dingy drapes filtered gray light, painting the walls inside his bedroom with bluish bleakness. Hastily propping himself on an elbow, he searched the bed. The hooded Bears sweatshirt was crumpled there. Empty. No trace of the baby. Still, Corbin swept his hands across the bed, searching the sheets, the floor, and beneath the bed. But he knew it was useless. He exhaled and sank onto the edge of bed. He rubbed his eyes, which felt scalded and swollen. If he'd been crying in his sleep he felt as though a reprisal would take little effort. He stifled the urge. After a time Corbin shivered and reached for the hooded sweatshirt, foolishly expecting some residual warmth there. Nothing. For no reason he could think of, Corbin wearily slipped the sweatshirt over his head, pausing when he caught a whiff of ozone. It *was* warm inside. He allowed himself a sad, thin smile before shuffling out of the bedroom and into the hallway. He sighed, appraising the splintered wood scattered on the floor and the obliterated state of closet door.

Corbin broke his lease early but had saved enough money to cover the fee, along with enough cash (some of it left over from Barb's generous compensation) to privately replace the sliding door panel in the hall-way. Corbin enlisted a few acquaintances from the moving company to help him pack his things—not much—into a moving truck. As he la-beled the boxes with a black magic marker, he thought of the old woman down the hall.

On his last day he stopped by Barb Whitaker's apartment. She opened the door almost immediately, as if she been anticipating his appearance and had been eyeing his approach through the peephole.

"Hi," he said.

"Good morning, Mr. Corbin." She glanced past him. "I've noticed you've been very busy lately."

"Yeah. I'm headed out of town. Back home."

Barb frowned and opened her mouth to say something, but Cor-bin politely cut in. "Listen, I was wondering if you could do me a fa-vor."

Barb's face twitched with kind-natured suspicion. "Certainly."

From his pocket Corbin withdrew a pair of keys to his apartment. "I have to turn these in before I leave. The building manager told me to slip them in the drop box by his office." He spun one of the keys and detached it from the ring. With a crooked smile he said, "I told him I'd misplaced one of them." He extended the key toward Barb. "But I thought you could use this, maybe snoop around the apartment after I leave, see if there's anything interesting or familiar in there."

The old woman's conspiratorial smirk widened into a smile as she ambled forward and almost bashfully accepted the key. "Well," she cleared her throat, "I don't know what to say."

After a few seconds, Corbin exhaled. "Me either." He smiled and extended his hand. "Maybe just goodbye is the only thing to say."

Barb nodded at that and gently clasped Corbin's outstretched hand. "Well, goodbye." They shook on that.

Corbin let go, turned to walk away but paused. "Oh, I almost forgot. You might want to take a peek in the hall closet." He sustained a stare for a few silent seconds until he was sure the subtext had sunk in. Barb nodded, glanced at the key, and smiled. Corbin waved and said, "There's an old vacuum in there."

As he descended the steps in the shadow-dim stairwell on his way to the lobby, Corbin was certain that no one would ever see Barb Whitaker again. And he was happy for her.

Corbin heads south, back home to Colfax, and uses what money he has left to make the first month's rent on an apartment on the out-skirts of town. At night, at ease in the solitude of his surprisingly com-fortable apartment, Corbin uselessly contemplates his incompetence as a partner, but thinks he might have been—in some course-corrective scenario—a decent dad. At night, Corbin sometimes wears his hooded sweatshirt to bed. And when his fitful mind grows restless from dwell-ing on a regrettable succession of images, actions, and words, he pulls the thick cotton hood over his head so that the fabric envelops his face in shadow. And then Corbin feels himself sinking, shrinking, and ac-cepts the sensation of unanchoring his conscience and suspending his perception as he gives himself over to the vast, breathtaking darkness within—an all-embracing blackness broken only by the mercury-glitter perturbation of spangle-swirled starlight. From the empty rhythm of seething silence comes the contented cadence of delicate respiration— the soft susurrations and echo exhalations of a peacefully sleeping baby.

THE HATCHET

On the last of October
When dusk is fallen
Children join hands
And circle round me
Singing ghost songs
And love to the harvest moon;
I am a jack-o'-lantern
With terrible teeth
And the children know
I am fooling.

        —Carl Sandburg, "Theme in Yellow"

It was still dark, just before six in the morning, when Brian Cline steered into the driveway of the Hoffman House. A brisk wind drove dervishes of rust-colored leaves across the beams of his headlights, which partially illuminated the decaying face of the house. After all these years, and as opposed to the meticulously maintained homes in this neighborhood, it was still difficult to decipher whether anyone occupied the dwelling or not.

Despite his bouts of vertigo when gazing at the place, he somehow knew he would not be alone in thinking this place empty, or at least devoid of any human habitants, for a staggering number of decades.

He was certain this was more than just a fragile trick of the mind. If, for instance, he were to ask a mailman about the house, he imagined the man would acknowledge delivering bills and parcels; but when pressed for an address or details about the house, he'd become embarrassed and troubled that he could supply no such thing. Neighbors might swear they'd seen FOR SALE signs fluctuate in and out of the front yard, yet could never name a real estate company, nor would they be capable of providing a description or name of the families who'd lived there throughout the years. They'd frown and think for a few seconds before disregarding it with a mental shrug. It was as if the entire property resided in a faulty pocket of perception, and only solidified in the flat light of unsettled scrutiny.

He'd been doing this a lot lately—these little self-dare staring contests with the house. Each time, he lost. Brian thought about calling his younger brother, Drew, but had no idea of what to say that didn't sound desperate or unbalanced.

For the past two decades, Brian had intermittently returned to this place—by car only, never on foot—and he rarely pulled into the driveway.

The Hoffman House was one of the first houses built in this subdivision shortly after World War II. Brian's grandparents—both long dead—had once lived in this neighborhood. So by and large, many houses looked similar, all affecting the one-story uniformity of the '40s and '50s. Except this one. This one was an architectural anomaly.

Over the years, and unable to avoid dwelling on the house, Brian had done some research. It was something called a Dutch Colonial Revival, a barnish thing with a steeply pitched gambrel roof and a second floor containing several sharp-edged dormer windows. And as opposed to the ranch- and cape-style houses throughout the neighborhood, this was a two-story anomaly of brick and shingles, yet it somehow remained inconspicuous in its not-rightness.

If asked what bothered him so much about the aesthetics of the property, Brian could certainly point out the untended yard, the broken troughs of gutters hanging askew. But when his mind lingered on these details, the memories would contort themselves, and on his next impulsive drive-by he'd see these things corrected, only to be replaced by a broken window or some other element of neglect.

Brian thought: It does change; it gets bigger by increments, makes asymmetrical shifts from time to time. Its dimensions were the same, but there was something disturbing about them.

Reflection had a way of distorting perception. Brain had read about this phenomenon before, about how dishonest human memories can be. Some scientists asserted that the simple act of recalling an event could actually change the shape of that memory in the brain. Details and narratives become altered. Essentially, the more a person thinks about the memory, the less accurate it becomes.

As is the case with so many structures that existed in the mind of childhood's memories, things had the tendency to look smaller, shrunken through the eyes of adulthood. Idly, he wondered how he might explain something like this to his fourth-grade social studies class. He could easily make the comparison of returning to a building that had long been severed from one's mind—a school, a church, a distant relative's house—but they were just children themselves. And besides, Brian had never left Sycamore Mill, and had grown along with most of the town's changes.

Something moved up in one of the dormer windows on the second floor. Brian bristled, looking, scouring the upper level of the house, wondering—for the thousandth time—if he was wrong, if people lived here, if he was trespassing. Brian put the car in reverse and was about to take his foot off the brake when he saw the fingers gripping the curtain.

It wasn't much, barely noticeable, but the longer Brian stared the clearer it became. Four gray fingers were parting a faded drape, exposing a thin slit of the house's lightless interior.

His heart surged. Brian thought of Drew. Brian thought of their mother.

Brian pressed a button on the driver's side door and rolled down the window. Squinting into the chill air, he spit into the driveway, afterwards wiping his lip and narrowing his eyes on the window.

Slowly, suggesting no alarm or urgency, the hand slid down and disappeared. The dingy gray curtain swayed for a moment and was still.

Brian took a deep breath and removed his foot from the brake, giving the house one last baleful glance as the headlights crossed over the structure's façade. With the tree-shadows overlapping against the front of the dwelling, the effect was that of a veil covering the house. And through the veil, the house was staring back. Brian steered away, certain it was watching him leave.

In 1987, Halloween fell on a Saturday night. With no school or getting up to catch the bus the next morning, this—like the Friday-night celebration the year before—promised to be a true holiday for children.

But as a twelve-year-old, Brian Cline had a choice to make.

For weeks his father had been hinting that Brian was getting too old to go trick-or-treating. When, at the dinner table, the subject of Halloween emerged, Brian's father would remind his eldest son about his age: *"Don't you think you're getting a little old to be getting dressed up in a costume? Drew's only eight . . . he has a few more years until he grows out of it . . ."*

Brian often relied on his less-overbearing mother for help, and she would always make an effort to soften her husband's heart. But lately, even to Brian's pre-teen ears, Kathy Cline's well-intentioned defenses resulted in a sort of Mary Poppins coddling. And with that doting came shades of shame. Still, he wanted to go. He didn't want to miss out on the candy, or maybe seeing one of the few friends from school. He didn't want to miss out on all the fun. Brian understood he could either mollify his father or please himself. But it wasn't until the night before Halloween that he'd had an idea. Their mother usually escorted them on their annual evening rounds, trailing along in the car or on foot. But if Brian volunteered to watch Drew, to babysit his younger brother, then he'd pacify his dad with the act of appearing as a responsible sibling.

Because they lived out in the country, the Clines only received the occasional trick-or-treater, so it had been a tradition to trick-or-treat in their grandparents' neighborhood—lots of houses, lots of candy.

After brushing his teeth before bed, Brian found his father working at his lamp-lit desk in the downstairs den. "Dad?"

Gordon Cline made a *hm* sound and glanced up from his papers. Brian was not surprised that his workaholic father was occupied with some business-related task on a Friday night.

"Dad, I have a question."

"Sure."

"I still want to go trick-or-treating tomorrow night."

Gordon slid his glasses to his forehead and passed a hand over his face. "All right," he exhaled, leaning back in his chair, his expression suggesting disappointment; but it was a familiar disappointment. Brian could cope with that.

"But I was thinking that I could watch after Drew."

His father's brow twitched. "What do you mean?"

"You know . . ." Brian fiddled with a pen on the edge of the desk. "Mom usually takes us trick-or-treating, but I thought I could take

Drew; that way mom wouldn't have to."

His old man smirked—his tone was playful, as if not falling for Brian's attempted sincerity. "You mean so *you* can still get dressed up and go trick-or-treating."

Brian was quiet. He thought about answering but could only summon a sheepish smile.

His dad scratched his forearm. And again: "Don't you think you're getting too old for this?" Brian shrugged, sincerely not knowing how to say no. "If you're still trick-or-treating like a kid, how do you expect to watch after another little kid like Drew?"

Brian gestured awkwardly. "I just—" There were no words. There hadn't been since his father began posing variations of the question: *When are you going to grow up?*

It was quiet for a long time before his father spoke. "Do you really think you're up to taking care of Drew?"

Brian nodded eagerly, trying to contain his glee. "Definitely."

His father slid his reading glasses back on his face. "All right." A spring creaked as he rotated his chair and returned to his work. "Just make sure it's okay with your mom."

Brian started away from the desk. "No problem. I promise."

His father concluded the conversation with the same curt *hm* sound that had started it.

The next day was Halloween, and the boys spent Saturday tinkering with their costumes. Brian was going to be a hockey-masked slasher like Jason Voorhees in the *Friday the 13th* movies. He'd found some old coveralls in the basement and was going to use one of his plastic Army knives as an accessory. Drew wanted to be a werewolf after begging for an elaborate mask he'd spotted at the drugstore. It was a bit too big for Drew's head, but their mother bought it anyway.

Evening settled in after a day-long interlude of gray skies. While their mother was loading Drew into the car, Brian examined the plastic play-knife in his hand. He considered how juvenile the accessory must look in contrast to the rest of his costume. A thought struck him. He ran around to the side of the house and trotted into the shed. His father's tools were hanging on a neatly arranged shadow board. Brian scoured the wall, settling on a carpenter's hatchet. Suddenly dizzy with how deadly the thing looked, he imagined the startled glances he might get from passing strangers. He removed the small axe from the wall pegs, checked its weight, and gingerly slipped it into the inner pocket of his overlarge coveralls.

The car's engine was running as Brian jogged up.

"Forget something?" his mother said, pulling the seatbelt across her chest.

Brian glanced at the plastic play knife, but felt the weight of the hatchet shift inside his jumpsuit. "Yeah. I found it." He looked over at Drew. His younger brother was clutching an orange pumpkin pail. He was wearing the wolfman mask. The little boy tilted his head back, and from the snarling rubber snout came the child's version of a howl.

Brian Cline arrived in the parking lot at Sycamore Mill elementary. Daylight was just beginning to tinge the cloud-heavy sky. It'll be overcast today, thought Brian. Given that it was Halloween, the notion pleased him.

He turned off the car and pulled the key from the ignition. He checked his phone, hoping to see a returned message from his brother. Nothing.

Drew and his family lived down in Florida, far away from the Midwest and its trappings. Shortly after moving to Sarasota, Drew had once joked that he favored the ebb and flow of the ocean as opposed to the ebb and flow of small-town seasons. Brian had sent his younger brother a text message the night before, asking if they planned on coming up during Thanksgiving or Christmas; but what Brian had really been fishing for was an invitation to go visit them, to get away, the get out of town for once. For a long time, maybe.

Now a neuropathologist, Drew was busy most of the time. Brian was used to that. But when his younger brother had not responded to his message, Brian grew antsy, sending him another text. This one was a cheery one about Halloween, and whether or not he was going to take his two girls—Brian's nieces—trick-or-treating. Brian had no children of his own. And just as sure as Drew always knew he'd become a doctor, Brian knew he'd never be husband material, let alone father material. It was something he'd discovered in the solitary wake of his dozen or so failed relationships. Over time, his students had filled the void.

Brian watched the screen on his cell phone fade back to black.

Clenching his teeth, he slipped the phone in his pocket.

There was a large laundry basket in the backseat of Brian's car, which he now withdrew and hefted up to his chest. The basket was stacked high with Halloween paraphernalia—posters, wall-hangings, plastic pumpkins, rubber bats, a life-sized skull along with a jumble of disassembled bones.

As Brian walked toward the front door of the school—the school where he'd been called Mr. Cline by his fourth-grade students for the past ten years—he listened to the anemic hiss of the wind in the trees, the autumn-dry rustling of leaves chattering across the asphalt.

Walking down the hall to his classroom, Brian saw another teacher. The teacher, a cheery old woman who taught second grade, was smiling and appeared ready to greet Brian when she caught sight of the laundry basket brimming with morbid decorations.

"Good morning," Brian said, his voice echoing down the hallway.

The woman's smile re-emerged. "Good morning, Mr. Cline."

Brian slowed as he neared his classroom door, trying to balance the basket while fishing his keys out of his pocket. Although he heard her footfalls continue down the hall, Brian sensed the woman faltering. "Let me help you this," she said, rushing over to pull open the door.

"Thanks, that's very kind of you," said Brian, giving the older woman a warm grin. She was eyeing the basket again.

"Don't worry," Brian said with an air of mock conspiracy. "I won't tell if you don't."

Unsure, the woman's smile flickered and faded. Something in Brian's eyes, perhaps. Something in his face. She appeared ready to comment, but Brian had already set the basket down on his desk. "Happy Halloween," said Brian, and allowed the door to close.

As they neared the neighborhood, Brian began to see the children in the street, rushing from house to house, parents lingering on the sidewalks. The neighborhood contained curvy lanes, which created tree-lined tunnels connecting one portion of the addition with the other. Things like small side-creeks and footbridges made all this feel like a village rather than a middle-class subdivision.

Brian's mother slowed the car to a stop near a curb, under a pale orange streetlight, and shifted the car into park. Drew unbuckled his seatbelt and grabbed the door handle.

"Now you boys just hold on just a second," said Kathy, and proceeded to remind the boys about what they'd discussed during the drive. "I'm only going to be gone an hour or so."

Brian gave a distracted glance at his watch and nodded.

"No problem," he said.

"And I want you to meet me right here."

From the backseat Drew said, "You should come with us, Mom."

Their mother smiled. "But I don't have a costume." She tousled Drew's hair. He was clutching the werewolf mask in one hand. "Besides, you boys will have more fun without me."

"Come on," Brian said to Drew, trying to sound like a doting big brother rather than an equally eager kid. "If we wait any longer all the candy will be gone."

Mrs. Cline craned her neck toward Drew. "You listen to Brian, okay?" The little boy nodded.

The interior light came on as the boys bailed out of the car.

Mrs. Cline stretched across the front seat and rolled down the passenger window. "Come here, Brian." Brian tilted his hockey mask up on his forehead. "I'm being very serious about this. I want you to keep an eye on Drew."

Brian bobbed his head. "I know, I know." He glanced around. Drew was awkwardly tugging on the large wolfman mask. He shifted back to his mom. She said, "I'm really proud of you."

Brian had the urge to lean in and give his mom a parting kiss on the cheek, but he had the mortifying split-instant image of someone from school seeing him. "Thanks, Mom," he said, and slipped his mask over his face.

She looked past Brian and shouted at Drew. "Mind your brother and stay out of the street, all right?"

His voice muffled slightly by the rubber wolfman mask, Drew said, "I will." He waved. "I love you, Mommy."

Their mother's response was partially drowned when a car roared past, its windows rolled down, rock music blasting. The car was loaded with what looked like teenagers. The guy on the passenger side leaned out and screamed, "Fags!" Seconds later, Brian saw a cigarette sail into the street, the orange speck exploding in a dandelion burst of embers. The music and chortling spilling from the vehicle's open windows echoed into the neighborhood before receding.

Brian looked at his mom; her expression suddenly seemed reluctant. "Don't worry, Mom," said Brian, placing his hand on the lip of the passenger door. "We'll stay on the sidewalk."

After a moment, she gave the boys a weak smile. Again she reminded them of the meeting time here at the corner, under the light, and then once more fixed her eyes on Brian. "You take care of him, Brian." The older boy did his best to assure her. "This could be a really good way of showing how grown-up you are." He nodded at that too, wondering if it were true.

"I love you both very much."

Drew was inching away, but called over his shoulder, "Love you too, Mommy."

Brian put a hand in the air as his mother pulled away from the curb. He watched the car's taillights shrink until those glowing red dots had disappeared completely. Drew, already making his way down the leaf-littered sidewalk, called out, "Come on!"

Brian jogged up behind his little brother. "Hey," he said, unzipping his navy blue jumpsuit. With a flourish, Brian presented the hatchet. "Check this out."

"Whoa!" said the little boy, slowing to a stop and lifting up his werewolf mask. "Where'd you get it?"

"Dad's shed."

After a moment Drew said, "Won't he be mad?"

Brian snorted a laugh, allowing the moonlight to glint off the blade. "What the old man doesn't know won't hurt him."

Drew was quiet for a few seconds. "Can I see it?"

Brian was already shaking his head. "No way." He let the hatchet swing casually at his side. "It's too dangerous." Drew began to protest, but Brian said, "Let's go," and quickened his pace.

As they sauntered up to the first house, Drew said, "Brian?"

"Yeah?"

"What's fags?"

Brian thought about the car of taunting teenagers, shook his head, and smirked. "I'll tell you some other time."

The two brothers—a hockey-masked slasher and a pint-size were-wolf—bounded up the front porch of a house, and simultaneously cried, *"Trick or treat!"*

The morning bell rang and Brian took attendance. He rose from his desk, appraising the wondering faces of his students as they gazed at the decorations. "Good morning, everyone." The kids responded. Some of them were smiling. Some looked a little unsure.

One of the girls in the front row raised her hand. "Mr. Cline?"

"Yes?"

"My mom said we weren't supposed to have Halloween parties this year."

Brian smiled. Though he never intended this to be a party, he knew what she meant. Honoring a "spirit of equity," the school's administration had strictly prohibited any sort of Halloween activities in the classroom this year. "You're correct—or rather, your mom is correct." He paused for a moment before turning and approaching the dry-erase board. The black marker made squeaky strokes as he slowly wrote the word *Samhain*.

Understanding that he had already taken this too far, he gently placed the marker on the sill, turned, and surveyed his students. "Does anyone recognize this word?" The kids' expressions ranged from rapt concentration to sleepy boredom. Brian tilted his chin. "This is pronounced *sow-win*, and it was a Celtic festival." A pause. "It was a harvest celebration, a time marking transition, when ancient people believed that the curtain between our world"—he made a gesture around the classroom—"and the world of . . . spirits was particularly thin."

A few kids nodded.

From the pocket of his khakis, Brian withdrew a slip of paper. "I want to read something to you," he said, the paper crinkling as he unfolded it. "This was written by a man named Robert W. Chambers." He cleared his throat. "'As the fallen leaves career before us—crumbling ruins of summer's beautiful halls—we cannot help thinking of those who have perished—who have gone before us, blown forward to the grave by the icy blasts of death.'"

Brian looked at his students. The classroom was silent. He took a deep breath and said, "The Halloween *we* know has become a distortion." Quiet. "We've"—despite himself, he couldn't help lumping the kids into his generalization—"become repressed."

Another frowning student raised their hand. "What's repressed?"

"It means that we have difficulty dealing with the reality of death." He tried taking a casual tone but failed.

After a silent moment, one of his boys said, "I just like getting free candy."

There was a titter of cautious chuckling. Brian nodded patiently, giving his students a sporting smile. "Halloween has become a consumption ritual for *us*. It's been trivialized by"—he struggled for an appropriate word and lunged at the first one that came to mind—"consumers so that we can better mask our own mortality." He unintentionally raised his voice. "*We've* forgotten," he said. "*Your* parents have forgotten." He went on like this for a while.

Brian happened to glance over toward the classroom door. The principal, a guy named Wilkes, was standing on the other side of the narrow window.

Brian hadn't realized it, but they'd wandered onto the street of the Hoffman House. The orange streetlights were spaced farther apart here, and some appeared not to be working at all. The lack of light paired with the large trees hanging over the sidewalk gave the lane a night-woods effect—beyond the screen of hedges and shrubs, amber light glowed from houses as a silent invitation to trick-or-treaters.

But up beyond its wrought-iron fence, the Hoffman House was so dark it nearly blended with the night. Disoriented, Brian slowed down.

Drew slowed too and said, "What's the matter?"

Brian frowned. "It's just . . ." He looked up and down the street. "I thought we were in a different place."

He turned around and peered at the house. Brian nearly suggested that they keep moving, but had another thought—the notion of showing up to school Monday morning and the only Halloween story he'd have to share was that he'd babysat his little brother. Brian scanned the front of the Hoffman House.

Pulling up his mask to get some fresh air, Drew said, "Come on."

"Wait a sec," Brian said. "Do you know what this place is?" He gestured toward the house.

Drew shifted his plastic pumpkin pail from one hand to the other, giving the house a wary glance as he shuffled closer to Brian. "No."

No one knew for sure, but the prevailing tale was that someone named Hoffman had died in there decades ago. Brian was prepared to say, *The kids at school say it's a haunted house . . . it's been haunted since the day they screwed in the hinges on the front door . . . and whatever is in there eats little kids.* But then he saw the way Drew was looking at the house, and knew he wouldn't have a chance of getting up to the door if he spooked the kid too much.

Brian jerked his head toward the house. "Come on," he said, hefting his grocery bag full of candy. "Let's give it a try."

"But it's all dark," said Drew. "There's no lights, they don't want trick-or-treaters."

Brian pulled a face. "Jeez, Drew, it's no big deal." His little brother was shaking his head; the little boy's expression looked like a reaction to a bad odor rather than genuine dread. With a wide smile Brian said, "Don't be such a baby."

Drew looked up at his brother, held his gaze for a moment, and then returned his attention to the house. "I don't . . . like it," said Drew, moving away from the wrought-iron fence.

Brian lifted the hatchet. "I'll let you carry this." The rectangular blade shone in the weak light.

Drew tilted his chin and smiled. "Seriously?"

Brian shrugged. "Only if you go up there and knock on the door a few times."

Drew's smile faded. "Are you going with me?"

"Of course."

The little boy was quiet for a few moments before his grin resurfaced and he extended his hand. Brian quickly pulled the axe out of reach. "Will you knock on the door?" Drew hesitated, but ended up nodding. Satisfied, Brian smirked and handed over the hatchet.

Drew held the hatchet in front of him. "Cool."

Brian returned the hockey mask to his face. "You better turn back into a werewolf," he said, indicating that Drew should pull his mask back on.

With his free hand, Drew shifted the mask back on and followed Brian.

Instead of walking up the driveway, Brian cut through the front yard, where several large trees created a low, bare-limbed canopy.

Passing through the shadows of the front yard, things became quiet. Brian had the sense—or the not-right sense—that he was moving past layers of unseen curtains. The wind had died down, and he could no longer hear the voices of other trick-or-treaters in the neighborhood.

He stopped a few feet from the front porch.

Under his hockey mask, Brian licked his lips. "Okay"—he canted his head toward the front door—"give it shot."

The snarling werewolf mask trained itself on Brian. "Aren't you coming with me?"

"I'm here, aren't I?" Brian flitted his hand. "Come on, I'm not leaving you. And besides," he gestured, *"you're* the one with the hatchet."

Taking a deep breath, Drew walked up on the porch.

Brian was only a few feet from the door himself as he watched Drew reach out and press the unlit doorbell. No sound issued from within the house.

Drew spun around. "See?"

"Try knocking," Brian said.

Drew obeyed, giving the paint-flecked door three small raps.

Neither boy budged. The wind was in the trees, their limbs sending bars of restless shadows across the front of the house.

Brian peered up toward one of the second-floor windows, fixed his gaze, and froze.

A pale shape—not necessarily a face or a body, just the grayish flash of a *thing* moving—had momentarily appeared in one of the upper windows before disappearing. Brian stared, narrowing his eyes, trying to understand what he'd seen. Suddenly, to describe it to his own confused mind, he had the image of dark water, as if the pane of glass was a transparent barrier in an ink-filled aquarium, containing some skittish gray thing.

Brian bristled as Drew gave the front door three solid raps with his small fist. "Trick or treat," said the little boy.

Movement now in the first-floor window—the folds of the faded drape swaying. Brian was certain he'd seen fingers withdraw from that dark slit.

"Drew," Brain said, disturbed to find his voice no more than a breathy croak. He took a few steps forward to grab his brother's flannel shirt. "Drew, we should—"

The weathered doorknob creaked and turned, and with mesmeric slowness the door simply eased open, widening to expose the unlit interior.

The inside of the house was a confusing jumble of dark folds and jagged silhouettes. Brian thought he could make out a hallway corridor and staircase railing, but aside from that, the interior contained only heavy darkness.

Without looking, Drew took a step back, but slipped when his foot came off the front concrete step, spilling his candy-filled pumpkin pail. Brian rushed forward. He crouched and clutched hold of his brother, but faltered before he could haul him to his feet.

Down the dark passage of the hallway, something was moving—a writhing, huddled shape crawling. Again Brian had the notion of something in the water. But the image refined itself now.

He'd seen his mother poach eggs for breakfast, dropping them in the steaming water, the translucent whites spilling out in cloudy threads.

Threading—that's what this thing was doing. Brian was watching something murky and gelatinous forming itself into a tendril-edged mass of shadow—something bleeding itself into a single shape. Suddenly, it reared up, the dark thing taking up the space of the entire threshold.

A gray-fleshed arm shot out from that darkness. The pale limb was inhumanly long, and its out-of-proportion fingers wriggled and skittered with arachnid-frantic movements.

Brian hoisted Drew back with an uncoordinated tug, and the boys spilled into the front lawn.

Brian scrambled to his feet but was again hypnotized by the thing in the doorway. It had a face now. Or rather, something that had once been a face. What he saw now was a malformed skull in mid-decay, flecks of gray flesh peeling from the bone. But its enormous eyes were impossibly alive—slick and searching in their lidless, rot-rimmed sockets. Within the ever-shifting blotch of darkness, Brian caught glimpses of gray skin, fragments of a body, what may have once been a man.

He had enough time to see the thing's oversized arm extending again, the hand reaching out to clutch hold of Drew. Too late.

Brian watched his little brother raise the hatchet.

The blade glinted for a moment just before Drew took an awkward swipe at the thing. Brian heard a moist *slish* sound as the hatchet connected with something, and saw a pale flash as the thing recoiled its now mangled hand. Those unblinking eyes were lolling in their sockets, darting around frantically. The eyes settled on Brian. To Brian, what existed in that lingering stare was not fear or pain or panic. Its eyes—the only thing alive in that decaying mask—somehow looked pleased.

A hissing sound emerged, something between a rattle and the insectile clicking of a cicada.

Brian bolted forward, grabbing Drew's flannel shirt and dragging him back. Both boys spun around and rushed across the yard.

Once they rounded the wrought-iron fence and hit the concrete, Brian broke out into a sprint and made sure Drew did the same. He gave a hasty look over his shoulder at the house. The porch was empty. The front door was closed.

They slowed down when they started seeing trick-or-treaters again. On the sidewalk, Brian lifted his hockey mask to his forehead, placing his hands on his knees and moving toward a shrub, preparing to vomit.

Drew tugged off his werewolf mask and let it drop by his feet. He was sniffling, his cheeks smeared with tears. "Brian," the little boy mumbled, his lips quivering. "I didn't mean to." His voice broke as he began hitching sobs. "Are we in trouble?"

Brian stood up. He noticed Drew's hands were empty. No candy. No hatchet. He wanted to cry too. He reached out and gripped Drew's shoulder. "Just relax, okay?" He scanned the neighborhood, wondering if he was going to hear the sound of sirens. Brian pulled his brother to his chest, embracing him, and needing a hug himself. "It was that guy's fault for trying to—"

Drew bristled and pulled away. "Guy?" said the little boy. "What guy?"

Brian could only blink. "The guy who came out of the house."

Drew stared at his brother. "It was an old lady." The little boy was on the verge of tears again. "She was in a"—he fidgeted—"a hospital dress or something." Drew looked over Brian's shoulder, as if seeing it again clearly. "It . . . it . . ."

Brian gently gripped Drew's arm. "You saw a woman in a hospital gown?"

Drew wiped his nose with his sleeve and nodded. "It had . . . blood on it." Brian's neck went cold. "When she reached out . . . I don't know . . . I thought she was going to hurt me." He sniffled, his small chest rapidly rising and falling. "Brian—her fingers . . ."

Brian blinked, raising a hand to stop him. For a long time, the boys stood in silence. Eventually Brian said, "You're right." Drew tensed. "That lady was trying to hurt us. It was my fault for bringing the hatchet, but it was her fault for trying to grab us."

Drew narrowed his eyes on his brother. His lower lip trembled. "What are we going to do about Dad's hatchet?"

Brian shook his. He spotted Drew's mask on the ground. "Come on," said Brian, reaching down and picking up the mask. He handed it to Drew. "We need to go meet Mom."

As they ran, Brian thought he heard the wail of sirens echoing somewhere in the distance.

The elementary school's principal was a younger guy named Wilkes, not much older than Brian, who even in the midst of tense conversation had a tendency to flash wide, irritating smiles.

The children had been dismissed for the day, and within minutes Brian was paged to the principal's office over the intercom.

He sat there now across from this man's desk. There was another person from the front office present, a rigid non-speaking female counselor. Brian supposed they needed to make this official with a witness. Brian declined any union representation. He scanned the office, noting a small paperweight in the shape of a Christian ichthys.

"Our policy has been clear," said Wilkes, leaning back in his chair. He was a smaller man—a small man in a big suit. Brian mentally amused himself with the notion that this guy wore a sort of costume on a daily basis. "This Halloween *party*"—he scratched at the air with his fingers, indicating the scare quotes—"you conducted in your class-room—"

"It wasn't a *party*," said Brian, imitating the other man's gesture.

Wilkes continued, "That may be true, but it was a flagrant violation of our standards." Over in the corner, the female counselor pursed her lips and jotted something on her notepad.

Brian rested his elbows on the arms of the chair. Although he and Wilkes were roughly the same age, Brian felt he was being spoken to as if he had no understanding of his actions. Yes, he understood this was considered gross insubordination. Yes, he understood how this would surely undermine the policies of the administration.

Maybe Wilkes is trying to give me a chance to defend myself, thought Brian. Maybe he wants me to verbally braid my own noose. Maybe.

As he listened to the principal with growing agitation, Brian had a dizzy moment where he actually imagined that he was twelve years old again, sitting in his father's office, being berated for some trivial mistake.

At the end of the mostly one-sided conversation, it was determined that Brian would be suspended pending termination.

No surprise. It was about what he'd expected.

Brian and Drew waited over two hours for their mother, neither wanting to run the risk of abandoning their spot to make a phone call. They sat on the curb, watching the number of scurrying trick-or-treaters dwindle until the sidewalks were empty and the houses were dark.

Eventually, headlights fell on them, and the vehicle came to a jerky stop. But it wasn't their mother. It was their father.

Gordan Cline stumbled out of the car. "Boys," he said. Their father left the car door open as he crossed through the headlights, nearly falling to the curb next to them. His eyes were red and swollen. He touched the boys' heads and face as if to make sure they were actually there. "Boys," the man stammered again, and this time his voice broke. His lips trembled and he began blinking rapidly. "Your mother—" His voice was hoarse. Drew was frowning—confused, not understanding. Brian knew.

Kathy Cline died at the hospital later that night. On her way back to
the neighborhood to pick up her sons, a drunk driver had careened
through an intersection, smashing into Kathy's vehicle with horrific
velocity.

Neither of the boys mentioned trick-or-treating again. Or the
Hoffman House, for that matter. Brian thought he understood that
what had happened that night had been some sort of violation, and he
thought they were being taught a lesson. He often wondered if Drew
believed the same thing.

Even on the morning of their mother's closed-casket funeral,
Brian had discreetly examined the newspaper, trying to find anything
about an attack on an elderly person in the old neighborhood. Nothing.

After Brian turned sixteen and received his driver's license, he'd
several times worked up the courage to drive by the Hoffman House.
On each occasion he merely slowed the car. Everything was the same.
But that wasn't quite right. Brian had the idea that the house was
watching him, playing possum.

Drew's personality had grown colder as he grew older, becoming
more clinically solemn and withdrawn. He seemed gravely intent on
producing scientifically sound answers to difficult problems, so it was
no surprise when he moved away to attend medical school and later
become a pathologist.

As the years passed, family members who dared speak of that Halloween in 1987 as if there had only been one tragedy that night. But
Brian and Drew knew better.

Brian pulled into the parking lot at the local hardware store around five
o'clock that Friday evening. Halloween.

Back at school, he'd left all the decorations hanging in his classroom and only toted a small box of belongings to his car before driving directly to the hardware store.

Brian pulled up the collar on his jacket as he crossed the parking
lot. The kids around town would have to bundle up tonight.

A cashier in a red vest greeted him as he entered. Brian smiled
warmly and nodded. Yes, he knew what he was looking for. No
thanks, he didn't need any help.

Brian slowed his pace as he approached the hand-tool section, reverently inspecting the selection of hatchets.

The Hoffman House stood before a curdled backdrop of slate-colored clouds. Brian sat in his car. The engine was off.

Again, Brian called up the memory—a memory that had taken on variations over the years. He sees the dark cloak of shadowed tendrils covering a shape of bone and dead flesh. He sees the old woman— he'd always thought of it as Drew's witch—in her blood-soaked hospital gown, her hair hanging in wiry clumps. But in his worst recollections, the thing that appears at the door is no monster at all, but simply a feeble old man—confused, fumbling out of the darkness.

But Brian's mind no longer permits this trick, and the scene sheds itself, revealing its true face beneath the mask of memory.

He missed his little brother. He missed his mom. Brian took a hasty swipe at his eyes. There was a brown bag on the passenger seat. Brian reached over, the bag making a parchment rustling as he withdrew the hatchet.

Brian got out of the car, giving the neighborhood an uninterested glance. His heart began to surge as he crossed the leaf-blanketed yard, the rest of the world became obscured by an unseen screen.

Brian approached the front porch and looked up to one of the second-floor windows. Something was standing up there. Unclothed. Its gray flesh was shaded here and there where the withered skin was stretched over ridges of misshapen bone. Prodigious eyes. The thing's angular face was smiling, leering.

Brian clenched a fist to knock on the door, but thought better of it. Instead, he clutched the hatchet and kicked in the door, the paint-flecked panel of wood easily splintering from its age-rotted hinges.

For a split-instant, it was the normal interior of an outdated house. But all that grew murky and indistinct. As if the sun were setting with startling swiftness, shadows clamored and stretched over one another.

Brian swallowed, licked his lips, and whispered, "Trick or treat." He hefted the hatchet and strode through the threshold, disappearing within the overlapping shadows.

THE JELLYFISH

This is it. This is where I'm going to die. On a gray-brisk November morning, Paul Dawson walked into the forest clearing. He'd been hiking for a little over three hours, trying not to dwell on painful images of his two daughters, trying instead to preoccupy himself with what comforting image he would cling to as he slammed the black door on his ridiculous life once and for all. In the end, not long now—hemorrhaging blood and embracing his final seconds of consciousness—Paul chose the jellyfish.

Earlier—following a pre-dawn breakfast of sloppily swallowed vodka, and a cheerfully vague e-mail addressed to his family and acquaintances—Paul's journey to the clearing had been a forty-mile blur of taxis, gas stations, and hiking along the snaky feeder roads fringing the outskirts of the massive forest preserve.

He'd been making headway, but, once inside the woods, walking felt more like wading as he slowly progressed through the dense terrain of gullies and undergrowth. As intended, Paul had given a wide berth to any sort of conventional trail, avoiding main thoroughfares, lest he cross paths with a hiker or, worse, a ranger doing some routine snooping. This place had a reputation for people executing this sort of thing, even more incentive to forge ahead and find his own special place, even more incentive to put distance between himself and himself—everything that made him ashamed to be Paul Dawson.

On any map of the state, the Marion Shaekel Wilderness Area was a 13,000-acre inkspill of dense forest, intertangled with 39 miles of trails and campgrounds. Instead, Paul followed his gut, guided by the intrinsic sense that he'd *feel* it when it was right, intuiting his way into the overgrown innards of the forest.

And this was the spot. Now, as Paul appraised the clearing, surveying the open pocket with quiet contemplation, a memory emerged. He was a kid, must have been twelve or thirteen, a summer night in the small town where he'd grown up—the town he'd never left. He was with a group of flashlight-toting boys, vaulting the low, wrought-iron fence crookedly framing a church cemetery on the farmish outskirts of the town. They called it, simply enough, the graveyard game. The boys would stand along the fence, their backs turned and their eyes closed, while a single member selected the name and date on a tombstone. When the name was announced the boys would scatter, flashlight beams dancing and darting from marker to marker. The idea was that when the name had been found, the winner would yell, "Grave robber!" But instead of rushing, Paul would simply stroll up and down the aisles, calmly reading the names etched in stone, changing course when the inexplicable urge moved him, sort of *feeling* where the name would be. More often than not (and barring one of the neighbors or the caretaker hollering threats of calling the constable) his flashlight beam would settle on the selected name.

"Grave robber," he said softly. Paul lingered in that memory a moment longer as he considered the clearing before him, a peaceful spot wreathed by a rim of trees, their remaining rust-colored leaves laced together by dark branches. Paul exhaled a short-lived puff of visible air, savoring the cemetery stillness, the hauntedness of this place.

A huge tree had fallen and now lay stretched across part of the clearing. Paul approached the tree and casually placed his duffel bag on the enormous moss-covered trunk. His hand was shaking slightly as he unzipped the bag and withdrew the silver revolver.

Paul went back, seven years earlier, to the day he'd acquired the weapon. It'd been Father's Day, and Steve Spencer—Paul's former father-in-law and Molly's retired-cop dad—had jabbed a heavy bow-wrapped box at his son-in-law. In his thirty-one years, Paul had never fired a gun. Astonished, Paul had followed Steve out behind the house, across a stretch of property to an impromptu firing range. Following Steve's gruff instructions, Paul braced, aimed at a coffee can placed on a hay bale, sighted, and—his mouth dry—squeezed. The recoil from the revolver caused Paul to flinch violently, the gun nearly bucking out of his hands. His father-in-law was laughing, his meaty hands spread over his generous belly. Despite this, Steve encouraged Paul to keep the gun—"for home security," he'd said—but henceforth eyed his son-in-law with what Paul believed was a mix of disappointment and disgust, and the older man never failed to slap Paul heartily on the back when he mentioned the incident each Father's Day. And each Father's Day Paul had constructed his own list of barbed responses. But Paul did what he'd done for so many years—with his father-in-law, with his wife, with his bosses. Paul cooperated. He kept his mouth shut and swallowed his pride.

Paul clicked open the revolver's cylinder and looked at the six unblinking eyes of the bullets' brass primers. "What are you staring at?" he mumbled, his voice sounding weird in the quiet clearing. Speaking now to no one, Paul wondered if he'd been more vocal, if he'd been more assertive, if his mind and his mouth had had a better relationship, then some of the problems in his marriage would have never emerged. "You have no imagination," Molly had said during their final fight, the one resulting in her packing up and shacking up with a guy from her office, the guy who was now her new husband.

Hell, Paul thought. *Nothing I said or imagined could have saved us.*

Now, framed by the black borders of exhaustion and half-drunk desperation, Paul saw a jittery home movie of his family as it had been, still intact, still in one piece, during one of their first vacations together; and he saw his girls as they had been—two kids on the beach, building a sandcastle, achingly brilliant sunshine highlighting the rippling water.

Again Paul steeled himself against these sentimental phantoms. In this world, it was what was *real* that mattered. Things—*money* things—that Molly clearly found more reliable than anything Paul could offer, and it was *real.*

Paul slapped the revolver's cylinder shut and inspected the remaining contents in the duffel bag.

He pulled out a plastic baggy containing several critical pieces of information—Social Security card, account numbers—to help expediate his identification someday. Years from now, he hoped. When his girls were older. He paused a moment on his driver's license. "This is who I am, folks," Paul said. *No,* he thought, *this is who I was.* He gave a morose smirk at the organ donor designation on his driver's license before withdrawing several lengths of bungee cord. The plan was simple: Secure the bungees to the lower bole of a tree and wriggle into them, snuggly strapping himself in place, still somewhat concealed yet readily available for scavenging denizens. Paul looked up at the overcast sky between the thinning, interlaced branches, and closed his eyes.

The gunshot made him flinch. With breathtaking abruptness, a single shot exploded across the forest. Paul's eyes went wide, reacting as if his own revolver had inadvertently discharged; but no—the report, now wavering to a dying echo, had come from somewhere nearby.

Wide-eyed, he scanned the clearing, already abandoning his plan. The most important thing right now was getting the hell out of here. But before he could get moving, Paul was frozen by another sound—a rhythmic twig-snapping and leaf-crunching, something big steadily cleaving its way through undergrowth. And then he saw a dark shape bouncing, swiftly separating from the crowded backdrop of tree trunks.

A massive deer bounded into the clearing, its powerful legs stabbing at the leaf-peaty earth as it charged ahead. He stammered and staggered backward, but ceased his retreat as the deer inexplicably faltered and stopped, its body going rigid and its black eyes locked directly on Paul.

The ginger-colored animal was panting, each snorting huff sending ghosty streamers into the air. Paul too was breathing in panicky puffs as his gaze flicked back and forth between the deer's eyes and its formidable crown of antlers, the multi-pronged rack branching out on either side of its head. Paul glanced down at the deer's torso, to the dark red smudge near its ribcage. The gunshot, the wound, and the deer's sudden presence made sense, but those thoughts collided with something dissonant: *Why did it stop?* Paul focused on the deer's black eyes and stopped blinking, stopped contemplating what was happening.

The clearing began to change. Light was fading, dimming, as if a curtain of coal smoke were drifting up from the forest floor. Shadows began blending together, turning everything into a dark canvas behind the deer, which stood motionless—staring, bleeding, panic-stricken, yet somehow . . . proud.

Paul was seized with an overwhelming sensation that he was moving in two directions: being dragged forward—his consciousness magnetized toward the buck's black eyes—and sinking backwards, as if gently floating on his back.

And then he thought about his mom.

Thirty-three summers before, when Paul was five, his mom had taken him to a local pool for swimming lessons. He was a nimble kid, eager, energetic, and when it came to swimming he was a natural. But he dreaded floating on his back. The combination of touching nothing and hearing his respiration coming in amplified gasps evoked a sort of reverse claustrophobia, causing him to splash and thrash upright, desperate to find purchase on something stable, something tangible.

Paul was experiencing this precise sensation now—pressure overtaking him from beneath, surrendering to the buoyant embrace of water.

As the last of the light dimmed from the clearing, he began enduring a flashbulb barrage of images, memories.

Paul saw—and saw *through*—his child-self propped up on a pillow in his bed, running a fierce fever, his mother rushing into the darkened room and placing a cool washcloth on his forehead—the boy-Paul feels the sudden urge to vomit, and suddenly he is a college student, throwing up in the toilet at his apartment, too drunk for his own good, and then Molly is there in the bathroom, appearing disappointed but amused as she cleans him up, helps him to bed, and then Molly is on his bed—*no*—Molly is in a *hospital* bed, Paul is next to her, clutching her shoulder and stroking her forehead as she pushes their first child into the world.

Paul felt something scalloped loose from his mind.

He was unaware of the tears that had begun to stream from the corners of his unblinking eyes as he continued to be bombarded by half-forgotten memories and emotions; and then it was all blurring together—he was a child, boiling with fever; he was a college kid, regretting his irresponsibility; he was a man grateful for the ordinary and significant opportunity to be called *Dad*. And while a portion of Paul's mind was experiencing all this, the other part continued its descent, falling backward, fathom after fathom, into amniotic blackness. And then Paul imagined the warm scene of his daughters building a sandcastle on the beach, his youngest daughter jumping up, running toward him, crying, mumbling something about a sting, a red, blossom-shaped blotch on her leg. As if to grasp those phantoms, Paul unconsciously raised his arms, reaching out.

The concussive stutter-crack of gunfire filled the clearing.

Paul—the *seeing* part of Paul that had been drifting toward the deer—was instantly yanked back now; but before that conscious presence could fully return to his body, he felt a punching thud pierce his upper chest. He had time to watch the deer twitch, stagger, then both he and the big buck fell, Paul collapsing to one side of the moss-covered log.

He was staring up through the branch-knotted canopy, at the shards of gray sky between the boughs, yet somehow he could still see himself down there, lying on his back on a bed of damp dead leaves. In an almost adrenal rush of awareness, Paul began to understand that the seeing thing, the thing seeing him, hovering in the clearing had a shape—a formation of sensate dimensions. Paul initially registered a sort of giant, all-seeing umbrella. But that wasn't quite right. Now his mind desperately clung to something that had nearly gone into mental atrophy: his imagination. As inexplicable as it was, Paul surrendered rationality, and the indistinct thing floating in the clearing rapidly took the shape of a massive black jellyfish.

The giant bell-shaped hood glistened in the gray light, its long black tentacles dangled beneath it, whipping languidly as it floated contentedly over the clearing. He could see everything within the jellyfish in a dome-shaped panorama as it narrowed its attention to the far side of the clearing, where the deer was thrashing and making choking noises, its antlers whipping at the air, its black eyes electrically alive with terror. There were now several large wound-smudges along its torso.

Now there were voices, and the jellyfish rotated its awareness again. A man came jogging out from the far side of the forest, swatting at the tangled foliage; he was toting a large machine gun, what—with Paul's help—the jellyfish coolly recognized as an assault rifle, an AK-47.

The man was dressed in dark clothing—ball cap, camo sweatshirt, camo pants—and he was wearing a backpack. He was a youngish guy with a narrow, clean-shaven face, tall and thin, what some people might call lean and wiry; but upon closer inspection, the man's eyes were underlined with dark crescents, and his sallow skin was stretched too tight over his cheeks and chin, things Paul associated with poor health or meth use. *An undertaker's apprentice.*

Another man emerged now, breathing heavily, clearly trying to keep pace. This one was wearing a logger's jacket. Unlike his partner, he was wide and burly, and had what looked like a week's worth of whisker-stubble on his too-fleshy jowls. He reminded Paul of a cruel Bassett hound.

"Goddamn it, Roger," the younger one said. "Thought I had him on the first shot."

The bigger man, Roger, panted as he spoke. "Don't . . . make no sense," he said, slinging his own rifle over his shoulder. "Why the hell was it just standing there?"

The slim one was already shaking his head. "Don't know. Don't matter." He paused, caught his breath and wiped his nose on his sleeve. "Maybe it knew it was as good as dead." And then he raised the machine gun to his shoulder and marched over to the dying deer.

"Don't shoot the fuckin' thing again, Blake," Roger said wearily, "unless you want to send out another goddamn invitation." The bigger man walked forward. "Just get it over with—quietly. Or I'll leave your ass out here to carry the whole thing back to the jeep yourself."

The other one—*Blake*—shrugged. "Fine by me." He looked over at his partner and flashed a grin, his teeth resembling irregular rows of infected corn kernels. "But I ain't sharing none of the profit." Roger snorted and stepped further into the clearing. The deer had slowed its flailing but was still mewling.

"Hurry up," Roger said, glancing around the clearing. "I ain't in the mood to run into a ranger."

"Yeah, yeah," said Blake, resting the machine gun against a tree. He slipped off his backpack and began scrounging through it. After a few seconds he produced a tool. A rusty hacksaw.

Paul remained mentally and physically severed: still helplessly seeing *through* the jellyfish, while his brain—secure in his paralyzed body—continued *feeling*, adding voice to what he was watching.

Suddenly, a few of those long black tentacles hanging under the jellyfish's gelatinous dome writhed and drifted out, extending to the hunters' foreheads, and Paul was bombarded by awareness. It wasn't quite omniscience, but what Paul sensed was intent—this was a kind of game or contest. The deer was a prize. *A piece of the deer.* He was gripped by the revelation of what they meant to do. A wild swirl of nausea flooded his unflinching body.

Paul watched helplessly as the jellyfish considered the deer's black eyes.

A few times as a boy, Paul had gone night fishing with his father at a pond just outside of town. They both carried flashlights with them on the boat. Once, struggling to lure a worm, Paul had fumbled his flashlight, dropping it in the water. He watched as the light danced and wobbled, the glowing beam fading as it sank into the murk. It felt as if it had lasted an excruciating amount of time, the helplessness of it, but it had disappeared faster than Paul could hitch in a breath.

Paul could sense the deer's life-light fading now, and he hoped the animal was far enough from the surface not to experience fully what was about to happen.

Blake approached the weakened buck cautiously, circling for a moment before savagely seizing a tangle of antlers and pressing a boot against its thick neck. The animal let out another shriek as Blake unceremoniously placed the hacksaw along the deer's throat and began sawing, the hunter grunting with each clumsy stroke, the rust-mottled saw—steadily streaking with gore—roughly serrated through the deer's neck, just under its jaw, as its black eyes continued to stare in hopeless astonishment.

Abruptly the jellyfish's sight zoomed in to a torturous proximity, its vision magnified close enough to see green grime under Blake's fingernails. It flashed over to Roger and watched the big man spit a viscous stream of tobacco juice, a string of spittle catching on his beard as he barked instructions at Blake, then it flashed back down to the deer, hovering inches from its face. Paul saw a few pearls of moisture racket off the animal's glistening nostrils as Blake struggled to saw through bone and sinew.

Paul wanted to close his eyes, but it was the jellyfish that was observing, absorbing everything with detached avidity.

After ripping through a clinging portion of meat and skin, the deer's head—along with its prized rack of antlers—was torn free. Blake let out a whooping cheer and hefted the spiky crown.

"All right, that'll do," Roger said listlessly and gestured toward the backpack. "Get it wrapped up so we can get the hell out of here."

Blake obeyed, still showing his infected-corn grin. From the backpack he unfolded a murky tarp, along with a length of rope, and set to work on packaging the trophy rack.

The jellyfish scanned down to the deer's body, and Paul was made to watch the deer's dismembered form for several repulsive moments. Gouts of blood pulsed from the ragged wound on the deer's neck. Only minutes before the deer had been standing twenty yards away, stoic, its deadly, umber-smudged antlers forked out like upturned talons. Now it was in two pieces—part of it being wrapped in filthy plastic, part of it lying on the ground, ejaculating blood. It looked like a botched autopsy, a madman's tantrum.

The jellyfish shifted its attention from the dead animal and began drifting away, making a sleepy retreat from Roger and Blake and returning to the air above Paul, who was again *seeing* it and seeing *through* it to himself—the pale, lifeless thing lying on the ground that was called Paul Dawson.

The jellyfish began descending and its black, slender tentacles began merging, twining together conically, converging on Paul's face. The twisted tendrils extended to his forehead and began corkscrewing, sinking in with drill-bit precision, but instead of pain Paul felt a washcloth coolness spread out over his brow as he watched the gelatinous form contracting and funneling. And just as the last of the jellyfish's bell-shaped dome contorted and sank into his brow, Paul blinked, sucked in a stream of cold air, and had the fierce urge to . . .

"HEEELLLP!"

The echo of his scream faded. Lying on his back, concealed by the fallen tree, Paul could only hear curses being traded and the clack of a gun being cocked. And then there was something else: Now, with consciousness and corporeality reunited, Paul was consumed by radiant pain in his upper chest. He ran an uncoordinated hand over the wound, his palm coming away crimson.

In time there was the cautious crunching of underbrush. Blake appeared, emerging from over the top of the log, eyes wide and wild, his machine gun shakily trained on Paul.

"Please," Paul gasped, raising his blood-coated hand. "Please . . . have to get . . . help."

Blake continued staring, repeating the same expletive. Finally he called out over his shoulder. "Roger—get your ass over here."

Roger ambled into view, sidling up next to Blake. They inspected Paul like two fishermen who'd reeled in an aquatic oddity.

"Where the fuck did he come from?" Roger said absently.

"Jesus," Blake mumbled. "Some goddamn hiker."

Roger leaned down over Paul and spoke slowly. "Where the fuck did you come from?"

Paul hooked his fingers over the bullet wound. "Please"—gasping—"losing blood . . . need to get . . ." but the words died away. Gauging Roger's uninterested expression, Paul became icily aware that his pleas were drifting toward uselessness.

Roger exhaled and pivoted, scanning the clearing, whipping off his ball cap and wiping sweat from his forehead. Paul stared at the man, awestruck with the man's bully-distilled features.

"Roger," Blake said, gun still aimed at Paul, "what are we—"

"Shut up," Roger said calmly, smoothly replacing the ball cap. He came forward and rested his boot on the log beside Paul. He said, "Now why are you all the way out here, fella?"

Paul again stared at Roger, trying to calculate how this was going to end. After a stretch of silence Roger began flicking his eyes around Paul, settling on something. "Blake," Roger said, gesturing toward Paul's unzipped duffel bag. "Go over there and fetch that bag." Initially Blake didn't move, only flinched a nervous glance at Roger. "Do it, boy," Roger said. Blake cursed, lowered the gun, and tromped over to where Paul had dropped his bag. Paul and Roger continued staring at each other.

"The hell . . ." Blake was frowning as he lifted Paul's plastic baggy full of personal information.

Roger said, "Give it here." He slid his hand into the baggy and withdrew the driver's license. "Paul . . . Dawson." After reading quietly for a few seconds, Roger twitched a frown and said, "New Bethel. Hell, that's forty miles or better." He inspected Paul. "What are you doing this far south, Paul Dawson from New Bethel?" With his boot resting on the log, Roger's posture, expression, and tone resembled a drowsy, small-town sheriff.

"Roger," Blake said, and held up Paul's revolver. The two shared a quiet moment before Roger glanced back at Paul.

"Well well," Roger said. "Now what would a guy like you be doing with a sweet piece like that, Paul Dawson?" A bird gave up a throaty squawk high up in the trees. Roger snorted. "I'll tell you something, Blake, this guy ain't no hiker, and he sure as hell ain't no hunter. So I'll ask you again—what are you doing all the way out here?"

A rational part of Paul—a part that he had neglected in the years, months, and days leading up to his grim adventure—was overwhelmed by the alien urge to survive, the urge to formulate a cogent plea to these hunters. *No, not hunters,* Paul thought soberly. *Killers.* And with that, what prevailed within Paul was another foreign desire—the desire *not* to cooperate. Right now, the only thing more hateful to him than the disappointment of his own life was the horror of ending it on their terms—begging, helpless. He lingered on the jittery moving portrait of his girls on the beach, the sandcastle, the laughter, the lapping waves, his daughter crying after getting stung on the leg by a jellyfish.

"Came out here to . . ." Paul murmured. "Came out here to . . ."

"Came out here to what?" Blake blurted.

"Came out here to . . . collect fossils." Silence.

Blake's gaunt face screwed up. "What the fuck? Fossils?"

Paul mumbled, "Arrowheads," and smiled, blood staining the front of his teeth. "Arrowheads and trilobites."

Something passed over Roger's face. "Quit your jawjacking, Blake."

But Blake ignored him. "What the fuck is the gun for?"

"For protection," Paul said, still smiling.

"From what?" Blake said.

Now Roger was shouting. "Shut the fuck up, Blake."

"Protection from . . ." Paul said thinly, and his smile faded as he blinked back and forth between the two men. "Animals."

Roger's expression grew vacant, unimpressed; but Blake still looked confused. "Roger, this guy—"

"Shut your mouth," Roger said with dangerous finality. He took a deep breath and then leaned in on Paul, his voice a hangman's whisper. "You're going to fucking bleed to death out here, pal." Paul stared. "But I figure that's what you came out here to do in the first place.

Isn't that right?" Paul said nothing. "Well, don't you worry. I have a feeling you're going to get your wish."

Paul blinked and licked his lips. "Maybe," he said, extending a finger toward Roger's young partner. "But I know Blake's name."

Blake bristled, hugging his gun close. "What's he talking about?"

Roger sneered. "He's saying that if somebody finds him they'd know about us because of the goddamned slug in his chest."

Paul, lucidity wobbling momentarily, wondered about how much blood he'd been losing. Again, he suffocated the urge to ask for help. He pointed at Blake and said, "Grave . . . robber."

Tearing his boot away from the log, Roger said, "Blake, hand me that revolver." Blake did so. Roger flicked open the cylinder, which he eyed briefly before slapping it shut. As he stomped over to Paul and trained the revolver on his face, the husky man's expression seemed to say, *Come on, fella, beg for it.* He wondered: *Beg for what, my life or the end?* Accepting the end—whatever that meant—was easy. Paul had been dwelling on it, had been inwardly practicing it, for so many months. But the difficult part now was accepting that these two men would continue doing what they do, would continue *being.* Paul wanted to deny them one more thing, wanted to deny them another trophy.

Everything slowed. Paul grinned as Roger thumbed the hammer and braced his arm. "So long, asshole."

Paul closed his eyes, but in the interminable blackness beneath his lids he saw a flicker and was overcome with the inexorable urge to *push.* Since the jellyfish had pinwheeled into his mind, it had excavated something. Fertilized something. The jellyfish hadn't just appeared, it had emerged, had awakened. He pushed. Memories seized him—*sick in bed as a kid.* He let out a wheezy breath and pushed again. *Molly in the hospital, Paul telling her to*—push. *His daughters, the sandcastle, the ocean, the jellyfish.* Paul clenched his teeth and *pushed.*

The jellyfish propelled itself from Paul's forehead, stretching out long and black, reacquiring its enormous form as it floated back out into the clearing.

Roger, gun still bearing down on Paul, blinked and hesitated.

"What is it?" Blake said.

Roger glanced around uneasily. "Nothing. Just thought—" he trailed off. "Thought he . . . did something."

Paul saw the jellyfish as a solid thing—vivid—sharp and crisp as Kodachrome, rapt by the inky beauty of it. He watched it drift into the clearing, hanging eight feet from the ground.

In one shaky movement Paul reached over and scrabbled at the side of the moss-covered log, hauling himself up, getting an elbow on top of the log. Clearly startled by the erratic movement, Roger braced the revolver with both hands and stumbled a few steps backwards, while Blake retrained his gun in Paul's direction.

The jellyfish had sailed over to the other side of the clearing, making a bobbing descent to where the deer's corpse lay in a pool of blood.

The jellyfish sank, its slender tendrils converging on the deer's torso, the thread-fine tentacles swiveling and corkscrewing, disappearing into the body. As it had done with Paul, the obsidian dome began contorting, shrinking, and sinking into the ginger-coarse fur of the deer. Then it was gone.

Paul was hunched over the log, wheezing. Roger spoke up. "All right." He strode forward. "Enough pissing around." He took aim at the back of Paul's head.

A thickly moist gurgle issued from across the clearing.

Whereas Roger and Blake hadn't *seen* the manifestation of the jellyfish, they had unmistakably *heard* this.

Going rigid, Blake said, "The hell was that?"

Roger jerked his face toward the sound as it erupted again. Another wet, lurching sound, and this time Paul watched as the deer's body twitched. Roger and Blake were staring in the same direction. Another violent shake from the carcass, which grew into a convulsive shudder. "Roger . . ." Blake began, but his voice died away.

The husky man hitched in a breath, but stifled speech as the deer's slender legs spasmed, flicked, and drew up under its torso. As if startled from a nap, the headless carcass lurched up onto its hooves.

Blake bristled and whimpered something as both he and Roger shuffled backward.

The carcass quaked. From within the hacksawed wound emerged a gelatinous blackness, amorphously oozing out between severed arteries and ripped muscle. Paul flicked a glance over at Roger and Blake, who were staring, seemingly paralyzed.

The gelatinous blackness hung out of the wound, then, in a snake-strike flash, clusters of black tendrils spilled forth, stretching out and writhing at the air, as if testing it, or tasting it.

Paul recognized the slender appendages—tentacles that had been hanging like a poisonous skirt beneath the jellyfish; now they trembled and began bifurcating, separating, merging in clusters to either side of the undulating pseudo-skull.

Paul's vision dimmed on the fringes, and he shook away another bout of light-headedness. Refocusing, he saw that the tentacles had now elaborately braided themselves together, imitating an enormous crown of black antlers with Rorschach symmetry.

"Goddamn it, Blake," said Roger, "get that rifle." With that, the deer's body bristled, the black-pronged rack seemingly intent on the source of the voice.

Paul watched Blake bring the gun to his shoulder with quaking hesitation.

The deer carcass took a few stilted steps forward, its hooves stabbing with mincing baby-steps. It stopped and started again with more stability, more precision.

"That fucking thing is de—" Blake began, but before he could finish the deer sprang forward, advancing across the clearing in a bolting lurch, leaping over thick underbrush with its black antlers thrust out as it charged ahead. Roger had time to fire two haphazard shots from the revolver before the carcass jumped up in front of Roger, its legs kicking, hooves slashing. Paul watched one of those hooves come down in a vicious arc across Roger's cheek and collarbone, instantly lacerating a long patch of flesh. Roger howled, grabbed his face and fell sideways.

Blake was screaming now, the deer carcass flinching and pivoting in his direction. Blake leveled his rifle on the deer but made the mistake of blindly retreating backward and was tripped up in a thick thatch of fallen branches and low vines. The machine gun chattered a series of haphazard shots as Blake pitched down, his frantic screams lost under the stutter of gunfire. As furious as the sound was, it suddenly ceased as the clip was expended, leaving only Blake and his screams as he struggled to free himself from the tangle of underbrush.

The deer advanced, charging full tilt, its prongs thrust forward combatively as it bore down on Blake, who screamed and wept, thick strands of saliva clinging between his irregular rows of yellow teeth.

And then the deer leapt up and fell on him, its forelegs stomping his chest and stomach, antlers whip-goring the young man. And with each stabbing plunge Paul saw that the venom-barbed tentacles were leaving ropy, livid streaks. The bruised marks on Blake's face and throat appeared to swell instantly into varicose welts.

Blake was still struggling, the deer carcass still mauling him, when a single shot rang out. Paul flinched and saw Roger, now up on his knees, a trembling arm extended with the smoking revolver. The wound on his cheek and jaw had opened thickly, blood streaming down and soaking into his logger's jacket.

Three more shots pealed out, rocking the deer's body each time. The carcass lurched back and staggered away from Blake.

Roger shakily made it to his feet. He stumbled forward, his eyes, shocked and glazy, danced around the clearing and found Paul, who was fighting to remain draped over the tree trunk. Roger's expression was absent and impassive as he raised the revolver, brought its barrel level with Paul's face, and pulled the trigger. The gun's hammer snapped repeatedly on empty cylinders with each frantic pull, and it took Roger a moment to hurl the gun at Paul, missing him, the useless weapon tumbling off into the underbrush. Roger began hobbling over to Blake, casting a wary glance at the deer carcass, which was on the ground now, the black antlers receding into the wound.

Blake was crying, his welt-lashed face stricken with each anguished plea. "Oh, Roger . . ." Blake moaned. "Roger . . . my eyes, Roger . . . oh Jesus . . . burning . . . it . . . can't breathe."

Roger muttered something as he pulled Blake to his feet, clutching one of the young man's arms and awkwardly hoisting him up beside him, cradling the young man as his legs wobbled beneath him. Roger gave Paul a glance as he began carry-dragging Blake out of the clearing, the younger man sobbing incoherencies. Soon, Roger and Blake's dark clothes blended with the huddled tree trunks, and then they were gone. Periodically, an agonized scream echoed into the forest, but even those eventually ceased.

The dim rim around Paul's field of vision had worsened, his breath grew meek. Instead of pulling himself up onto the log, he let go and dropped down, falling on his back.

Silence settled in the clearing. Silence and darkness.

Consciousness ebbed and flowed, he dozed and was shaken awake by bouts of cold and feverish quaking. With the occasional rustle-hush of leaves from the upper reaches of the trees, the clearing was quiet, peaceful, which made the abrupt presence of the jellyfish hovering above him all the more startling.

It rose up from the lower portion of Paul's eyeline, floating languidly, swimming in the air four feet above him, its delicate tentacles hanging below it. He thought about his daughters, and regret was replaced with a sober sort of calm—the jellyfish sting, Paul wiping away tears, telling her it would be all right. *I promise.*

The jellyfish descended, its skirt of tentacles converging. He winced as the tendrils sank in smoothly, streaming into the wound as its globular hood contorted, crumpled, and slunk into Paul's chest. His respiration became rapid, and he could hear a wavy thrumming in his ears.

He felt pressure from below and from the sides—the overwhelming sensation of floating on his back. He smiled and closed his eyes.

Paul shivered awake, his body tensing, causing his mattress of dead leaves rustle.

Through the lattice of burnt-orange leaves clinging to dark branches, he noticed that the gray sky was now pale blue, and the position of the sun suggested afternoon rather than morning.

Paul swallowed and aimed his face down to inspect his chest. Blood had dried and stiffened across his sweatshirt; he carefully lifted his fingers to where he'd been shot, feeling only chilled unbroken skin. Paul rolled to his side and rose up on his hands and knees, catching his breath and licking his lips.

Head muzzy, he pulled himself up. Paul took a few mincing steps forward and spotted the silver glint of the revolver. He hefted it, ran his fingers along the cylinder, and checked to ensure it was empty. He dropped the gun into his duffel bag and surveyed the clearing. The deer carcass. Paul sought the half-wrapped tarp, hefted it, and brought it over to the desecrated corpse, settling it down carefully alongside the torso.

Paul retrieved Blake's machine gun, stabbing the butt of the weapon into the damp earth, and started digging.

Hours later, Paul Dawson—covered with dirt, his face sweat-streaked with grime—was walking through the woods. The light was beginning to retreat and the shadows were creeping long. He walked earnestly, with purpose, passing part of the time by wondering if Roger and Blake had made it out of the woods; and if they had, would they find him sooner or later? The notion made him smirk. With the sky dimming into lavender-fringed pastels, Paul hiked on, moving so swiftly and so smoothly that, when he closed his eyes, it felt like floating.

WHAT HAPPENS IN HELL STAYS IN HELL

Thus bad begins, and worse remains behind.
—*Hamlet*, Act 3, Scene 4

The principal of Clarke Ridge High School has two hours left as an independently functioning organism—two hours left to exist as something other than *food*. This is the way his world ends: He is preparing to close his office when the secretary calls out from behind the receptionist's counter: "Mr. Wilkinson?"

With his hand on the doorknob, the young principal tries, and fails, to sound professionally serene. "Yes?"

Mrs. Welch pivots and examines a slip of paper. "That gentleman from the Army called for you again."

Wilkinson is slowly narrowing the space between his office door and the jamb. "What gentleman?"

"William Craft. He says he's been calling and e-mailing you for several days."

Wilkinson faintly recalls the name. "Did he say what he wanted?" He hopes his tone implies that she better make it snappy.

"No," says the secretary, clearly taking the hint, returning her glasses to her face and her fingers to the keyboard of her computer. "Just that it was urgent."

Wilkinson thanks his secretary and finishes closing the door.

Silence. He knows the peace of his office will be brief. And despite a tedious to-do list of parent phone calls to return and discipline reports to manage, he savors the tranquil moment nonetheless.

Wilkinson sets his coffee mug on his desk and walks over to his aquarium, scanning the pristine tank of tropical fish before sprinkling in some food. Smiling, he watches the flakes float down.

Wilkinson straightens his tie and settles down into his chair, swiveling toward the computer. He maximizes and opens his e-mail. A new message. Wilkinson notices the last name, Craft, and has another flicker of guilt for not returning the man's phone calls, but it had been a mercilessly hectic week. The principal passes a hand over his generously tanned face and clicks open the message:

"I encourage you to read the rest of what I've written here, but the most important thing is this: You have to stop Lonnie Meadows from entering your school." Wilkinson's leather chair creaks as he leans closer to the screen.

"I'm not sure what he intends to do, but I'm certain you'll regret permitting him on the premises. He's been calling me for the past few weeks, saying he has a plan, something to do with a recruiting session at your school. I've tried listening. But it's not the same Meadows. It's not the same guy I knew from combat. I started ignoring his phone calls, just like you've clearly done with me.

"Before I go on, I want to jog your memory. My name is William Craft, formerly staff sergeant William Craft. Now, I am no longer a sergeant of any kind, nor a soldier. I am a coward. And if you'd seen the things we'd seen, you call yourself a coward too.

"I'm sure you've heard about that staff sergeant, Robert Bales, the monster who murdered all those women and children in the Panjwai district back in March, 2012; and I've often wondered if he'd ever been assigned to a place just north of Ceghak, in the Oruzgan province. The military would never release that information, just like they'd never release the truth about the details of our last mission—the one where I lost Meadows as a combat comrade and a friend and maybe a human being altogether."

Wilkinson is still frowning at the message on the monitor, still reading the strange e-mail, when the morning bell rings. Over the PA speaker, a student begins reciting the Pledge of Allegiance. Wilkinson refrains from standing and placing his hand over his heart, but mumbles along with the oath. With the previous messages, Wilkinson had suspected that Craft, because he claimed to be affiliated with the Army, was contacting him about scheduling a recruiting session with some of the students. But Wilkinson had assumed that his secretary would take care of the arrangements. Now Wilkinson was relieved that he'd never taken the phone calls or returned the messages. This young man was obviously unstable. Wilkinson takes a sip of coffee, winces, and reads on . . .

If you don't take this seriously, that's up to you. If you're still reading, it's probably too late. Like me, you may find solace in Eliot's wisdom: "This is the way the world ends—not with a bang, but a whimper." I know the poem "The Hollow Men" has nothing to do with what follows, but the words have drifted in and out of my mind since witnessing the horrors of war.

If you are still reading, then maybe there's something within you willing to give me the benefit of the doubt. In that case, I'll get to the point: I met Lonnie Meadows about seven years ago. We joined up around the same time, right after high school. We endured boot camp together, we were deployed together, we were even assigned to the same squad during our second and final tour. Our squad's job was to work with tribal leaders and villagers as security advisors.

I would take you directly to the events in that unnamed village just north of Ceghak, but I also need you to know—and anyone else whom you choose to share this message—that Meadows was my friend.

In high school, I'm sure Meadows would have given me a hard time. As a principal, you would surely have classified him as a hood. But within the great equalizer of the military, I guess I had proven myself a worthy ally. After trading a few boot-camp insults with Meadows, we became fast friends and, to my surprise, remained friends long after our initiation.

During our downtime—and when he wasn't either arguing with or sleeping with his girlfriend, Brittany—we'd made a habit of driving aimlessly around the backroads of the countryside, splitting a twelve-pack or trading sips from a pint of Beam. Meadows had been driving this particular night. This was long before he'd received the extensive wrist-to-elbow tattoos, and his unmarked and uninked forearm was slung over the steering wheel. He glanced over at me and said, "You know, Craft, you and me, like, complement each other."

It was one of the rare occasions when Meadows had something thoughtful to say, but one of the common occasions when he'd been drinking heavily. "Well hell, man," I said. "I'll take that as a *compliment*."

Meadows ignored my joke about the homonym. "No, no. It's

like"—he winced and shook his head—"I don't know, it's like we're a ying yang or something."

"*Yin* yang," I corrected him.

Meadows had just taken a swig from his bottle and frowned at me. "That's what I said." I smirked and took a pull from my own beer. "Anyway," he continued, "I just think that we get along because he fit together, you know. Like puzzle pieces."

This was interesting. Poignancy and articulation were not things that my friend, nor my battle comrades, took the risk of conveying. "How do you mean?"

Meadows shrugged. "Shit, man, I just don't think, in any other situation, without the Army holding us together, that we would be able to tolerate each other."

I said, "I'll drink to that," and did so.

"It's sort of like, I'm the muscle and you're the mind." We both chuckled.

"Yeah," I grinned. "But I can still kick your ass."

Meadows laughed, wiping beer from his chin with the back of his hand. "I'd like to see you try. Then you'd really have to write everything down in your little journal—I wouldn't leave you enough teeth to tell your stories."

My grin flickered and faded. Though no one had ever read my journal—the closest anyone has ever come is you reading this excerpt—I was certain he'd seen me scribbling in it from time to time. It was one of the only habits that maintained my sanity during boot camp and combat; and it was a habit—like the habit of Meadows's friendship—that endured long after.

Meadows would have been too drunk that night, and I wouldn't have been drunk enough, to supplement Meadows's admission with this: You and I are cowards, and we're both terrified of the same things.

But now, as years have passed, I would have preferred to end that drunken conversation, like so many that followed, by saying something kind. Something that might have saved my friend's life.

Principal Wilkinson minimizes the message, rolls his chair away from his computer, and slowly swivels toward his office window.

Movement out in the guest parking lot catches his eye. Two men—both dressed in Army fatigues—have emerged between the rows of vehicles. Recruiters, of course. He recognizes the stout, blond one as Jason Noble, who has visited before; but he doesn't know the other one, the tall guy sporting a crewcut.

The principal shifts his attention to his fish tank, meditating on the graceful movements of those brightly colored creatures. He decides that he'll forward Mr. Craft's message to the local recruiter. Wilkinson doesn't want to jump to conclusions, but this—this story—is clearly, and perhaps understandably, the result of post-traumatic stress.

He gazes at his fish tank. After several thoughtful minutes, Wilkinson reprimands himself for even considering the notion that a soldier would take advantage of a recruiting opportunity to harm young people.

The principal takes a quick drink from his coffee, walks over to his office door, and peers through the window. Mrs. Welch is chatting with the two recruiters, who appear to be concluding the sign-in procedure. As casually as possible Wilkinson opens the door and wanders over to the reception area.

The blond man, Noble, finishes signing in and rests the pen on top of a clipboard, thanking the secretary as he lifts a tote filled with promotional posters and other giveaway material. As a pretense, Wilkinson strolls over to a filing cabinet and randomly opens a drawer. As the men exit the office, Wilkinson sneaks a peek at the name patch on the right breast of the tall, crewcutted recruiter, and is relieved to read the name Santana. Wilkinson halfheartedly notes that young Santana is quite pale, perhaps even sick. Dark curves of exhaustion or sleep deprivation underline his eyes, and his complexion is waxy, as if running a fever. Santana, who'd been resting his forearms on the receptionist's counter, smirks at the principal, who returns the silent gesture with a tight nod.

The two recruiters exit the office as Wilkinson attempts to inconspicuously observe their behavior. As he watches them through the wide office window, Santana turns and winks at the principal before disappearing down the hall with his companion.

Mildly embarrassed for gawking, Wilkinson shuts the filing cabinet.

"Did you need something, Mr. Wilkinson?"

The principal clears his throat. "No. I mean, no, I found it."

Back in his office, Wilkinson drops down in his chair, now fully committed to notifying someone about this. But before he does so, he maximizes Craft's message, scanning the e-mail, scrolling down until he reads . . .

Our unit was operating in a place called Sangin, in the Helmand province. We'd only been there a few weeks, but had already accumulated an unusual number of injuries, mainly from ground-based bombs and IEDs, what the military and media are calling "signature wounds": two legs blown off at the knee or higher, accompanied by damage to the genitals and pelvic region.

It was late morning, and most of us—Meadows, Ricketts, Harper, and Flood, our translator—were gearing up for a routine patrol, when Lieutenant Strauss approached.

"There's been a change of plans, gentlemen," said Strauss.

"Surprise, surprise," mumbled Marcus Flood, our squad's interpreter. Flood always wore these big, black-rimmed spectacles, and I used to muse that he looked like a young Marvin Gaye sporting a pair of Buddy Holly's eyeglasses. "Strauss is changing shit up again."

Under his breath, Meadows said, "You mean we're finally getting out of this fuckhole?"

I grunted softly as the members of our team closed in on the lieutenant.

"We've been selected for a scouting mission in the Deh Ravod region," said Strauss, sounding more out of sorts than usual. "It's about eighty miles up river." The river was the Helmand, but—like so many ancient Afghan habitations—I'd never heard of Deh Ravod.

After a terse briefing about what to expect, Strauss asked us if we had any questions. As usual, none of us did. We split up to gather and prep our equipment.

I found Meadows in one of the temporary storage facilities, sullenly inspecting his gear. All the guys handled stress differently, but you could always count on Meadows to deliver some sort of farcical bravado during this period preceding a mission, which, if for nothing else, brought us a few grim laughs before rolling out. But Meadows had grown more withdrawn during this particular deployment.

"Hey, man," I said, glancing around the room, making sure we were alone. I slipped off my backpack and propped it against a crate. "You all right?" My friend grunted something as a response. He had his back to me, but I could see he was inspecting his machine gun. "Listen, if you want to talk—"

Meadows viciously slapped a clip into his M-4 carbine. "What the fuck is wrong with you?" he said. It was a legitimate question. I didn't know how to answer it then and I wouldn't know how to answer now. Usually, I'd shrug off one of Meadows's tantrums. But this deployment was different. I didn't want to give up so easily.

I said, "You still have time to say something."

Meadows turned to face me, baring his teeth, his breath coming in quick hisses. But there was also something that passed over his face, a brief batting of eyelids as if he were struggling to say something. I continued, trying to take advantage of his inward division. "I'll go with you right now, man. We won't even notify Strauss, you can request to speak to another OIC."

After a quiet moment Meadows said, "Don't fucking talk to me like that." His voice was low, almost a whisper. "Don't talk to me like I'm some character in one of your stories."

I frowned, gently lifting open palms. "Meadows, I didn't mean—"

"Don't give me that *I-didn't-mean-anything* bullshit." Meadows raised a tattooed forearm, his index finger aimed at my face. "Everything you say means something else. All your fucking observations and questions and"—he waved a hand toward the personal gear I was leaving behind—"all those anecdotes you keep in your diary."

My journal was tucked away in my duffle bag. Meadows knew that little secret about me, but I also knew that Meadows was carrying a secret of his own.

I read a statistic a few years ago that during one particular month more soldiers had committed suicide than had died during combat— the figure was something like 24 suicides to 16 deaths. A lot of these cases had endured multiple deployments and were unable to cope with what they'd witnessed during that time—comrades torn to pieces by landmines; black clouds of flies floating over corpse-filled trenches; women, concealing IEDs beneath their burkhas, obliterating themselves in marketplaces; the bloated and shrapnel-riddled bodies of toddlers. All this was supposed to be left behind. It felt as if the Army had misappropriated the slogan that Vegas uses to summon tourists: *What happens in hell stays in hell.*

Therapists went on to cite the stigma associated with soldiers seeking treatment. I'd seen it—the leadership shaming soldiers who exhibited any sign of mental frailty or emotional weakness.

Meadows had attempted suicide several years earlier. It had been between deployments. He'd returned home and discovered that his fiancée, Brittany, had done "something stupid" with one of his friends. Meadows never elaborated. He didn't have to.

Meadows disappeared for a few months. When he finally resurfaced, he was sporting several elaborate tattoos on his left forearm, mostly tribal stuff. On the inside of his forearm was the inked-in script, *Not with a Bang But a Whimper.* Meadows never mentioned T. S. Eliot before; he said he just liked the way it sounded.

I met Meadows at a pub one evening. That's when he shared his story.

A few days after finding out about Brittany, Meadows had rented hotel room. Cosmically intoxicated, he stripped, slid into the bathtub, and slit his wrist. Meadows said he woke up, shivering in the tub and smeared with dried blood. He thought the alcohol would have thinned his blood enough to galvanize the process. Meadows had smirked then at the end of his confession. "Guess I'm just too tough to die." The reason it didn't work, I had the dark urge to say, was that he didn't cut deep enough to sever the radial artery; but it wasn't an appropriate time to be pedantic.

Meadows never mentioned any of this to our superiors. And he quite literally tried to cover up the incident by getting wrist-to-elbow tattoos on his forearm to hide the scar. And each time I attempted to reprise the issue, Meadows would respond as he was doing now.

"Don't ask me what's wrong," said Meadows, "you know what's wrong." He returned to inspecting his equipment.

"They won't force you to fight if you self-identify." Meadows paused in mid-movement. When he looked at me, his expression was a complex arrangement of hate and helplessness. "You said one time that you and I complement each other, right? Like a yin yang, remember?" I licked my lips and continued before he could speak. "So if you're in trouble, let me be the side that helps."

Meadows grunted. "Help how? By doodling in that fucking diary?"

"No," I said, adjusting my Mollie vest, "by having the balls to tell the truth."

We were quiet for a while. Meadows loaded the small grenade launcher. He placed his weapon on the table, giving up a weary smile. "There was a time"—he swiveled his head, glancing around—"that I thought being a soldier was the best way to show my family I wasn't a total fuck-up." He ran his fingers over his forearm, tracing the scar that'd been camouflaged by a swirl of tribal tattoos. "How are we supposed to go anywhere, let alone home, after seeing the things we've seen?"

Just then Ricketts and Harper burst in at the far end of the room. "Look alive, ladies," said Ricketts. "Strauss says we're pulling out."

And that was it. As the other soldiers appeared, Meadows changed, resuming his role as our squad's hostile and heroic joker.

Meadows slung on his remaining gear, looking over his shoulder at me as he walked away. Loud enough so the other guys could hear, he said, "You going to stay here and doodle in your diary, or are you coming to fight some bad guys?" I clenched my teeth. Ricketts and Harper laughed simultaneously. One of them yelled, "Queer."

The last thing I glanced before walking out of the facility was my rucksack, mentally staring through it to see my tattered journal, hating myself and the things that book contained—the good things I'd witnessed during our missions: snapshots of friendship, selflessness, loyalty, compassion. I wanted to burn that goddamn thing and fucking kill Meadows myself.

Six hours later we were just north of a place (according to Flood) called Ceghak in the Oruzgan province. Before this, our Chinook landed in the planned location of Deh Ravod, but after Strauss spoke with the tribal leaders, he split our unit in half, the rest of us proceeding ten miles west across the river. A few times during the trip, I noticed that Flood, through a combination of frowns and wrist-watch inspections, appeared increasingly confused about our coordinates.

It was late evening when our aircraft descended into a narrow pocket near the mountains. I'd glanced over at Meadows several times during the flight, but, like the other guys, his eyes were hidden behind his M-frame sunglasses; but sunglasses became useless as the helicopter sank down, the mountain shadows rising up, creating the illusion that twilight had rushed over us in a matter of seconds.

After landing in a desolate, sun-cracked plain, the engines were cut and the rear loading panel was lowered. Outside, Lieutenant Strauss called out for the translator to accompany him.

We headed north now, just west of the river, toward a narrow pass in the mountains.

Marching gave me time to think. I wasn't humiliated that Meadows had "outed" my journaling, my private writing, my amateur ambition to emulate Ernie Pyle—whatever you want to call it. I was demoralized by the notion that all that work didn't matter. I had believed that the recorded observations would refine my thinking and might help my comrades make sense of the trauma all around us. I know that at one time I may have stumbled on some sort of metaphors for war, but I don't feel like articulating them anymore.

I flinched when I heard, "Hey," hissed from behind me. Meadows. I was still furious, but it was a familiar and complicated emotion when dealing with my friend.

"What the hell do you want?"

Meadows had removed his M-frames, and his dark eyes darted around. "When we get back, after this, I'm going to talk to somebody." We walked on for a few seconds. As if I didn't comprehend, Meadows added, "I'm going to get help when we get released."

I thought about that for a moment. "If we get released in one piece," I said, meaning for it to sound more lighthearted than it did. Meadows simply nodded and looked away. I felt like doing something, patting him on the shoulder, maybe; of course this would have been wildly inappropriate. "If you're serious about that," I said eventually, "then I'll go with you." In the rapidly receding light, Meadows squinted over at me. I shrugged. "There's some stuff I need to get off my chest." I glanced around at the other soldiers—Flood, Ricketts, Harper. "I think there's stuff we all need to talk about." We walked in companionable silence as Strauss led us north for another hour or so.

A man emerged from the rocks up ahead. He was dressed in dark, dusty villager garb, and he began gesticulating and babbling something in Pashto. As opposed to most of us, Strauss fully seemed to expect this. Our lieutenant never drew his handgun, but simply raised a wrinkled sheet of paper. The stranger inspected the ragged paper, said something else, and began walking in the direction from which he'd emerged.

The village, primitive even by Afghan standards, nearly blended in with the dark and jagged folds of mountain stone as we approached. The most prominent structures were composed of some sort of mold-mottled stucco or clay. Surrounding the village proper was a jumble of crudely assembled shacks and huts. It was very dark now. Orange light from various fires sent flickering shadows against the cul-de-sac of rock walls that rose up around the habitation.

Strauss ordered us to hold our position on the perimeter and motioned for Flood to accompany him. Our translator was inspecting a small handheld device (likely a navigation instrument), the illumination glinting off his glasses. Flood seemed to hesitate before jogging forward to catch up with our lieutenant.

There was a rush of movement and chatter from one of the outbuildings as a gray-bearded man confronted Strauss and Flood. The man was wearing a wide, dark turban and was dressed in a long white bisht—certainly the village elder or at least some sort of governor. But I was less focused on the man than on his entourage. To my surprise, he was not surrounded by Kalashnikov-toting bodyguards, but rather a procession of burkha-clad figures. These women—what I presumed were his wives—were startlingly tall, towering over the governor. Their unusual height, paired with a nearly imperceptible swaying—as if engaged in some silent chant—added to my unease.

A large fire illuminated the village elder and his escorts. Strauss raised his voice a few times while Flood seemed to play peacemaker. Eventually, Strauss sent Flood back to our group.

The scowling translator would have strode right past me, but I stopped him with an urgent whisper. "What'd he say?" Flood ignored this and continued walking, so I followed, jogging up behind him. "What the hell happened?"

Flood stopped. I had never seen our calm-and-collected translator so hostile. For an instant, his expression suggested that—whether verbally or physically—he was going to lash out at me. But Flood finally blinked and licked his lips. "I'm not sure . . . exactly." I opened my mouth to ask why but he cut me short. "The guy's talking in some sort of mishmash of Pashto, Uzbek, and . . . something else I don't recognize."

I glanced over my shoulder. The other guys in the squad were holding their positions, while Strauss continued speaking with the elder, his contingent of black burka-clad women swaying around him. Again I appraised the translator. "What are we doing here?"

Flood grew more agitated. "We weren't supposed to leave Deh Ravod—we weren't supposed to split the squad. Ceghak wasn't part of the plan."

Strauss raised his voice, and Flood looked past me to see what the problem was. He was about walk away, but I grabbed his arm. "What is that guy saying to Strauss?"

Now, physically halted, Flood looked genuinely pissed. But he didn't pull his arm away, not yet. Through clenched teeth he said, "I'm telling you—I . . . don't . . . know." Flood flicked a glance over at Strauss. "The old man's not one of our informants. In fact . . . Strauss doesn't seem interested in the Taliban at all."

I didn't have much time. "So what—"

"Goddamn it, Craft," said Flood, yanking his arm from my grip. "The guy keeps saying something about . . . an exchange."

Not unusual. Most of our intelligence resulted from one sort of symbiotic trade or another. "So what?"

Flood discreetly unholstered his Beretta, checked the clip, and re-holstered the handgun. "He keeps using a word I can't figure out." Flood began to walk away, but stopped. "The closest thing I can figure is that he means"—he shook his head—"*fish.*"

Strauss called our unit over, ordering us to follow him deeper into the village. Sunlight, along with the purplish streaks of twilight residue, had completely disappeared. The village was a jumble of fire-pit painted stone and sharp-edged shadows.

The village elder did not budge as we marched past him and his entourage. Closer now, I found myself having difficulty even making eye contact with the black-clad figures. I'm about six feet tall, but these figures were at least two inches taller than me. I could hear the elder mumbling something. He seemed to be solemnly appraising us, examining each one of us. Maybe he was just doing a head count.

I peered directly at one of the faces of the burkha-covered sentinels, scrutinizing the thin-slitted opening in the mask. The eyes and skin were all wrong. Not only did they never blink (nor really look at anything, for that matter), but there was a waxy quality about the eyelids and surrounding flesh. I had the notion that, if touched, the whitish tissue would have the same fat-flimsy texture as uncooked bacon. And the eyes were cloudy and too bulgy, as if milky marbles had been hastily inserted in the sockets of a wax dummy. I looked away.

As we passed I noticed the smell—something nice, like lavender, mingled with something fetid, like sun-spoiled shellfish.

We were snaking our way between the shacks when something occurred to me: I hadn't seen any kids. Children, in almost all our encounters, were always part of the backdrop. But here. But here, the absence of children was distracting.

Strauss stopped at a canvas-covered hut and again split-up our already meager team, ordering Flood and several others to stay behind. The rest of us followed the lieutenant into the hut. I gave Flood a lingering look as I passed, which he returned with a hard-to-read expression—something like reluctance, disgust, and (I like to think) a signal of vigilance. *Watch your ass, Craft.*

The interior of the fire-lit tent appeared as you'd imagine. Shadows. Clutter. Dust-grimed faces, but still none of them children. Because it was adjacent to the mountain, one of the walls was all stone. A large, intricate carpet was attached to the wall. Strauss silently regarded the few people in the hut before walking over to the rug and yanking it aside, revealing the large, open mouth of a cave.

Strauss ordered on our night-vision goggles. "Ricketts," Strauss called out, waving the soldier forward to take point. Both men clicked on low-watt flashlights to provide faint ambient illumination. Single-file, we followed each other into the tunnel.

We shuffled through a warren of twists and turns for over thirty minutes. The cave floor throughout was dusted with sand, making the downward-sloping path easy to distinguish. Meadows was a few paces in front of me. Gradually, the cave grew colder and the walls began to glisten with moisture. I caught the mineral whiff of water.

Up ahead came a sudden rustling of equipment and a rush of whispers. Instinctively, I crouched and braced my weapon. Strauss, his coarse voice echoing through the cave, said, "Hold your fire! Hold your fire!" Nothing happened for a few long moments. Then, through the green-glowing screen of my goggles, I saw them.

Three of the towering, burkha-covered figures were moving toward us. Moving isn't the right word—gliding, almost floating. Strauss barked out another order to hold fire as the black-caped shapes silently swept past. In the green glow, I watched them—their masks, that narrow strip exposing that flimsy skin and unblinking, milk-murky eyes. As the final cloaked figure drifted by, I noticed something on the cave floor, some sort of dark liquid streaking a trail behind the retreating figures. When they disappeared I again paused on the lines of the inky, foul-smelling excretion. I nearly let go of my weapon in favor of clutching my nose and mouth.

In a few seconds we were moving again. The ceiling and body of the cave opened up into a wide passage. Strauss called for us to stop and ordered Harper to the front. Again: traded whispers. Harper nodded, hefted his weapon, and hunched low, moving quickly around a ragged crook of cave wall.

I imagined Meadows up there—our squad's hero, grip tight on his carbine, molars clenched like vices, eyes narrowed on the point of attack. I, on the other hand, continuously had to coax myself into action to avoid being court-martialed for disobeying a direct order.

The screaming started without any sort of preceding commotion. There was a sporadic cadence of gunfire, but it was brief. My heart surged and my stomach lurched when I heard Harper begin to articulate the word *help*.

But Strauss remained silent and unmoving. At one point I saw Ricketts try to stand from his crouched position, and Strauss turned around and growled something at him. Ricketts lowered himself again.

Harper's cried for help deteriorated into tormented, inarticulate shrieks. I had the nauseous notion that he was caught in some sort of spiderweb.

We all tensed as faint light blossomed up ahead, a pulsing glow that seemed to grow in intensity along with Harper's insane screams. As the light grew brighter, I pulled off my goggles. The greenish-blue light soon swelled strong enough for me to see the detail of my team-mates' faces. So it was the screaming. I know that now. Some sort of connection between the ferocity of the screams and the brilliance of the light.

Meadows was looking back at me, staring at me over his shoulder. There was something in the angle of his neck, a small shift of his chin, an unspoken question: *If I make a move, will you back me up?*

Meadows was also asking to get court-martialed or possibly shot. I meant to give my friend some sort of response, but I stayed still. Eventually Meadows took his eyes away from me.

I was expecting a delay, but Meadows simply sprang forward, gun trained in front of him, defiantly sprinting ahead down the tunnel, the blue-green light casting his swift-moving shadow against the walls. "Goddamn it, Meadows," growled Strauss as the insubordinate soldier ran past, disappearing around the rocky elbow of cave wall. Strauss, gesticulating with his handgun, spun on the rest of us. "No one move—no matter what you hear, no one move. Stick with the plan and hold your positions."

Mercifully, Harper's screams were drowned out by the resumption of gunfire. Meadows. Even at this distance I could hear the jingle of fired casings bouncing off the rock. The sound of machine-gun fire blended with my racing heart. Meadows had asked for my help. He'd asked me to be something other than a coward.

I shoved myself from the cave wall and lurched forward, racing past my comrades and the screaming and cursing Strauss. I can't be certain, but I believe I heard our lieutenant shout, "You're not part of the plan!"

Not slowing, I rounded the corner and hunkered into my weapon. The machine-gun fire suddenly ceased along with the pain-laced soundtrack of Harper's screaming. But I could hear the lapping and sloshing of water now. The flickering, algae-tinted light throbbed within the narrow corridor.

Another sharp turn, and I drew up on an open space and tried to make sense of what I was seeing. Positioned in a shadowed alcove was part of an Army MLRS—a multiple rocket launcher system. It was just the loader module, twelve square compartments that usually contained M270 rockets. There must have been another entrance somewhere big enough to haul this thing in here. I didn't care about logistics at the time, I don't care now. I crept closer, trying to get a better look at the rockets inside.

I could see the tops of their heads. The corpses of children—the youngest probably around seven years old—were fit snugly within the dozen rocket compartments. Their pale faces were quite distinct in the diffuse glow. Some of their eyes were open. Some had died with agonized expressions.

I staggered backward, trying to stay on my feet. I was seized with the need to cry, to weep openly, to sink down onto the sandy floor and cover my face. Strauss's shouts echoed down the corridor. I tore off my helmet and flung it at the rocket module, steeling myself with a scream before running toward the light.

The tunnel dead-ended in some sort of grotto. The concave wall was textured with large, polished rocks, like cobblestones, and their slickness glistened with reflected light pulsing from within a wide pool. Harper was on the narrow shore. Still alive, he clawed at the sand as he tried to pull himself away from the water. His lower legs were missing and his hips and pelvis were connected to something. I followed the ropy line of gore to the shallow pool.

My first thought was that I was looking at a large, bobbing black raft. But then my mind reconciled the true contour of the presence in that shallow pool.

I have privately described it as an enormous octopus, but that's not quite right. I've spent countless nights searching images on the Internet, trying to capture the anatomy of this thing. The giant creature in the grotto was nearly identical to a cephalopod called the vampire squid.

The thing's head was shaped like a bulbous helmet skirted with writhing tentacles connected by glistening webs of black flesh. Its huge round eyes glowed beneath the surface of the water like two blue-green lanterns.

I shook out of that semi-trance and reached down to grab Harper, but the sucker-studded tentacles spasmed and recoiled, pulling the still-mumbling soldier into the pool. The luminescent glow grew more intense as water sloshed and Harper's body disappeared.

A furtive movement to the left pulled my attention from the creature. About fifteen yards away lay Meadows, face down near the muddy rim of the grotto pond. A dark, cloak-covered shape was draped over him, squirming over his throat and torso.

I raised my weapon and strode forward. "Get the fuck away from him!" I screamed, my voice ricocheting around the cave. As I closed in, the black-robed figure slid off my friend's upper body and stood, rising up to full height. The thing raised some sort of appendages beneath the fabric, though too snaky to be actual arms. The narrow slit of its mask exposed the emotionless eyes and pale, pickled skin. I aimed the machine gun at its chest and squeezed the trigger, not releasing until I'd depleted the clip.

I stumbled forward and grabbed Meadows's vest, dragging him away from the bank, his nose was bleeding, his face and mouth streaked with some sort of black liquid. But he was breathing.

And then my friend opened his eyes. He no longer had pupils or white sclera—they were glassy and black. Meadows took in a sharp breath, his open mouth exposing the black stub of tentacle where his tongue should be.

Then came an explosion, and my world swirled to darkness.

Everything that followed exists in my mind as a slashed, hastily edited reel-to-reel film: Flashlight beams. Smoke. Ricketts and Strauss screaming . . . someone dragging me by the collar of my uniform . . . the maze of the cave. And then I hear Flood, our translator, shouting at Strauss. The village . . . soldiers firing on burkha-covered figures . . . vibrations and thrumming from a helicopter . . . a spotlight casting brilliant light throughout the village. (I realize it was the witnesses, perhaps even Flood—along with my insistence that I remembered nothing—that saved my life.)

I feel my body being loaded into the chopper. My eyelids flutter as I struggle to remain conscious. And just as the pilot begins to take off, I look over and see Meadows being hauled on a stretcher by two soldiers. Both of us are on our backs, and even at this distance I can see that he's staring directly at me. His eyes are normal again, but his features are all wrong. Hollow. At the last moment, just as I lose sight of him, a malignant grin stretches across my friend's pale face, and I see his sharp teeth begin to part in what was certainly a laugh.

While this confession is a manifestation of my coping, it is also, like most of my earnest scribblings, an exercise in futility. If Meadows is in your school, it's too late. And if you're still reading this, it's too late for me. I plan on pressing the SEND button seconds before lifting this 9mm and punctuating this whole thing with a worthwhile gunshot.

Wayne Wilkinson has read enough. With an expression of contempt, the principal nudges the keyboard away and scoots his chair back, swiveling around to search for solace in his aquarium. Though the message is obviously indicative of some post-traumatic stress, Wilkinson feels foolish for allowing this young man, Craft, to occupy so much of his time and attention with this bitter nonsense. Wilkinson nods to himself absently—he'll contact the police department and notify them of a threatening e-mail he'd received from a former soldier, quite likely suffering from PTSD. Hopefully, someone will be able to get Will Craft the help he needs.

Still, something lingers.

The secretary is on the phone as Wilkinson approaches the counter. "Brenda," he says.

The interruption, along with the rare use of her first name, causes the secretary to place the caller on hold. Twitching a frown, Mrs. Welch says, "Yes?"

"I'd like to see the sign-in sheet from this morning."

Still frowning, the secretary reaches over and retrieves a clipboard. "Certainly. Is there a problem?"

Wilkinson flashes an unsteady grin. "No, no," he says, sliding the clipboard closer and inspecting the names there. "Just curious about something is all." The principal squints at the list, his eyes hanging on the names Noble and Santana.

"Are you looking for one of the recruiters?"

Wilkinson raises an eyebrow, answering her question with a question. "Funny you should ask. Did either one of them act strange to you?"

Mrs. Welch exhales and casually crosses her arms. "Well, which one? The blond one or the one with the tattoos?"

Wilkinson feels a rill of ice trickle down his spine. *Tattoos.* His eyes dart down to the clipboard and search for the room number to which the recruiters had been assigned.

"Mr. Wilkinson, is there a problem?" repeats the secretary, but he ignores her as he rushes out of the office.

And then he's jogging down the hallway, his polished loafers squelching over the high-gloss floor.

Principal Wilkinson reaches the classroom door just as the first screams issue forth.

He falters for a split-second before yanking open the door.

Most of the students are running toward him, others are on the floor, clawing at the carpet as they attempt to escape the thing at the front of the class. Unblinking, his mouth hanging open, Wilkinson steps into the room even as students bump and rush past him. He absently notes the blond recruiter, Noble, slung over one of the desks, thick cords of his insides snaking out from beneath him. But it is the thing that had once been a soldier named Lonnie Meadows that occupies his attention now.

It's covered in Army fatigues, but most of the flesh, as if a castoff cloak of skin, is sloughing away in sinewy clumps. Barely recognizable are the tattoos on the outstretched arm. Branches of slender tentacles have escaped through the lacerated and split tissue there, and several of those oily appendages have wrapped around the legs and torsos of several screaming teenagers.

Surrounded by shrieks and pleas, Principal Wilkinson shuffles to a stop, paralyzed by the glowing eyes of the thing that was Lonnie Meadows. Blue-green light begins escaping through the thing's slowly opening mouth.

With a graceful, almost erotic uncoiling, one of the glistening tentacles slithers across the floor and wraps around the principal's calf. Wilkinson tries to scream, but instead feels himself fall to the floor, collapsing not with a bang, but a whimper.

THE DAY OF THE EARWIG

This. Is not. A ghost story. Although the town of Deacon's Creek, despite having evolved in more insidious varieties, is a sort of ghost when compared to the vistas of our collective zeitgeist. No, this is not a ghost story. What you are receiving is more like a transmission—static-lashed and insubstantial.

According to the bucolic bylaws of this community—which mechanically championed earnest work, conservative values, and a pious terror of the Old Testament omnipresence—Luther Hume, at his age, should have already graduated from an upstanding university, should have moved out of his dad's house, and should be honorably maintaining a job that could lead to a reputable career that, in turn, could in time sustain a steadfast marriage and support a nuclear family. You know the script: the children here would then be instilled with the regional litany of previously listed values, and the cycle would begin again, again. And if you deviated from the Deacon's Creek conformation (as so few had)—well, that was yet another sort of story.

Instead, this is where we find Luther Hume: it's midmorning, July, and our young man is nursing a lukewarm hangover, occasionally squinting against the brutal blue sky as he skims debris, dead insects, and a discarded condom from an in-ground pool in the back yard of an opulent, Craftsman-style bungalow located just a few blocks off Main Street. The surrounding tree-lush streets are lined with affluently similar homes—aesthetically arresting exteriors, meticulously manicured lawns, and fussy landscaping. Again: you know the script.

After taking another lethargic swipe with the long-handled skimmer, Luther paused, running his fingers through his disheveled hair. He looked as if he belonged skulking around a skate park, except Deacon's Creek had nothing that resembled a skate park and Luther loathed skaters and all species of hipsters. His hair was crewcut petulant—high and tight on the sides but topped by bladed bangs, sort of a malignant but ultimately reluctant Mohawk. And to accent the air of anti-community militance, Luther wore a pair of his dad's old dog tags (which his father had long ago allowed, although he had also long ago acknowledged that the adornment was far from sincere) that evoked a quiet sort of hostility, honoring an anti-authority irony.

Though the home's resident was not currently occupying the up-scale dwelling, the house was owned by a widow named Irene Crawley. The condom, for a brief period the night before, had been owned by Luther.

Misty. He might call her later, see if she wants to play house again later tonight.

Was he a criminal? Not really, just your average, small-town parasite.

Luther was in mid-movement, taking another pass at the debris with the skimmer, when he glanced up at the house, involuntarily cocking his head as he gauged the certainty of what he was seeing. Through the kitchen window, in that area where the kitchen sink would be, a dark form materialized, graying into a substantial figure as it moved closer to the sun-glinted glass. And now as Luther focused on the figure, faint definition emerged—pale skin, a nimbus of white hair . . . the flash of spectacles reflecting sunlight. An old woman. Mrs. Crawley (only recognizing her from photos and in-town encounters over the past two decades). She was not smiling.

Luther swiftly arranged the scenarios, skimming through a poten-tially problematic script. But the fact of the matter was that he was cur-rently doing the job he'd been asked to do. Even so, he was ready to deliver as many ad-lib lies as possible to get on this old woman's good side.

As Luther registered the presence he was instantly vigilant about appearing outwardly innocent—he produced a wide smile, raised his hand in a cheery wave—*just your friendly neighborhood Boy Scout, ma'am.* An awkward span of seconds passed before the woman responded by raising her own hand—what was certainly her hand but, because of the misty reflection, appeared nothing more than a gray branch of arthritic talons, and those talons beckoned Luther toward the house.

Luther set down the pool skimmer on the concrete walkway and began sauntering toward the house, accidentally catching his sneaker on the stack of cleaning equipment and chemicals, cursing under his breath when he remembered—too late—the condom.

Even as familiar as he'd become with the house in the past few weeks, he still marveled at it with covetous contempt. Luther's grandmother used to call this mannered part of town "Ersatz Evanston." Luther had once asked what she'd meant by that, and Gladys Moira Hume, his dad's mom, had explained that the neighborhood resembled some of the housing pockets on the northside of Chicago, in the hamlet of Evanston.

Luther, in his twenty-three years of existence, had never been to Chicago, and had only occasionally traveled to the nearest big city. Caught in the Midwest murk between Cincinnati, Louisville, and Indianapolis—in a vague spot a more creative tongue might have termed the Bemused Triangle—he'd passed through large cities before, but Chicago was out of his depth. He did not go on to ask what "Ersatz" meant, but had the sense that his grandmother laced it with a large dose of good-natured sarcasm.

And impressive as all this was, Luther had often suspected that some underlying self-consciousness impelled this immaculate profusion, as if something fundamentally necrotic existed in the collective core of Deacon's Creek, and this architecture was all merely an anaesthetically manifested antidote. For Luther, the problem was very simple: everyone here was afraid. Everyone clung to a pastoral codependence on a mediocre status quo. Again—not Luther's words. Inebriation fostered an atrophy of articulation. Luther, in the best way he could privately convey, thought of the town's backwardness as an illness, but lacked the lexicon to directly call it a bucolic cabal.

And Irene Crawley was one of the predominant elders in Deacon's Creek. He knew that solely because of his own grandmother, Gladys Hume, who had also been one of the community's influential matriarchs and who was now flanked by other bygone townsfolk out at Evensong Cemetery.

Luther's father was co-owner of one of the town's more established real estate agencies. Last spring Luther had begun overhearing snatches of conversation about the Crawley house—the old widow woman, Mrs. Crawley, was going to live with her son and his family down in Alabama. The short version: the old woman moved out and the house was put up for sale. Luther's dad got the gig as listing agent to show the home to potential buyers.

So far, no bites, just a few nibbles. "You'd think somebody could convert it into a bed-and-breakfast or something," Curt Hume commented, standing at his desk in the den.

One afternoon a few days later, Curt stopped Luther as his son was walking out of the house. "Got a second?"

Luther shrugged but kept shuffling toward the door. They hadn't spoken in a few days, not since their last nasty verbal tussle. "Sure, but I got to split."

Curt was a craftsman when it came to engaging potential buyers and sellers throughout town and in the outlying communities, but he regressed to a boot-camp awkwardness when interacting with Luther. "Yeah, well, I won't keep you. I just—well, I've been so bogged-down about showing this Crawley house. I was wondering if you'd like to make a few extra bucks."

Being several states and hundreds of miles away, Mrs. Crawley's son had proposed that the agent (Curt) arrange for someone to act as a temporary caretaker for the property. Crawley's son had made it clear that there would be no compensation, but Curt would secure his position as the listing agent.

Here was the offer: someone stops in a few times a week and cleans the pool and details the yard at the Crawley house—roll the push-mower over the lawn, pull weeds from the flagstone sidewalk, that sort of thing.

Again: the Crawley son was not offering money. Curt was the one providing the stipend, and Luther instantly registered pity braided in his father's proposition. Nevertheless, Luther twitched the bangs off his brow—"Sure"—and proceeded out of the house.

And so it went that Luther would occasionally retrieve the ancient push mower from the small shed out back and mill around the yard. He'd skim and clean the pool, making sure the chemicals were in proper proportion. He had no clue what the hell he was doing. *pH levels?*

It didn't take long for Luther to flirt with the idea of actually getting into the locked home. Not long after this novel notion, Luther, one morning while his old man was in the shower, helped himself to his father's cell phone and discovered the three-digit code to the bulky lockbox on the front door: H . . . A . . . G.

Luther had cased the house for an electronic alarm system and found none upon his first unofficial break-in. Initially it was just Luther. He'd wait until dark, until after the lights began winking out in the elderly-affluent neighborhood, before parking the car down the street, taking a stroll along the sidewalk, keying in the code on the lockbox, and blending into the black house like a resident wraith. Of course, Luther always left the lights off, using only a small flashlight or the illuminated screen from his cell phone to navigate the dark home. There were quite a few rooms in the belly of the house with no windows, and Luther discovered a study with a leather recliner and a television.

Luther would toke up (beforehand, of course, on the drive over or something) and get comfortable in the study, sometimes bringing along a slim bottle or a flask and getting dreamy drunk in the dark, windowless room, his face silvered by coruscating light from the TV.

One night, Luther—sitting in the leather recliner, eyes slit-lidded—was aimlessly flipping through the late-night channels when he stalled on a public-access channel airing a program called *Mother Mary Angelica and the Nuns of Our Lady of the Angels Monastery*. The elderly nun—or mother or sister or whatever you called her—was wearing the full outfit, her wrinkled, plumply jowled face framed by a headpiece and black veil. Luther momentarily pursued and gave up on recalling the word "habit" for the costume nuns wore. And in addition to the cloaked uniform, the old nun was wearing a black eye-patch, which fascinated Luther as he floated on a cloud of inebriation. The nun was seated in a chair on a studio set profusely with pastels, directly addressing the camera. Luther thumbed up the volume and listened. She was doing a monologue about something, that one glassy eye blinking at the camera with soft-spoken sincerity. From time to time a tremor of gaspy, almost mournful agreement—*"Amen . . . Glory to God"*— came from the studio audience. "Most of us live in the worst moment of our lives over and over again," said the eye-patched nun. "At this moment, here I am talking to you . . . don't weigh yourself down with yesterday or tomorrow . . . be like Jesus today . . . Jesus showed me the way (*Amen*). Remember, my dear friends and family, be a child of light . . . do not tolerate darkness. Stand tall, not in disobedience but in truth—truth is truth, and we must teach truth (*Amen*). And truth is light and truth is joy and the truth is happiness. If you want to be filled with the joy Jesus promised, we must speak the truth from our hearts and live the truth . . . be generous . . ."

Whatever. Luther had numbly moved his thumb to change the channel when, with absolutely no transition, the nun leaned forward and scowled directly into the camera. Directly toward Luther. The old lady's expression contorted, and her wrinkle-pinched face, hooked nose, and bony chin appeared almost liquidly to penetrate the screen as she said, "How would you like it if a stranger was desecrating your house without permission?"

Fumbling with the remote control, Luther lurched upright, but as he did so he noticed a strange, fabric resistance over his forearms and swept a startled gaze over his body to discover a black material draped over his chest and legs. A nun's robe. Something chaffed his forehead. With a shiver of nausea, Luther slapped his palm to his brow—the movement impeded slightly by those heavy sleeves—feeling the constrictive hood and the hem of the white coif and hanging veil. And then something on his sternum caught the blue light from the TV: a silver-beaded rosary attached to an ornate crucifix resting cock-eyed on his chest.

Luther gasped and spilled out of the chair and onto the floor, clawing at the costume and the rosary. He rolled and squirmed and stopped, bringing stillness back to the small room. He was on all fours, gazing at a gray blanket that he now remembered had been thrown over the back of the recliner. His heart was beginning to slow to a mad but manageable rate, and he took a shuddered breath, his hand shakily going to the silver device looped around his neck, dangling in front of his face. In the soft light Luther hesitantly inspected his father's dog tags, chromed in the blue glow from the television, making sure they were precisely the hostile accessory he'd intended them to be and nothing more. He ran his thumb over the aluminum, over the indented name there. Curt T. Hume.

For the next few days Luther abstained from partaking in any herb.

He let Misty Chambers in on his little house-sitting secret a few days later. And together, in the dark, they had found more entertaining ways to play house. Luther and Misty—an unambitious Bonnie and Clyde. But that sort of symbiotic indolence infused their entire relationship, and it was as though one was waiting for the other merely to shift a degree one way or the other so that moving on—in one way or the other—would be made less arduous.

Misty, in her current social incarnation, was not the type of girl you invited to a sit-down dinner in your house—at least not in this town. Misty, by all accounts, was indeed considered a slut in high school, and the appellation—earned or otherwise—remained with her long after. She had done nothing to repair her reputation and didn't appear to be in any hurry.

But let's get back to *now*—to the backyard pool—to the face in the window.

As Luther approached the back porch he mentally rifled through the inventory of last night's trespassing: The house was spotless, he was certain—in fact, his meticulous assessment of the place was the thing that kept his recent intimate intrusions with Misty Chambers in a threadbare balance. It had occurred to him that if he'd been this thorough with the rest of life he might actually be building something that could enable him to get out of town.

In the backyard pool area, a few wood-planked steps led up to the screened-in porch. Inside, a short corridor that gave into a laundry room and then a few paces later into the kitchen was separated from the porch by a pair of French doors, which slowly opened with a genteel squeal. The feeble-gaited woman emerged.

"Hi there," said Luther—a simple greeting made salesman-saccharine by its intonation. "I hope I didn't startle you." The woman said nothing as she continued to hobble forward. "My name's Luther Hume, my dad—"

"I know your father," Mrs. Crawley said, her warbled voice sounding frail and phlegmy. She stopped moving a few feet from the screen door, appraising Luther.

"Cool." The sound of a lawnmower buzzed to life in one of the adjacent yards. "So I was just cleaning the pool, making sure it looked nice for the agents showing the house. I think your son and my dad had discussed—"

"I'm aware of the arrangement."

Luther nodded and cleared his throat. "All right." He involuntarily looked over his shoulder at the pool, squinting against the sun before turning to peer again at the small old woman on the other side of the screen, the mesh of dark material making her features and body language difficult to gauge. They stood this way for some time; the lingering silence and steadfast staring nearly coerced Luther to drop the altar-boy act entirely. He held fast, jabbing a thumb at the pool. "I don't know what it is, but even with the plastic cover that pool collects a lot of bugs."

Mrs. Crawley said, "Must be the heat. I've seen it like this before."

It's about time you chimed in, chatterbox. "Is that right? Well, I'm new at this whole pool-boy thing, so I hope you'll not judge me too harshly."

"Putting in a pool was my son's idea." Luther wasn't sure but thought he'd seen the porcelain flash of teeth in what might have been a smile. "In my opinion it's more trouble than it's worth."

Luther bobbed his head and rubbed his chin. "Yeah . . . I can see your point." He glanced around, but the tall wooden privacy fence prevented him from seeing the street or neighboring yards. "Well, I'll just be wrapping up here."

"Is he paying you?"

Luther had started edging away but stopped. "Pardon me?"

"Your father." She shuffled closer to the screen door, and now Luther could see that her expression was not as severe as he'd initially thought; in fact, she was wearing a pleasant, lopsided grin. "You don't mean to tell me that you're slaving away in the sun for *free*."

Luther rubbed the back of his neck. "Oh, no, ma'am. He's giving me a small allowance."

She nodded slowly at that. "Would you like to add a few more dollars to that allowance?"

Luther bowed his lower lip. "Sure—what can I do?"

Mrs. Crawley smiled, "Backbreaking work, I'm afraid." She chuckle-sighed at that—"Oh, I'm only fooling you"—and made a hobbling retreat away from the screen door. "It won't take long. Please"—she summoned with that thin hand—"come inside."

Now that's brilliant, thought Luther. *Invite some hood into your house to do a few odd jobs. Jesus—don't you watch the news, lady? I'm going to con you out of your life savings . . . I'm going lock you in the basement and strip all the copper wire from the house . . . I'm going to bind and gag and torture you and make off with all that jewelry in that coffin-size armoire in your bedroom . . .*

This town, simple as it was, had never been much in the way of secular street-smarts. Luther gave a last glance at the pool area before mounting the concrete steps and opening the flimsy screen door, stepping into the porch—a large, cool box filled with russet shadows. Of course, he already knew the French doors gave into a narrow hallway that led into the kitchen, but he followed tentatively, as if unaware of the house's layout. *The key is to act like everything's new and remarkable—you can't even hint that you know your way around this place.*

She walked ahead without waiting for him. Luther moved slowly into the corridor. "Hello?"

"In here."

When Luther emerged he saw Mrs. Crawley standing at the far end of the kitchen, near the wide threshold that opened into the body of the house. A shaft of mote-swirled sunlight angled through a window above the kitchen sink, glowing on the hardwood floor and tingeing the space with a sepia staleness.

Luther made a show of appraising the immaculate kitchen. "Wow, I wish my kitchen looked like this."

"Oh?" In the dimness it was still tricky for Luther to assess her attitude toward him. Mrs. Crawley smiled, her small teeth catching some of the light. Though she was on the other side of the kitchen, Luther noted the details of her appearance: the top of her prim nimbus of white hair came about to his sternum, her head supported by the wrinkled stalk of a neck, her back hunched slightly. A typical old lady. Now all he had to do was get out of here and break the news to Misty that they would *not* be enjoying a session of aquatic sex this evening. The old woman said, "What does your kitchen look like?"

Luther grinned. "I don't know, just"—he gestured awkwardly— "small, I guess." But there were other words on the sharp tip of his tongue; and if he'd tried harder, as he rarely did, he would have conjured the terms *lonely, comfortless, abandoned.* Luther couldn't remember the last time he and his father had eaten a meal together at the kitchen table—likely the grim lunch following his grandma's funeral roughly a year earlier. They hadn't really spoken on that occasion either.

In the intervening years following his mom's walking out—
sneaking out, really, as there was no demonstrative spectacle of her
leaving—the house that Luther and his father, Curt, occupied became
a museum of sorts, aesthetically minimalized by a pair of provincial
bachelors—a father-and-son Odd Couple made uncomic by a tacit dis-
like for each other—their cohabitive dwelling made cold and quiet by
domestic disuse. And just as Luther, seventeen by then, was beginning
to get more comfortable with asserting his deteriorating opinion of his
dad (Curt Hume was no dandelion, but the shame and humiliation of
his wife leaving the way she did was exacerbated by the bridge-table
gossip all over town, and the guy's spirit had simply been deflated—
Luther did not know the word, but he wanted to describe his old man
as emotionally exsanguinated), his grandma Gladys got sick, too sick to
stay alone. Curt suggested she come live with them. And even as her
health irrevocably declined over the next few years, Gladys Hume
acted like a geriatric generator in their home, positioning herself most
days at the kitchen table, writing letters to acquaintances, talking on the
phone, playing cards with loyal friends who were mobile enough to
visit. She was usually the first person Luther saw in the morning before
leaving for school and the last person he saw before going to bed. In
the limited years she was with them, Luther had begun thinking of her
as a sort of lighthouse attendant, making sure Luther was on the
straight and narrow, making sure he could find his way home.

But as Luther's local reputation began to depreciate, as his and his
father's relationship became more eloquently adversarial as those relationships are wont to do, the lighthouse glow began to wane within
Gladys. Eventually, the table was frequently empty at breakfast, and
merely a microwave light was left on for Luther at night, often along
with a note on the table—a few kind words scrawled in that loopy,
elderly script. Sometimes Luther paused and read the note, most times
he was too messed up to care.

"Small?" said Mrs. Crawley, rousing Luther from his vivid reflection. "Bah," was the old woman's good-natured dismissal. "I'm sure
your home is lovely. If there's anything I've learned about the character of a home, it's not about the size or the ornamentation, it's about
the memories you fill it with that give it true energy and personality."

Which edition of Chicken Soup for the Soul *did you steal that chestnut from?* "That's a really nice way of looking at things." *More like* Chicken Shit for Soul.

Luther had been so preoccupied with playing the part of haplessly cordial handyman that he was only now beginning to notice the smell. A tremor of electric panic pulsed through him—his first thought was that he and Misty had left out some food that was now permeating the room with the subtle aroma of putrid produce. He gave a furtive assessment of the kitchen but saw nothing noticeable on the counters or on the table. Besides, they'd been careful. So what was it? Maybe, thought Luther, he was just paranoid. Maybe it was simply the old-skin scent of the elderly.

To dispel the silence, and out of genuine interest, Luther blurted out, "So what brings you back to town?"

Irene Crawley hobbled a few paces and rested her withered hand on the smoothly curved back of a chair. "Robert—" she said but interrupted herself with a ragged succession of phlegmy coughs. She recovered after a few moments. "Dear," she said, blinking rapidly. "Robert, my son, has to attend a seminar at a university in . . ." Suddenly, she steadied her rheumy eyes on Luther. "It's not important." She smiled. "My eldest found it incumbent to return me temporarily home so I could be taken care of while he and my daughter-in-law and their family were away."

Quilt-thick quiet again hung between them. Luther: "So you said you needed help moving something?"

"Well I'm afraid *I* won't be of any *help,* but yes, I'd be grateful if you could move a piece of furniture for me . . ." Her voice trailed off as she twisted at the hip and commenced her fragile ambulation, leading the way into a dark hallway that connected to the family room.

Luther followed, his sneakers squelching slightly on the glossy planks of hardwood flooring. But as he rounded the corner of the murky, pictured-framed corridor he nearly collided with Mrs. Crawley, who'd stopped and was pointing at a stretch of unlit hallway, toward the study and first-floor bedrooms. Luther and Misty had, many times in recent weeks, acquainted themselves with these private recesses of the home. Looking into the dark alley of the hall, Luther had the crazy notion that the eye-patched hag dressed up like a nun was down there sitting in the pitch-black den, waiting for him to open the door, a widening shaft of pale light slowly throwing itself across the floor, to the folds of her black cloak, across her gray, grinning, expectant face. *Glory be to God.* And why then, in his imagination, would she be salivating? Luther dusted away the dumbass idea.

As we said, Luther and Misty had been cautious. No lights, save for Luther's small flashlight or the glow from their cell phones illuminating their surreptitious illicitness. Mostly they used the floor. Sometimes used the couch. But never on the beds. On several occasions, however, they'd wandered deeper into the house, up to the second floor, the mercury light from their mobile phones throwing shadows into strange angles, as if matte-black figures were stealthily shifting out of sight at the last millisecond; as if something—the uncatchable presence of black-clad vandals, perhaps—had preemptively beaten them to occupying the house.

"My husband, Harold, was born in this house, right back there"— a crooked finger extended toward the gloom—"in the master bedroom." She let that sink in for a few beats. "It was quite a common occurrence back then."

"What was?"

"Giving birth in the home."

The image of placenta-stained sheets and a blood-soggy mattress—whether in the nineteen-thirties or any other decade for that matter—gave Luther the creeps. *They probably washed and reused that stuff for years. Sweat and piss and shit and umbilical gore.* "You're kidding."

"Not at all. It really is amazing, isn't it?"

Amazing that people used to give birth in the same bed in which the baby was conceived?—Yes . . . stunning. "It certainly is."

The old woman's hand balled into a fist and went to her mouth, and her frail frame was again wracked by a succession of wet-ragged coughs that echoed down the tall rectangle of hallway.

In the white-noise distance of memory Luther heard his own grandmother's coughing, often between laughter, when he was in a nearby room, watching a basketball game or sketching pictures in his room.

Luther frowned. "Are you okay?"

But as the wet coughing resumed, the small knobs of her shoulders shaking, Luther narrowed his eyes. With each succession of coughs he watched Mrs. Crawley's body dim out, going visually staticky—not transparent like a ghost, but similar to how the low-quality, antenna-TV images used to act when you slapped the top of the television. Luther endured a nervy pull of panic and made another mental note to take it easy on the psychoactive sleep aid of cheap pot.

After a few moments Mrs. Crawley recovered and the blurry distortion seemed to cease. "Heavens, excuse me. I can't seem to shake this stubborn cough." In the muted light, a pale hand directed him to the next room. "Come agrog." For the first time, it occurred to Luther that the old woman might be having a tidy little stroke. *Agrog?* She cleared her throat—"I beg your pardon. Come *along.*"

The hallway opened into the living room. Like the rest of the old, opulent home, the living room—a great, squarish space furnished with comfortable seating areas and accented with ornate wood trim—was immaculate and decorated in the photo-ready arrangement of slick magazines. Built-in bookcases were imbedded on two sides of the walls. On a few occasions, using the weak light from his small flashlight or cell phone, Luther had eyed the titles of these tomes with a petulant expression, as if those thick, gold-gilded spines—*The Brothers Karamazov . . . The Red and the Black . . . The House of the Seven Gables . . . Melmoth the Wanderer . . . Don . . .* something—were provoking him to do, well, something. He hadn't read these books, and while he was certainly literate he didn't really know *how* to read them. In the end, like everything else, his fury was fleeting. *Fuck. You.* Privately, Luther had tried to articulate the vague notion that his lack of ambition was more than just laziness, that there was some sort of—*what's the word?*—*current* here in Deacon's Creek, some sort of restrictive energy. And though it was far beyond his lackadaisical lexicon, he would have loved to capture the notion and isolate the phrase "existential eddy."

"You must be a busy boy."

Luther slowed. "Huh?"

A knobby, pointing finger. "You keep looking around . . . like you have somewhere to go."

Luther chuckled. "Oh, no, ma'am. Just admiring your home. I don't have anywhere special to be," he said with a salesman's flourish. "Let's see this massive piece of furniture you need moved." *How the hell can I get out of here?*

"Oh . . ." She batted a hand at the air. "You've already helped us out so much by taking care of our home." Mrs. Crawley slouch-hobbled deeper into the living room. "But I need your strong arms and sturdy spine to move this grandfather clock." She indicated the far side of the room, near another hallway. "It's a valuable keepsake that belonged to my mother. She brought it over from Rotterdam, believe it or not, back when the family came over."

Thanks for the minisode of Antiques Road Show. "Wow. That's really impressive." Luther rubbed his palms together, ready to get to work.

Luther surveyed the space, pleased with its pristine state. On the far end of the room was a bulky fireplace, the mantel and hearth composed of large stones mortared together with pretentious asymmetry. The old woman stopped in front of the fireplace, hunched down, and began examining something in the charred chamber. "I knew Gladys, you know."

Frown lines and a nervous smile appeared on Luther's face— *Gladys?*—and it took him a second to realize that she was talking about his grandma. "No—well, I guess I knew that. Didn't you go to the same church?"

Crawley nodded her tiny head but continued inspecting something in the fireplace. "Oh, but we knew each other long before. We attended grammar school together. Harold and I knew your grandfather, too."

But Luther already knew most of this. Decades earlier, his grandmother Gladys had run afoul of the town elders and matriarchs by apparently expressing some of her more progressive ideas of social and religious reform—Luther had gathered this from snatches of stories and casual conversation—and she'd paid the price: not exactly outright ostracization, but a more sophisticated sort of social banishment that Luther could identify with, though he imagined his grandmother reacting with more dignity and class. Deacon's Creek did not take to criticism on general principles, but its response was more pronounced when dissent came from one of their own. Either way, she seemed unshaken.

"Really?" Luther slipped his hands deep in the pockets of his baggy shorts. "I guess I shouldn't be surprised, as small as Deacon's Creek is."

Crawley straightened a bit and made a noise—*"Hm"*—that Luther couldn't tell was an affirmation or that she simply couldn't hear. "For these last few years we were widows together."

Oh, brother, here we go. "Grandma lived with me and my dad for a while." Inadvertently Luther almost added, *After mom left,* but decided to leave it alone.

"Oh yes, yes, I had heard that," she said, her back still to him.

Luther removed a hand from his pocket and shoved his fingers through his hair. He was prepared to navigate his way toward a conclusion of this little discussion when he looked across the room at the coffee table. Luther, his lips slightly parted, blinked a few times and stiffened, his blood seeming to congeal.

In a synaptic flash, his memories of the past ten hours—from this very instant to his activities last night—underwent an instantaneous reversal: following Crawley into the living room, into the house . . . lazily cleaning the pool . . . drowsily driving to the Crawley house . . . his father's baritone voice booming down the hall at home—". . . *you need to make sure the yard and the pool are in fine shape for the showing this afternoon* . . ."—a few black hours of sleep . . . drunkenly creeping into the house . . . kissing Misty goodnight, part of him wishing she had some more self-respect, wishing she wasn't so sexually indecent . . . sex in the pool . . . sex on the floor of the living room in the dark . . .

And Luther paused on this scene, seeing with heart-lurching clarity the mistake he'd made. He remembered Misty, the flashlight throwing strange light on her nude body, lying on the floor, propped up on her elbows, preparing for Luther to ease into her. But as he does so he sees her reach up, taking hold of his dogs tags and removing them. *We're supposed to be quiet, right?* He can hear the jingle of the ball chain striking the imprinted plates as she settles them onto the coffee table.

And that's where the dog tags lay now, exposed, casually coiled on the high-gloss coffee table. Luther made a movement, but Crawley twisted around from the fireplace, regarding her guest with a warm smile. "Did you hear what I said?"

Luther severed his attention from the coffee table. "Hear?"

"Did you hear what I said?"

He cleared his throat. "No, ma'am. Pardon me, I missed it."

"I said that your grandmother always spoke fondly of you."

"Oh?"

Crawley's expression grew thoughtful. She shuffled a bit, stretching her birdish arm out toward the fireplace mantel for support. "She delighted in talking about you—your hobbies, your artistic tendencies." She looked at Luther, glassy-eyed. "Grandchildren, if old folks are fortunate to live long enough to watch them develop, can be a wonderful reward."

Luther swallowed hard and nodded, watching for the woman to became distracted long enough for him to scoop up the dog tags. "I couldn't agree with you more."

"My son's children"—the old woman shook her head and looked past Luther—"are some of the most ungrateful and spoiled specimens of young people I have ever encountered."

Luther was trying to re-establish his composure and casual tone. "Really?" A regretful click of the tongue. "That's a shame."

Moisture appeared at the crow's-feet folds at the corner of her eyes. "They try to avoid me. I sit in a room they've prepared for me and they walk right past the door, hardly saying a word." Her gaze wandered for a moment but connected with Luther. "Sometimes I think I'd be better off as a ghost."

Luther had been panic-pedaling toward a solution for swiping up the dog tags, but now he let that go, removing his grip from his present obsession and letting his mind coast.

Now he thought about a toffee tin filled with cash.

Shortly after Luther's grandmother moved in with them she had arranged for a small portion of her pension and some other retirement allocations to be mailed directly to their home. Each month, Luther's dad would cash the checks and deliver the money to Gladys. Yes, it was a small amount of cash (just enough to make her feel safe, he thought later), but Luther only needed a little, twenty bucks here and there—for a bottle, a bag of dope, whatever. He knew she kept the money in her bedroom, in a toffee tin stashed in the center drawer of an antique vanity. Like all lazy thieves, Luther was certain she'd never notice, and by the unwavering state of her warmth and earnest innocence—*Are you still practicing your drawings? Are you going to go back to art school?*—Luther was confident she never suspected a thing.

In the end, it was congestive heart failure. It was morning and Luther was the only one in the house with her. Luther's father had called to see how she was feeling. Luther, groggy and fussy from being roused from sleep, went in to check on her. Sun streamed into her room, making the death smell something discordant, perverse. There was a wet clicking in her throat that he mistook for shallow breathing. He couldn't get her to wake up.

A few days after the funeral, Luther weakened under the weight of curiosity about how much money remained in the toffee tin in his grandmother's bedroom. Eventually, he grew eager enough and unforgivably desperate enough.

With the exception of the bed being stripped from where the paramedics had removed his grandma, everything in the room was the same. Without giving the strange sensation of compunction too much consideration, Luther strolled over to the mirrored vanity and carefully (*Why carefully? No one was home*) pulled open the middle drawer. Reaching in, his fingers did not touch the cheap metal corner of the toffee tin but something else. The papery corner of something. A large business envelope. He warily withdrew the swollen device, instantly imagining it bloated with money. *She must have cashed out the entire account,* came the reprehensibly giddy possibility.

Luther unclasped the envelope, widened the mouth with two fingers, peeked in, and frowned. Cautiously, he began removing what he thought must be financial documents. Instead, what he extracted was a stack of drawings. Up to this moment he hadn't invested a second thought about what had happened to them: he'd simply discarded them, left them neglected on the kitchen table—a six-year-old boy's pencil sketch of a statue in the city, a ten-year-old's strangely detailed rendering of a bat, an adolescent's wasp, a cluster of bare trees with leaves scattered around their roots. Art assignments from elementary school, projects from high school he thought he'd pitched. All painfully amateur.

His grandma Gladys had used jute twine to bind the thick stack of drawings and sketches together. Luther had never seen the envelope in the drawer before, and its mere existence now was a crystal-clear transmission that connected with gut-wrenching resonance. *She knew.*

Inside the envelope was one last thing, an index card with a single scrawled line, *Glory be to God for dappled things,* along with the initials *GMH.* He'd automatically assumed they were his grandmother's initials. Luther had dismissed it, slid the contents back into the envelope, and hid the homemade booklet in his bedroom, thinking about the situation as little as possible during the following year. Liberal quantities of pot helped. Drinking proved to be a useful distraction. And Misty's kinky physical allowances occupied the remaining space of his hollow conscience.

Now, Luther was recollectively yanked away from his grandmother's empty room and back into Irene Crawley's living room.

The old woman gave a ragged cough into her liver-spotted fist. After a while: "I know it may be difficult for you to discuss, but I understand you were with your grandmother when she passed on."

From far away, Luther heard the echo of that boggy noise in grandmother's throat, heard the panic in his own voice as he called his father, incapable of knowing how to help. He looked down at the dog tags. "Yes," he said, "that's true." The ensuing silence urged Luther to add, "I couldn't get her to wake up."

The old woman's voice sounded weird now. "She thought you were something speckled," said Crawley, and then corrected herself. "I mean *special*. She thought you were something special. Did you know that?"

Again Luther wondered if the old woman was having some sort of health event, and he was about to ask if she was feeling all right when the old woman teetered, barely clinging to the fireplace mantel. Luther rushed forward, scooping one arm up under the woman's armpit before she collapsed with too much momentum. She weighed very little. "Are you okay?" Of course she was not, but it was all he could think of saying.

Irene Crawley's breathing had grown staticky with congestion. She let go of the mantel and sagged against Luther's chest. "Not . . . feeling . . . as spry . . . as I used to."

Something flared in Luther then—a lukewarm anger at Irene's son for replanting her here in Deacon's Creek and leaving her alone so that his family could go on some sort of trip. Why had he brought her home to fend for herself? The small old woman rested her scrambled white hair against Luther's sternum. "You mustn't . . musn't . . . take your family for granted . . . no matter how small or insignificant it may seem . . ."

"No," agreed Luther. "No, you can't." He began edging away from the fireplace with the intent of settling her on the sofa, the awareness was very real that he needed to call his dad or an ambulance or something. "You might feel better if you sit down." His attention grazed the dog tags, but he just as quickly dismissed them. "We probably need to call somebody."

Irene's body sagged but, somehow, grew strangely heavier. Her voice quavered. "Someone's calling right now," she said. "Can't you hear them? They're talking about you and me this very instant . . . how you're carrying a sick old woman to a sofa." Luther didn't respond as he continued carrying the sick old woman to the sofa. There was a moist clicking in her throat before she said, "Did you ever . . . pay me back?"

Though still hoisting the woman, Luther froze. "Pardon?"

Something else was in Irene's voice now—something like mischief stitched with meanness—"Did you ever pay *me* back?"

Luther kept his eyes on the cushions of the sofa. A dizzying thought poured into him: *She's been here the entire time—she's been in the house while Misty and I* . . . "Pay you back"—he licked his lips—"for what?"

And then Luther angled his face down as Irene Crawley simultaneously looked up at him.

It was not Irene Crawley. Instead it was the exaggerated, gray-and-waxy deathbed face of his grandma Gladys—eyes rheumy and sunken in purple-rimmed sockets, her semi-translucent skin riddled with branches of dark-colored veins. Her lips were curved up in a giddy rictus, exposing glistening teeth, their stunted size and blunt shape resembling perverse, oversized baby teeth.

Luther was paralyzed, still cradling the thing in his arms when it started talking again, its mock-infantile voice twined with a vibrating buzz. "You should have paid me back when you had the chance." A puff of compost-fetid breath escaped its chapped, rapidly moving lips. The corpse's long-fingered grip tightened around Luther's waist as he began to struggle. "I knew you were stealing from me, boy . . . boy . . . *grandboy* . . . I could have told your father, but *no no no* . . . I didn't . . . I was charitable . . ." The thing's voice began deteriorating into something high-pitched and keening, but its spoiled face and bugged-out eyes were still trained on Luther. "Your little talisman won't help you now . . ." Luther didn't care about the damn dog tags. *"And your whore is in for a pleasant surprise she finds what we've left of you . . ."* As a punctuation to this Luther felt the elderly thing's arms constrict with scream-worthy strength, but the cry was stifled by the sensation of additional appendages coiling around his midsection. The septic tank smell worsened. The thing imitating his grandmother began to convulse and shiver as the bad-transmission flickering of her body resumed. But this time Luther could see what was underneath.

The rattle-shock sight of segmented legs momentarily slowed his struggling—caramel-colored appendages had extended through the grafted image of flesh and fabric along either side of her—*her?*—ribcage. But it really wasn't a ribcage, was it? Luther saw now that there had never really been clothing or flesh. Luther continued a futile fight with the shiny, brown-shingled exoskeleton of the insect wrapped around his waist.

Still towering over the thing, Luther spotted a pronounced set of pincers at the ass-end of its pill-shaped abdomen, each curved pincer the size and shape of a large farming scythe. But that was not the worst.

Glory be to God . . .

His grandmother's face remained as it was in its deathbed defilement, as if something had impishly undone all the work of her coffin presentation. That wasted mask—the bulbous, eager eyes, the sharp, incisor-stunted teeth—was fixed on Luther at a hungry angle, and an aroused cicada buzz swelled within the room.

. . . for dappled things . . .

As if pressing against aquatic resistance, Luther felt himself lift his leg and kick out toward the fireplace, solidly connecting with the stone hearth and heaving his weight backward.

The insect cleaving to Luther with its gray-grafted skin was still holding fast, and the momentum of the kick sent both of them to the floor, the hybrid horror of bug-and-grandma landing on top of him. Luther's panic included everything except a scream as he wriggled and flung his arms—his knuckles struck the leg of the coffee table, he arched his back to stretch out toward it. In a desperate, wrestler's lurch, Luther ground down his shoulder and pivoted his upper body to caterpillar-crawl away from the thing.

The dog tags slid off the coffee table, falling to the carpet with an aluminum jingle. Luther's fingers clawed at the necklace, and with jittery coordination he got the ball chain wrapped around his fist, the sharp-edged plates protruding between his knuckles.

A well-placed punch may have done the trick, but a punch punctuated with a dull-razor laceration had a more pronounced effect. Clenching his teeth and again facing the exaggerated death mask of his grandmother, Luther struck out with several mad slashes, the thin blades connecting, one swipe in particular opening a ragged, diagonal gash from eyebrow across the nose and down to its lower lip and chin.

The noise it emitted was either pain or surprise, but it was not human—a sub-audible keening that filled Luther with images of lightless tunnels choked with oily, carapaced profusions of skittering, chattering, beetle bodies trampling one another along with the black soundtrack of clacking communication.

The thing rose up just enough for Luther to get his palm under its chin. He pivoted and shoved the thing off of him, sliding out and pushing himself up to all fours, his sneakers finding traction on the carpet as he raced out of the living room in an unsteady, headlong sprint, racing through the darkened corridor. But as he propelled himself across the hardwood floor of the kitchen, Luther slipped, his sneakers catching with a yelping squelch, flailing his arms to hold his balance and teetering toward the lip of the sink to steady himself. It only took a half-second glimpse, but it was sufficient. As though regurgitated from the garbage disposal, the sink contained a blossom-shaped stain and a dark streak of viscous liquid, as though a wide-bristled brush had been used to paint a single bar of foul-smelling, coffee-colored slime.

Luther sprang away from the sink and advanced through the threshold of the back porch just seconds before he heard the maniacal typewriter clacking of skittering legs on the kitchen floor. He was through the French doors and in several strides had reached the screen door, when he felt the pill-shaped form strike him low on his back, slender appendages wrapping around his torso. The momentous impact sent Luther hurdling forward, the unlocked rickety screen swinging open in a wide swipe. Luther careened off the porch steps and clattered to the concrete walkway surrounding the pool. He felt the

metallic sourness of blood on his lower lip where he'd struck the concrete, his arms shot out to grab anything, and he succeeded only in
knocking over the stack of chemicals and cleaning supplies, toppling
them into the pool as he struggled to free himself from the segment-
slender legs.

The thing on his back loosened its grip long enough for Luther to
roll on his side.

The broadcasted illusion had ceased entirely, and now the thing at-
tacking him was simply a slick-plated bug reeking of rot and clinging to
his midsection.

The false flesh of his grandmother's face had disappeared and was
replaced by features honoring the insectile aspect of the rest of its
body—the whirring antennae, the bulbous, obsidian eyes, the fine
filaments and shivering feelers quivering within its moistly moving
mandibles.

Luther made a final pivot-yank with his upper body and felt himself falling, registering descent a millisecond before being enveloped by
water. The insect unclasped Luther, who bobbed out from the water
with a violent swipe at his eyes, gasping for air and steering toward the
edge of the pool, hauling himself out and ass-scooting away from the
water.

With fluid fury the insect writhed to find purchase on something,
but struggled too long where the chemical spill had been most potent.
Finally, one of its numerous legs caught hold of the ladder, and it clattered out of the pool. Now—still catching his breath in sharp
hitches—Luther saw the entire insect. About four feet long, the oily
segments and caramel-colored plates of its exoskeleton reflected the
summer sunshine with an almost hypnotizing luridness as it made a
skittering retreat from the pool.

He pushed himself off his rear end and sprinted toward the tall
gate of the privacy fence, looking over his shoulder to see the insect
scuttling toward the bushes, disappearing near the crawlspaced founda-
tion of the home.

Luther felt the self-preservative compulsion to run, sprint, scream,
and swing his fists, but he faltered on the sidewalk outside the house,
the lacy awning of overarching tree limbs shading him. He could still
taste chemicals on his lips, smell them soaked in his clothes.

Luther skimmed the exterior house, looking from window to window; but his appraisal finally settled on the lower skirt of the home where the decorative shrubs surrounded the structure. He heard something rustling in the shrubs—heard something twitching the leaves in the trees all around him: normally he would have disregarded it as a squirrel or a bird, but he was now uncertain about the true source of the sounds. The thought of overlarge insects smoothly creeping along the limbs of the elms and sycamores urged Luther to keep moving.

Suddenly there was dull pain in his hand. Luther looked down— his dad's dog tags were wound around the knuckles of his clenched fist, a small rill of blood dripping between the seams of his fingers and freckling the unflawed sidewalk.

His car was parked down the street around the corner, and Luther started off in that direction, his sneakers squelching with moisture. But once the urge to run had ebbed, what flowed in to replace it was the simple need to tell someone—to ask for help, to confide in a companion. Luther shuffled to a stop and turned to examine the house from a distance, and considered the icy emergence of the sobering realization: *Who the hell do I have to tell?*

Later that afternoon Luther will work up the courage to return to the house. Of course he won't enter it—he watches the house with the dread of a self-conscious matador eyeing an unblinking, red-eye rabid bull—but will simply clean up the mess of spilled chemicals, finally retrieving and disposing of the discarded condom just before the scheduled house showing. Before he leaves, he steels himself to check on the screen door, which is still rickety but sturdy along its hinges, and locks the French doors from the outside.

That same evening at his own house, Luther walks down the hall, cranes his neck into his dad's den, and clears his throat. "Hey."

Curt Hume is at his desk, his back to Luther, his broad shoulders blocking the monitor that throws a blue glow against the wall and ceiling. He doesn't miss a beat with whatever he's working on and continues pecking at the keyboard without turning around. "Hm?"

"I . . ." Luther edges across the threshold, "I . . . was just curious how the showing went today."

Curt stops typing now and rotates his head a degree or two. After an uncertain moment, he says, "I don't think they're going to make an offer. Said they were looking for something with more warmth, can you believe that?" The steady typing resumes. "Why the sudden interest?"

Luther makes a clueless gesture. "Like I said, just curious."

His dad slowly swivels partway around to look at Luther, giving his son a crooked smirk. "Looks like you still have a job."

Luther blurts a nervous laugh. "Yeah." He turns to leave but hesitates. He licks his lips. "Thanks, Dad."

Luther walks down the hall, the quiet corridor catching the clack-clack echo of his father's fingers on the keyboard. *Clack-click . . . clack-clack-clack . . .*

A few nights after the incident at the Crawley house, Luther is in his bedroom at home. Driven by a complicated urge of remorse and motivation—the latter having gone into almost absolute atrophy over the past few years—and with the snaky haze of chemical influence beginning to dissipate, Luther finally grows ambitious enough to investigate the source of the scrawled line that had been haunting him for a dozen months—*for dappled things . . .*

At his computer, Luther types the phrase into the search engine, seconds later retrieving several responses that connect to the initials GMH. It's a poem, something titled "Pied Beauty" by a guy with the last name Hopkins. Luther opens up another tab to look up what the hell *pied* means before reading the poem in its entirety.

> Glory be to God for dappled things—
>   For skies of couple-colour as a brinded cow;
>   For rose-moles all in stipple upon trout that swim;
> Fresh-firecoal chestnut-falls; finches' wings;
>   Landscape plotted and pieced—fold, fallow, and plough;
>   And all trades, their gear and tackle and trim.
> All things counter, original, spare, strange;
>   Whatever is fickle, freckled (who knows how?)
>   With swift, slow; sweet, sour; adazzle, dim;
> He fathers-forth whose beauty is past change:
>   Praise him.

It doesn't mean a damn thing to him. Though he has the sense, an uneasy tickle—*am I a dappled thing?*—that there is a riddle in here. But more than anything, he feels as if it were a final, forgiving embrace from his grandma. Hesitating, the next thing he types is "earwig." After a long time he shuts down the computer. He thinks he'll read more about this Hopkins guy and earwigs tomorrow. He has to start somewhere.

Yet outside Luther's immediate perception—on a similar, overlapping frequency in which this narrative is being transmitted—and yet not so far away from the double-exposure reality in what Luther has so often imagined a life that may have been—staticky snatches of voices briefly emerge: moments of formal clarity: fleeting threads of thought (. . . *I was drowning in the ocean under a bone-toned moon* . . .), conversation—a broadcasted news report, perhaps . . . it's difficult to hone in on the context . . . but there are words, voices . . . or rather a mystical con-catenation—fleeting as it may be—of conveyance . . . of *mechanisms by which these parasites are commanding . . . hosts . . . remain unsolved mysteries . . . it's co-opting pre-existing behavior . . . modified organisms are more complex than we had previously believed . . . Ampluex Compressa . . . in at least some of the cases . . . these parasites produce neurotransmitters or hormones that mimic host hormones . . . example of external control . . . Plesiometa Argyra . . . a different species . . . able to control . . . Hymenoepimecis Argyraphaga . . . via injection into its brain . . . and force it to enter its nest to become food and shelter . . . Leucochloridium Paradoxum . . . for insect's larvae . . .*

And in that dark concert on the black plane of all-inclusive con-sciousness, the transmission fades, ebbs from perception, deteriorates into the mandible-chatter of insectile clicking and clacking, where the white static of this hissing transmission transitions into the seething sustention of white, inkless space . . .

ABOUT THE AUTHOR

Clint Smith is a winner of the annual *Scare the Dickens Out of Us* ghost story contest (for "Dirt on Vicky," in this collection). His fiction has appeared in numerous journals and anthologies, including the *Weird Fiction Review* and the *British Fantasy Society Journal*. Clint lives in the Midwest, along with his wife and two children.

Ghouljaw: The Soundtrack, by Allen Kell of Shadeland, is available for purchase on iTunes, cdbaby, Spotify, and other sites.